PATHS UNBOUND BOOK 1

THE FURY SHE HOLDS

MILLI C. VIEIRA

DEDICATION

For the little girl who never stopped dreaming.
For the young woman who needed an escape.
And for the new mother who lost herself.
Keep dreaming.
Keep searching for your place.
Keep following your heart.
I see you. I am you. We did it!

Content Warning

The Fury She Holds takes place in a world consumed by evil of all shapes and sizes. Should any of the below topics or themes be upsetting to you, please find another great adventure to get lost in.

Strong Language
Substance Abuse/Alcoholism
Open-Door Spice
Graphic Violence
Abuse
Child Abuse (implied)
Sexual Assault
Rape (attempted)
Implied Grooming
Kidnapping
Torture
Death

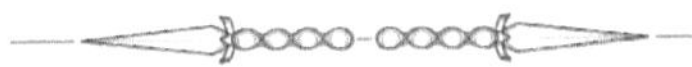

1

Charred flesh always coated Talwyn's nostrils and ruined her appetite, but nothing would stop her from melting the skin off Pochette's bones. In the alley below, he arranged for an ambush in exchange for a measly bag of coin. Tonight, Pochette would burn, and Talwyn would make sure of it.

Torchlight illuminated Pochette's gnarled hand. His thumb pressed a slip of paper against his palm while his other fingers clawed the air, useless.

Talwyn grinned to herself at a distant memory; one with threats, promises, and a kiss from the cold steel of her dagger.

A cloaked figure stood opposite the thug. It took the paper with an eerie grace that sent chills down Talwyn's spine. "You guarantee she'll be here." Its voice echoed through the alley, a muffled, emotionless sound.

Pochette's balding head nodded once. "I can give you the others, too." His voice shook with unease. "But you need to get me out—tonight." He searched the alley nervously. His good hand fiddled with a loose button on his faded green jacket. Patches and stains littered his once-luxurious suit. Yet, it would still sell for a week's worth of meals in the docks.

Talwyn seethed on the rooftop. If she hadn't already planned the man's demise, he would have just sealed his own fate. She crouched over the eave. Her well-worn black leathers clung to her body in the humidity and drowned her in darkness on the moonless night. A hood concealed the mahogany-dyed hair that clung to her neck. The handle of her dagger offered comfort against the rage warring within her.

"That was not part of the deal. We have no use for the others," the cloaked figure said impassively.

Pochette spluttered. "Then I'm a dead man. I'm exposed. My men are vanishing. Even if you take her tonight, the brats will suspect me."

His companion reached out its arm, an offering concealed beneath the voluminous sleeve of its dark cloak. "Then I suggest you run."

A wooden door smacked against the side of a building, followed by a commotion outside a tavern opposite the alley. Pochette jumped and cowered in the shadows. Two figures, hanging onto each other, cackled and stumbled down the cobblestone street.

Talwyn's ears perked at a familiar presence on the rooftop. Carrick's massive form crouched beside her, and she inhaled a relieved breath. Their plans were moving along smoothly.

Pochette hesitated, shifting his bulbous frame from one foot to the other. Another roar of laughter filtered into the alley, and he swiped his companion's offering. Coins clinked within the leather pouch as Pochette hugged it to his chest. Without a farewell, he hobbled out of the alley and down the street.

The cloaked figure dissolved into nothing but shadow, and Talwyn gasped. Whoever Pochette had involved himself with knew magic more powerful than she'd ever seen.

"Bastard," Carrick growled. "He deserves less than you're giving him."

"He'll suffer all the same. Still no information on his companion?"

Carrick shook his head, his attention locked on the spot where the cloaked figure once stood. "Rain will be interested to learn it can disappear, though."

Talwyn nodded. "Send Egan to sniff around the surrounding area. Maybe it left a trace of some kind. You and the twins search for any others nearby, then meet me at the Kiln."

Carrick grabbed her arm. "We stick to the plan. No wise ideas this time." His deep brown eyes reflected the orange glow of a distant torch.

She scoffed. "You know better than to give me orders." She turned without another word.

Talwyn trailed Pochette from the rooftops. His portly figure hobbled down the empty street at a snail's pace thanks to years of overindulgence in food, ale, and debauchery. His labored breath echoed through the alleys, leaving a trail for Talwyn to follow.

Silence ruled the night as if the docks knew its tyrant's power had run out. Not even the Netters rolled their carts down the cobblestone streets in search of homeless women to fill their brothels.

Pochette had established power long before Talwyn made a name for herself recovering stolen items, stealing secrets, and making another's problems disappear. He made it clear he didn't appreciate her interference when he put his greedy hands on her and forced her into a deal. In another life, Talwyn would have cried herself to sleep when the monster had violated her, but Talwyn had survived on nothing but stubbornness and hatred.

Whoever she could have been had died on the cobblestone streets of Meladair. The night he touched her, Talwyn washed the feel of his calloused hands from her body with more ale than she had ever consumed before. She burned the clothes without a thought and scratched herself raw. Pain offered more comfort than the feeling of her cotton shirt caressing her cursed skin. The next night, she stalked Pochette back to his home and watched him go about his evening. He ate and drank as if returning home from an honest day's work. While he slept, Talwyn wore an indent into the leather wrapped around the hilt of her dagger. A fresh image of the man's future suffering accosted her with each grating snore. Before the end of the week, her dagger met his flesh in a vow of more to come. Tonight, she would fulfill that promise.

Pochette ran right into her trap. On the street ahead, Talwyn jumped to the ground using the edge of the roof and the building's windowsills. She waited in the shadows until Pochette came into view. When he stepped in front of the open sewage drain, Talwyn ran full force into him, ramming her shoulder into his ribcage, earning a deep grunt from the man. She shoved, and Pochette cried out as he fell toward the hole in the ground. He pitched sideways and disappeared into the darkness below. Another of his cries echoed when he splashed into the tunnel.

Talwyn descended after him, landing on her feet as she pulled a dagger out of its sheath. "Get up," she hissed, her blade aimed at his throat.

Pochette struggled to his feet and gulped audibly.

She nudged him east. "Walk."

"You can't kill me." His shaky voice didn't match the conviction of his words.

She jabbed the weapon toward his back, and Pochette flinched away. "You and I both know that's not true."

"My men will burn your little crew alive."

Talwyn laughed humorlessly. "They'll never get the chance."

He made a few more attempts at intimidating her, but eventually the echo of his efforts died along with his hubris. They walked the remaining distance to the Kiln in silence. Carrick waited at the steel door, his hulking frame leaving little space to pass through. Pochette eyed him warily as he approached, halting inside the entryway. Carrick kicked him in the lower back, and the man stumbled to the ground, sprawling in the center of the room.

Unlike the stone tunnel outside, steel lined the large, domed area. There were no windows or other doors this far underground. The only breaks in the metal were a grate in the ceiling's center and another on the floor directly below. Torchlight reflected off the walls, disrupted only by smoke stains and char marks. Black soot powdered the ground.

Carrick placed a wooden chair over the grate in the center and hefted the now blubbering captive into the seat.

Pathetic, Talwyn thought. *For all the violence he's brought to the docks, the rat can't handle any directed at him.*

Carrick located the hooded figure's leather pouch and stashed it in his pocket. He nodded to Talwyn when he finished tying Pochette to the chair.

She dipped her head in response before he left the room and closed the door behind him. She stepped up to Pochette and noted the wet spot between his legs with disgust.

"Tying me up? Too weak to fight me honorably?" Sweat dripped down his temple.

"The time for honor has long passed, Pochette. I thought I made that clear at our first deal." She nodded to his right hand, clawed around the arm of the chair.

"You're nothing. You'll never have the power I have. The docks will *never* let a *woman* replace me," he snarled.

"We don't need a power-hungry tyrant." She eyed the spot on his pants. "With you gone, its people will have the freedom they deserve."

"Then you're prepared to face the evil I've kept away these last twenty years? Without me, they'll destroy everything I've built."

"If your measly crew of criminals kept this so-called power out of the docks, we'll have no issue protecting the people." There had been no indication of a foreign power reaching Meladair. Warring factions in the southern kingdom were the closest indication to any sign of conflict, but Talwyn had no reason to believe they made their way north.

"Then you're a fool."

She slammed a dagger down on each forearm, and Pochette's scream echoed off the walls. "The only fool here is you." He flinched at her proximity. "How many girls have you taken to your bed? How many did you steal off the streets and sell to the highest bidder?"

"I haven't touched a single—"

"Your recent *chastity* does nothing to fix the twenty years of damage you caused. How many women still remember your stench on their skin? Are a few years enough to atone for that?" She spat at him. "Your reign is over."

"Then do it already! Get it over with!" he yelled at her, flinching when she shifted one of the blades.

"But it's so much more fun when you suffer." Her lips pulled up in a wicked grin. "Tell me," Talwyn's fingers twitched, eyeing his damaged appendage, "can you still feel with that hand?"

Pochette's wide eyes darted around the room, uncertainty lining his brow.

"It's been almost six years to the day since I vowed to remove it. Do you remember? Do you remember what that hand did?"

"I—"

"Of course you don't. But I remember. And I remember my promise the night I gave you that scar." Talwyn steeled herself against the feel of his skin under her fingers, about to drag a nail down the faded white line on his swollen hand. She stopped short, swallowing and flexing her fingers. Instead, she asked, "Why did you finally decide to sell me out? Why now? What changed?"

"Bitch!"

A third dagger met the meaty flesh of his thigh. When his pained howls ceased, she leaned close. "Don't be brave now. You're going to die anyway. The question is how quickly I send you to the hells." She gripped the leather handle of her weapon, a mischievous tilt to her mouth.

He panted, eyes squeezing shut. "They want you."

"Who?" Her eyes narrowed. She shook the dagger a fraction, and Pochette cried out, straining in the chair.

"Apparitions! Faceless copies!" he yelled through clenched teeth.

"Copies of *what*?" Talwyn spoke each word carefully.

"Mages. That's all I know. More powerful than anything this kingdom can handle. They come from nowhere. They can't be found until they find you." Pochette's face turned red as he stumbled over his words. A vein bulged in his forehead.

"We'll see about that." Talwyn paced the small room. "Why me?"

"A red-haired woman."

The hair on the back of her neck prickled. She resisted the urge to touch it. He couldn't possibly know she dyed her red locks.

"I know. I know you hide your true identity," he continued. "The elixirs and dyes you purchase from the alchemist—you're not as secretive as you think."

"What of it? Anonymity is the only way to survive in these slums." Talwyn bit her lip. Dealing in the docks made many enemies, and her unique features would be a dead giveaway even in darkness, never mind daylight. She often cursed the gods for giving her hair the color of the setting sun and eyes brighter than a gold coin. Once a month, she drank an elixir to keep her eyes dark and soaked her hair in a dye that stunk of rotten plums. She made the alchemist swear to secrecy in exchange for a hefty bag of coin, and he'd promised the best formula she would ever find.

Pochette chuckled darkly. "There's more to you than meets the eye, isn't there Little Fury?"

She didn't bother arguing with him. It didn't matter that he knew she had elemental magic, let alone that he had correctly guessed she was a Fire Fury. What concerned her was *how* he knew and who he already told.

"Don't tell me you believe the rumors. Fire Furies all but died out long ago."

"You think you've kept yourself hidden. But I know what you are. When they asked for the red-headed woman, I had prepared to give them whomever. But my men saw you in the woods. They saw what you can do and that blazing hair of yours to match."

Talwyn clenched her jaw. She'd been careless. Two weeks ago, a bounty that had been particularly troublesome lured her into the trees and attacked her from above. After chasing the man for hours, her patience reached its end. She flicked her wrist and set him aflame. The fire consumed him in minutes, but she cursed herself for the extra time it took to hide the body and scorched earth.

Pochette smirked. "Even now, I can see the red peeking through. Did you forget to color your hair this week? I'll bet it'll be as red as the Pyrie before the week's end."

She exhaled a breath to calm the building rage within her. When Talwyn learned that Pochette planned to sell her out, she threw herself into controlling her magic. With each session, she further reined in her fury and started burning through her elixirs. By that night, one treatment only lasted a day or two. She clenched her eyes shut, willing them to remain dark brown. "*No red. No gold. No fire,*" the memory echoed in her mind.

Pochette laughed. "They're going to find you and sell you off. And this name you've made for yourself at the docks will vanish. Your pets will be slaughtered without you to protect them, and you'll be used up, locked away in some dungeon until they have need of you. Perhaps the young king is looking for a fiery redhead to fulfill his fantasies."

In a movement faster than his eyes could follow, Talwyn wrenched a dagger out of Pochette's forearm and held it to his throat. "They will never touch me," she seethed, heat warming her chest. She'd been keeping it at bay up until now, but he knew exactly how to get under her skin. Her fury raged to be set free, pounding against the walls she'd built around it long ago. It uncoiled past her core, down her limbs, and made her fingers twitch. She stared into his beady eyes, her fist hovering over his mangled one. "A promise made is a promise kept," she whispered and opened her palm to release her fury.

The orange glow of her flame shone on his face before he registered the pain. She watched his smug grin fade to horror as his gaze darted to his melting skin. He writhed in the chair, eliciting an ear-piercing howl.

Talwyn sneered, her hatred leaving her devoid of any remorse for the man whose touch had haunted her since she was nineteen. Her fury consumed his hand until nothing but a charred husk remained, and Pochette collapsed in the chair. With an effort, she snuffed the flames, gritting her teeth against the tide still pressing against her defenses.

"No more," he whimpered. He begged again and met her gaze. Pochette's jaw dropped. What color was left drained from his face. "No," he gasped, "no, it's not—It's not possible! Your eyes! You're—" His own widened further. "You're *her*. *That's* why they want you! They know! They know who you are!"

Talwyn blinked in confusion. "They know nothing," she muttered, wiping her blade on a handkerchief. "I am no one." She pocketed the cloth and replaced the weapon in its sheath.

He howled madly. "You're a memory, a whisper on the wind! They've found you."

Irritation flared alongside her fury. She found no enjoyment in ending a man lost to madness, but Talwyn could no longer hold back her magic. She retrieved her other two daggers, eliciting a momentary shriek from Pochette before he returned to his blathering. She wiped his own blood on his shirt before returning her weapons to her belt.

"You were dead, and they've found you!" he crowed.

"Then I'll see you in the hells." She clasped both hands around his neck and released the inferno raging inside her.

He choked on his manic laughter once, twice, and then coughed up black smoke that reeked of melted flesh. A moment later, his head shot back, a wall of white flame erupting out of his mouth, his eyes, every orifice on his body. Talwyn watched him, hands still on his neck, the flames licking her face in a gentle caress, until his convulsing stopped.

She walked out of the Kiln without a backward glance to the pyre behind her. Her boots splashed through a large puddle, and her attention flicked to the mirrored surface. Her hands, clenched at her sides, were untouched by the fire. Even her hair remained unaffected despite the blaze that washed over her. The familiar warmth of her fury-heated leather jacket embraced her. She remained untouched by the flames save for the bright glow in her gold eyes.

Glass shattered somewhere in the tavern. Talwyn stared at the table before her, lost in thought while she sipped ale in a dark corner. An imperfection in the metal cup scratched the skin along her thumb. It did not bode well that Pochette knew her secret, and Talwyn couldn't understand why his likening of her to the Fury of legend grated on her nerves. Fury was rare magic, and some humorless gods thought to gift her with control over the element.

"You're brooding." Carrick dropped two new pints on the table, sliding into the seat across from her.

She waved the metal cup away. "The fool spouted nonsense."

"Did he tell you who brokered the deal?"

"Mages, that's all I know." She shook her head. "Did you find anything?"

Carrick pinched his thick lips into a thin line, his focus on the door. "Egan found no trace. None of us did." His forehead wrinkled. Carrick had been outraged when he learned that Pochette planned to betray them, though Talwyn herself had expected it to happen years ago. His boyish face contrasted the rest of him. The muscles covering his upper body flexed as he sat stiffly in the chair. His knee bounced under the table, bumping Talwyn's own. "The pouch held five pieces of the king's gold."

Talwyn stilled. "You're sure?"

Carrick nodded and slid one toward her.

She dragged it across the table until it fell into her waiting palm. A flaming willow tree witnessing two crossed swords shone in the low tavern candlelight as if the fire on the coin itself flickered. "So, our new cloaked friends may not be from outside the kingdom after all." She pocketed the coin and took a large swig of her drink, making a face. The liquid had gone warm during her musings. "He called it an apparition."

Carrick swore, scrunching his button nose. "What in the hells is that? And why would Pochette negotiate with one?"

Talwyn hesitated. She wondered this as well. Thanks to its lack of resources and poor state, the kingdom had gone unnoticed by the outside world for the last twenty years. If they believed Pochette, the apparition connected to something that could spell danger for the docks and Meladair as a whole. "Any word from the coven?"

Carrick frowned and shook his head. "No one's seen or heard from the witches in over eight weeks. You don't think anything has happened to them, do you?"

"They're likely in hiding." Talwyn didn't voice her thoughts. If enemies were nearby, their friends with earth-given magic might have found trouble.

"Does this change things?"

Talwyn bit her lip. Plans had been set in motion months before their discovery of Pochette's betrayal. They originally decided the docks needed a change of hands, and the rendezvous tonight merely pushed things along. But they hadn't prepared for a new, more powerful rival.

Egan and the twins joined the table, interrupting her thoughts.

"Could you two have been more obnoxious?" Egan teased the twins, presenting a platter of food. His short, lithe frame snuck past Talwyn into the chair beside her, and his plain features twisted into a mocking smile.

Sybil scoffed and held her hand over her heart. "We were tasked with keeping watch at Gale's tavern. Nothing, and I mean *nothing* is more conspicuous than a sober patron at Gale's." Her beak-like nose turned up at the smaller boy. Given her unusual height, Egan could only peer up her nostrils. Sybil leaned her broad shoulders over the table and turned her attention to Talwyn. Her hair, so black it swallowed any surrounding light, fell in front of her face. She flipped the shoulder-length waves back over her shoulder. "Nice to see you awake for once, Talwyn. How does it feel to be sober?"

"I've built up enough reserve magic to take care of one thug," she responded. She chose not to respond to Sybil's question. "Do I have your visions to thank for moving things along, or did your little act get out of hand?"

Sybil winked. "I can neither confirm nor deny whether my actions were part of the plan or merely a stroke of genius."

Sybil's air magic made her a seer, lending her glimpses of the many possible outcomes in a yet unwritten future. Despite her words, she would have known if her drunken act would reveal their presence or move things along.

"And where were you?" Sybil pointed a roasted pigeon leg at Egan.

"In the shadows, as we all should have been," Rainier chastised in a raspy voice.

Sybil's twin, Rainier, could not be more unlike his sister, with broader shoulders and black hair roughly cut at his ears. Where Sybil was boisterous, Rainier was observant. Where Sybil acted on pure instinct, her brother made precise calculations before taking the first step. His gift was no different. Sybil's magic allowed her to see another's future like the branches of a tree all based on a single decision. Rainier's allowed him to influence others with only his voice, his magic carried on the wind that gifted it to him, and his victim would do whatever he said as if they had come up with the idea on their own.

They had been an interesting addition to Talwyn's little gang. It appeared the gods had gifted each power with a purpose. The impulsive one received the ability to see consequences, while the methodical one received the ability to make choices for others—they balanced each other out. They bickered more than anything, but their fierce loyalty to each other and the rest of the crew was invaluable.

"Then why did you join in with the act?" Sybil retorted. "If I didn't know any better, I'd say you enjoyed it." She tore off a large chunk of meat and sat back in her seat.

"You gave me no choice. I had to make sure my cocksure sister didn't draw the attention of every drunken fool in the establishment. You'd do well to remember that not everyone knows you can kill a man without blinking. We didn't have the time nor the space to clean up your messes tonight—"

"Enough," Carrick interrupted. His attention remained on a crowd growing at the entrance.

Talwyn withheld a groan. In full metal armor stood Daire, the captain of the palace guard, and Talwyn's most annoying mistake. He carried his helmet under one arm and rested his free hand on the pommel of his sword. His eyes twinkled as he approached.

The captain was handsome enough. Growing up training with the king's knights had sculpted his body into a muscular physique worthy of making even Sybil swoon. His thick, chestnut hair fell over his eyes, and his thin lips curled into a hungry smirk that grabbed Talwyn's attention as a young teen.

They'd formed a friendship after he happened upon her at the royal stables, and years later it had turned into something more. She would study his pointed nose, his hard jawline, and get lost in his sky-blue eyes. But at some point, the confident teen had turned into a misguided young man. Instead of swapping stories, he criticized Tal for her actions, and the fantasy extinguished. When she ended their little fling, he had the nerve to be sad about it, which infuriated her.

Carrick rolled up the sleeves of his loose cotton shirt and faced the newcomer, his muscles on full display.

"Tal, you're looking wonderful tonight." Daire flashed what he believed was his champion smolder, and the twins groaned audibly while Egan did his best to dissolve into his seat.

Talwyn took another gulp of the warm ale and slammed the cup on the table. "Go away, Daire. I'm busy." She sighed at the cup, refusing to meet his eyes.

He placed a hand on his metal chest plate, feigning hurt. "Am I that unwelcome? Have you forgotten our time together already, my love? I certainly haven't." He leaned into her ear and whispered, "I still dream of my name on your tongue, your gasps in my ear as I—"

Tal jerked her head away from the captain and pushed him. Carrick stood up, nearly knocking the table over, and bumped Daire with his chest. "Captain or not, your rank means nothing to me," he threatened. "You'll listen to Tal, or you'll get out."

Daire sneered at Carrick. The two towering men stood eye-to-eye, but Carrick bested the captain in muscle. Several of Daire's regiment had scattered around the tavern, hands on their swords, ready for a fight.

"Enough." Talwyn sighed. She stepped between the two men and pushed Carrick back into his seat before turning to the soldier. "What do you want, Daire?"

"A word... alone." He narrowed his eyes at Carrick.

"Fine. *Alone,*" she emphasized the word, nodding at his watching soldiers.

Daire nodded and his men swiftly found their own spots around the tavern. He walked out the door and away from anyone within hearing distance, Talwyn close behind.

When she'd had enough, Talwyn crossed her arms and stopped. "I think this is sufficient."

Daire turned with a smirk on his lips. "You always did try to control the situation."

"And you always assumed I'd fall in line like one of your subordinates."

"A woman's place is at her man's side, not fighting his battles," he shot back. Besides Tal, the women in his life had been decorations for their husbands to flaunt around like some kind of trophy, never speaking, never doing anything without the man's permission. Their time together had no effect on his narrow-minded views.

She glared at him. "My food is getting cold."

Daire sighed and changed his tone. "The king is looking for a wife."

"Wasn't he already betrothed?" King James was barely three years older than her; a child compared to the rulers of the surrounding kingdoms. He remained unmarried and had a reputation of using his position to his advantage with the ladies of the noble families—married or otherwise.

"He's broken the engagement."

"So?"

"*So*," Daire began, "there will be events held in his honor to help him find a wife. His counsel is pushing for a profitable marriage with a foreign royal, so he's agreed to a masquerade to host ladies from the surrounding kingdoms."

Tal inspected her nails. "I don't see what this has to do with me."

"As captain of the palace guard, I will be invited as an esteemed guest. And I am expected to bring my own lady to escort."

She paused her annoyed theatrics and peered up at him. "Your own lady?"

"Yes, Tal." He sighed, exasperated.

"I'm no one's lady."

"Well, clearly, we'll need to work on your appearance and behavior, but I have the palace dressmaker at my disposal, and he can work wonders. And as long as you don't speak to anyone, the night could be quite enjoyable."

Tal barked out a laugh. She had been a fool to let their friendship mature into something more. Clearly, the man could benefit from actually listening to himself. "I thought I made it clear that I despise being used."

"Used? Tal, this is your chance to get away from the docks. I'm offering you an advantageous marriage, that—"

"Marriage? Again? You think I want to marry you? What we had was a fantasy of your own making, Daire. Look at me." She held out her arms, displaying her leather pants and lack of corset or skirts, her belts and straps with multiple sheaths for knives and daggers, her messy hair and dirt covered skin. "This is the real me, a bounty hunter. Not some shy little mouse for you to play with or show off to the vultures at your table. Let it go. I will never be the lady you wish me to be. Go find some innocent brat to spoil with your wealth and big ego. I want none of it." She turned to storm off, but he grabbed her arm. On instinct, she used her free arm to unsheathe a dagger and held it at his exposed throat.

Daire tensed, but to his credit, he didn't let go of her arm. He gulped before saying, "Do you really want to spend the rest of your life having to carry blades out of fear? I could protect you. You'll never want for anything." The misguided sincerity in his gaze infuriated her.

"If you think I carry these out of fear, then you know nothing about me, especially not what I *want*." She tore her arm out of his grasp and stomped back into the tavern.

In her anger, she slammed the door open, causing everyone to jolt and stare at her. She seethed under their gazes and clenched the dagger still in her hand. A few soldiers reached for their swords until their captain appeared behind her.

"I'll await your answer," he said quietly enough for only her to hear. With a single gesture, he signaled his men to follow him out of the establishment.

At their exit, Sybil yelled, "And stay out, ya lumpish milk-livered pignut!" A roar of laughter erupted, followed by a few cheers of, "Here, here!"

Talwyn stalked back to the table and took the pint Carrick had offered earlier, still untouched. She chugged the drink whole and plopped down with a belch.

"What did he want?" Carrick asked, a hint of irritation still in his voice.

"He wants me to marry him," she said flatly and was promptly showered with ale as Sybil spit out the swig she had just taken.

"He proposed? Here? At the tavern?" Egan asked, incredulous.

"How romantic," Sybil added while wiping spittle from her chin.

Tal took a cloth from Carrick's outstretched hand and wiped her face. "And he wants me to attend the king's masquerade ball as his guest."

"A king's ball? This is the first I've heard of it." Rainier prided himself in learning information first. He wouldn't take it lightly that he wasn't already aware of the event.

Talwyn nodded. "The king ended his engagement, and the ball is to help him find a new one."

"Ah yes, because every lady wants to be paraded around like a goat at an auction for some greedy royal to decide if she's ripe enough to sink his cock into." Sybil stole her brother's drink and ignored the incredulous look he gave her.

Talwyn snorted. "I told him as much."

"I wonder what motivated the king's decision," Rainier considered aloud. "But an invitation to the ball could be useful."

"I'm not going. I refuse to be dragged around on his arm like some sort of prize he's won. And accepting such an invitation would also mean accepting his proposal."

"You don't want to get off the streets, Tal?" Egan asked in a tone that often came off as timid. But where Rainier observed his surroundings, Egan silently controlled his impulses. He was the perfect ghost during jobs, but when emotions ran high, he lost himself to his own demons.

His exact ability remained a mystery. Nevertheless, in a fight, Tal wanted him on their side. When she accepted their last member, Egan confided his fear that he would one day give in to the rage and never find his way out. She promised she'd never let that happen, but now she wondered if the boy, only eighteen, hoped to find a way out of life by the docks. If he never had to fight, would he never have to worry about losing himself?

"I would never be accepted by them. I have no delusions about what I am and do not have the self-control to hide it." Her eyes softened at her young friend who nodded and sat back.

Talwyn sighed and pinched the bridge of her nose. Her head felt like it had split in two. Using her elemental fury shouldn't exhaust her the way it did lately, but she had been distracted with Pochette's betrayal. She had always planned to end his life, and her crew ultimately decided this summer would be the time to do it. The docks needed someone in power who would help the poor, not steal from them. They worked painstakingly among the shadows to put themselves on top, but the added surprise of the mages disrupted their plans.

She remembered what Pochette said about her hair color bleeding through and set a mental reminder to get more elixir from the alchemist. She'd finished the last of the eye drops after returning from the Kiln, her eyes now the same deep brown as Carrick's. She would need to have a not-so-friendly chat with the old man. The blasted mixes he'd been giving her lately washed out sooner and sooner with each application. She suspected he altered the formula to rob her of her coin.

Something else bothered her, nagging at the back of her mind, but every time she reached for it, the thought slipped away. Something Pochette had said needed to be addressed. They needed to return to the tunnels and make plans for the retribution. They'd anticipated Pochette's men taking revenge, but she needed to go over the plans again, needed to be sure they accounted for every lackey, every hired servant, until they were sure they wouldn't be caught unawares. The nagging thought tickled her mind again, and she focused on it; a whisp of a word reached her tongue.

"Fire!" A man burst into the tavern screaming the word. "They've burned the docks! All of Pochette's is in flames!"

2

By morning, nothing but ash remained where any establish-ment associated with Pochette once stood. Every man under his employ was either missing or growing cold in the gutters. Talwyn and her group of misfits had spent the better part of the last eighteen hours picking through the rubble. They had no death toll, having found the countless bodies were blackened and mutilated beyond recognition. They'd seen more death in one night than the last hailfire outbreak.

Smoke burned her throat as she walked through the remains of Pochette's gambling den to the rectangle that used to be his office. The scavengers already scoured the place, leaving nothing but cinders and footprints. A bloody, charcoal-coated hand poked out from under a blackened wooden beam. Tal stepped around it, noting it ended at the wrist. She nudged the burnt seat of a heavy desk chair with the toe of her soot-covered leather boot, not sure whether to be angry or relieved. If her friends had their way, she would have woken up this morning as the queen of the docks. Now, she was queen of nothing but ash.

A light breeze sent more dust and sparks swirling up around her and she covered her face to avoid breathing it in. Her eyes followed the dancing embers as they aimed for the clouds. A large weeping willow stood sentinel on a distant hill, mocking the current state of the docks. As children, she and Carrick would trek to the base of the tree and watch life continue below them, a king and queen on their earth-made throne. The tree would listen as they exchanged grand plans of the future, plans that never came to be.

Behind her, Carrick bent down to a frail old man sitting on the ground, his blistered hands held before him. Carrick offered his waterskin and pulled a jar from his pocket, applying the pink healing salve to the burns. Tal doubted the old man knew Carrick used half the week's salary to buy it.

Exotically sweet spice carried downwind. Without looking, she asked Rainier, "Did they leave anything behind?"

"Nothing important. And *no one* either." Rainier, along with the rest of their crew, had gone searching through another of Pochette's establishments. "They were thorough. Destroyed the ships and the distillery too." Unlike the gambling dens and whore houses, the ownership of the ships and distillery, were not public knowledge. Rainier, however, had known about all of Pochette's endeavors for years. The crew should have taken control over it all that morning.

"Damn. They could have at least left the ale."

"They got Greggs."

Tal spat. "Good riddance." Greggs tracked everyone's debts for Pochette and, while he never carried out punishment, he most certainly enjoyed watching. He also happened to be their link to Pochette's empire. "I don't care if he sold us information. Once we were in, he would have been disposed of too. Any sign of Duncan?"

Pochette's muscle and right-hand man wanted to end Tal's life in the most drawn out and sadistic of ways ever since she permanently disfigured his boss. Pochette had held him back partly due to the violent promise Tal had left him with. His fear of her wasn't far off, but she didn't so much have a plan in place as she simply didn't need protection.

"Duncan and his two guards are still missing. That's two weeks now. He might have left before Pochette brokered his deal."

"Even if he's dead, there's no chance we'll identify him among these." She gestured to the limbs and torsos littering the street. Her mind swirled with the implications of the attack while her gaze lost focus on the silent scream of agony on a bodiless face among the ash.

Rain bit his lip as if contemplating his response. "How are you feeling? Did the training help build your reserves?"

Tal nodded absently. "I'm awake at least. I still have some fury left in me before I'm fully drained. It's getting easier to build up enough reserves to last a week or so before I need to rest."

His teeth worried on a single spot on his lip until it started to bleed. "Good. After this, I wouldn't advise you to drain your reserves. If something happens, we can't have you comatose for days on end."

Tal's fury flared in her chest. "It's not like I can control it. You know better than most that magic doesn't work the way we want it to, and the price is steep." She narrowed her eyes at him, noting the flare in his nostrils, but he didn't respond.

After hearing of Pochette's betrayal, Tal increased her training tenfold. She'd been in and out of consciousness almost every other day, then would throw herself right back into training. By the night of the rendezvous, she could burn down a small building without blinking. She eyed the remnants of the empire that ruled the docks not twenty-four hours prior, the empire she should be taking control of, all burned to nothing.

"This changes things," Rain voiced Tal's thoughts.

She nodded. "We should see if the others have found anything."

They'd made a home for themselves in the underground sewage system. No one bothered them. The smell alone deterred most of the riff raff, and others who lived underground wished to be left alone. After nearly two decades, they'd learned which tunnels were no longer used, cleaned them up, and founded their own little haven. A large opening had been turned into a sort of gathering space.

Blankets and hay-stuffed cushions sat atop crates that acted as seats and a table, where Egan placed a plate of bread and cured meats. Carrick stood against the far wall with his arms crossed. Sybil cleaned her boots with a dirty rag while Rainier read through the notebook he kept as a ledger.

Egan tossed a gold coin next to the plate. "Found a few more of these among the rubble."

Rainier leaned forward and snatched up the coin. He turned it over in his hand. "More of the king's gold."

Tal caught the coin when Rain tossed it to her and ran her thumb over the raised image on the side. "What would Pochette's businesses be doing with coins containing the king's seal?"

Rain shrugged. "Could be nothing more than money passing hands at one of his businesses. Could be something else. Now that they're reduced to smoking coals, it'll be more difficult to find out."

"Greggs should have mentioned it," Carrick growled.

Rain shrugged. "Either he didn't think the particular type of gold in the business mattered, or he betrayed us as much as he betrayed Pochette. Nothing we can do about it now."

"Well, at least we don't have to worry we'll be gutted in an alley by one of his men," Egan mused.

"Don't be so sure," Carrick warned. "Not all of them are accounted for."

"I don't believe that a single one of them is gone until I see their lifeless bodies floating down the Taralin." Tal picked at soot under her nail with a knife.

Egan tapped a spot on the stone floor. "Who do you think did it?"

Tal flicked her eyes to Carrick, who answered for her. "Mages, if what Pochette said is true."

The twins stiffened at the word and exchanged a glance.

"I think it's time you tell us what happened in the southern kingdom," Tal said. A sense of foreboding filled the room.

Fifteen years ago, Rainier and Sybil showed up at the docks in the bottom of a cargo ship. They were frail from poor nutrition but fierce as a pair of tigers backed into a corner. At just thirteen years old, their father paid one of the ship's crewmen to hide them on board, handed them packs of essentials, and said good-bye. Until now, no one pestered the twins about their story, and they never shared it.

"The mages didn't come as dignitaries with grand announcements and celebrations. One night, they just appeared," Sybil began. "For weeks before, maybe months, those with elemental magic went missing. Most of the time, anyone who would have witnessed it was found dead—stabbed, poisoned, burned, you name it."

Carrick met Tal's gaze, and their conversation of the recent bounties and missing witches replayed in her mind. The disappearances had already started in Meladair. They'd been hired by one family to locate a mother, then a son, a sister, and soon, the numbers became too large to keep track of. While disappearances weren't uncommon between the trafficking rings, Netters, and general criminal activity, no one suspected any outside forces. But those disappearances, now coupled with the long silence from the local witch coven and this new information, spoke volumes.

Sybil continued, "At first, we thought it was infighting. Magic governed our society, and power often changed hands. It got to a point where we didn't know what to do, so we hid anyone with magic who couldn't fight. Then they started sending their apparitions—faceless copies who would speak as if without a soul. They wore long dark cloaks that would have been much too hot for the climate. They met with folk in secret and offered coin in exchange for information on the whereabouts of anyone with an ability. But those who completed their end of the deal only lived long enough to see their reward go to waste and were soon found suffering the same fate as the others."

"And those who refused didn't make it to sunrise," Rainier added.

"Did you get a good look at the reward they offered, where it came from?" The weight of the king's coin in her pocket pressed against Tal's leg.

Sybil frowned while Rain merely shook his head. "It's unlikely they'd have the same gold, if that's what you're thinking." He held up the coin still in his hand.

"What of the mages?" Carrick interrupted.

"Tensions grew for weeks, and then one morning, the sky filled with smoke. Father woke us up and ordered us to get dressed. It was chaos—people running, screaming all around. The dead were everywhere—people we knew, people we grew up with. Dismembered bodies, severed heads on spikes in front of their homes, left on display." Rainier's tone was grim. When the others said nothing, he continued. "Word had been sent to the king weeks before, asking for help, but it never came. Non-magical folk weren't often trained to fight, and since most of those with abilities were missing or dead, we didn't stand a chance."

Tal had heard whispers of magic folk more powerful than the gods, but she had chalked it all up to myth. "Where could someone get such power?"

"Pain." Sybil pursed her lips at some vision the others couldn't see. "Even if our warriors were able to get close enough, they had one chance to get a killing blow. Anything less just made the mages more powerful."

"You mean blood magic?!" Carrick turned to Tal. As children, they'd snuck around the docks and often heard stories from the other kingdoms. At the mention of blood magic, a hush would fall over the conversation, and Tal would shiver against an unnatural chill, as if the gods themselves cursed anyone who dared speak of it.

"That can't be. It's forbidden." Egan shook his head.

Sybil answered with a somber stare.

Tal didn't believe in legends, but the danger stood before her. "Can we kill them?"

Rainier tilted his head. "If you get past the countless apparitions, dodge the spells and curses, and strike true? Sure. They're still mortal. One or two didn't make it out of the battle, but for every one of theirs we killed, hundreds of ours were lost."

A power like that could destroy their weak northern kingdom without any resistance. "How many mages were there? Maybe we're lucky and only have to deal with one. Have you heard anything from the southern kingdom since?"

The twins shook their heads in unison, but Sybil spoke. "They mostly sent out their apparitions. We only ever saw a few actual mages—they wielded all the magic." She clutched the ash-covered cloth in her fist. "Our village was destroyed by the time we got to the ship. Based on what we learned in the weeks before and then afterwards on the ship, the same thing happened to several villages along the path from the eastern kingdom to the southern kingdom. All taken out within a week of each other. But there's been no word." It had been fifteen years since they stumbled out of the belly of that cargo ship. If their father hadn't come for them yet, the likelihood of him ever coming at all seemed nonexistent.

"That is what I don't understand—from what Father told us, the southern kingdom was always at war but always from within. Power always switched among the families. And then one day, this unknown outside faction comes in, and no one talks about it?" Rainier clenched his fist. "Did the mages stop traveling south? Did one of the remaining villages stop them? And why didn't the king send help? If the warring families suddenly united, maybe we could have won. Bleeding pigs, how could they sit back and let the surrounding villages get destroyed?!"

No one had an answer for their conflicted friend. In the last fifteen years, no whispers of a conquering foreign power had reached Tal's sources. That this bloodshed happened within that time left her uneasy. The conversation created more questions than answers.

"Is it possible they cast some sort of illusion spell to prevent anyone from seeing the true devastation?" Egan mused.

"Do you know how powerful of a spell that must be? To prevent all traders and travelers from seeing a massacre of whole villages?" Rainier lost his composure and yelled at their young friend.

Sybil put a hand on her brother's arm. "We don't know if anything happened to him. For all we know, Father managed to force them underground. There's still a possibility—"

Rainier ripped his arm away from his sister and stormed off in the direction of his room. No one spoke for several breaths. Rain rarely showed emotion, but they never spoke of their home before now. It made the appearance of the mages at the docks all the more concerning.

Tal, Carrick, and Egan sat motionless while Sybil described the apparitions. "Human copies of the mage who created them—even down to their cloak. Except, their faces." She shook her head, eyes widening at some horror Tal couldn't see. "Nothing. No eyes. No nose. No mouth. No features whatsoever." She gripped the back of her neck and refused to look at anyone in the room. "When they spoke, you could hear how empty they were."

Tal compared Sybil's memories with her observations from the night before.

But since only Pochette got close enough to the apparition, the burning of his buildings and killing of his men weren't enough to indicate that mages were in Meladair. Tal was proof of at least one Fury alive with the power to set an entire building ablaze. Though, to their knowledge, there were no others in the kingdom, and she was the only person brave or powerful enough to take on the now-dead king of the docks.

Sybil described the breadth of the mages' power. As they escaped the village, she watched as a man's head had been severed from his body by a mere swipe of the mage's cloaked arm. A couple running across the street were caught in a wall of flame that erupted from under the enemy's cloaked hood. Syb and Rain witnessed another mage attack with three different elemental powers—something that should have been impossible. The unease in Tal's stomach solidified to something akin to fear, a feeling she wasn't used to.

"Do we think these mages are connected with those from the southern kingdom?" Carrick voiced the question Tal had been toying with. They didn't know how many mages were involved in the deal brokered with Pochette.

Sybil shrugged. "It's possible. A secret society of the most powerful magical beings taking out any possible threat would make sense. Then again, we've never heard of anything like it."

Egan tilted his head. "What would a secret society of mages want with Meladair? We barely have enough food here, let alone gold or any other resources. It makes more sense that the two situations are unrelated."

"We have to assume the worst. Do we really want to let our guard down on the chance this mage is acting alone?" Rain stood in the entrance to the common area, leaning his shoulder against the stone. He'd attempted to return as his collected self, but his hunched shoulders belied his irritation.

"So that's it then?" Egan asked, incredulous. "We just accept that we're being invaded? And what about our plans?"

Tal scoffed. "What plans? There's nothing left of Pochette's empire, nothing to run, nothing to rule over. Hells, if the gangs aren't running for the mountains already, they'll surely destroy each other in the fight to claim the throne of the slums."

"Has anyone actually seen a mage in Meladair?" Carrick sounded skeptical.

Tal shook her head. "If what Pochette said is true, he only interacted with the apparitions."

"But if an apparition is present, a mage can't be far. From what we saw, a mage could only project an apparition the length of twenty buildings." Sybil sharpened one of her knives while she relayed the information.

"Any witnesses still alive only saw cloaked figures before the fires started. Apparitions are incapable of producing magic, so unless they set the fires without it, unlikely given how quickly and completely everything burned, mages were in the streets last night," Rain concluded somberly. He crossed his arms and clenched his fists.

Pochette's warning about the evil he kept at bay echoed in Tal's mind. What had he done to protect his empire? Did the mages destroy it and leave or were they here to stay? She beseeched Sybil wordlessly, and the seer nodded. "Shit." She bit her lip. "Can you see anything? Do we know why they're here?"

Sybil narrowed her eyes at the blank space in front of her. Her lips pursed and nostrils flared, and then she shook her head. Despite her powerful gift, she could not see futures for strangers unless they linked with someone she knew and only if she focused on the right person and the right events. Even then, there was no guarantee the future would reveal itself. When Tal mentioned that the unknown apparition searched for a red-head, Sybil stared at her with a strange look on her face. But when Tal questioned her, her friend kept silent.

"Someone should inform the king." Egan stood as if he would be the one to do it.

Tal sighed. Egan was the most naïve of the group. He still believed the king would help or cared at all. "The docks have been rotting for years with no help from the palace. The nobles are too busy attending their balls and eating their fill to give us a second thought." No one of status had ventured to the slums or offered any kind of aid, least of all the young king who wasted his days on pleasures of the flesh. No, they were on their own.

"Even if one of us could somehow get word to the palace, do you really think they would believe us?" Tal sheathed her knife and stood. "Until we know more, we need to be careful. We have to assume they're taking anyone with abilities. Sybil, Rain, you know more than any of us how dangerous this could be. Be vigilant. No one goes out alone at night. And we take it easy on the bounties. Small jobs only like we had planned while getting used to the businesses. Even without taking over Pochette's establishments, we have enough to manage for now."

"The same goes for you too, Tal." Carrick notched a brow.

"I can hold my own."

"Be that as it may, if what Pochette said is true, then powerful mages will be looking for *you*. Have you ever gone head-to-head with a mage? I'd rather not test your strength, if you ask me." Carrick crossed his arms.

"I am not some princess needing a bodyguard. I did just fine on my own before you four showed up, and I continue to do just fine when you're all doing your own thing," she ground out.

Talwyn had few memories of her life before a fisherman named Waltford picked her up with the rest of the rubbish at the docks nearly two decades ago. He took her in, fed her, clothed her, and let her sleep in the corner of his one room home. But he never let her leave and never gave a reason. "No red. No gold. No fire," he would say in his simple-minded language. One day, he went out and never returned. After seven days, Tal ran away and lived on the streets, scrounging for food and hiding from the Netters.

Carrick spotted her long before she noticed him. Days without food left her collapsed in an alley. He offered her bread and fresh water when she was too sick to find her own and carried her back to his hideaway under a dock where he nursed her back to health. His gentle nature and strong presence broke down her walls. By the end of the week, they were inseparable. As much as Talwyn refused to let anyone think of her as fragile, she would never fault Carrick for his protectiveness over her.

"I'm okay with holding off on taking over things, since every one of those businesses and persons are gone. But regardless of who is after you, we need to figure out what to do about these mages." Rainier tapped his ledger, as if the numbers in the book would give them a plan.

"We do nothing." Talwyn stood with her arms crossed. All eyes landed on her.

"Tal, we can't ignore them as a threat," Sybil said gently.

"Did you forget what happened in your village? We are not kings with armies at our commands, nor are we assassins. We are bounty hunters. We do not stand a chance against beings powerful enough to destroy entire villages in one night. And it's not our job to keep the peace."

"I thought we were prepared to do just that when you killed Pochette," Egan added quietly.

"We were supposed to keep his businesses running and the gangs away from the common folk. *That plan* never included outside forces, and now all our allies within Pochette's gang are gone too. It's just us. Pochette had hundreds of men, and *he* couldn't keep the mages out. Besides, he was dead whether I delivered the blow or not. If he thought they were going to let him walk away, then he deserved what he got."

"So, you would sit back and let them destroy our home? You'd watch the world burn and do nothing?" Carrick asked.

Her eyes shot to his and the hurt in them gripped Tal's heart enough to steal her breath. Carrick had always been supportive of her choice to lay low. She always said, "Helping others is the best way to get yourself into trouble," to which Carrick would tease that *he* helped her. She never had much of a response to that, but she would be forever grateful for his kindness that day.

She knew this went against everything they'd agreed to, but Tal never wanted any of it. "We do nothing. When the mages are gone, *then* we can revisit this ruling business. Until then, we lay low and avoid capture," she repeated, ending the conversation. She left them there, in one of the dead-ends of the underground sewage system and retreated to her room.

3

Coals still glowed in the ruins the next morning as Tal trailed behind Carrick through the ash-covered streets. He stopped next to a mule-drawn cart with two children sitting within. The father pulled at a large stone blocking the cart's path. Carrick helped remove the stone while Tal scanned the children. Their clothes needed washing, and soot coated their faces. Three cloth bags and a crate of food sat in the cart between them.

"Where you headed?" Carrick asked.

"North," the man said. "Our home burned down in the fire. There's nothing left for us here."

Tal noticed the burns on his arms. One of the children's faces bore an angry red rash and scorched hair on one side. Tear tracks marked her cheeks, and she gripped Carrick's jar of pink salve in her tiny fist.

"Take this." Carrick handed the man two pieces of coin, and Tal shook her head.

The father pushed Carrick's hand back. "No. Thank you, but we will manage. Thank you for your help." He climbed into the cart and urged the mule onward.

"That bleeding heart of yours is going to give away all our money," Tal teased while they watched the small family go.

"They're not the only ones leaving." He nodded toward the pier, where people boarded an awaiting ship with nothing but the clothes on their backs.

Tal surveyed the ruined buildings. A man dusted off a wooden sign in front of what used to be the tailor's shop. Another added pieces of broken wood to a basket. Children dressed in dirty rags hopped from a fallen stone to balance along a charred wooden beam. "But more are staying. They'll pick up the pieces."

"And what if they attack again? How much more of this can these people take?"

She sighed and pinched the bridge of her nose. "What can *we* do Carrick? What power do we have against these mages? We're just a bunch of misfit orphans who've managed to scare a few thugs into leaving us alone. We'd be signing our own death bounty if we even thought of standing against them."

"We'll be signing our own death bounty *and* everyone else's if we do nothing and let them tear this place apart." He gestured to the still-warm coals behind them. "And what if they're the ones responsible for all the people going missing lately? Are we going to give up on the poor souls?"

She hadn't given up on them. She needed to find them—if nothing more than to prove that their kingdom could still be safe. Despite those leaving now and the countless others before them, life could continue in Meladair. It always would for Talwyn. This was her home. She sighed but didn't say anything.

He wrapped an arm around her shoulder. Despite being two heads taller and nearly twice as wide, his enormous presence gave Tal stability. His companionship made the difficult life in the docks enjoyable. The gods had smiled down on her in that one moment where he chose to befriend her. Without him, Tal would have left long ago or joined the dead.

She sighed. "We'll continue to look for the missing, but we won't engage with the mages. Not unless they are a direct threat. Okay?"

"You got it, Tal." His voice revealed his doubt of her conviction.

"I mean it. We stay away from them. Your dreams of being king of the docks died with Pochette's businesses."

He nodded. "Sure. Whatever you say."

Tal jabbed his ribs with one of her knuckles. He flinched away before messing her hair. She slapped his hand away, laughing with him. The moment faded quickly as the scene around them came back into focus.

They continued through the devastation, watching the ships come and go in the distance. Rubbish floated down the river. Children played among the soot and grime while people all around picked up the pieces of what had been destroyed. And the sun set over the dirty, crime-filled town they called home.

They returned late, expecting everyone to be asleep. A high-pitched sob echoed through the tunnel. Carrick's brown eyes mirrored her own confusion. They each drew a weapon, preparing for a fight. The voice came from Egan's room, a dead-end covered by a torn and weathered blanket.

"I tried to stop them, but they just pushed me back. They didn't even have to try that hard." The child hiccupped. "My stupid knife didn't even reach them. They took her and laughed in my face."

Talwyn sheathed her dagger and pulled the blanket back. A small boy, about eight, stood opposite Egan at the table. He faced away from them. His clothes hung in tatters over his skeletal frame, while filth covered his clothing and every inch of his exposed skin. His short blonde hair had been cut at odd angles as if someone had hacked it away in haste.

"Took who?" Carrick said, all business and booming power.

The boy jumped and turned his tear-stained face to the sound. Talwyn had to bite her lip to stop herself from gasping at the boy's state. Even more dirt and grime covered his face, save for the streaks made by his tears. His cheeks were sunken from malnutrition, and his eyes bulged. He had scrapes and cuts all along his exposed skin, some new, others in various stages of healing or infection.

The boy stiffened when he saw Talwyn. The children of the docks knew her to be cold and unforgiving. She'd used them on numerous bounties throughout the years as an easy source of information. It hadn't been easy to gain their trust, but once she'd earned it, a basket of food was all she needed to get them to talk. No one ever looked twice at the children; they certainly wouldn't suspect the sickly orphan was about to sell the exact details of their crime for a loaf of bread.

"My sister." He sniffed, holding his chin high. "The baker said you're looking for his niece. Can you help me?"

Talwyn clenched her teeth. *Another kidnapping.* She stepped to the child and bent down on one knee. "What's your name?"

"Janin." He sniffled again. "Can you help me?"

Talwyn avoided his plea. "How old is your sister?"

"Five."

"They're taking five-year-olds now?" Carrick interrupted. "When will this end, Tal?"

Talwyn ignored him and continued her line of questioning. She kept her voice calm as much to help him as to organize her thoughts into a plan of action. They *would* find this one. They *would* bring her home. "Who took her?"

"Mages. Two of them," Egan spoke for this time.

Tal jerked her attention to Egan.

"And they had two other men, but they were strange," the boy continued.

Tal attempted to keep the unease out of her voice when she asked, "Strange how?"

Janin sucked in a breath. "They had no faces."

Carrick and Talwyn locked eyes then. Any hope the mages had left dissolved in an instant. Her whole world began crashing down. She couldn't ignore the coincidences and cursed herself for not investigating the prior disappearances further. But Sybil hadn't seen anything to suspect a connection to the mages that attacked her homeland. Why would they venture this far north? What would they want with the common folk? Could all of those missing have magic?

"Where were you when they took her? Which way did they go?" Talwyn formed a plan in her mind. She just needed to know where to look, and she could get the boy's sister back.

"We were in the alley behind the bakery. That's why the baker came out. He heard us screaming." Silent tears streaked down his face, but his voice stayed even.

Talwyn nodded. "Good. Did you see which way they took her?"

His face crumpled. "They threw her in a cart with the street rubbish. I think they're taking her to the incinerator." Janin sobbed, and Egan came around the table to put an arm around the boy.

Talwyn and Carrick were on their feet, walking swiftly in the direction of the twins' corridors. The entire kingdom once sent their rubbish to the incinerator to be burned and then dumped into the Taralin River, but it had been abandoned long ago.

"Why would they go there? It's a dead end," Carrick spoke more to himself than to Talwyn.

If the mages took the girl to the incinerator, it meant only one thing. "Because they have no plans of taking her out of the docks."

"What in the hells is going on? It hasn't even been twenty-four hours, and it's all going to shit. Murdering children? Do you really think they're capable of that?"

"We don't know anything about them beyond what the twins saw years ago. And you can bet your ass they're powerful enough to instill fear in more than just some dockside thug like Pochette." They split at the end of the tunnel. Talwyn tore the ragged blanket from the entrance to Sybil's room.

"I heard. What's the plan?" Sybil stood with her foot resting on the chair similar to the one in Egan's room. An assortment of knives, daggers, and other weapons lay on the table as Sybil strapped each one to a hidden sheath on her body.

"The incinerator. We need a way in and a way out."

Sybil nodded. "On it."

4

Talwyn found Carrick and Rainier down the tunnel going over the known details.

"There's a series of rooms like our Kiln where they burned rubbish. If they are holding her anywhere, alive," Rainier paused, "they'll have her there. The main incinerator is outside. It's too public. Anyone nearby would hear her screams."

He didn't need to say it, but Talwyn knew he expected they would be torturing the girl. *Damn Rainier*, she thought. They needed to get going.

They convened in Egan's room briefly. He would stay with the boy, while the rest went after his sister. There wasn't time for good-byes or assurances. Talwyn gave Egan a nod and headed back through the tunnels.

Sybil joined the remaining three in step and motioned where to go. "There's an open sewer under the building that leads to the river. We should be able to access the inside through there."

Talwyn nodded and adjusted her course through the tunnels. They would reach the facility quickest by sticking to the waterways.

Noises fell flat as they ran. The river swallowed echoes, wrapping a blanket of unease around them. Evidence of other underground dwellers littered the ground, but their progress was unimpeded. No curious eyes tracked their movements; no street urchins scrounged for scraps. No one dared venture out now, and an eerie sense of foreboding settled over Tal. Their journey to the incinerator passed without obstacle, and their quickened pace calmed her nerves. She needed to keep her head clear if she hoped to get the girl out alive, to get all of them out alive. They planned as they ran.

Sybil couldn't see outcomes without knowing the location, and she'd never been inside the building. They would be entering blind, with only split-second warnings from the seer if they even had that kind of time.

Talwyn readied herself, keeping her breath steady and searching for her fury within. She would need to conserve her magic until absolutely necessary. One mage would be difficult enough to manage. They knew of at least two who took the girl. If they found more, their fates were left to the gods.

Despite being abandoned long ago, the smell of rotten refuse permeated every inch of the structure. Her eyes watered as she waited for direction, wondering how the stench could be worse than their tunnels.

Unsurprisingly, Rainier knew the layout. With his palm, he directed them where to go once they got into the facility. Sybil's predictions were spot on, as usual. No one waited for them at the sewage entrance, and they found a loose grate to climb into the heart of the building. Once in, they stayed close together, daggers and knives out, Carrick at the front, Talwyn and Rainier flanking him, and Sybil at the back. A single word from her guided them on which way to turn. Apprehension alone filled the silence filtering through the corridors. Sybil would warn them of any traps. She would know that much at least.

A man yelled incoherently up ahead, and their progress stopped. Talwyn eyed Sybil. "I don't know." She shook her head.

A green flash illuminated everything, and more shouts echoed down the corridor. Torches along every wall erupted in flames of the same emerald color. Metal clashed, followed by a child's scream.

As one, they turned right, and the chaos came into full view. Faceless men wearing deep green from head to toe crowded the corridor. Some lay on the ground unconscious or bleeding. Others were locked in a swordfight with someone out of view. One figure's hood remained down. As he turned, his blank face came into view. Where eyes, nose, and mouth should have been sat only a blurred picture of mottled skin, like trying to remember a face, but not quite recalling it. Apparitions overwhelmed every space, the deep forest of their cloaks punctuated by the gray of the floor or the occasional flash of red.

The group sprinted together, jumping into the fray.

Talwyn fought with barely contained fury, throwing her whole body into the brawl. "Where is the girl?" she cried out after stabbing one enemy through the spine. She screamed, aimed for the most painful blows, tore her knives through flesh, and allowed the apparition to get close enough to nick the skin so she could stab them in the heart.

"Behind the swordsman! Backed against a wall." Sybil leered at the apparition in front of her before running at him and ducking at the last minute. Her blade came up and connected with the figure's middle. It doubled over, and she stabbed again until it fell. She yelled, cackled, and taunted each copy of a man. She threw her knives without looking and struck true. "He's trapped if we don't help him."

Carrick fought with brute force, punching, slamming faceless heads into walls, and pulling bodies onto his short sword. "I thought that's what we were doing!" he called back.

Rainer danced into view. He avoided a blow with a graceful spin, his weapon continuing the movement until it connected with flesh. He parried and side-stepped around assailants, slashing as he went, aiming for the most vulnerable points. In between jabs, he spoke under his breath at the next assailant, telling him to stab his own throat, then commanding the next to attack his fellow apparitions.

Beyond, Talwyn caught glimpses of a lone swordsman, dressed from head to toe in a deep red leather, his hood pulled back, a mask of the same color covering the lower half of his face. His dark, unkempt hair whipped this way and that as he fought, and his graceful form exposed a lifetime of practice. Tal took a moment to admire how expertly he dodged the attack of one apparition, using his momentum to slice through the chest of another, then bring his sword back around and sever the neck of the first. Tal whistled in admiration.

"There!" Sybil threw a knife toward the swordsman. An apparition stepped in its path, unaware of the flying weapon, and crumpled on the ground before it could take another step.

A few paces in front of the body sat a malnourished little girl about five years old, covered in dirt, grime, and blood spatters from the fighting. Her blonde hair would have been curly if it wasn't matted. She sobbed, head swiveling back and forth between the swordsman and his attackers.

He fought well, taking on multiple assailants at once, but they outnumbered him five to one and backed him into a dead-end. They weren't going to make it to the pair at this rate.

"Carrick! Make a path! Syb, take the lead!" Talwyn slipped on a dark puddle. She used the momentum to thrust her dagger into the nearest apparition.

With practiced familiarity, they regrouped and barreled through the enemy toward the lone swordsman. The onslaught of forest green assailants continued, with even more appearing at their backs where none had been before. Talwyn searched for the source, but they appeared out of thin air.

"Where the hells are they all coming from?" Carrick threw a cloaked figure to the ground.

"The mages!" Rainier blocked an overhead swing with the weapon in his right hand and stabbed under his attacker's ribs with the one in his left.

"Find them! It won't stop until we kill the mages!" Tal screamed as an apparition grazed her thigh with something sharp. She thanked him with a slice across his gut.

"There's no time! Get the girl and get out!" Sybil's voice grew hoarse.

Carrick swore and barreled further, pushing and stabbing. Sybil ran along the space on the wall, throwing knives, ducking, pausing, and side-stepping, until she crouched next to the child huddled in the corner, sobbing beside the red swordsman.

"Where the hells have you been?" he bellowed, felling one enemy after another. A gap in the surge afforded him the chance to breathe and his gaze locked with Talwyn's. "It took you long enough!"

Confusion made Tal pause. "To your right!" she warned.

He threw up his sword just before being bludgeoned over the head. He stumbled back, swinging, and his blade hit its mark. He gave Tal a wink before returning to the fight.

Sybil protected the girl from an overhead blow. "You knew we were here."

"I went ahead when I saw you enter the building," was his reply between sword strikes.

"Let's go Syb!" Tal ordered before avoiding an overhead attack. "They aren't slowing down!" A cry rang out and Talwyn spun to find the source.

"RAIN!" Sybil's voice dripped with fear.

Rainier pulled a dagger out of his ribcage.

Talwyn locked eyes with Sybil, willing her to search for a future.

"The mage. Third room. Go, now! Rain, get up!"

"Quit pestering me!" he yelled back, his brotherly banter eliminating any concern for his condition.

Tal found the room Sybil had indicated. The door held no window, but she trusted her friend wouldn't send her to her death. She tore open the door and threw a knife into the darkness. A cry rang out as a searing pain clawed at her mind.

The clamor beyond the door lessened, and Carrick yelled to retreat. She thanked the gods and hoped they'd make it out safely. The pain increased, and she let out a strangled scream. Her fury begged to be let loose, but she couldn't, not yet.

Two mages took the girl. If she used up all her energy on one, they would never make it out. She ignored the pain and ran into the room in the direction she threw her knife. She swiped in a wide arc, hoping the mage had no experience in battle and would be frozen in place.

The gods must have favored her because she hit something soft, the pain in her head lessening. She slashed and stabbed again and again, stopping only when the pain dissipated completely.

"Tal! Time to go!" Carrick's voice carried over the fighting still going on.

"Leave you fool! What are you waiting for?" She leaned against the wall. A moment. She needed a moment to regain focus. Her mind felt fuzzy against the sudden deluge. She blinked away the lingering tears and breathed deeply, gagging on the stench of blood, garbage, and ash.

"We're waiting for you, you flaming dewberry! Get off your ass and get out here!"

Tal steeled herself and rejoined the chaos. To her dismay, the death of one mage did little to tip the scales in their favor.

"I can't carry her and fight them off!" Sybil held the girl over her shoulder and struggled to keep her safe.

"I can." Carrick reached for the girl, but Sybil stopped him.

"No, we need you at the front. It's too dangerous for her there." Sybil ducked under a swinging arm. She kicked the figure in the knee and shoved her knife into its neck.

"Go! I'll hold them off," the stranger yelled, stabbing a figure where its face should have been.

"Suit yourself!" Sybil adjusted her hold on the girl, hiding behind Carrick's wall of a body, the stranger protecting her back.

Talwyn hurried to Rainier's side, his movements slowing. His knife-work grew sloppy, and his breath labored. She made to put an arm around to steady him, but he pushed her off.

"I'm fine," he growled and kneed an assailant between the legs, causing him to double over onto the knife Rain held upright, slicing the creature's throat.

Carrick swore ahead of them. More apparitions blocked their exit.

Sybil hefted the crying girl higher on her shoulder and searched for another. "This way!" She rushed down the opposite corridor, away from their escape route.

"There's too many, we'll never make it." Carrick backed toward the direction Sybil pointed.

"Go," the stranger said, clearing a path for them.

"Don't be a fool. You're no match for all of them," Talwyn said as she headbutted an especially annoying apparition who didn't react to any of her slices across his chest.

"I held them off just fine before you four showed up," he grunted, using his second blade to kill two apparitions at once.

"Even if we heed his advice," Rainier blocked a downward strike and shoved his knife into the assailant's ear, "he wouldn't be enough to let us get away." He relied strictly on physical attack now—the wound to his side rendered his manipulation useless.

Conversation halted while they continued to fight. Sybil said nothing, an answer itself.

"Take the girl," Talwyn commanded. "Go. Now."

"Tal, no!" Carrick reached for her.

"Get them out of here, Carrick." She spared her friend a glance while waiting for Sybil, who searched through Talwyn's possible futures from this one decision. Tension and worry filled Carrick's features. Tal hoped Sybil saw a future that lasted more than a few minutes.

Sybil nodded, indicating the right decision had been made, one that didn't necessarily guarantee their survival, but the right one, nonetheless.

"The roof," she said. A clue for where Talwyn and her strange companion would find an escape. "Don't unleash it," she said as a farewell before putting forth her full effort into their new path, Rainier behind her.

"Dammit Tal. You come back to us. You hear me?" Carrick shoved his shoulder into Talwyn's nearest attacker and gripped her arm. His chest heaved, and adrenaline shook her arm in his grip. The intensity of his gaze held her for a breath until he broke eye contact and released her to punch an apparition in the head.

"Go, you big oaf. They need you!" She pushed him, too pumped with adrenaline to wonder what type of good-bye this was. She didn't watch them go. They would be safe with Sybil guiding them. Instead, she threw herself into the fight, screaming, stabbing, punching, anything to gain an inch.

"Are there stairs?" she called to her new companion.

"How the blazing hells should I know?"

Of course he has no clue, she thought. *What kind of a fool runs into a fight with two mages without a plan?* She ran through what she knew of the incinerator. *The chimney*, she thought. If the incineration rooms were like her Kiln, then every room had a large chimney for smoke to escape. She could climb up there and find a way off the top of the building, but first they'd need to lock themselves into a room without any apparitions. *Fantastic.*

A blow to her head knocked her to the ground, and four apparitions descended upon her. She punched, stabbed, and kicked, but they persisted. She screamed out of sheer frustration, wondering how Sybil saw her out of this mess.

Three of her attackers were knocked to the side with the fourth being sliced across the middle. A hand reached down, and the red swordsman pulled her to her feet.

"What's the plan, princess?"

"We lock ourselves in one of the rooms, and don't call me princess," she growled and threw a high elbow behind her.

"A little forward don't you think? At least tell me your name first." He side-stepped and let an apparition stumble forward, then thrust his blade behind him, stabbing the attacker in the back.

"You don't need to know my name." She ignored his humored comment and searched for a door.

"No?" He guffawed. "I like a woman with a little bit of mystery."

"I liked you better when you didn't talk," Tal shot back, taking a slice to her forearm. "Dammit!" She sheathed one of her daggers and grabbed the man by the arm, ducking under a swinging blade and pulling her companion into the nearest room. They thrust the door closed against an incursion of assailants, stabbing and shoving hands, arms, and legs until it closed.

There weren't any locks for a room that held burning trash. She searched for something to wedge against the door and found a slim piece of metal nearby. Using her toe, she dragged the metal close enough to grab and jammed it between the door and its frame. It wouldn't hold, but it helped. She prayed the remaining mage didn't start creating assailants directly within the room.

"Get that grate down." She pointed at the center of the ceiling where a flimsy vent covered their escape.

"Flaming hells." He pulled down his mask. "You won't be able to hold them back," he warned. His full lips were set in a line, and his green eyes met her glare with concern.

"Watch me."

Still leaning against the door, he put his hand to his chest. "Oh dear. I think I've just fallen in love with you."

"Blazing pigs, get on with it!" she yelled, and he jumped into action. The door shook behind her, and the metal wedge slipped the slightest bit. She swore under her breath and placed her hands against the door frame.

No red. No gold. No fire.

Forgive me Syb. It's the only way, she thought. Sybil's cryptic message before she left had warned Talwyn not to unleash her elemental magic, but she had to do something to buy them enough time to climb to the roof. She flicked a quick glance to her companion to ensure his attention remained occupied.

His back was to her as he sized up the distance to the grate. The leather suit left little to the imagination. He put his hands on his hips and his back flexed against the material.

Tal blinked to regain focus. With a deep inhale, she turned back to the door. As carefully as she could manage, Talwyn placed the palm of her hand against the latch and focused her element into the steel, welding the door to its frame. The weight of her limbs grew with the effort as if the magic turned the blood in her veins to stone. She hadn't had enough time to rebuild her stores since Pochette's death. A fire hot enough to melt steel sapped too much of her energy, especially one concentrated in such a small area, and she still needed to climb the chimney to the roof. She made quick work of the hinges and rested her back against the door, exhausted. Perhaps the gods would finally send her good fortune and let her sprout wings. She huffed at the thought, which caught the attention of her companion.

"Care to share?" he asked. He removed his belt, and Talwyn's brows drew together. "I need to loop the grate to pull it down."

"You ever think of jumping?" Talwyn's voice was haggard, her exhaustion ready to devour her.

"A good fighter *and* smart. I'd ask you to marry me here and now, but I'm afraid we'd have to ask one of those green blokes outside to marry us, and I'm not sure they would be happy if we invited only one of them."

"Blazes, do you ever stop talking?" If he took much longer, he would have to carry her out, and she could imagine what he would say to that.

"Absolutely!" he said between leaps, reaching for the grate. "When my mouth is otherwise occupied." He smirked at her.

"You're terrible at jumping," she cut at him.

"But I'm an expert at *so many* other things... like embroidery," he retorted playfully.

With an effort, Talwyn pushed herself off the ground and stumbled over to him, putting more weight on her left leg thanks to an exceptionally deep gash on her right thigh. "Lift me up."

"Oh, this is getting interesting." He gathered his hands for her to step into and hoisted her up. Talwyn hooked her fingers in the slots and wrenched. The cover came free and crashed to the ground.

"Hells, woman, you're covered in filth, and you reek of rubbish. Do you bathe in the stuff?" He turned away from her thigh, gagging.

"Welcome to the docks, your highness," she jabbed, mocking his earlier use of a royal address. "Did you not see the countless apparitions I gutted mere minutes ago?"

He coughed and let his hands drop her, grabbing her around the middle before her feet slammed to the ground. "Did you say apparitions?"

Tal's hands flew to his chest, and she winced at a sharp pain in her leg. "Yes, they're created by the mage. Didn't you see they were faceless?" Her eyes flicked to the arms still wrapped around her and back to his face just in time to see his own eyes leave her mouth.

"I was too busy slicing and dicing," he responded and Talwyn rolled her eyes. "A mage?"

She pushed away from him and let out an exasperated sigh. Placing her hands on her knees to hide their shaking, she took a moment to muster the energy to climb the chimney. "Lords, did you throw yourself into this mess without a moment of planning? Did you know anything before coming here?"

He crossed his arms, and the muscles strained against the material of his suit. "I knew a child had been taken by four men. I can take on twice as many without injury. It should have been easy to save her," he said, all playfulness gone from his voice.

"Lucky for you, her brother thought to come find me. Otherwise, you both would be floating in the Taralin by sunrise." Talwyn pushed off her knees and eyed the opening.

"And what makes you so fearsome that he would seek you out?"

"Pray you never find out, highness," she used the name again and noticed the muscle along his jaw tense. "Come. Lift me up. We haven't got much time. If the mage ventures out of his hiding spot, we're done for."

"You're going to tell me about this mage when we get out of here." He cupped his hands again and lifted her, higher this time, so she could pull herself into the chimney.

"Thank the gods," she sighed. The brick-and-mortar chimney supplied enough inlets to wedge her fingers and feet. "Give me your belt," she called down.

He tossed the well-made leather up to her, something she considered stealing once they escaped. It would fetch enough coin for almost a month of meals. Using the hilt of one of her thicker knives, she banged another into the mortar, the loop of the belt held within the blade, a makeshift rope for the swordsman to pull himself up. Her limbs shook with the effort of holding herself after sustaining injuries and using her fury with such concentration on the door. It need only hold a little longer. Then, the apparitions could barge in all they wanted. They would find no one in the room.

She ignored the pain of her injuries, placing her remaining knife in its sheath, and made the slow climb up the chimney, which, thankfully, was only a few shaky steps before she reached the opening at the top. She pulled herself up over the ledge and toppled out onto the sloped roof, barely holding onto the brick chimney to keep from sliding off.

The swordsman followed her with much more grace and handed her the other knife, having pulled it out of the mortar. She noted he once again wore his belt. *Damn*, she swore to herself. *I'll have to steal it another way.* "Clever thinking, given that I'm terrible at jumping." He pulled her to stand and beamed.

Talwyn swayed on her feet, and he held her middle to steady her.

"Are you injured?" His eyes scanned her body.

She waved away his concern. She still didn't know who this man was, or what his connections were. It was best if she kept her power-induced exhaustion a secret and he thought of her as a fighter out of the slums.

He searched for a way down. "How far is your refuge?" he asked. "Where are you meeting your friends?" he added when she arched a brow at his word choice.

"If we can make it to the tunnels, we should be able to go un-detected," she breathed. The longer they delayed, the less likely she would be able to make it back on her own two feet.

The man steadied her briefly before stepping to the edge. He shook his head. "There's no way around it. We're too high up. We'll have to jump into the river. Can you swim?"

"Fabulous," Talwyn said. The incinerator sat atop a fifteen-foot cliff above the Taralin River. With the height of the roof, they had at least a thirty-foot drop, with a necessary ten-foot leap outward if they didn't want to splatter across the rocks below. Then there was the added problem of the current. The northern ocean fed into the river and encouraged the waters south into the temperate seas.

Metal groaned in the room below. "I'll take that as a yes," the swordsman said. He reached below her shoulder with one arm, steadied himself, and they ran full speed toward the edge of the roof, leaping at the last moment.

Talwyn didn't have time to think of the drop. She only felt the deep relief in her legs when she no longer had to bear her own weight. Her companion reached around as they fell and gripped her belt. When they crashed into the water, his arm ripped from under her shoulder, but a tug at her waist told her he held fast to her belt.

The icy water was painful enough to make her gasp, but her ex-haustion kept her mouth shut against the wave that crashed over her head. Her limbs wouldn't respond. She was dead weight, and sleep called to her. The cold eased her further into it like a gentle embrace against her aching muscles and lacerations. She had almost forgotten all the slices she had received. Carrick wouldn't be happy about that. He would be even more unhappy that she was about to let herself drown. Hells, he'd bring her back from the dead simply to kill her again out of anger. She imagined what he would say as sleep threatened to pull her under.

A watery roar and a gasp interrupted her peaceful thoughts. The maroon swordsman had pulled them both to the surface, even with her dead weight against him. "Hells, woman, I thought you said you could swim?" He had her back pinned against his chest with an arm looped under her own.

"I never said I could," she drawled sleepily with much effort.

"Is that sarcasm? She has a sense of humor? Lords, take me away before I sell myself to the devils for her."

Talwyn's lips twitched, and she let the infuriating man pull her to safety, for even if she wanted to help herself, her body had finally given out, and the darkness consumed her.

5

Talwyn groaned. Her body felt like lead. As sensations returned, the pain overwhelmed her. She panted with the effort to roll to her side, groaning once more.

"It's about time you woke up," Sybil called from outside the makeshift curtain wall of her room.

Talwyn pushed herself upright with shaking arms. Her leathers lay in a heap on the ground. Someone had changed her into a white cotton tunic.

Carrick placed a pitcher of water on the table opposite her. He sat beside her with a full cup and held it to her lips. She gulped quickly and spilled water down her chin.

"You didn't listen, did you?" Sybil crossed her arms, leaning against the wall. Her tall frame took up much of the vertical space. When Tal didn't answer, she sighed. "How much fury did you use?"

Tal finished the water, and Carrick helped her scoot back against the wall. "Enough to weld a steel door shut. That's it." Her voice grated against her throat.

"That's. It?! Why in the blazes did you think I told you not to unleash it? Hmm?" She threw her hands in the air. "What if someone saw you? What if someone finds the welded door? There are no other Furies in the kingdom, Tal." Sybil huffed in frustration. "I need to think." She left Talwyn alone with Carrick.

"How long?" Tal croaked.

Carrick left her bedside and crossed the room. "You've been out for two days," he said while refilling her cup.

She sighed noisily. She'd been building up her power for weeks, and yet one concentrated use knocked her out. Perhaps she'd used it too soon after her attack on Pochette.

Carrick returned with another full glass and scrutinized the lacerations along her arms and legs. The tunic did little to conceal her bare limbs, but she didn't move to cover herself. Carrick had seen her strip nearly as many times as she'd seen him. Modesty was not a trait afforded to those who grew up owning only the clothes on their backs. "I thought you were a better fighter than this," he said, handing her the cup.

She ignored his question long enough to finish the second glass and handed it back. "They're superficial cuts. I left an opening so they would betray their weak side." She did her best to hold her chin up, but her head fell back against the stone wall. She closed her eyes, wondering if sleep would come once more.

A hand on her knee made her flinch, and she opened one eye.

"Superficial?" Carrick said.

Above his hand, stitches held a long gash together. "Shit. I forgot about that."

"You're cut up worse than a pig at the butcher's, Tal."

She sighed. "I'm fine. I made it back."

"Unconscious. You made it back unconscious and only because Faron brought you back," he snapped.

"Who?" she asked without caring, her eyes closed again.

"The swordsman."

"Ahh, you mean the dewberry who ruined our perfect rescue plan and then tried to play the hero."

"I mean the swordsman who pulled you out of the Taralin and carried you through the tunnels until he ran into one of us. He'd been walking for two hours."

She lifted her head. "Two hours? Damn. I would have left his ass."

"This isn't funny Tal."

She ignored his irritation. "How did he carry me? Over the shoulder? Across both forearms? I wonder if his muscles ache. Serves him right, the dingbat."

"Tal," Carrick said, his voice pleading.

She sighed and rested a hand over the one still on her injured leg. "I'm sorry. You had to go, and someone needed to stay behind to make sure you got them out." Tal and Carrick both knew he needed to go. Both Sybil and Rainier were nearly useless, with Sybil carrying the girl and Rain injured. If either of the twins fell, he would be able to get them back up. Talwyn would have only been able to burn everything to the ground and then pass out.

Carrick sighed and hung his head. "The moment I got them to safety, I went back, but you were already gone. The apparitions and mage had all disappeared. I thought they'd taken you."

"Hey." She squeezed his hand. "I'm okay. I got out, and they don't know where to find me. They probably don't even know I'm the one they're looking for. For all they know, I was just a random person trying to help."

Carrick hesitated. "There's a reason Sybil told you not to use your element." Talwyn narrowed her eyes, but he ignored her. "You can join us, Rain," he called.

Sybil's brother edged into the room looking worse for wear. His tall form hunched, and his inky black hair hung in his eyes. Sweat glistened on his skin in the candlelight, and blood soaked through the cloth wrapped around his torso. He held his side and eased himself into the chair at the table, wincing as he did so.

"Rain, you should be resting. Do we not have any healing elixirs?" Tal admonished.

"So should you. And I'm fine." He attempted to sit up straight and grimaced, resigning to rest an elbow on the table. "They're searching for something. The girl won't say much, but we know the mages thought she had it." He winced again, shifting in his seat.

"You're assuming they're after other Furies? Is that it? We have no proof."

Carrick frowned. "Sybil saw a vision of you. She can't make much sense of it, but it has something to do with you, a group of nobles..." he paused, "and the Pyrie." He met her gaze.

Tal stilled at the name. Pochette mentioned it before he burst into flame. She bit her lip. "What's the connection?"

Rain took a deep breath and stopped short, grabbing his middle. "As kids we were told a story about the Pyrie, a Fury from eons ago. Some call her the original, others say she was the most powerful of her time. The legend says the power drove her mad, and she tried to destroy the world."

"So, what happened to her?"

"Another elemental betrayed and killed her."

"What does this have to do with me? Do you think I'm about to go mad, too?"

He sighed, frustration creasing his brow. "Power is dangerous, especially when it's untamed like yours. You know that better than anyone. I only remember pieces of the story we were told as children, but there's a reason generations of people passed it down. I need to learn more, but I can't help but think this is a warning."

"And the nobles?"

Rainier shook his head. Sybil's gift created more questions than answers.

Tal's arms shook as she pushed to her feet. She grunted. "I need some food."

Carrick helped her to the table as Egan arrived with a plate overflowing with a meal worthy of a king.

"Go rest," she dismissed Rain as he stood slowly.

Egan paused at the door. "We've got your back, Tal. Whatever it is." He gave her a small smile and followed Rainier down the tunnel.

Carrick handed her a fork and motioned for her to eat. "We need to take this seriously," he began, but Talwyn waved him away. With a sigh, he changed the subject. "Faron has been wandering the taverns searching for you. I told him to stay out of the tunnels if he knows what's good for him." He didn't wait for a response and left Talwyn to finish her meal in silence.

———

Using her fury left Tal ravenous. She asked Egan for a second plate before energy returned to her limbs. And after gulping down half of a healing elixir, she made her way through the tunnels, her wounds mostly healed.

She found the children in one of their storage rooms. Rainier's various glass bottles sat against the wall; the large crate that used to contain them overflowed with hay. Egan's oversized blanket cocooned the children sleeping there. It wasn't permanent, but it would work until they could figure out what to do.

"Evania. That's the girl," Egan said behind her.

"How is she?" Tal asked without taking her eyes off the sleeping forms.

He stepped next to her. "She screams in her sleep, clings to Sybil, and won't let anyone leave her by herself—not that her brother will let her out of his sight. He thinks it was his fault. He tries to act tough, but one crack in his armor, and the boy will be a blubbering mess."

"Will they eat?"

Egan nodded. "They're skin and bone. Covered in bruises. Evania flinches when anyone besides Sybil comes near. They won't tell us, but we suspect they've been abused. Sybil's been using her visions to figure out who did it. I'll take pleasure in shaving the skin from their bones when we find out." He paused, steadying his breath and turning his thoughts away from violence.

Talwyn gave him a moment to reign in his inner beast.

"They mostly sit together and watch us, but they've begun to play a little." He paused, gathering the courage to say what Talwyn knew the whole crew felt. "We can't send them back to the street," he pleaded. "They won't make it on their own."

She pursed her lips. "Have the others been told of the danger?"

"I warned what orphans I could find to stay out of sight. They'll tell the others."

Tal nodded. Helping those like Evania and Janin had been the plan all along, but not in this way. They were supposed to funnel money from Pochette's businesses back to the poor. They were supposed to keep the gangs out of the docks. Taking children into their care asked too much. The docks held enough orphans to fill the tunnels to the brim and with not enough people able to care for them. If they took in one, how could they say no to the rest? And what kind of life could she give them? Dishonesty, danger, and violence found them at every turn, even with the absence of Pochette's men. Would it be fair to pull two children into that kind of life? And were her friends responsible enough to care for two children? What would they do when they had to leave for a bounty? Would someone have to stay behind to watch the kids? She surely couldn't bring them along.

Talwyn sighed. For now, the children were safe, and they had more reason to keep them in the tunnels than to send them away.

She put a hand on Egan's shoulder. "They'll stay for now until we find them a better home. Rain is resting tonight. The children won't be alone. Come on. We have a maroon swordsman to find."

Sybil stayed in the tunnels, claiming she had an irresponsible redhead to have visions about, but Carrick refused to stay back. So, Talwyn, Carrick, and Egan took to the streets. They chose to buy a pint at Gale's Tavern first. It stood far enough away from the entrance to their particular set of tunnels, and their well-dressed target would expect them to slum with a rowdier crowd.

"He probably thinks we're scoundrels," Talwyn said.

Gale's always guaranteed a good time. The owner, Gale, a woman with enough muscle to give Carrick a fair fight, communicated with her patrons through the use of force, and often destroyed her own furniture to do it. On any given night, they would be sure to see at least two brawls, one person leaving with a black eye, another missing a tooth, and patrons often hoped to receive the honor of being literally tossed out the door by the burly woman. Tal always chose Gale's to let off steam. But it wasn't the place to find their swordsman.

They tried two other taverns, having a pint or two at each, until they decided on a better tactic. Grabbing a few things to go, they took to the rooftops, positioning themselves so that together, they could see the entrances to four taverns. Talwyn tipped her pint six buildings to the north to Carrick. He held a bit of bread up by way of greeting and then waved west to Egan, sitting cross legged and feeding a black bird that joined his perch.

Talwyn leaned back on one elbow, one leg bent underneath the other. Stars dotted the night sky, and she beamed at them. A warm breeze blew her hood back, revealing her greased hair. Out of dye, Sybil had given her a handful of black tar to spread on her fiery locks. Somehow, over the last two days, the brown color had completely leached from her hair and her own natural red burned with all its glory. She would have to wear her hood up until she could confront the alchemist.

She gulped more ale, dropped the nearly full cup, sloshing some over the rim, and fell onto her back. She would likely fall off the roof before she found her target. Carrick would have a hell of a time getting her down. A carefree laugh escaped her lips at the thought. Carrick, her constant, her savior, always worried about her safety more than she did. She wasn't ready to give him up, but one day, she hoped he could go his own way, if he ever chose to, and wouldn't feel guilt at leaving her behind.

Unlike Tal, Carrick wasn't meant for life on the docks. Maybe she could convince him to go to the mountains, perhaps take the children. He could build a life there, and Tal would visit to share stories of how they ruled the slums. She could even help the poor blunderhead find a wife.

Tal imagined Carrick charming some poor soul, stumbling over his words, his big frame always getting in the way. She lost herself to a belly laugh at her poor friend's expense, even if he didn't know it.

"How could such a fierce fighter giggle like an innocent child?"

Talwyn shot to her feet and swayed. She swore as she stumbled, and a hand caught her by the elbow.

"Careful there!" He steadied her.

Talwyn fumbled for her knives, but her damned fingers slipped over the handle. The intruder grabbed her wrist and chuckled. The red swordsman, Faron, bowed his head in greeting, and she scowled. He had no mask, and his hood remained back to reveal his face in the moonlight. Hells, he was handsome, too handsome for his own good, and he knew it. His jawline could cut glass, and his eyes drew her in with their ridiculously long lashes. Her drunken state muddled the green of his irises in the moonlight, but she could see the stars reflected in them. She tried to tell herself it was the ale, but she didn't want to look away.

"What a poor lookout you are, drunk and stumbling nearly to your death." He laughed. "Were you planning to sleep off the ale up here?"

"Well," she slurred and wrenched her arm out of his grasp. "You want me? Here I am." With a flourish, she spread her arms wide and not-so-graciously fell to her backside.

"Alive and well, I see." He sat beside her and took a piece of bread off her plate, earning himself another scowl. "Glad to see your ailment left that beautiful frown untouched."

"What are you talking about?" She ripped the bread out of his hand before it reached his lips and tore a bite off with her teeth.

Faron let his mouth hang open as if waiting for the bread, then curled his lips into a mischievous smile. If possible, it made him even more handsome. He rested his forearm on his knee and turned his head to her. "You know, I'm sore in places I never thought possible thanks to you."

"That is entirely too much information. What you do in the confines of your bedroom has nothing to do with me," she drawled. She needed water. Instead, she shoved more bread into her mouth and nearly choked on the dry grain.

Faron howled with laughter. "Oh, you have a foul mouth, don't you? Is that the thanks I get for carrying you, sopping wet, through sewage for hours? I could have left you in the river, you know."

She swallowed with difficulty. "Why didn't you?"

He dropped the humor from his features. "Why would I?" He met her stare, blinking.

Tal's eyes wandered to his lips. She licked her own and smirked when his gaze flicked to the movement.

His answering grin tugged at the corners of his lips, and he grabbed meat off the plate. He lay back and turned his face toward the sky, an arm under his head. "I'm glad to see you are well. And your companions? The girl?"

"They'll live," she replied, searching the rooftops for Carrick and Egan. She expected them to join shortly.

"I've heard the stories of how elementals had built the city, how Furies ran the incinerator endlessly, and Hydras would send waves of water taller than me through the tunnels. Until that night, I'd never seen those places for myself."

"Yeah, well they're long gone now, so it's all left to ruin."

His leather suit creaked when he rolled onto his side and propped his head onto his hand. "I never asked, but how did you manage to block the door?"

Tal hiccupped. She scowled, warning her companion not to react. The distraction allowed her sluggish mind a moment to think of a lie. "A bonding paste."

He nodded, not questioning her any further. "And here I thought you held it by sheer strength. Lucky you had the chemical on you." He rolled to his back. His chest heaved as he sighed. "I'm Faron, by the way."

"I've heard."

"I believe this is the part where you offer your name."

"And I believe you're wrong," she said tartly.

"You're not easy to talk to, are you? I thought it was a fighting thing. You know, too busy to make conversation while saving the world. But you're still tight-lipped as ever." He sighed and sat up. "Thank you for coming to my aid." His tone had lost its humor.

Talwyn bit her lip, holding back a snide remark. "We went for the girl. There wouldn't have been so much trouble if you hadn't interfered. What were you thinking going in alone?"

He hesitated. "I was trying to help."

"Yes, well, running into danger alone like that is the best way to end up floating down the river."

A head popped up by Tal's feet. "Yeah, Tal. Maybe you should heed your own advice." Her young friend turned to Faron. "The name's Egan." He smirked and hoisted himself up onto the roof, followed by Carrick who placed a pitcher of water on the eave before pulling himself up too.

Tal grabbed for Egan's feet, and he danced out of the way. "Ale is making you brave, little devil. I think I like you better sober and content to worship the ground I stand on." She accepted the pitcher from Carrick and gulped greedily, avoiding Egan as he tried to nudge her shoulder.

"My new friends." Faron nodded. Egan mirrored the greeting, but Carrick, who had likely been the one to pull Tal's unconscious form from Faron's arms, merely pursed his lips. "How lovely to find you here." He grabbed Talwyn's pint of ale from earlier and sipped greedily, earning a cold stare from Tal. "Now that I see you're all well, I'd like to chat."

Talwyn's drunken snort was the trio's only response.

He continued, "I'd like to know about these apparitions you mentioned, and the mages."

"What of them?" Carrick asked, still standing. He didn't seem too pleased to be talking to the swordsman.

"What do you know about them?" he asked.

"Why do you want to know?" Carrick retorted

"Usually when someone asks a question, the other person answers it. I believe you are instead asking another question." Faron raised his brow, the picture of nonchalance and unbothered by their thin layer of hostility. He finished the pint and set it down. "I would hope that my attempt at rescuing the child is evidence enough that I have only the best intentions."

Egan spoke up this time, "Usually an answer to a question is expected to be direct rather than skirting around the issue. And you being there doesn't prove you were trying to rescue the child."

"I brought the sleeping goddess back unharmed," he countered.

Talwyn ran through the facts. The mages hunted her. If he'd been in league with them, he would have had the perfect opportunity to take her after they jumped in the river. Her gut told her to trust this man even if she didn't have all the information yet.

"The apparitions were human copies created by magic. A mage, a powerful one, can create an apparition that is essentially human, except that it can only exist as long as the mage does. If you kill the mage, the apparition ceases to exist. Otherwise, it fights and bleeds like any man."

"How have I never heard of these?"

"Do you live in a cave?" Carrick offered.

"Apparently." He scratched his head. "And what did the mage want with the child?"

"Mages," Talwyn corrected him. "There were two."

"Were. Because you killed one of them," he said it as a statement to which Talwyn nodded.

She felt Carrick tense behind her. By the twins' admission, mages could be the most powerful magic wielders of their age. She somehow managed to kill one without her fury. *A fluke*, she thought to herself. *I just got lucky.* Earlier, Carrick tried to use this to prove they could handle the mages themselves. She wouldn't hear any of it.

"Okay, so what did the *mages* want with the child?" Faron repeated.

Talwyn hesitated. Revealing the mages were after her would lead to too many questions. And that still didn't explain what triggered the mages to take Evania in the first place. She settled for a half-truth. "She said they were searching for something. They thought she had it, but that's all we know."

"Have you noticed any disturbance in the industrial district?" Carrick asked out of the blue, referring to Pochette's businesses.

Talwyn whipped her head around to scowl. She hadn't planned on telling Faron about that detail.

Faron hesitated. "I've seen the smoke. Are these mages involved?"

"They burned a thug's empire to the ground in a single night. You didn't think anything of it?"

"I was on my way to investigate but happened upon the girl and her captors first. I take it you weren't expecting this attack? Have the mages been here long?"

"Our first sighting happened the night everything burned." She didn't feel the need to mention the weeks and months of missing persons. "Why am I getting the impression this is all new to you?" Talwyn asked, suspicious.

"Where I come from, conversations stick to superficial things—clothing, sex, scandal. Dangerous groups, powerful magic, and violence are taboo." He tried to grab the last piece of bread, but Talwyn snatched it first.

She sneered, popping the bread into her mouth, to which he chuckled and dropped his head.

"And where exactly do you come from?" Tal said around the oversized bite.

Faron peered at her out of the corners of his eyes. "Your dreams." He winked.

Talwyn blushed, blaming it on the ale. "Non-answer," she muttered.

"I'm from the house of Dohaern." When all three of them offered blank stares, he added, "The noble household." He received silence once more, so he tried again, "From the King's court?" Talwyn blinked, and he sighed deeply. "My family estate is to the north of the palace. You really haven't heard of me?"

Tal took a swig of water while Carrick shrugged. Egan spoke for the three of them. "To be honest, we only know the king's name because his guard likes to prance around the taverns claiming they're his favorite."

Talwyn nearly choked on her water.

"What are you doing at the docks?" Carrick interrupted.

"Getting myself in over my head apparently." Faron rubbed his neck and shook his head. "What's your involvement in all this?" He gestured around at nothing.

"We're not involved. We protect what's ours. And the docks and everyone in them are ours." Even in her state, Tal noticed how the noble's frown lifted when she spoke.

"Perhaps it's time you come out of your tunnels." He stood. "I'll come find you if I learn anything." The swordsman walked backwards to the end of the roof.

"No. You won't." She narrowed her eyes playfully.

"Stay away from the ale, and perhaps you'll be right. Gentleman, it's been a pleasure. Milady." He bowed, then straightened with a wink and hopped out of sight.

Tal rushed to the edge of the roof, worried for a moment that he had jumped to his death. She huffed a laugh when she caught him leaping down from the window ledges. When he reached the bottom, he pulled his mask up over his mouth, saluted her, and ran off into the darkness. Tal shook her head, picturing all the reasons Faron of Dohaern hung around the docks.

The next morning, Talwyn woke with a pounding headache and a fierce desire to empty the contents of her stomach. She shook her head at the pitcher of water Carrick left on the table and changed out of her clothes from the night before, opting for a loose fitted shirt and trousers, before heading out in search of her friends.

Laughter drew her to Rainier's room. She pulled back the tattered blanket covering the entrance to reveal the group inside. Rain, who must have taken a healing elixir, sat up in his bed, an arm over his bare middle, watching the children dance and play together. Sybil hummed a tune and drummed on her thigh while Egan whistled along.

Evania and Janin held hands as they spun in a circle, their eyes bright. They each wore one of Egan's loose shirts to replace their own tattered clothing. Tal smiled as Evania's blonde curls bounced around her smiling face, recognizing a reddish sheen as the locks caught the torchlight. She noted the distinct smell of lavender in the room and couldn't help but wonder how much one of her friends had paid the alchemist for a hair salve. Someone must have taken the time to brush out the knotted mess.

Not twenty-four hours ago, Egan told her how afraid the two children were. She smiled along with them while they played. She could imagine what they had been through living on the docks. Talwyn had lived it herself. If it weren't for Carrick, she probably would have died from the influenza all those years ago.

Her face fell thinking of the life Evania and Janin would likely lead. If they survived, they would either be caught by the Netters, barely living as human dolls to be used by foul men, or they would have to turn to a life like hers. Violence was a guarantee. The only question was: would they be the victims or the aggressors?

Tal regarded the state of their home. The tunnels weren't sanitary or comfortable by any means, but they had a roof over their heads and a safe place to sleep at night. A part of her wished she could do that much for the children, maybe for others. Life as a hunter grew in her bones, but it wasn't meant for the rest.

She thought of the conversations they had over the last few months—the more recent growing pressure to involve themselves in matters that would surely get them all killed. They wanted to intervene, but she hesitated. They'd spent years building this fragile life. What would happen if they got involved? What would happen if they didn't? She took in the scene around the room: at the children dancing, Sybil's joyful smile, Rain nodding his head to the music, and Egan whistling happily. Carrick rested against the wall, eyes closed, his face relaxed. She would give anything to protect this moment, to create a life as carefree as this for her friends.

Her thoughts darkened as the images of the last few days came to mind. A few hours after Pochette warned her of the coming evil, so much destruction rained down on not only the docks, but her specifically. If the mages wouldn't leave, she couldn't ignore them. As much as she wanted to keep her head down, life told her at every turn to look into herself and learn what she was meant for.

Sybil lifted her head, her black hair brushing her cheek. Talwyn locked eyes with her and she knew her friend had a vision. Sometimes Sybil sought them out, other times they demanded her attention all on their own. Tal watched warily as the seer crossed the space and stood beside her.

"A vision?" Tal asked.

Sybil didn't turn, instead she continued to watch the children dance. "You must train more."

Tal pushed off the wall she had been leaning against. "Is danger coming?"

Sybil's deep brown eyes sought out her own. "It's already here."

6

"Absolutely not. He lied to us last time, and I will not scare a servant into keeping quiet simply because the sod can't discern basic kindness from romantic advances." Tal pointed her fork at Rainier and shook her head. "If he's too afraid to properly find other men of his persuasion, he can figure it out on his own. It's not our job to clean up his mess."

Rain's quill scratched across his list of outstanding bounties. "Well, we're getting backlogged and haven't had payment in days." He skimmed the list on the table in front of him. A plate of sausage and cheese sat between him, Tal, and Egan. They convened in the tavern by the butcher's, their usual choice to talk business. "The satchel on the south pier had a letter," he said, his tone less than hopeful.

"Oh? And what new bounty do we have this week?" Tal asked.

"Apparently, one of the lesser gangs doesn't like the new leadership. We've been challenged to step aside." His tone lacked the seriousness of his words.

Tal scoffed around a bite of sausage. "What leadership? We have no empire, no business, no men. If they wanted, they could just claim the title."

"It appears the gang leaders are still holding to their promise to stick to their territories. It's the lesser grunts who have an issue."

"That's their problem. Let them fight it out. We have other things to worry about before entertaining this ruling business."

"Agreed. I just thought you'd like to know since they put a bounty on you." He smirked at the cynical turn of Tal's mouth.

"Who do they expect to fill the bounty?" Tal shook her head. "Sometimes I wonder if these dullards know which end they piss out of."

"The price is... considerably high, and we're running low on healing elixirs." He scratched a note into his book.

"I'm still waiting on payment for Brott's bounty," Egan offered. "That bird was not easy to find, and he keeps giving me the slip."

Tal stabbed a chunk of cheese. "He thinks he can avoid paying you because you won't break his hand. I'll send Carrick to collect." It wasn't the first time someone refused to pay, but Egan forgave too easily. "Anything else?"

"Just the bounty for the cheating husband," Rain said.

Tal sighed. "I haven't figured out his punishment. It needs to be something his wife can dole out."

"Narcolepsis?" Egan asked, scratching behind his ear.

"So, he'll fall asleep when he visits his mistress? I think we need something a little more vengeful."

"Well, I think your options at this point would be Marjoramint or Emetikos. Though, I'm guessing a permanently limp member isn't harsh enough." Rain closed his book.

"Emetikos it is then. Shall I warn the wife about the vomiting?" Tal stood and gathered her things from the table.

"I doubt she would invite him to her own bed, but yes, I would recommend it."

Tal nodded. "I'll ask Septimus for another crate of the healing elixir," she said, exhaustion dripping from every word. In light of recent events, she would probably need to ask for two. While the problems of men filled her pockets, they emptied them at an equal rate. She wondered if the world would be better off if she burned it all to the ground.

There was no clearer indication of an alchemist's skill than the color of their wares, and Tal's alchemist sold only the most vibrant solutions. She stood at the long wooden counter in the small shop and eyed the cubicles filled with jars of every color liquid and cream. There were no labels, but Septimus, a scrawny old man with a long gray beard tucked into his belt, grabbed a vial off the shelf without hesitation and placed it on the wooden counter with a solid *thunk*. The single gulp of yellow liquid swirled with bits of red.

A glint at the top of the wall caught her eye. A small jar held a sparkly gel, the blue color like the far end of a sunset where the day finally accepted its fate and succumbed to the darkness of night. "That one's new."

Without turning around, the alchemist said, "Aconitum. Highly poisonous. I've created a jelly-like paste that delays onset of symptoms for twelve hours, but *death* is delayed for at least twenty-four. It mimics consumption and dysentery. Great for secret assassinations. Tastes like licorice. Any amount ingested will kill the target, but not before the twenty-fourth hour. The smaller the dose, the more painful and drawn out the death."

"How do you know what it tastes like?"

Septimus blinked at her.

"Sounds lovely. I'll take that and half a dozen healing elixirs."

"Gracious me!" He gasped and placed a hand on his heart. "You and I have a longstanding agreement not to impede on the other's business, but what bounty of yours deserves such a gruesome death?"

"Fine." She rolled her eyes and pocketed the Emetikos, not questioning how the old man knew she needed it for a bounty. "How many doses will he need?"

"Just the one. I do not sell weak mixtures here."

"Then how do you explain my hair and eyes?"

Septimus sighed, exasperation dripping from his tone. "My dear, I sell all manner of wares that can make your dreams come true or be your worst nightmare. But I do not suppress magic, certainly not fury like yours. If you wish to be rid of the effects of such power, you will need to learn to control it and not let it control you. Now, I have something else for your eyes, but you won't like it."

Tal narrowed her aforementioned eyes at him. She never revealed that she had magic, let alone that she had fury. If he shared her secret, Tal would be in grave danger.

"Oh, don't look at me like that." He wagged a finger at her. "I've known about you since the first time you entered my shop, and I haven't uttered a word of you, your specialty, or your raggedy crew to anyone." He turned and hummed, packaging the healing elixirs, including a small jar with a dropper of warm brown dye for her irises.

She watched the man closely but saw no sign to indicate a lie. Her payment scraped the counter when she pushed it toward him.

"A pleasure as always, Miss Talwyn," he said as he pocketed the coin and then disappeared behind a door in the back.

Tal stashed the glass vials in a satchel over her shoulder and returned to the tunnels, anticipating the ice-like sting Septimus warned would accompany the new formula for her eye color.

Evania and Janin fell asleep early that evening, and everyone joined together in the common area. A plate of jerky sat on the crate-turned-table. Rainier lay across a pile of hay and blankets while Egan and Carrick kicked a hard ball back and forth. Sybil sharpened her knives in the corner, a frown on her face.

"Septimus knows about my magic." Talwyn sat cross-legged on the floor, sewing a patch into one of her shirts.

All activity halted.

Carrick's shoulders hunched against the tension filling his muscles. "Is he going to be a threat?"

Sybil tapped her head. "He's on our side, for now."

"How long has he known?" Rain asked.

"No idea, but he says I need to control it, or it'll burn right through his formulas."

"Then we work on controlling it." Sybil didn't look up from her weapon.

"Isn't that what she's been doing?" Egan stopped the ball when Carrick kicked it to him.

"Apparently not enough." Tal sighed. "I'm not sure what more I can do."

"You continue to train," Rainier said. "I think the warnings about madness in Sybil's vision alone is enough to prove how necessary it is."

"I'm not going to go mad," Tal grumbled to herself as she set her sewing aside and pulled a strip of leather out of her pocket. She placed it in front of her, and everyone returned to their tasks. While she attempted to ignite the strip with her magic, the effort sapped her energy with each strike. She warred between frustration and reassurance, knowing each attempt built a tolerance.

"Try not to grasp the magic. Let it flow through you." The metal of Sybil's knife scraped across the whetstone.

Tal ran a hand through her hair. "What does that even mean?"

Rain rested his elbows on his knees. "You're thinking too much of your magic like something within you. Imagine it's a part of you. When you want to use your fury, it's as easy as lifting your hand, as easy as breathing."

She paused and considered his words, reluctant to let go of the hold she had on her magic. Then, with the words "part of me" repeating in her head, she took a deep breath, imagining it flowing through her like her own blood and forced it out quickly. A stream of fire appeared two paces from her mouth and careened toward the leather. It blasted into the fabric, incinerating it in place. The stream continued across the small space, setting fire to hay and blankets alike.

Rain yelped and rolled off the burning pile while Carrick and Egan jumped into action stamping out the flames. Sybil didn't do so much as look up from her seat on the opposite wall. Frustrated, Talwyn swore at herself, slapping at a half-burned blanket.

"That's new." Rainier winced and smacked an ember off his trousers.

"You breathed fire!" Egan exclaimed, putting out the last flame and coming to stand beside Talwyn. "Do it again!"

"Absolutely not!" Talwyn asserted, aghast. She would set fire to the lot of them if she tried again.

"Come on! That was incredible!"

"It could prove pretty useful in a fight." Rain nodded with approval, but edged his way to the room's exit, destroying all of Tal's self-confidence. Sybil sat yet unmoved while Carrick came to Tal's other side.

"Not here. I don't think we can afford to keep replacing blankets." Tal considered the Kiln, but she didn't want to get too far from the children.

"Over the water then," Carrick said. His big brows pulled down in concentration. The setting sun would be level with the water's surface, sending fiery reflections everywhere. No one would notice an extra flame or two.

Egan bounced on the pads of his feet like a giddy child, which helped relieve some of the worry coiled in her chest.

They marched to the tunnel opening over the river, and Tal's heart raced as her friends gathered around expectantly. She gave the group a tentative smile, and took a deep breath, focusing on a piece of rubbish floating down the river. Heat built in her chest until it climbed up her throat. With a huff, she breathed a fiery stream past her target. It skipped across the surface before it dissipated. Despite the feat, she couldn't help but notice the tightness in her chest. She was still holding back.

Silence filled the space between them for three breaths. Then Egan let out a cheerful holler and threw his hands in the air. Rain whooped and Carrick put two fingers in his mouth, sending a shrieking whistle across the river. Sybil and Tal laughed, in awe. Tal's friends patted her on the back, ruffled her hair, and told her to do it again.

She managed to breathe a streak of flame three more times before she started to feel its effects. Her breathing labored slightly, and her hands shook, but she tried to hide it. She ignored the knot in her sternum altogether. Everyone still cheered, calling out pieces of rubbish for her to aim at, betting on distances, sizes, and how long she could go without collapsing from exhaustion.

"We're going to need that," Sybil said to no one. The comment sobered Tal immediately as she recalled Sybil's warning from the other day.

"What's that supposed to mean?" Egan's tone bordered on accusation.

The seer raised a brow and waited for Tal to respond. She continued when Tal crossed her arms and sighed. "We can't wait around for the mages to find us. It leads to nothing good. It's time to go hunting."

Five pairs of eyes searched the space around them with anticipation. "No more keeping our heads down?" Carrick asked in a low voice.

Tal avoided his gaze. "I'm not fighting back. I just don't want to be caught off-guard. We need to know for sure why they're looking for me."

"And then?" Rainier asked with expectation. He opened his mouth like he wanted to say more but closed it with a shake of his head.

"And then we make sure we're prepared when they attack." Tal knew they hoped for more, but she'd been through the argument before. They were only five people, barely into adulthood. They may have been in over their heads when they decided to take over Pochette's empire. Perhaps the gods had been trying to say as much when everything fell. They had no connections, no armies, and only enough money to live comfortably in the slums. This wasn't a decision Tal should be making alone, but her friends seemed too eager to save the world. Her eyes pleaded with Carrick for help. *This life we've made is everything to me. I can't risk losing it*, she wanted to say.

"So, we do what we can to protect what's ours," he said with finality, leaving no room for argument.

Tal held his gaze, relief washing over her until a gentle smile pulled at her lips to match the one he gave her.

They jumped into planning. Sybil provided input on what visions she'd seen, and everyone else filled in the blanks, focusing on the most recent one first.

"How are we supposed to learn where the nobles fit into all this without looking suspicious?" Talwyn mused. "We can't just waltz right up to the palace and ask for an audience with them."

Rainier tapped his chin with a finger. "We need a way to eavesdrop without being noticed. The masquerade ball will be the largest gathering of nobility for a while." He gnawed at a spot on his lip.

"You think we could sneak in?" Talwyn asked.

"Us, yes. But you're going to walk right in." Rainier smirked. "It's time for you to accept that invitation."

Sybil burst into laughter, stood, and walked out of the common area, doubled over at something only she could see.

Talwyn held up her hands. "Woah, woah, woah. You mean for me to *attend* the ball? Are you nuts? I'll stick out like a noble at the docks."

"That's what I'm counting on." Rain stood and began pacing. "Do what you do best, and you'll be the perfect distraction for the rest of us to gather information." His voice held a command that had Tal forgetting about her reservations. "Keep Daire occupied, and keep your magic controlled. Remember, as far as we know, the mages can only identify you with your red hair. We'll grab an extra potent hair elixir, and you'll be able to walk right by anyone without notice."

"Just don't talk to anyone," Carrick said with a hint of mirth in his voice, and Tal shot him a glare that promised violence.

"I, for one, cannot wait to see you in a dress," Sybil added, entering the room with a red face and a glint in her eye.

7

They outnumbered her, and Tal reluctantly agreed to their idea. With a goal in mind, their plans solidified quickly. Sybil would attend as Tal's chaperone. However, she would quickly make herself scarce to start searching for information on the Pyrie or mages in the offices and library. Egan would infiltrate the kitchens to talk to the palace staff. And Rainier procured an invite for himself as some unknown noble from a distant land.

Tal suggested Sybil attend as a potential bride presented by her brother, Rain. She argued their near-identical resemblance would not go unnoticed, but the roles were decided. Rainier reminded her that he needed to make nice with the bachelors to get invited into a separate room for private conversation, and he couldn't do that while pretending to watch over his sister. Since Carrick's size made him too conspicuous, he found a position as a footman for another guest, which would allow him to stay outside and listen to conversations with the guards and coachmen.

Tal thought she had the hardest task of all. She found Daire at the horse stables inside the eastern wall of the palace grounds, readying his mare for a ride—a beautiful, white Friesian named Aggie with an even temperament. She'd been a gift from the king upon Daire's appointment. He coveted the horse almost as much as his own position.

He stood brushing the mare in only his trousers and leather boots, his training tunic hung on the stall. The early summer sun glistened off the sweat dripping down his muscled back, and Tal remembered the days they would sneak away to the woods. He had been her first, and while she never held any delusions about settling down, when they got along, she'd been content. His opinions on political and social matters ultimately put a rift between them.

She leaned against the wood post by the stable doors with her arms crossed while he brushed Aggie. The horse noticed Tal first and huffed a few times, nodding her head. *I knew I liked you for a reason,* she thought. She missed the mare.

Aggie whinnied and stepped toward Tal.

"Woah there, girl. What are you all excited about?" Daire asked the horse. He still hadn't seen Tal yet, so she cleared her throat, and he turned his head. His face lit up when he noticed her. "I don't usually see you around here anymore," he said by way of greeting.

"I missed my horse." Tal stepped closer to pet Aggie's snout. The horse closed her eyes and snuffed, nudging Tal's hand.

"Your horse, huh? If I remember correctly, she was gifted to *me*."

"Perhaps, but Aggie chose me." Tal shot him a sly smirk.

Daire put a hand to his bare chest in mock injury. "Aggie, my darling, is that true? Have I been betrayed?"

Aggie answered by taking a step further into Talwyn's space and nipped her ear with her lips. Tal tilted her head and nudged the mare.

"After all we've been through?" He threw his arms wide, but a smile lifted his lips. "That hurts, Aggie. That really hurts."

Silence filled the space between them while Tal debated how to broach the subject of the ball. Instead, she asked, "What have you gathered about the fires at the docks?"

He straightened, and his face hardened. "You know I can't discuss that with you."

"But you *are* investigating it."

"Is that really why you came here?"

"No." She hesitated.

Daire broached the subject for her. "Have you changed your mind?"

"You mean you haven't asked someone else? It's been weeks, and the ball is tomorrow. The dress—" Tal waited until the last minute to seek out the captain in hopes that his invitation to her had been given away.

"Tal, there is no one else. The dress has been ready since I asked you. The dressmaker has been waiting for you for a final fitting." He took a step toward her and reached for her arm, but she stepped out of his reach. "My offer still stands, all of it." His smile softened, but she saw a hunger in his eyes while he waited for her answer.

"Daire, I want to be clear—"

"Just say yes, Tal," he interrupted. "It's okay to want to be taken care of."

"I'm not marrying you." She crossed her arms. "I don't need to be taken care of. I'm only going to the ball."

Daire thought for a moment. "Okay, only the ball," a mischievous gleam reached his eyes when he added, "for now."

"I'm serious. I am not accepting a marriage proposal. And if you try anything, one of my knives will find their way into your side."

Daire released a thunderous howl. "Hells, Tal, you always were so violent. I only meant that you'll enjoy the ball, and perhaps you'll change your mind about... the rest."

"Not going to happen." She started walking away, ending the conversation.

"We'll see!" he called. "I'll have the dressmaker call for you tomorrow."

Tal waved him off and left the palace grounds.

***

Egan and Carrick left before the sun came up. Rainier left after breakfast to bring the kids to the baker's wife, who had graciously agreed to take them in for the time being, and Sybil went out briefly to pick up her own dress. She returned empty-handed about an hour before they needed to leave and winked when Tal eyed with suspicion.

The pair met the dressmaker at his shop before lunch. The sprite-ly middle-aged man with salt-and-pepper hair and a black pencil mustache tugged, nudged, tsked, and harrumphed for three hours. Tal grumbled through the whole ordeal, growing more and more frustrated at how much fabric they draped over her, then again as they pulled her hair into a beehive and added color to her cheeks, lips, and lash line. Sybil enjoyed every minute of it. The only blessing had been that they offered her endless glasses of champagne. She was practically cheery by the time they'd finished.

In a periwinkle tulle gown that looked like clouds draped over a waterfall, stood a very annoyed but slightly buzzed Talwyn. The sweetheart neckline met an abundance of cascading fabric and bil-lowing sleeves in an off-the-shoulder style the elite would find scan-dalous, much to Tal's delight. Unfortunately, the sleeves drooped down her arms, and she constantly had to pull them back up. The bodice hugged her middle and then exploded in vertical waves of more periwinkle tulle in a princess silhouette. The fabric itself felt surprisingly light, but all the layers underneath more than made up for it.

At one point, Sybil dressed in her own simple gown of gray and white with a square neckline and tapered lace sleeves. She whistled at the sight of Tal. "Never in my life did I expect to see you in something so... big."

"This will be the only time you'll see this, so you better enjoy it while it lasts," Talwyn replied. "These sleeves are so impractical. It feels like I have a mule tied to my hips. And how am I supposed to sit with this vice around my middle?"

"You're missing one thing." Sybil pulled a thin, tube-like flask out of a pocket in the folds of her dress and handed it to Tal. "It's already filled and should fit right between the breasts." She winked as she handed it to Tal.

Tal smelled the liquid inside and gave her friend a conspiratorial grin. "Where did you manage to get raspberry mead? I thought it all burned with Pochette's distillery."

"I promised not to tell. I had the flask specially made for tonight just in case those royals don't know what a good drink is."

Tal slipped the flask under her corset and blew the seer a kiss. "Now, how the hells am I supposed to take a piss in this thing? Why would they give me all this champagne if I'm expected to just hold it?"

Sybil snorted and motioned to a back room that held a chamber pot for Tal to squat over.

Tal gave a disgusted snarl. "And why do you get to go without sleeves? I'm already sweating."

They helped each other pin their masks in place. Sybil's was a simple, flat gray while Tal's matched her dress in color but covered half her face with an abundance of feathers.

When the carriage arrived, Sybil unceremoniously shoved Tal through the coach door and plopped all the extra fabric into her lap. By the time they reached the palace, Tal was ravenous, and her fingertips buzzed with the alcohol in her blood.

Daire waited by the front steps in the last rays of sunlight, the picture of a perfect gentleman. His stiff black and red suit looked new and tailored to fit his muscular frame. His simple red mask with spiraled gold embellishments dipped down at the end to highlight the square of his jaw. It clashed with her dress.

"It looks lovely on you." His gaze roamed over her appreciatively.

"I can hardly move in this thing, and it takes an army to put on. You're lucky I had no idea what it would look like before they dressed me."

He notched an eyebrow when Sybil emerged from the carriage. Tal pulled his attention back to her by resting a hand on his arm. "She's my chaperone. Show me this palace of yours."

Once inside, they walked through a great hall with ceilings higher than most of the buildings in the docks. Tal narrowed her eyes at the grandeur of it all. *You could fit half the docks in here*, she thought. *What a waste of space.* She sneered at the golden candelabras, the ornate furniture, the curtains made from the finest linens and silks. All the kingdom's money went to *this*? All around, guests were grouped in conversation, showing off their wealth while well-dressed servants presented trays of food and wine. Among them, Tal caught sight of Rainier's dark tresses. He locked eyes with her, tapping the drink in his hand. She gritted her teeth, turning away from the ostentatious display.

Daire stood tall beside her, his arm held out, displaying her like some kind of living ornament. He fit in here or at least tried to. She tsked and rolled her eyes.

A servant with a tray of small brown sausages walked by, and the smoky aroma instantly made her mouth water. Her stomach growled to prove a point. A small plate of fruit appeared in front of her. Daire held the food with an encouraging nod. "The freshest berries you'll ever have," he said.

Tal reluctantly chose a red one. When she bit down, a rush of sugary sweet juice hit her tongue, and she groaned.

Daire smiled triumphantly. "I can provide you with food this sweet anytime."

"If I marry you," she finished for him. When Daire didn't deny it, Tal shook her head but eyed the nearby servants in search of more food. She grabbed a plate or cup off any tray that passed by and relished the flavor of each without care of how audibly she enjoyed the taste. She commented none-too-quietly about the small portions and earned herself a few stares from nearby attendees. Servants started to avoid her, but Tal managed to snag a few slices of bread from one as he passed by.

Daire regarded her with weary eyes. "Please try to behave," he whispered.

Tal paused chewing for a moment, wondering how best to tell him to screw off, but caught an approaching servant out of the corner of her eye. She inwardly delighted at the horror on Daire's face when she grabbed a glass of wine off the passing tray and drank the red liquid in three gulps. Sybil's choked chuckle reached her ears as she set the empty glass down on the frightened servant's tray. She turned back to Daire and spread her arms wide. "I am a picture of utmost civility, my lord," she mocked, bowing her head and giving him an evil grin.

Daire ushered her through a nearby door that led to the ballroom below a sweeping marble staircase. She marveled at the size of the structure as they walked past and then balked at the ballroom itself. With black, red, and white marble floors, and ceilings several stories taller than the last, the room could easily fit over two hundred people. Floor-to-ceiling glass windows cast a rainbow of shadows on the guests while chandeliers with rows of cascading crystals reflected the light into hundreds of vibrant prisms around the room.

Large tables stood near the edges with glass plate settings. A string quartet sat at the back of the room playing a beautiful, melancholy melody. Daire guided Tal with a hand on her elbow to a table near the musicians while other guests filtered into the room.

"Where did Sybil run off to?"

"How should I know? You're welcome to go looking for her." Tal could feel the effects of the wine and regretted her impulsive decision to chug the drink. She sat back in her seat and prayed dinner would be out soon. A few servants passed with more trays of bite-sized morsels, which she grabbed greedily whenever she could. Daire attempted to make small talk but gave up when Tal responded through a mouthful of the most delicious meat she'd ever tasted.

The rest of the guests at their table arrived in pairs and gawked at Talwyn with wariness or outright disgust. They whispered behind their hands and stared at her. At some point, the music stopped, and a herald announced the arrival of King James. Everyone stood. Daire grabbed Tal by the upper arm and pulled her to stand as well. They stood too far back for her to see anything, but she expected the king to be just as haughty as the rest of them.

When the food arrived, Talwyn instantly took back every terrible thing she said about the masquerade. She had never seen so much food, never smelled anything so decadent, nor tasted anything so divine in all her life, and probably never would again. She devoured every last bite with a vigor that earned her even more stares. She eyed a long, thick, green fruit on her plate that appeared to have warts.

"What's this?" She pointed at the object.

"It's called a pickle," a gentleman said hesitantly. The woman gripping his arm smacked him and turned her disgust back to Tal.

It smelled of vinegar, and Tal shivered involuntarily. She gripped the pickle like the handle of one of her daggers, waving it around. It felt unexpectedly stiff in her hand, and Daire reached to put her arm down. Tal met his disapproving gaze and bit into the food with a satisfying *crunch*. A wave of gasps around the table drowned out the string quartet. The bitterness made her mouth water, but it didn't stop her from licking her fingers after the last bite. Daire once more tried to rein her in by suggesting she use a fork but gave up and slumped in his chair in defeat.

After finishing her plate, Tal downed another glass of wine, feeling refreshed with her full stomach. She stood and stated that she needed to relieve herself. Daire blanched, mortified. He didn't bother escorting her.

Tal stumbled toward the washroom at the direction of one of the ladies at the table. She bumped into chairs, other guests, and even managed to knock a tray of cheese out of a servant's hands. She apologized and continued on her way.

She exited the ballroom at one of the back doors that led to a corridor filled with rooms on one side and entrances to a grand balcony on the other. One of her sleeves caught on a stone statue, and she pulled at the impractical fabric in frustration. She pushed both sleeves up over her shoulders, gathered her skirts, and stomped down the hall. With the washroom finally in sight, she cursed at her tulle prison, fully intent on escaping the suffocating ballroom for the rest of the night.

8

S tumbling out of the room, Talwyn's thoughts warred between subjecting herself to further judgement from the haughty nobles or escaping outside for fresh air. She cursed the last glass of wine that sent the hall spinning. She hoped her barbaric display had caused enough grief for Daire that he wouldn't notice her friends within the palace. Carrick's disapproving sigh echoed in her mind. No, she'd caused enough trouble tonight. Any more opportunity and Tal might be forcibly removed. She turned to the north side of the hallway and pushed through the glass doors out onto the now-dark balcony.

She breathed in the clean air and noticed a hint of something floral. The stone railing felt cool against her fingertips. A light breeze lifted the stray hairs from her neck and disturbed the feathers of her mask, tickling her flushed face. Her sleeves slipped further down her arms, and she grunted as she shoved the fabric back.

Her dry tongue stuck to the roof of her mouth. After a quick glance to ensure no one watched, she dug around in her bosom to find the metal flask that had slipped further into her corset during dinner. After a terribly inappropriate display, she had the flask in hand and sipped the honey sweet liquid, a delicacy at the docks. The bottles rarely appeared in taverns before and never would again now that the distilleries were destroyed. She sighed and leaned against the railing, savoring each sip.

Out on the lawns below, the moonlight revealed a path snaking around fountains, stone statues, trees with benches beneath them, and in the distance, a large maze grown out of shrubbery. Tal wondered what she would find within. A small voice in her head whispered of a beautiful flower garden, and she longed to prove the voice right.

She finished the last of the mead, replaced the cover, and returned the flask to its hiding spot. She leaned over the railing, lost in thought, when her foot slipped out from under her. Both feet lifted off the ground, and she began falling over the railing.

Tal cried out. She grappled for balance when an arm reached around and pulled her back toward the balcony floor. A man in a white, navy blue, and gold suit and matching mask set her back on her feet.

"Careful there!" the silky voice warned. His attire was simple yet elegant and held markings that indicated his high rank. Tal lifted her chin and swayed on her feet. He stood a head taller with dark hair that peeked out over the edges of an oversized mask, but the finer details escaped her. "Are you well?"

"Perfectly fine." She brushed her skirts. "Just sampling the wine a bit too enthusiastically."

The man chuckled. "It is well made." He leaned an elbow on the stone railing. "It can be quite strong."

"So, it would seem." She leaned onto the rail, mirroring him, but only to hide her poor balance. She didn't bother informing him of the mead she had just finished. "Thank you."

"What for?"

"For catching me."

"It is what any gentleman would do." He smiled, not in the possessive way Daire sometimes ogled her, but genuinely. "May I ask why you aren't enjoying the company of the other guests?"

"The only thing I would enjoy is shoving some of that minced meat pie in their faces, then finishing their plate for them."

A surprised laugh escaped from the stranger's lips. "I would love to see that."

"Was that not proper? Hells, how does anyone survive these things? More food than could feed an entire village, and they choose to nibble and gossip. If we could have something like this at—" She paused, stopping herself from revealing her lack of title.

"I agree. Pretending to enjoy their company is excruciating."

"You don't have to agree with me. You look like you fit right in."

"It's an act."

Talwyn swore she saw him wink. A voice from inside caught her attention, and she stiffened. Through the glass, she could see Daire opening door after door, searching for her. She peered out over the maze with a sinking feeling in the pit of her stomach. She wanted very much to get away. "Would it be against the rules if I explored the gardens?"

"If you're with me, there are no rules."

Tal narrowed her eyes with a mischievous grin. If he was taunting her, she didn't care. Daire yelled her name again, and she wasted no time. "Right then," she grabbed the gentleman's hand, "come on!"

She stumbled over the steps, and she dragged him down with her. At the bottom, she kicked off her shoes and continued onto the grass. She ran until they were out of sight of the stairs. A shriek of glee escaped her, and her companion followed.

The mysterious noble laughed with her but slowed to a stop near a row of red tulips. Tal halted and turned to him. Breathlessly, she said, "Come on, I'll bet you've never felt grass this soft beneath your feet." She lifted her skirts ever so slightly and scandalously wiggled her naked toes at him.

He appeared unbothered by her behavior when he replied, "These boots are the work of a demon. Once they come off, I'll never be able to get them back on. I'll spare you the horror of my bare feet."

"Spoilsport," she teased. She walked toward the wall opposite him where sunflowers reached her height and beyond. She stood on her tiptoes to smell the flower and promptly lost her balance.

"Oof!"

A hedge eased her fall, her drunken limbs doing little to save her. She exploded into another fit of giggles despite the branches scratching the exposed parts of her face and sticking in her hair.

Strong arms pulled her out by the waist and set her down on the grass. The noble sat next to her with concern on his face. "Are you alright?" he asked.

"Never better," she replied, unable to keep from smiling. Tal lifted her arms above her head and fell back onto the grass. She sighed then, letting the world spin around her. "You know, I thought I would hate coming to this, but right now, it's not so bad."

He eased himself down beside her. "I have to agree with you."

"Do you attend these often?" she asked the stars.

"Only if I have to. I usually try to sneak away when no one is watching." His silky voice drifted around her.

The night sky spun as she breathed in the unfamiliar smell of grass. Her companion's quiet breaths drowned out the couples chatting on the balcony.

Fabric scraped along his arms when he propped himself to face her. "Did you fall asleep?" He chuckled.

"No." She paused. "Simply enjoying the quiet."

The melody from the string quartet filled the space between them. "This is quiet to you?"

She could feel him watching her. She wondered why he entertained her, but a warm wind blew, and the thought evaporated. Thanks to her numerous drinks that evening, she didn't care much about anything. "It is," she replied.

Daire called her name from the balcony.

She groaned. "It appears I'm missed." She struggled to stand. Her companion sat transfixed as if he couldn't curb his curiosity for the guest who clearly didn't fit in. The man who invited her happened to be the lowest in status at the masquerade, and she didn't deserve to be at *his* side, much less with the man sitting in front of her, whoever he may be. "Thank you for... catching me." She attempted a slight bow, which earned her another chuckle, and she realized she should have curtsied instead.

"It's been a pleasure." He bowed his head, and Tal tore her eyes away with difficulty.

She reached the balcony and Daire turned in her direction. "Where have you been?" he hissed. "I've been looking all over for you." He reached for her elbow, but she pulled away.

"I needed fresh air."

"You're drunk," he snapped.

"What else is new?" She waved him away. Daire had spent enough nights with her and her friends to know she wasn't one to hold back on ale. Why would wine be any different? She started toward the ballroom.

The quartet picked up its tempo. Daire sighed. "The dancing is starting. At least come inside and have one dance with me."

"You know I don't do these silly things. I don't want to be paraded around, and, as you clearly pointed out, I'm not at my best." She pushed through the doors into the ballroom, and the upbeat waltz carried on the stuffy air.

Servants bustled about cleaning tables, the clinking of dishes adding to the din. Groups of ladies stood on the edge of the dance floor eyeing groups of men opposite them. She caught sight of Rainier, who tilted his head and scrutinized her scowl. She shrugged, trying to convey that she was a lost cause for the night, and headed for their table. On the ballroom floor, couples danced in perfectly choreographed synchronization. Men dipped and lifted their partners whose dresses billowed out like puffed pastries.

She reached the table and plopped into her seat, noting the plate of cake, pastries, and a bowl of vanilla pudding at her setting. Daire sat down with finesse.

"I made sure they saved some for you." He nodded stiffly at the desserts.

"How gentlemanly of you," she replied. "Thank you." However much he grated on her nerves, Daire knew how much Talwyn relished sweet treats. She ate in silence, savoring the taste. Two songs passed before she attempted conversation. "So, tell me." She searched the faces at the table. "Have any of you heard anything about mages kidnapping women in the docks?"

Daire choked on a sip of water and had to dab at his jacket with a napkin. "Talwyn." He chuckled nervously. His eyes darted from one appalled expression to the next. "That is not the proper topic for such a setting."

"But certainly, it's the perfect opportunity for it. It's not every day I'm surrounded by such esteemed company. Perhaps some of our friends," she gestured to a noblewoman who clutched her jeweled necklace, "have heard something."

Daire leaned in close and whispered in her ear, "This is not the place. Drop it."

Talwyn opened her mouth to respond when a newcomer cleared his throat. She felt Daire stiffen beside her.

"May I have the honor of a dance?" asked her savior from the balcony, standing to her left. His eyes remained on her, his right hand held outward.

Talwyn searched the faces all focused on her. "With me?" she asked, a bit confused.

In the new lighting, his mask served as a ridiculous distraction. It obscured the shape of his face, hanging just over his upper lip and revealing only a strong jaw and the lower half of a handsome smile. With a nod, he answered, "Absolutely."

Talwyn shook her head slightly. "I'm sorry, but I don't know the dances. And I still haven't finished my dessert." She gestured to the bowl of pudding in front of her.

"Don't be silly, my lady," Daire said loudly. "Of course you would like to dance." When Tal glared at him, he whispered, "Go. You cannot refuse him."

"What?" she whispered back, incredulous.

"For once, just listen to me, and dance with him." The vein in his forehead bulged.

Tal gave him one last glare, ate a heaping scoop of pudding, and stood, throwing her napkin down. The surrounding guests whispered with renewed vigor as she passed. She skirted the table and took the arm of her new dance partner who guided her to the marble floor. When they reached the middle, the music switched to a livelier tune. The man turned to face Talwyn, placed his hand in the middle of her back, and held her other hand in his own.

"I warn you," she started before he guided her through the first few measures, "I don't know any of the steps."

He smirked down at her. "Then it's a good thing you've had plenty of wine to loosen your feet." Sparkling blue eyes met her own. For a moment, Tal forgot why she protested.

He pulled her through the first spins, and she stumbled along with him. His hand at her ribcage guided her in the correct direction, and he used a tilt of the head to hint at any turn or spin. "I'm afraid I didn't get your name."

"Is it necessary? We'll likely never see each other again." She stepped on his foot and mumbled an apology.

"Oh, I don't know about that." He ignored her misstep.

"I can almost certainly guarantee it." She let him pull her into a spin that left her dizzy, and she cursed herself for having to lean into him to keep from falling over.

"I'd love to see what sort of fun you get up to when it's of your own choosing." His eyes gleamed in the shadows behind the gold mask. They weren't the cerulean of Daire's irises, but a deep storm of cobalt that held too many secrets in their depths.

"I doubt you could handle my type of fun." She gave what she hoped was a wry smile, but she may have lost control of the muscles in her face. *Damn that wine*, she thought.

Her partner leaned in close as the song came to a close and whispered, "Why don't you give me a chance? You may be pleasantly surprised."

Tal blushed. She realized they'd stopped moving. The music had paused between songs, and the whole of the dance floor had their eyes on her. She let go of his hand and took a fumbling step backward. "Thank you for the dance. My apologies for your shoe."

"It was a pleasure, my lady." He bowed.

Tal turned and stepped right into Daire who swept her up into his arms and pulled her into another dance without giving her the chance to refuse. He led her stiffly, and she stumbled more under his guidance. "Daire, I need to sit." She felt hot. The dancing only made it worse. Her head spun.

"Just one dance," he said, more a command than a request. "You are *my* guest after all."

Tal ignored his tone because the wine sloshing in her stomach suddenly demanded her attention. "Daire, I'm serious. I don't feel well."

"Well, if you hadn't had all that wine, then maybe—" He stopped abruptly when the aforementioned wine forced its way out of Tal's stomach and onto the front of his jacket along with pudding, cake, pastries, and bits of her dinner as well. Tal heaved twice more and met the horrified captain's gaze. Guests all around gasped and backed away, murmuring about Tal's disgraceful behavior. The music stopped, and everyone stared at the couple and the mess between them.

Tal grabbed a handkerchief out of the front pocket of Daire's jacket and wiped her mouth. She attempted to give it back to him, but the disgust on his face had her dropping it in the puddle growing between them. Servants hustled into action, surrounding the pair with rags, pitchers of water, and buckets. They cleaned up the floor and Daire's jacket the best they could.

A hand reached into the fray and pulled Tal out. She stumbled into Rain's arms, and he whisked her toward the great hall. She didn't see the disgusted faces as they passed, nor did she listen to the whispers of how abhorrent her behavior was. Her stomach churned before they reached the grand doors to exit the palace, and she retched into a potted plant.

Outside, Carrick called out to them.

"I don't think Daire will be inviting her to any more balls," Rain said when Carrick reached them.

In a footman's suit, all black with gold stitching and buttons, Carrick was striking. It was a stark contrast from the cheap cotton he normally wore. For a moment, the world stopped spinning. "Hells, Tal. You reek."

She attempted a stabbing comment back but had to clamp her mouth shut around another wave of nausea. She let her head fall on Rain's chest, and he held her upright when her knees gave out.

"We'll take the coach," Carrick said. "I'll bring it back before everyone needs to leave." He scooped Tal into his arms and placed her into the covered coach. Getting through the narrow doorway proved much easier with Carrick's muscles forcing the billowy fabric through. Rainier stayed inside and produced a small vase for Tal just in case. The coach lurched forward with Carrick at the reins, and Tal blacked out shortly after. She didn't wake until mid-afternoon the next day.

9

"I don't see why you guys are mad. Tal created the perfect distraction for me to snoop around the palace," Sybil said around a mouthful of her dinner. She flipped a gold coin in the air then turned her attention back to one of the two books she'd stolen from the king's library.

They ate food from the nearby tavern within the privacy of their tunnels. Talwyn had avoided the crew until early evening when Rainier returned from checking on Evania and Janin. The baker's wife happily kept them a few days longer. Everyone agreed they couldn't just send the children back to the streets, and the tunnels weren't suitable.

"More king's gold?" Carrick asked.

Sybil nodded. "Hidden within the pages of a ledger."

"Did you find anything else?" he pressed.

"Written under the coin. A few transactions that didn't quite make sense—one particularly large sum said something about a trade with a country named Foederis. Ever heard of it, Rain?"

"No. Are you sure it's a country?"

"It was listed as the location and signed by someone named Sceleratus."

"I'll look into it. What were the other transactions?"

"A few trades for provisions, but they were either too large to be plausible, or for items that I know for a fact aren't available anywhere on this side of the Taralin and haven't been for quite some time."

Tal blinked. "Why did any of that stand out to you?"

"They're probably falsifying the ledger to track the money but hiding what it's actually being used for. It's not uncommon but could be worth investigating. Pochette had two ledgers—one where everything appeared lawful and one with the real documentation." Rain would have thrived in a greater kingdom. Thanks to him, Tal blackmailed Pochette into keeping his promise. One slip-up and his enemies would be sent a letter with some very incriminating information.

Egan stabbed a roll with a dagger and spoke around a large bite, "Are we saying that the king is involved in this since they're his ledgers and his coin?"

"They weren't necessarily *his* ledgers. Just ledgers in his palace." Sybil shrugged.

"We don't really know one way or another, but it's also highly likely someone else could be secretly sending money elsewhere and hiding the truth from the king with these false documents." Rain tapped his hand on his boot in thought.

Tal didn't like it either way. If what they found in the palace linked anyone to the mages, it spelled bad news.

"And I had another vision."

All eyes shot to the seer.

"I found a room with a long table and really nothing else. When I stepped inside, the vision hit me like a sack of stones."

"A new one?" Tal gripped her drink, unsure if she wanted to hear what Sybil had to say.

"The same vision actually, but one detail stood out."

"Are you going to elaborate or...?" Tal didn't have the patience for Sybil's annoying tendency to drag out her revelations.

"A window." She dragged out the word as if expecting the others to understand the significance.

Rainier pinched his nose. "Out with it, Syb."

His sister huffed and mumbled something about suspense and dramatics. "The window is to your right in the vision, the nobles behind you, and you're facing the Pyrie." She paused briefly to let that detail sink in, as if anyone else knew why it would be important. "That exact window is in that room."

"What? The same one?" Rain leaned in.

Sybil's head bobbed in affirmation.

"Why would Tal be in a room within the palace among a bunch of nobles?" Egan piped up.

"Hells if I know. All I know is that whatever happens, it has something to do with that room." She bit into a piece of bread.

"How did the vision feel to you?" Carrick questioned. "Could it still be symbolic, or do you think Tal will somehow find herself there?"

"Carrick, the Pyrie is dead. How would it be a literal vision if the woman is supposed to be there?" Tal's gentle tone contrasted her words.

Sybil patted Carrick's bulging shoulder when he shrugged. "It's okay, big guy. I'm just as clueless as you. I'll work on finding out more."

"Well, my part turned out pointless," Rain finally said. "The lords wouldn't stop criticizing the king or talking inappropriately about every woman that walked by. Aside from some mention of an expected invitation, they gave nothing away. I suspect they discussed it further when they left for drinks in the study, which I never got to." Rain side-eyed Tal, and she had the mind to grimace.

"What did they have to say about the king?" Carrick tilted his head.

Rain waved his hand. "Just how selfish it was to break his engagement. They think it ruined the alliance with the eastern kingdom and the trade agreements."

"The kitchen had a lot to say about that too," Egan added. "There was talk that only a fool or someone with no need for alliances would break an engagement."

Rain nodded. "It could lead foreign powers to speculate the king has something up his sleeve and turn unwanted attention to Meladair."

"Right," Egan agreed. "One of the cooks argued there's evil lurking already, trying to find out what he's hiding. They brought up the missing people."

Tal's eyes found Carrick's. She ground her teeth. Everyone had been affected by the disappearances. She had been searching for too long without finding a single person.

Egan continued. "One of the maids said one of her girls never showed up yesterday. She said the girl had as much fire in her as her hair color and probably ran off with the blacksmith's apprentice, but the cook thought otherwise."

Tal leaned forward. "Did they say anything else?"

Egan hesitated. "Ah, no. That was about the time when you, er..."

She threw her hands up in frustration. "Look, I told you guys it was a bad idea, and I would screw up royally. I don't know what Daire was thinking when he invited me."

Not one to put blame on Tal, Carrick reluctantly admitted to not having much time to gather information of his own. "Everyone was too afraid to approach me," he mumbled.

Talwyn turned to Sybil. "Why didn't you tell me to stop drinking the champagne? You knew this would happen, didn't you?"

Sybil waved her away.

Tal pointed an accusatory finger in the seer's direction. "And that mead! You knew. You knew I would drink too much. What vision did you see, Syb?"

"Don't blame me for your alcohol problem. I did my part for the night. I wasn't supposed to *actually* chaperone you."

"You're going to tell me," she mumbled when Sybil pretended not to hear her. "Rain, did you get a good look at the guy I danced with?"

"You mean Daire?" Rainier asked.

"No, before him. The guy in the white suit with dark hair. Some noble or something."

"You danced with someone else?" Egan asked.

"I didn't see, sorry," Rain replied.

"I thought you saw everything," Talwyn teased with only a little attitude.

"Tal, stop blaming the rest of us for doing our part. Rain engrossed himself in high society like he was tasked to do." Sybil sneered.

While Sybil's humor involved frequent teasing, this level of ridicule grated on Tal's nerves. "I wasn't trying to blame him. The guy saved me from falling off the balcony last night. He was a bit of a coquette. I just want to know who he was."

"You fell off the balcony?!" Egan leaned over the table.

Carrick ran a hand over his face. "Tal, what the hells did you do last night?"

"I think it's time she reevaluates her relationship with alcohol," Rain muttered.

"My relationship with alcohol is perfectly fine. And no, I did *not* fall off the balcony, Egan. Like I said, some guy in a white suit caught me before I did."

"And then he was inappropriate with you," Carrick added.

"You didn't give him a little show when you nearly fell to your death, did you? Or maybe you gave him a gracious thank you?" Sybil winked.

Tal wanted to throw her drink at the seer for her snide remarks. "Blazing pigs, Syb, will you stop?" She groaned and reined in the warmth building in the center of her chest. The champagne and wine had done a good job of tamping down her fury last night, but today it returned with renewed vigor. "He shared a dislike for high society and wanted to know more about me. I'm curious why he was so interested in me. He joined me on the balcony and then sought me out in the ballroom."

"You think he could have a connection with the mages," Rain surmised.

"Maybe. It's just a thought."

Sybil slammed her fist on the makeshift table. The wood cracked. "So, you *did* try to work last night!"

"Syb… why don't you give it a rest for tonight." Carrick, ever the peacekeeper, shot Sybil a warning look.

"Or some guy just took a personal interest in you," Egan offered.

Tal nodded. "Either way. I was too drunk to see him clearly, and he wore this ridiculous mask that covered most of his face. I doubt we'll see him again, but if we do, I'd like to be prepared."

"I doubt he knew who you were, and after last night, I don't think Daire will be quick to share that he invited someone from the docks. People would say he deserved to get vomited on for thinking a commoner could attend the king's masquerade." If Sybil had said it, Tal would have lost her hold on her fury, but level-headed Rainier gave his educated opinion on the situation. Tal swallowed and trailed her thumb nail along an imperfection in her cup.

Egan perked up. "Maybe Faron could identify him. He admitted to being in the king's court. I bet he was there last night."

He had a point. Tal hadn't even considered the possibility that their leather-wearing swordsman friend would be at the ball. They hadn't seen or heard from him since that night on the rooftop.

"Yes, the handsome one!" Sybil shouted. "Tal, why don't you go drink-for-drink with him, and see how much information you can get out of him!"

Everyone groaned.

"Will you drop it already?"

"That's enough."

"I swear, if you say one more word…"

"I think Tal is going to melt your hair."

———

Tal threw her dagger at the corner post of a leaning building. She had met her wit's end with Sybil's teasing, and the stuffiness of the tunnels made her nauseous. Carrick convinced her to join him above, and they wandered the streets chatting about nothing important. Tal commented on how dapper Carrick looked in his footman uniform the previous night, and the brute shoved her into an alley playfully. She stumbled a few steps but stayed upright and gripped the side of the building beside her for support. When she turned to step back into the street, an arm came around her throat, and something sharp pressed into her rib cage.

Tal stilled, quickly taking in the details of the situation. She had several weapons hidden on her, but she wanted to let this person think they had the upper hand. Sometimes these louts talked more than they should. She tensed, and her attacker took it as fear. His hubris loosened his grip and left him vulnerable.

"One move, and I'll puncture your lung," the deep voice hissed, a wretched stench wafting from his mouth.

Tal had to exhale to keep her nausea at bay. She instantly recognized Duncan, Pochette's bodyguard. He had been missing for weeks. It appeared he'd escaped the slaughter that the rest of his associates fell victim to. The man stood less than a head taller than her, but at least twice as wide.

"What do you want?" she asked calmly.

"They're looking for you. If I bring you in, they'll leave me alone."

Tal rolled her eyes. "Who's looking for me?"

"I am. But I'm not sure *he* knew that," a deep, silky voice said from behind them.

Duncan jumped at the sudden appearance of another person. He pulled Tal backward into the wall and tightened his hold on her, pressing the knife further into the material of her jacket. She winced. If he punctured the leather, she would pluck the hair from his nostrils one by one.

Faron stood in shadow, his hood pulled up and two swords in hand pointing at Duncan. He tutted. "I would release her if I were you."

"Shut it!" Duncan spat.

"You should listen to him, Duncan." Carrick leaned against the entrance to the alley, a picture of nonchalance.

"I'm not afraid of him." Duncan jostled Tal and he missed her hand slipping to the knife at her belt.

"No, but you should be afraid of me." Tal jabbed her knife into the man's stomach and twisted away from his blade. She wrenched her own knife downward until he released his hold on her neck, at which point she stepped back out of his reach.

"You continue to amaze me," Faron said to her. His hood shielded his face, but she could imagine the embarrassingly awestruck expression there.

Tal used her heel to kick Duncan in his open wound, and he collapsed onto the cobblestones, clutching his side. "Who. Is. Looking. For. Me?" she repeated slowly.

The thug must have been living in squalor for weeks. The beginnings of a beard covered his usually clean-shaven face, and his greasy salt-and-pepper hair stuck out at odd angles. His blue suit was unrecognizable. Scrapes and cuts covered his exposed skin. He breathed heavily, clutching the wound as blood seeped through his fingers.

"Looks like you haven't got much time," Tal said matter-of-factly.

"They'll find you sooner or later," he rasped.

Tal rolled her eyes. "Are you going to share who these friends of yours are, or should I open up that side pocket a little more?" She gestured to the wound.

Duncan grimaced. "Mages," he said with difficulty. "They wear dark cloaks with the hood pulled up."

"Have you seen their faces?" Carrick pushed off the wall and took two steps into the alley.

Duncan nodded.

"How many?" Tal crossed her arms.

"I don't know. I don't know!" he repeated frantically when Tal stepped closer, her knife aimed at his wound. "There was a new one every time—always one of their creations."

"How long did Pochette know about them?" Copper filled her nostrils and Tal flicked blood off her knife. If Duncan spoke the truth, she had no way of knowing how many mages were involved. She knew nothing about her enemy.

"Since he started at the docks, but they've been here longer," Duncan replied, his voice weak. His skin paled, and blood pooled beneath him.

Tal narrowed her eyes at the new development. "Why haven't they made their presence known until now?"

"Biding their time." Duncan slouched against the wall, and his hand fell to the ground, unable to press against the wound. He didn't have long.

She changed up her line of questioning. "Where did you meet them? Where can we find them?"

"Everywhere. They come to you." His speech began to slur.

"No hideouts? No underground crypts to hold prisoners?" Faron spoke this time.

Duncan offered a sardonic smile. "If there were any, the only ones who knew about them are dead," he said darkly, and his body slumped the rest of the way to the ground. He breathed heavily, closing his eyes against the pain in his side.

Tal swore. If she thought she could get any more information, she would have attempted to save the criminal, but he didn't even have ten minutes. She knelt beside his head and whispered, "You're getting what's coming to you, Duncan. The families you've stolen from, the women you've kidnapped and raped, the people you've sent floating down the Taralin, your punishment is nigh. Save a seat at the fiery table for me."

When he took his last breath, Tal wiped her knife on his sleeve and stood as she placed it back in its sheath.

"I take it you two knew each other." Faron used his sword to gesture to the body.

She turned to him then, noting his height and how tightly his leather suit hugged his muscular frame. She swallowed. "He was the bodyguard of a crime lord here at the docks. We had a few run-ins over the years."

"And this crime lord?"

"Sent to the hells."

Faron paused for a moment. "I would ask how he met his undoing, but I have a feeling I'm looking at her."

"Pochette reigned over the docks for decades. He stole, kidnapped, raped, murdered, you name it. His power and money kept eyes off him. He got less than he deserved."

The hooded figure nodded in response. His reaction gave away none of his thoughts on the matter, but she felt no remorse over her part in Pochette's demise. She only wished it had happened sooner. Life in the docks had hardened her against that sort of thing.

"I have some news," Faron interrupted the silence. "Is there somewhere we can talk?"

The three of them sat at a table in the back of a tavern near the south entrance of the tunnels. Faron grabbed an ale for each of them plus two more and sat opposite Tal and Carrick. His hood still concealed his face from other patrons, but Tal could see him clearly. Carrick insisted that Tal take the inside seat, and she rolled her eyes, but chose not to argue. She grabbed the ale from Faron and curled her hands around it, not sure she wanted any tonight. Her fury roiled in her chest, and she had plans to release it.

Tal eyed the two pints yet unspoken for, but Faron jumped right to business. "A servant girl at the palace went missing."

Carrick nodded. "We're aware. She never showed up for the king's masquerade yesterday."

Faron cocked his head, and his lips twitched. "Maybe I should address this first. Talwyn, what is your relationship to Captain Daire?"

"None of your business," she said.

Faron took a sip to hide his smirk. "I'm afraid your behavior last night may have ruined any chances you had of being his guest again."

"You saw me there?"

"How could I miss you?" His teeth flashed. "And I noticed your friends there as well. I think the king would be interested to know how all of you managed to sneak past the guards. One is concerning, but five? Someone might think that the captain of the guard is conspiring against the crown, if he gave you his personal invitation."

Tal sighed. Daire grated her nerves, but he was a good captain and loyal to the kingdom. She didn't want to get him in any trouble. "Daire didn't know we were all there. His invitation to me was purely innocent, and Sybil attended as my chaperone. That's all he knew."

"I think it says something about the captain if he doesn't know when someone sneaks into the palace."

"If you're here to make threats then we're done," Carrick growled as he leaned forward.

Faron waved his hand. "I'm only having some fun. But it is a safety concern for the king. I won't get the captain in trouble, but the king should be made aware of weaknesses in his security." He notched a brow as if challenging her to deny it.

Tal nodded slowly.

"Was your little stunt part of the plan?"

Tal peered sideways at Carrick and gritted her teeth. "I didn't anticipate not being able to eat all day."

Faron leaned against his chair and chuckled. "Are all women at the docks like this, or is it just you?"

Carrick's eyes flicked between Tal and Faron. He raised his brow a fraction, his silent question of whether she wanted him to intervene. When she shrugged, he said, "Are we going to continue with the small talk, or did you have something to tell us?"

He threw a hand up. "Apologies. The women I have the unfortunate task of interacting with are not nearly as interesting as you." He leaned forward, all eyes on Tal. "I'm intrigued."

"And I'm tired. Can we get back to the girl?" Tal sat back in her seat and crossed her arms.

"Right, the girl. Her name is Nola and she's a scullery maid. She's never been late or missing before. The other maids mentioned that she could often be found wandering around the smithy, talking to one of the blacksmith's young apprentices." Carrick and Tal exchanged a knowing look. This confirmed Egan's findings from the kitchens. "Apparently the boy has gone missing too, but no one seems to have noticed. The blacksmith said he's prone to forgetfulness and loses track of time. But he and Nola disappeared the same night."

"Is it possible they ran off together?"

He shook his head. "They boarded with other servants who said they barely have a coin to their name. The two were never seen leaving the palace that night, and no horses or carts are missing."

"If they didn't leave the palace, then where are they?" Carrick frowned.

Faron's attention caught two figures entering the tavern, and he waved them over to their table. "Perfect timing."

The two men sat beside Faron, each taking one of the remaining drinks. Carrick tensed beside Tal, who shifted in her seat with a deep exhale.

"I'd like you to meet—"

"Eddard." Tal eyed the man with the carefree smile and sandy blonde hair.

To his credit, Faron appeared only slightly taken aback. "You know each other?"

Eddard nodded. "We've met. How goes the horse riding?"

"I get in the saddle here and there. Find the perfect sunset yet?"

"Alas, I'll have to search another day."

Tal nodded. She met Eddard shortly after Daire had been appointed to captain. He was just as much a dreamer then as he appeared to be now. She turned to Faron. "What does a member of the king's guard have to do with this?"

"Did you know that the palace was built in an age of great espionage? It's riddled with secret tunnels, passageways, rooms hidden from the public, even dungeons that no one knows about. And thanks to your little incident last night, I did some exploring." He winked. "One of the tunnels led to an underground chamber where the two are being held."

"So, you just happened to find a secret tunnel that led you to a secret dungeon that held the two people you were searching for?" Tal didn't believe it for a second.

"What luck, right?" He tipped back his ale and ignored the skeptical expression she aimed at him. "Actually, no. I grew up visiting the palace and was a very curious child. What I just found is that there are others who know about the tunnels and are using them for nefarious deeds. The problem is, I need help. The boy appears to be hurt pretty badly, and the girl has been given a sleeping elixir. I can't carry them both out."

Carrick gestured to the two men sitting beside Faron. "It appears you already have help."

"Ed is going to distract the guards at the gate so we can get in and out."

Eddard beamed, but Tal eyed the other newcomer. He wore the fine clothing of a noble but took little care to present himself as such. His shirt lay open to a chiseled chest, the buttons undone and one even appeared to have been torn off. He had disheveled dark brown hair, and a bit of rouge colored his cheek in the shape of a pair of lips. Tal guessed he had just left some woman's bed. "And you?"

Unlike Eddard's childlike smile, this man's grin smoldered. "Waylon, milady." He leaned as far across the table as could be comfortable. "I must say, Faron. You never mentioned how beautiful this one is, nor how—" his eyes raked over Carrick appreciatively, "muscled that one is."

Carrick choked on his drink and spilled the ale down his shirt.

Faron blinked, unbothered by Waylon's behavior. "Waylon is great at distractions."

"Among other things," he interrupted with a wink, causing Carrick to erupt into another round of coughing.

Faron continued. "He'll help us avoid any altercations."

Tal turned her attention from Faron to his friends. "Weren't you just saying it's bad that we snuck into the palace? Now you're asking us to sneak back in, and help two prisoners escape? Does the king know they're there?"

Eddard gave Faron a side-eye while Waylon wiggled his eyebrows at Carrick, and the oversized man scooted closer to Talwyn.

Faron's eyes darkened. "I think there are some things going on in the palace that are being kept from him. He had no knowledge of the kidnapping until I told him." He clenched his jaw, and his brow ticked up a notch. King James, often referred to as the "boy king" by townsfolk, had a reputation for spending more time in high society and brothels than with his council.

"So, why doesn't he just release them then?" Tal asked.

He sighed, pinching the bridge of his nose. "Look, he doesn't know who to trust. We have reason to believe there are members of the council that are keeping him in the dark in order to undermine him. If they catch wind that he'd been involved in the release of these prisoners, they may suspect that he's onto them. He doesn't have the support he needs to remove these men from his council yet."

"And so, he's asked you to take care of it?"

Two of the three men lost patience with each passing minute. Faron adjusted his seat repeatedly while Eddard tapped his middle finger on the table incessantly. Waylon leaned back in his seat and didn't pay much attention to the conversation at all. Beside her, Carrick sat straight-backed, accentuating his muscled chest even more. Tal tried to indicate as much with a wide-eyed expression between him and Waylon, but Carrick only returned the look, seemingly misunderstanding her.

"The guard are controlled by the council. A direct order from James would need to be reported to them. I offered my help, thinking you might have the strength," he indicated Carrick, "and the stealth," his eyes returned to Tal, "to get them out quietly."

"And yet you have a member of the guard right next to you." Her expression softened when she turned to Eddard, and he smiled back as if they were talking about what to eat for dinner. Out of all the guard members Tal knew, Eddard was the least likely to reveal their secret rescue, but she wouldn't admit that.

"I trust both these men with my life. They'll ensure our escape is without conflict."

"And why couldn't the king order the guard not to say anything?" Tal leaned forward with her eyes narrowed at the noble. "What aren't you telling us?"

He clenched his jaw. "Do you know anything about the politics of running a kingdom?" He narrowed his eyes at her.

Tal hesitated. "No." She never had reason to venture far enough within the palace grounds to mix with those people, and she never had a desire to know anything about them. She didn't even know what the king looked like.

"I'll do everything in my power to get you in and out quickly without issue. I only need your help carrying them through the tunnels and out of the palace walls. I'll have a carriage waiting to take them somewhere safe once they're outside of the grounds."

"You're sure they're still there? We shouldn't encounter much trouble?" Carrick asked. He purposefully avoided Waylon's gaze.

Tal scrutinized him, still not sure about this plan, and the amount of trust they gave this near stranger. He may be handsome with his youthful eyes, dark hair, and sharp jawline, but she never met a noble who ventured to the docks, let alone one who asked for her help.

"They were there a few hours ago." Faron straightened.

"Alive?" Something about a woman in distress always swayed Carrick. Hells, the man couldn't stop himself from helping anyone in need.

Tal sighed with resignation.

Everyone leaned closer. "For now," Faron said through clenched teeth.

Tal watched as the muscle along his jaw flexed and relaxed several times.

Carrick stood. "Then we leave now."

10

They hurried through the streets in silence until they reached the outer walls. When the gate came into view, everyone slowed except for Eddard. He continued forward, and his gait adjusted to that of someone who had been drinking heavily. He stumbled up to the two guards and nearly fell into them. Tal couldn't hear what he said to them, but disruptive conversation echoed in the night. His arms waved around frantically, and he fell into one of the guards.

The four onlookers eased their way closer to the gate while Eddard created a boisterous scene. He pulled something out of his pocket and lifted it to his mouth. One of the guards gestured for Eddard to move on and was promptly showered from head to toe with spit. Eddard pointed and roared with laughter, leaning on the other guard for support. The man aggressively attempted to brush the liquid from his armor until he gave up and stomped away from the gate.

They inched close enough to hear the conversation between Eddard and the remaining man.

"It's not fair, Jens! You should have joined tonight." His drunken slur sounded just believable enough. Tal thought they may get away with it.

"Perhaps another time, Ed. Why don't you go sleep that off?"

"Sure, sure. But a man's gotta take a piss first. Could you help me out? The walls are spinning." He fell into the guard again.

Tal could hear the soldier, Jens, sigh heavily. He put an arm around Eddard and nearly carried him away from the gate.

They didn't need any more of a signal and rushed through. Faron directed them to the left where the buildings cast a shadow. They sprinted through the flat expanse of the bailey, and the great wooden doors to the palace neared for the second time in as many nights.

Tal and Carrick shared a curious glance when they veered away, following a downward slope along the main wall, away from the front entrance. After several minutes of slinking along, Faron stopped near an enormous drain surrounded by overgrown bushes. A slow trickle of water came through the grate and trailed a path toward the main gate, searching for a way to the river.

Faron and Waylon stepped into the water, gripped the bars covering the opening, and wrenched sideways. Metal on gravel broke the silence as the bars slid into a hidden pocket within the palace wall.

Tal's jaw dropped. She and Carrick exchanged shocked expressions while Waylon slipped inside. She only hesitated a moment before passing through the secret entrance. Carrick nearly filled the space but managed to fit through and stand at full height. The thick air stank of dirt and stale water. Tal blinked, encouraging her eyes to adjust in the darkness. Dripping water echoed off walls carved out of the earth until it was drowned out by the scrape of their shoes on the dirt floor.

Once Faron stepped inside, Waylon helped him replace the metal bars. "It's this way." He gestured ahead, stepping in front of them.

Waylon lit a torch on the wall and guided the group forward. Tal stepped lightly over the uneven ground. The winding path of the tunnel split into different directions—some sloped further down, burrowing deep into the earth, and others had steps that disappeared as they curved up and around hidden corners. Still, other paths continued into the darkness with no apparent end. Occasionally, a rat scurried across their path, or Faron swiped at a cobweb, but they didn't encounter anyone else in the near darkness.

Unease flipped Tal's stomach. *If Faron wanted to do anything, he would have already*, she reminded herself. Beside her, Carrick held a tight grip on his sword and his eyes darted up and down the tunnel, tracking the movements of the other two men as they walked. Tal suspected his thoughts mirrored her own.

When the dirt wall transitioned to a masonry of carved stones, moss, and mud, Faron stopped and placed his ear against it. The soft trickle of water at their feet pierced the silence—not even a breath rose above the quiet stream. A dark line traced the change in masonry in the shape of a rectangle, revealing a hidden door.

Faron turned then, torchlight flickering across his features. "They're behind this wall, in a room to the right. They should be alone, but if not, be ready." He nodded at Carrick's sword, and Tal took two of her knives from the sheaths at her hip.

Having placed the torch in a sconce above his head, Waylon gripped his own sword, his face devoid of the earlier flirtation. Faron braced himself against the man-made wall and pushed with a grunt.

Slowly, with the grating of stone that echoed back the way they came, the door opened. It scraped against a large hanging tapestry and opened their view to a dim hallway. Like the tunnel, it too had been dug out of stone, but with thick wooden doors set in the wall, torches, and a wooden bench at the other end, next to an even larger door. That one appeared to be the entrance.

As soon as he had enough space to slip through, Waylon disappeared. Faron followed, sword in hand. A moment later, Waylon's voice rang out. "Empty."

Talwyn went next, Carrick at her back. She searched in each direction despite the reassurance from Waylon. Tal's heartbeat pounded against her chest.

Faron ushered them down the hall to the second cell on the right where a simple metal latch kept the prisoner inside. Metal bars set high in the wooden door gave little view of the pitch-black interior. Faron wrenched the door open.

Tal grabbed a torch from the wall and shined it into the room, if the tiny space could be called that. The smell of blood and waste hit them like a punch in the face, and Tal held the torch higher. In the left corner, a crumpled form lay motionless. The once cream and brown clothes of the blacksmith's apprentice were stained with dirt, blood, and gods knew what else.

Faron rushed over to him, gently placing a hand on the boy's shoulder. He jerked, the first sign that he still lived. "Luan," Faron whispered, "where's Nola?"

The boy whimpered, a sound more like an exhale that faded until he gasped in another breath.

"We're getting you out, but we aren't leaving without Nola. Where is she?"

Carrick met Tal's gaze and tilted his head toward the hall. When she nodded her understanding, he disappeared to check the other rooms.

"They took her," Luan whispered into the back wall. He curled around himself, flinching away from Faron's hand.

"Who took her?" Faron gentled his voice.

"Cloaks. Dark cloaks."

Faron turned to Tal, his eyes saying what he couldn't. It must be mages. They had been in the palace. Why were the boy and girl being held here? How did the mages know about this place? Did they have an ally within the palace?

"Where did they take her?" Tal asked, keeping her voice low.

"North. Silaron." His voice grew weaker, if that were at all possible. Tal wondered if he had much time left before he succumbed to his injuries.

Faron tensed at the mention of the girl's location. Tal had never heard the name before.

Carrick's hulking form filled the doorway. "The rooms are all empty. Waylon's gone down the hall."

"Do you have a healing elixir?" she asked her companions. When both of them shook their heads, Tal pursed her lips. She wanted to ask more questions. What happened? What condition would they find the girl—if they found her? Had he seen their faces? What did these mages want? What would they find at Silaron? But the poor boy didn't appear to have much more energy to continue breathing let alone explain everything. Tal stepped to the side. "Carrick, you carry him. Faron will show us the way out. I'll keep an eye on our backs."

Without a word, Carrick stepped into the room and knelt beside Faron. He assessed Luan's injuries before gingerly placing his hands below the boy's shoulders and knees. The apprentice let out a pained grunt and began panting as Carrick lifted him into his arms. A dark puddle filled the space where he had been laying, and blood dripped from his ripped tunic.

Talwyn gritted her teeth against the rage that fueled her fury at the sight. When Carrick turned with him, the boy's swollen and bloodied face came into view. He couldn't have been more than fifteen. She feared for the girl, Nola, and whatever state she was in. She stepped aside and allowed the men out of the room, with Carrick holding Luan like a sleeping child.

Waylon appeared by a door at the end of the hall. "Time to go. There's movement."

Without a word, Tal replaced the torch she'd been holding and returned to the hanging tapestry and their secret entrance. Faron helped her pull the stones to a secure close with a hooked metal fire poker that he grabbed from the ground just inside the tunnel.

They left twice as fast as before, and Faron didn't falter at any of the turns. When they reached the false sewer grate, Tal winced at how loudly the metal scraped along the stones. They stuck to the shadows through the grounds and reached the main gate. Without a moment's pause, Faron instructed them to head into the woods and follow the water, and he and Waylon would catch up. The two men approached the same two guards, arm in arm, singing a boisterous tune. Their distraction worked instantly, and the guards left their posts to guide the two men back within the grounds.

Tal and Carrick hurried to the trees surrounding the outer palace walls, a small stream of water flowing on their left. After a distance, they slowed their pace, and Tal broke the tense silence that hung between them. "Does any of this seem suspicious to you?"

"You mean why would a noble come to us for help?"

Tal nodded. "I want to trust him, but something isn't adding up." She paused, then said, "Perhaps it's because we're expendable? Should anything go wrong, no one will miss a couple of orphans from the docks."

Carrick grunted in response. They walked for a few minutes longer, their pace terribly slow as they picked their way over tree roots. A branch cracking behind them had Tal whipping around, knife in hand.

Without a greeting, Faron spoke, "When we reach the village, there will be a cart waiting to take Luan north to the mountains. They'll have a healing elixir for him. Whoever took him has connections within the palace, which means he can't stay here. I've hired a healer and her husband to care for him until he's well enough to find his own way."

"What about his family?" Carrick asked, carefully adjusting his hold under the boy's shoulders. He grunted softly, but didn't stir.

"He has no family."

Talwyn scoffed. "And you learned this when?"

"I met Luan three years ago while I acquired a new sword. He and I have spoken on occasion since then."

"Where's your friend?" Tal eyed the empty space surrounding him.

"He's gone to get Ed. Do you not trust me?"

"I could hardly say I know you well enough to offer my trust. Why are you so trusting of *me*?"

Faron chuckled beside her. "So cynical. I trust you because you help the lowly, even if it puts you in danger. Besides, I'm a great judge of character." He straightened with a hand on his chest.

"You don't think this appears suspicious at all?" Moonlight illuminated his handsome face, and Tal tripped on a tree root. He caught her by the elbow and only released her when she steadied her footing.

"Oh, I think it looks terribly suspicious. Who on earth is trying to frame the king by placing a tortured blacksmith's apprentice in a dungeon underneath the palace? I think we need to get to the bottom of this before it escalates."

"You know that's not what I meant. And what do you mean 'we'? *We* don't need to do anything. Carrick and I are doing you a favor. *We* need to get this boy to safety, and that's it."

Faron stopped walking, and the center of his brow pulled up in dismay. "You're not going to help me get Nola out?"

Tal stopped a few paces ahead of him while Carrick continued walking. "Do you know where she is?"

A shout in the distance forced them to quicken their pace and ignore the hanging question. When they reached the outskirts of the village, a cart waited for them, as the noble had said. An older man sat at the reins while his wife stepped down to greet them. She asked Faron questions about Luan's condition before hopping in the back of the cart where Carrick laid him. She uncovered a large crate filled with glass bottles of elixirs and salves.

Faron took Carrick aside and spoke too quietly for Tal to hear, handing him a leather pouch. The two exchanged a few short words, and Carrick left with a gesture to Tal to stay put. Tal watched him head south and disappear into the trees, then stood back as the woman pulled out several bottles and jars, poured one liquid over the cuts on his skin, applied a salve over the top, and instructed Luan to drink another.

"Brigid—" Faron began.

"Where's the girl?" the woman, Brigid, asked.

"They've taken her to a place up north," Faron answered. Something passed between the two that Tal couldn't discern.

"It is not safe for you to go after her. Hire another who has the manpower to deal with this." The old woman spoke to the noble as if she knew him well.

Tal contemplated the reason for this concern for the man beside her, not quite like a mother's worry for her son, but certainly more than what could be considered common for acquaintances.

Faron gestured to Tal. "I've hired the best bounty hunter in Meladair and her muscle. They are more than capable," he said with a wink, to which Brigid scoffed.

The healer rummaged through her cart and insisted Faron take a satchel filled with glass vials. She didn't describe the contents, but Tal suspected Faron already knew. He protested briefly but thanked her when she wouldn't take them back. He then went and spoke to Brigid's husband, who said they would ride further north and wait until sunrise. If the group had not rescued the servant girl by then, they would have to arrange other transportation for her.

The man urged the attached horse forward at a slow pace, so as not to draw attention, while his wife cared for the unconscious boy in the back of the cart. Shortly after, Carrick returned on a large horse with two more in tow.

"I sent a message to Rainier," he spoke to Tal quietly. "He'll meet us there if he gets it in time."

"Where?"

"Silaron, the royal family's holiday home," Faron spoke before Carrick could respond. "It's a two-hour ride from here. We should go." He mounted the brown mare and eyed the remaining horse meaningfully.

Tal briefly considered the significance that the kidnapped servant had been taken to one of the king's additional homes, but even Carrick seemed to urge her to get on the horse. She complied reluctantly and they set off.

11

"They're spaced three minutes apart," Faron observed.

The trio hid among the trees outside the property. Thirty paces ahead, Eddard stalked after a cloaked figure that patrolled the grounds. Lights shone through most of the windows of the four-story mansion. A shadow appeared in a first-floor window on the eastern side of the building. It waved and then disappeared again. Waylon had made it inside. Faron hung his head, hiding his smirk, and Carrick snorted.

"Guards are placed at each of the entrances. I don't see any among the grounds," Carrick added.

"Pretty bold of them to assume they don't need more patrols," Tal said.

"What worry do they have of someone rescuing a palace servant? This place is virtually unknown. It should have been abandoned nearly twenty years ago. Though it doesn't look like it's been abandoned at all," Faron added under his breath.

"A false sense of security. That's good for us. It'll make it easier to go unnoticed. Can we hope this also means there aren't hordes of them inside?" Tal asked the noble.

"There are no rooms underground. Everything you see is the whole compound."

"Well, they can't be watching from inside with the intent to create more apparitions at the first signs of an intruder." Carrick paused. "Both Eddard and Waylon made it through the grounds without issue."

"Maybe they are too bold for their own good. How much of an offense would the king take if he knew mages took over his holiday home? That is, assuming he didn't give them permission to occupy it in the first place." Tal's suspicion pulled a scoff from the noble beside her.

"The king would never consort with mages, especially those that torture and kidnap innocents," Faron huffed.

"That you know of," Tal muttered under her breath.

They reached the mansion half an hour ago and were no closer to discerning whether the abducted girl was inside or not. Tal and Carrick exchanged doubtful glances, knowing any conflict with mages would be dangerous, but Faron seemed determined to search the building regardless.

A tortured scream broke the silence of the starry night, and their attention shot to a window in the top corner of the west side. Tal noticed the ivy snaking its way from the ground up past the window to the roof.

"That's the queen's quarters," Faron said with a determined glint in his eyes.

"You seem to know an awful lot about this secret mansion," Carrick voiced Tal's concerns.

Without missing a beat, Faron replied, "Before King James's father took the throne, my family was close with the royals and other members of the nobility, as I previously told you." He met Tal's gaze. "They had a daughter a few years younger than me. When politics required our fathers meet, we often played together: the princess, King James—then a young noble—and me."

"So, this secret mansion is only a secret to commoners then." Tal searched Faron's face for a hint of deception.

"It is a secret to anyone who is still alive, save James, a few select advisors, and me, and now you, Ed, and Waylon. Everyone else who knew about the mansion died in a fire that burned down the east wing." He nodded to the opposite end of the mansion.

Tal narrowed her eyes at the east wall. The stone shone brighter in the moonlight, with considerably fewer vines snaking up its face. The framework appeared stunted, as if the structure used to be grander. The newer addition didn't fit the architecture or the quality.

Whispers from years past of the dead king began to make sense. "A tragedy," they would say. "His whole lineage, even the little one." Women gossiped over their baskets. Men harumphed at the new king without royal blood. The throne had been given to one of his closest advisors—a noble—and King James was that man's son.

She hadn't thought about the circumstances surrounding the throne but seeing where the man and his entire family met their demise humbled her, at least for the moment. She found the window at the west end of the house where the girl screamed in the room beyond—the queen's room.

For decades, perhaps centuries, the royal family would visit this mansion for a private summer getaway, and the queen would sleep peacefully in the room where one of her kingdom's servants was now being tortured. Who was that woman that perished in the fire twenty years ago? Would she turn her nose at anyone below her station, or would she protect all members of her kingdom, title or not?

"How do we know the king isn't somehow involved in the mages' presence here? It is his mansion," Tal said.

Carrick's body tensed with each new tortured scream from the window, but she wasn't about to blindly jump into a rescue mission against an unknown number of the most powerful and dangerous beings they'd ever heard of.

Faron sighed, exasperated. "We've been over this. The king has no involvement with the mages, nor would he ever contribute to the kidnapping and torturing of innocents. If he were involved, do you really think he would be hiding them in a secret dungeon or in his summer house? He would be better off creating a false story to accuse them of treason, not that he would even need to have a reason for any of his actions. But I'm telling you, he's a good man. He is not involved here. Are we done debating who is responsible? Can we stop them from torturing Nola now?"

Tal released a frustrated sigh. "If those vines are strong enough, I could scale them to that window." She nodded to where curtains swayed on a summer breeze.

"They'll hold. But I'll go first to eliminate the mages in the room."

"With all due respect, your nobleness, those swords of yours won't do any good from that window. By the time you get over the threshold, the mages inside will have already spotted you, sliced you open, and raised an alarm. We need the element of surprise." She pulled her daggers a few inches out of their hilt, letting the moonlight glint on the metal.

"Then I'll go," Carrick chimed in.

Tal patted his large bicep. "Sorry big guy, I don't think any vines would hold you. And there's no way you would fit through that window. You stay below to keep guard and run the girl to the woods once we get her out. I'll go first and take out the mages in the room. Hero over here," she gestured to Faron, "will follow after me, help me get Nola out of the room, and down to you. In and out. No heroics. No wise ideas to investigate or take out any more than we need to."

Carrick's mouth tightened in a thin line, but he stayed silent.

Faron's lips quirked into a crooked grin. "I like it when you give orders."

Tal ignored him but stuck her tongue out at Carrick. No matter how much trouble they found together, he would always try to protect her from danger.

A window on the west side of the building opened, and a candle appeared.

"That's Ed's signal. The patrols are gone." Faron tensed on the balls of his feet.

Tal pulled her daggers out. "How many mages are inside?"

"Only one way to find out," Faron said with a flourish of his sword and leapt out onto the open lawn.

Carrick swore and followed while Tal paused to smirk at the man bounding across the lawn, dressed head to toe in leather. She met her companions against the west wall, regarding the vertical climb.

They waited for a signal from Waylon to indicate he'd distracted the mages inside. Carrick faced the opposite end of the estate. "What kind of signal did he say he would give?"

"He didn't." Faron tested the strength of the vines.

Tal wondered how much longer they'd have to wait when a deafening *BOOM* shook the building. Despite the horror on his face, Faron gestured for Tal to climb. "Well, you can't miss that. Up you go, lovely."

Without a moment's pause, Tal stepped to the wall, quickly finding footholds.

The climb proved much faster than she anticipated. The ivy grew several inches thick from decades of neglect, and she easily slipped her toes among the foliage. As she climbed, the agonized screams continued, pushing her to move faster.

She reached the side of the window and carefully stepped onto the sill, the curtain obscuring her from the occupants inside. By the groaning floorboards and voices within, Tal guessed there were two others—one near the girl, and one straight ahead, likely by a door. Securing her footing on the ledge, she pulled two daggers from their sheaths. Tal crouched behind the curtain. A quick glance told her that Faron had climbed halfway up the wall.

With a deep breath and flip of her weapons, she pulled the curtain aside with her left hand, threw the dagger in her right across the bed, choosing to aim for the man's chest for a wider target. Before it hit, the dagger in her left hand soared toward the door, this time finding home in the second man's throat, his faceless head turning to her as blood gushed over his cloak.

She spared only a glance as he slumped to the ground. Then she turned back to the enemy at the bed. A hand lifted, his bloody knife pointed in her direction. His head suddenly snapped back, the hilt of her third dagger sticking out where his eye socket would have been. Tal stepped to the side of the bed where the girl, about sixteen, panted. "Nola?"

"Please. Please help me," she begged. Her clothes bore evidence of the torture she'd been subjected to; cuts and bruises littered every visible inch of her body. A sheen of sweat coated her face, and her cheeks were sunken from malnourishment.

"We're getting you out of here." Tal attempted to cut the ropes tying the girl to the bed, but nothing happened.

"They're spelled. You can't cut them," the girl cried weakly.

"I've got it," came a voice from behind her. Faron slipped into the room. His hood covered his eyes. He pulled a small vial of yellow liquid out of the satchel on his back, the same one the healer had given him, and poured three drops onto the bonds at Nola's hands. "Careful, this will burn if you touch it."

A fiery yellow glow spread from the spot where the drops soaked into the bindings. The ropes sizzled, emitting a green smoke that smelled of sulfur. Slowly, the rope turned black and then disintegrated where the liquid soaked through. Soon, the bindings broke apart, and Nola's hand fell from its bonds. Faron made quick work of the other three restraints. Tal's fury pressed into her chest and ached as if it recognized the liquid.

When Nola was free, Faron hefted her over his shoulder and went to the window. Tal stepped back into the room and pulled her daggers out of the mage and apparition. She wiped their blood onto their cloaks. Like all men, the mages bled red. The coppery smell gave no indication of the dark magic it summoned.

Her eye caught the burned bindings on the bedpost, and she paused. She carefully picked up the charred end of one of the restraints, noting how the remaining magic made the hair on her arms stand on end. She could feel the fury within the solution Faron used. Her own fury called to it.

Biting her lip, she reached for the bedpost and placed the tip of her finger against the magicked knot. She thought of the yellow glow of the solution as it ate through the spell and the rope together. She focused all her fury into her fingertip pressed there. The warmth in her chest trickled over her shoulder, down her arm, and reached her finger. She thinned her lips and flared her nostrils when the fury pushed into the knot. The rope began to sizzle. The charred smell reached her nose again as she watched her magic burn through the spelled restraints. A faint smile reached her lips.

The creaking door interrupted her thoughts, and she spun around, throwing a spike of flame without thinking. Her shot blasted into the door frame and sent splinters flying. Before she could attack again, the mage in the opening flung his robed arm in her direction, and her legs gave out. She tried to stand to no avail. The mage attacked again, and warmth spread down her arms.

She sat on the floor, her legs folded under her, her arms limp at her sides, and the pain hit. Her gaze fell, and she realized he'd sliced her open with each slash of his arm. Blood pooled beneath her, and dizziness consumed her. She struggled to stay upright when the mage stepped toward her, cupped her chin in his hands, and met her eyes. With his hood pulled back, she saw a middle-aged man, the hair at his temple graying from near black. His wrinkles deepened as his lips pulled into a wicked grin.

"Ah. I see we've had the wrong one all along. You weren't nearly as difficult as I thought you'd be."

Tal swayed, fighting to stay conscious.

He clicked his tongue and waved his hand, casting a spell that froze Tal in place, her back held straight by an invisible post. The weight of the spell bared down on her chest, making it hard for her to breathe. Copper filled her nose as blood warmed her legs where it pooled on the floor.

"Do you know—" The mage stopped and fell backward, the hilt of a dagger protruding from his skull.

The freezing spell cracked, and Tal collapsed. A familiar voice behind her swore, and Tal's eyes fluttered closed. Someone pulled her upright and a warm liquid trickled across her lips.

"Swallow."

More liquid met her tongue, and she choked on it.

"Swallow, dammit," the voice commanded.

Tal obeyed and quickly felt the pain in her limbs cease, but her moment of reprieve was short-lived. Her eyes shot open from the shock of fire that wasn't her own shooting up and down her limbs. A red, leather-clad shoulder pushed painfully into her stomach. Her legs were pinned against his chest. Her mind screamed in agony, but her body lacked the energy to react.

"Hold on," the familiar voice said.

Tal closed her eyes against the dizziness and pain. When she opened them again, the floor disappeared, and she hung four stories above the ground. She blinked, her mind an exhausted blank space, before closing her eyes again and letting her head fall against his back.

"You know, I'm beginning to think there's something between us, what with you falling into my arms every time we meet."

"Do you ever stop talking?" Tal managed to groan. The healing magic burned and itched as it stitched her back together. Her energy slowly returned as the pain lessened.

"Just making sure you're still with me," Faron said, relief in his voice. He continued their descent.

As they neared the ground, Carrick burst from the trees.

"What in the hells happened?" he demanded, reaching up to help Tal.

"Distracted," she offered in response. When she met his eyes, Carrick's widened, and he discreetly tapped his temple. Understanding dawned, and Tal dropped her gaze to the ground. *No red. No gold. No fire.* Her fury must have burned through Septimus's serum, letting the golden color of her eyes shine in the limited moonlight.

A shout from the fourth-story window pulled their attention. A blast of magic shattered the wall of ivy behind them and sent debris flying.

Without giving Tal a chance to object, Carrick scooped her up in his arms and sprinted across the lawn, Faron following close behind. Cloaked figures spilled out of the house and spread across the lawn, firing arrows and throwing daggers at them, but only the occasional spell aimed their way. Tal tried to reach her daggers, but her arms were pinned.

"Let my hands free," she tried to say.

An arrow flew past them from the line of trees, hitting an attacker square in the chest, followed by another that hit one in the shoulder. Waylon bellowed as he crossed the lawn, chased by three adversaries. Arrows quickly took down two as Eddard sprinted over from the west. He easily dispatched the third pursuer with his sword.

When the two reached the group, Faron yelled, "What kind of a signal was that?!"

"What do you mean?!" Waylon dodged a ball of what looked like ice that flew over his head.

"I said to distract them, not blow up half the mansion!" Faron yelled back.

"I was not given specifics!"

They reached the tree line where six horses waited. Carrick lifted Tal onto the nearest mare, and Faron climbed into the saddle behind her. She began to protest, but a figure leapt from the trees.

"Way to cut it close, as always, Tal," Rainier said, throwing his bow on his back and climbing onto the horse currently occupied by a better-looking Nola.

Her cuts had stopped bleeding, and she sat straighter on the horse, clutching an empty glass jar. Faron must have given her a healing elixir.

"Less than a handful of cloaks from what I can tell," Rainier told Carrick. "We need to outrun them. Can you manage a saddle this time?"

Carrick didn't hesitate to mount the largest horse. "I've improved," he said and kicked the animal into action.

The group set off into the woods as fast as the horses would take them. The one meant for Tal galloped without its rider at the back of the group.

They weaved in and out of the trees, avoiding stray spells and losing their enemy. When they could push the horses no further, their pursuers were nowhere in sight. Eddard and Waylon circled back to ensure they weren't being followed.

The sudden ending of the chase worried Tal more than anything.

"How are your wounds?" Faron asked. They had slowed to a walk.

"Better," she responded. The clip clop of the horse's hooves pounded in Tal's ears like a warning drum.

Carrick led the way, Rainier and Nola behind him. The servant girl had fallen asleep, and Rain held her head against his shoulder with one hand, the horse's reins in the other.

"When we meet with the wagon, I'll get you more healing elixir," he offered.

"No need. I'm healed enough until I can get to my own stash." She tried to sit straighter in the saddle and winced when pain sliced through her leg.

"Has anyone ever told you that you are terribly stubborn?" She could hear the smile in his voice.

"The girl needs it more than I do."

"What if the old woman has two extra vials?" Their horse slipped on a rock, and Faron tightened his hold around Tal's waist.

"That's doubtful," she said, painfully aware of his chest against her back. Healing elixirs were rare, especially effective ones. The power and ingredients needed to brew them were harder to come by than a bag of gold coins in the middle of the street. She wouldn't let anyone waste the elixir on her.

"Just as doubtful as you thought of my skills with a dagger?"

Tal smirked. She admitted to herself that it had been an expert throw, though she wished he had given the mage a chance to speak first. At least he had confirmed that the mages sought *her* and not simply anyone with elemental fury.

"Ah. So, my skills leave you speechless. I'll be happy to show you more sometime."

"More skills with the dagger?" she teased.

Faron leaned close to her ear and whispered, "Throwing daggers isn't the only skill I have."

His warm breath caressed her neck, and she had to fight the wave of chills that rolled down her spine. "Oh, you mean your skill with a sword," she replied coyly, knowing full well he most certainly was not referring to swordsmanship.

He chuckled in her ear. "Is that what you'd like to call it?"

Tal rolled her eyes even though he couldn't see. "Is this how you win over all your female conquests?"

"No conquests, just you."

"I hardly believe a member of the nobility doesn't take advantage of his status to pull silly little girls into dark corners to satisfy his unsavory desires."

"I'm offended you think so little of me, but I'd gladly let *you* pull me into a dark alcove to show me *your own* unsavory desires." His arms curled around her a fraction.

Tal sunk further into his arms, exhaustion pulling at her. "What I desire is a decanter of ale, a plate of pheasant and fresh bread, followed by a full night of uninterrupted sleep."

"Then the first round at the tavern is on me." He let the conversation fall away when Tal didn't respond.

They continued in silence and soon, the rhythmic clopping of the horse lulled Tal to sleep.

12

Tal limped past the blacksmith's shop. "Dammit," she grumbled. Her wounds weren't closing. Whatever spell the mage used had caused more damage within her limbs than a mere blade. She hoped the alchemist knew how to put her to rights. As soon as she convinced Septimus to create a new formula for his healing elixir, she would retreat to her bed for the next forty-eight hours.

A figure stepped out from the alley, and she scowled. "Go away, Daire."

"I need to talk to you," he said, his tone serious.

"I'm busy." She brushed past him, trying to hide her limp.

Daire kept pace with her. "I just need a few moments. I think you owe me that much."

Tal's anger flared, and she stopped short. She bit back the retort that sat on the tip of her tongue and glared at him instead.

"Join me." He nodded to a pier jutting out over the water. He waited for her to accept, his expression serious.

Tal took what should have been a deep, cleansing breath and exhaled aggressively. She hobbled down the street, the length of one building, crossed another street, and sat along the wall overlooking the lower docks, her legs hanging painfully.

Daire, who gave no indication that he noticed her obvious injury, sat next to her, tucking his captain's sword behind him. He hesitated only briefly, but turned to Tal and said, "I want you to know that I forgive you."

Tal cocked her head and gawked. "Excuse me?"

"I forgive you, Talwyn," Daire repeated.

She stared at him in disbelief. While there were certainly many things Tal had done to require forgiveness, his audacity to say it outright amazed her. No asking how she felt, no acknowledgement that he had unfair expectations, not even an apology for the ridicule she received at the ball even before she actually chose to be a nuisance.

She swallowed her anger and instead said as calmly as she could, "What is it exactly that you forgive me for?"

"Come on, Tal. You made a fool out of me at the masquerade; not to mention, you ruined my dress uniform. I've spent the last two days as the center of gossip because I brought a barbarian to the king's ball."

"Oh." Tal blinked. "Is that what you think of me? I'm a barbarian?"

"That's what the nobles are saying. I've had to make up this ridiculous story that you're recovering from the influenza after learning of your brother's sudden passing overseas, and you aren't yourself."

Tal couldn't believe she'd considered this fool a friend for so many years and then let him court her. "Oh, I'm sorry. I didn't realize your ego was so fragile that it shattered the moment any of those overstuffed pigeons realized you had relations with anyone less than nobility." She stood to go, wincing against the searing pain in her legs.

"Are you not remorseful over your behavior? You ate your meal like a dog that had been starved for days."

She stopped and turned. "Is that not what I am? When has anyone from the docks ever even *seen* exotic meats or a room with enough food to feed an entire village, let alone been invited to *eat* it? And the looks they give you if you actually do eat it!" She gasped dramatically and put her hand on her chest. "Heavens forgive me for accepting such a gift and enjoying it!"

She turned, but he grabbed her arm, right where the mage cut her open. She grunted and flinched in his grasp. Daire froze and gaped at her, noticing the tenseness in her body, the way her back hunched.

He pulled his hand away, and his eyes grew wide when he saw the fresh bloodstain from the wound he had just reopened.

"Who did this to you?" His voice deepened with rage, his eyes narrowing, and his jaw set. He tightened his hand over the hilt of his sword as if he would fight her attacker right then and there.

"A dead man," Tal said flatly.

"Does he have any accomplices?"

"Forget about it, Daire."

"I cannot stand by and pretend someone hasn't assaulted you. It's just as much an attack on me."

Tal guffawed at his audacity. "And how, Captain, do you gather that?"

"If you are to be my wife, I will not hesitate—"

"This again?" Tal's lips pulled up in disgust.

Daire paused, confused. He sputtered a moment, his mouth hanging open, then said, "I will not stand by while my future wife..." He let his voice trail off.

Tal eyed the water at her feet. If she had her strength, she would have thrown the imbecile into the river. "Is that why you wanted me at the ball? To show off your future bride? Unless you want me sharing how freely you throw your lot in with the riffraff, you'll forget about this laughable idea." She stepped closer. "Let me be perfectly clear: you do not, nor will you ever, have any claim over me no matter how many times you stuck your cock inside me." Daire winced, but she continued, "I will not marry you, nor will I marry anyone. I am not a piece of property to own or purchase, and I certainly will not be told what to do for the sake of your reputation. Go find some dimwitted little bird who is happy to sit quietly by your side and starve as you parade her around like a pony you won at a contest. Bring this up again, and I will do more than just ruin your dress uniform. Do you understand? Maybe, instead of worrying about me, you should be eliminating the mages."

The shock on his face quickly faded to hurt. His lips set in a grim line. "Who told you about the mages?"

Tal shook her head. Of course he would question her about what she knew. She didn't bother arguing. She probably should have felt badly for what she said, but she was tired, in pain, and the man needed to take a damn hint. Either he was too stubborn for his own good, or so thick-headed that he actually thought she would give in at some point. "Stop trying to be so *honorable* and find someone who deserves you." She didn't let him respond as she limped away.

Tal dreaded comforting the broken-hearted woman in front of her. She was not in the right mind to console anyone. She explained where the young woman's husband went every night, who he spent the night with, and gave her the bottle of elixir Septimus had promised would cause the man to become violently ill any time he became aroused. She expected the wife to break down crying, but aside from wiping away a single tear, the woman set her mouth into a thin line and nodded, taking the vial with a firm, "Thank you."

Tal hesitated. "You knew," she stated.

She nodded. "Ain't no woman who doesn't know when she's lied to. Thank you for tellin' me what I needed to hear." She cocked her head. "You don't remember me, do you?"

Tal studied the young woman's features, finding recognition but unable to place it.

"My father—" She hesitated, inhaling and raising her head. "You saved my mother when he was in a rage."

Tal's eyes widened, recognition blooming. Eight years ago, a ten-year-old beseeched Tal to stop her father who had been beating his wife. The village's sheriff wouldn't do anything, claiming what a husband and wife did behind closed doors was no business of his. The girl offered to pay the bounty with money she had earned selling flowers. After a quick investigation, Tal learned the man also had a gambling problem and had been hiding from Pochette because of the large debt he owed.

Tal would have waited to ambush him on the streets, but the daughter burst into the tavern one night, panicked. The bounty hunter finished her ale in a single gulp and stormed off toward the girl's home. She could hear the wife's screams all the way down the street. Tal sneered at the quiet homes nearby. Not a single person tried to help. Kicking in the door, she clocked the man in the jaw and broke his arm but not before he broke her cheekbone. Despite his size, Tal was the better fighter, and he was severely intoxicated. She dragged him to Pochette's gambling den and deposited the man in front of Greggs, the gangster's debt collector. She left without a word, the man's pathetic pleading following her until it cut short.

She found the little girl and half-dead mother at their home, still no help in sight, and dropped a healing elixir from Septimus that she picked up on the way back to the broken family. She assured the pair they would never hear from the bastard again and collected payment from the girl. Tal paused at the door when the mother cried that they were ruined and asked how they would survive without a husband. The daughter tried to console her mother, but the woman could only reply, "What have you done?!"

Tal waited long enough to ensure the woman wouldn't turn on her daughter, then returned to the tavern.

"You stayed," Tal said to the woman in front of her. "I would have thought you and your mother would go to the mountains."

She swallowed. "My mother didn't... get better after that night. She refused to leave and chose to wallow in her own self-pity. I did all I could, but ain't nobody who can force someone to live. When she died, the house became mine and has been since. The memories my children created there are enough." She tried to hand Tal the bag of coin she pulled from her pocket.

Tal shook her head. "You have a family to feed."

"And we had a deal. I promise, we'll be just fine. Ain't nothin' I won't do for those kids."

Tal reluctantly took the payment and whispered, "Make him regret it," to which the woman winked and turned, walking down the street. She walked with her back straight and head held high. Beyond her, the weeping willow swayed in a breeze Tal couldn't feel. If it could speak, it would surely have wise words to share, words Tal had no desire to hear.

So many left the docks over the years, running from their problems. The mountains offered a new life for anyone who fled. And here, a ten-year-old girl picked up the pieces left by the parents that abandoned her and focused on the love she had for her children. She held no bitterness, no rage, just moved forward. Tal's fury lay quiet in her chest, an odd feeling.

———

Tal limped home, distracted. She and the young woman were two sides of the same coin. While Tal fought tooth and nail to keep male influence out of her life, this woman accepted it and moved on when it no longer served her. She had never thought to consider that perspective.

That night that she helped the little girl, she bumped into Daire on the street. After seeing the swollen, broken skin and Tal's black eye, Daire fumed, asking who had hurt her, and Tal relayed the story. She had actually forgotten the bastard had hit her. Besides, it could easily be fixed by a healing elixir.

"Maybe this life is too dangerous for you," Daire had said. His lips thinned, and his grip on her arm grew a bit too tight.

Tal's mood immediately sobered. "Too dangerous?" Daire had never spoken to her like this before.

"It's not right for a woman to get into fights, much less have to defend herself against criminals."

"And who should I expect to defend me?" She tore her arm out of his grip and crossed them over her chest.

"What? Well—me!"

"You?! Why would I need you to defend me?" Confusion flooded Tal. Until that night, Daire would have shared an injury of his own from his training.

"Because that's what husbands do!"

"Husbands?! Who made you my *husband*?!"

It was the first of many conversations that shed Daire in a new light. Eventually, Tal stormed off. She was angry over many things, but mostly she was angry over Daire's sudden need to be the dominant member of this—whatever it was. The next time she saw the captain, she hadn't forgiven him, but he held her face in his hands, kissed the no-longer broken cheek, quickly healed from an elixir, and took her on a horse ride in the woods. She thought that would be the end of all this husband nonsense, and it was, until something else happened to trigger a similar response from him. The arguments became more frequent, and Tal quickly lost interest in the relationship while Daire continued to exert his male dominance over her. And now, nearly every interaction between them turned into an argument, and Daire still seemed determined to take responsibility for Tal after all this time.

Every argument with Daire flooded her mind, fueling her fury, along with each frustratingly painful step. She paused by an alley and took out yet another healing elixir. She'd sipped a single jar all day to no effect. Taking the stopper out, she upended the bottle and swallowed the shimmering yellow liquid in three gulps. Warm relief washed through her. She held up her still bleeding arm, examining where Daire's bloody handprint stained her sleeve. She carefully pulled the fabric back and watched the seeping blood slow, then stop, and the skin knit itself back together. She fought the urge to scratch the wound despite the feathered sensation there. Tal breathed a sigh of relief when the opening reduced to a single, angry red line. But the feeling was short-lived when the shock of an invisible dagger sliced down her skin and opened the wound for the hundredth time.

"Dammit!" She gritted her teeth and pushed off the wall. A dark figure stepped in her path. "Daire, I swear by the gods—"

"Are you alright?" Strong hands steadied her by the shoulders, avoiding her wounds.

Tal noted the way Faron regarded her with concern and scowled. "I'm fine. If you'll excuse me." She tried to side-step him, but he held onto her.

"You're still bleeding." His voice held concern while his face showed confusion. "The healing elixir didn't work?"

Tal sighed. "Whatever spell the mage used keeps ripping open my wounds. I need to see my alchemist."

"You can't walk in this state. Take a seat." He gestured to the wall behind her.

"I'm fine, really. Once I get the right formula, I'll be fine."

"I brought you something that might work."

Tal's shoulders slumped in defeat. Her body ached, her wounds burned, and not in the comforting way her fury did. She would rest for just a moment. She sank to the ground, and Faron joined her.

Faron pulled a vial out of his pocket. A golden honey hue replaced the sunny yellow of most healing elixirs. "I noticed last night that your wound still bled after the one vial. The king's alchemist owed me a favor. She said this should work against any internal injuries caused by blood magic." He pulled a brown leather knapsack from behind his back. "She also said a full stomach will help the elixir work faster."

The aroma of roasted pheasant and fresh bread hinted at the memory of their conversation from the night before. "No ale?" She smirked.

Faron reached into the sack and pulled out a canteen. "It's water."

"I don't need you wasting your favors on me." Favors always came with a price. Her wounds throbbed as if in protest.

"I offer it freely, I assure you."

She narrowed her eyes, wondering if he read her mind. She reluctantly took the vial and drank. The golden liquid warmed her tongue and tasted like spiced honey with a hint of rose water.

"It's the least I could do after your help last night. Thanks to you, Luan and Nola are safe and on their way to live in a quiet village in the mountains."

Tal nodded. She closed her eyes with the instant, sweet relief and comforting warmth of her wounds closing properly this time. The satisfying itch worked its way through her muscles. "The king's alchemist is almost as good as mine," she sighed.

"I'll be sure to pass your thanks along." Faron chuckled.

Her body relaxed as the pain subsided. She reached into Faron's knapsack for a piece of pheasant—wrapped delicately in brown paper and still warm. She tore a piece off, and the first bite tasted even better than the food at the king's ball. Tal rested her head against the building and closed her eyes, savoring the juicy meat. After another two bites filled with rosemary, thyme, garlic, and a few other flavors she couldn't identify, she opened her eyes to find Faron watching her. He rested an elbow against his knee, propping his head with his fist. His eyes softened, and the skin by them wrinkled in boyish amusement, but Faron's full jaw and prominent cheekbones were most definitely that of a full-grown man.

"Better?" he asked.

She nodded. "Better." She eyed his attire to avoid his gaze. "You're getting your expensive pants dirty."

"Goodness me! Not my expensive pants! What ever shall I do?! Oh right, I'll just burn them and order my servants to make me new ones. I've been meaning to yell at them for something anyways."

Tal's laugh died when she thought of the pompous socialites Daire had complained about, and she knew they would have done exactly that.

"I'm kidding, you know." He leaned over, careful not to bump her shoulder with his. "I made these myself."

Tal snorted around another bite of pheasant. "You did not."

"I did indeed. I learned so I could repair my red suit. Can't have anyone asking questions. And the only way to learn was to say I wanted to make my own clothes. So here I am!" He gestured to his pants with a flourish.

"I don't believe it. No noble would debase himself by making his own clothes."

"I guess I'm not a noble then." He winked at her. "But believe it." He pointed at the hem by his ankles. "If you look closely, you'll see that the right hem is a bit lower than the left. And I forgot to put a pocket on the right side." He pulled at the fabric by his hip to show her.

Tal chuckled. "And your maidservant let you wear them?"

"Oh, she tried to burn them. But I bribed her with chocolates for two weeks. Since then, she's taught me more, and I've made a handful more items, but these are still my favorite."

They sat in silence and listened to the gulls overhead, the sailors unloading their ships, and the townspeople passing by. Her mind quieted for the first time in weeks. As she relaxed against the wall, her shoulder brushed Faron's, and she didn't move away.

Faron rested his head back against the building and closed his eyes. His chocolate brown hair hung loose by the side of his brow, cropped close enough to avoid his lashes, but long enough to be disturbed by the wind. In the back, the length tapered and tickled the collar of his brown leather coat. He smiled at the darkness behind his lids.

"I can feel you staring," he said.

Tal paused for a breath. "You're tired."

Faron nodded. "Looking this good is hard work."

She scoffed.

"It isn't easy turning down so many beautiful women, you know." The teasing returned to his tone.

"So don't."

"I'm saving myself," he responded.

"For some foreign princess with a fortune and powerful kingdom to promise herself to you?" Her breath hitched at the intensity in his gaze.

"For a mysterious brown-haired beauty to take off her mask." He didn't lean into her or make any crude remarks. He only stared as his lips turned up ever so slightly.

Heat crept up her neck and into her cheeks. "Any chance she will?"

He turned back to resting his head against the wall. "She's untrusting, but I'm hopeful she'll let me in."

The sarcasm that usually littered her tone failed her. Instead, she searched for the words to fuel his optimism. "I'm sure you'll do everything in your power to make it so."

He lifted his head again, a boyish grin pulling at his lips. "Is that an invitation?"

Tal hesitated, unsure how to respond. She searched his face for something, anything to give her a snide remark to throw back at him. She bit her lip to keep from smiling and stood abruptly. "I need to get back." She handed the canteen back to him. "Thank you for the elixir and food." She turned without a good-bye and nearly sprinted home, noting the distinct lack of pain in her limbs, and the way her fury curled into her chest like a purring kitten.

13

Tal sighed and paid the barkeep for her drinks. It was well past the appropriate time to be walking alone at night, but she was no stranger to moonlit—and sometimes drunken—patrols. She hadn't tried to rope one of her friends into joining her. Her thoughts were too jumbled, jumping from frustration over Daire to thoughts of Faron for the last two days.

She stumbled over a stone and veered to the right thanks to the several pints of ale she'd had. To an observer, Tal looked like just another drunk who had nothing better to spend her money on. They didn't know that ale often kept her fury at bay. Some nights, she could sneak away somewhere to unleash it and calm her emotions, but the resulting risk of losing days at a time to pure exhaustion often stopped her. Other times, she could fight the frustration out without giving in to the magic's call. And then some nights, like tonight, she hadn't the energy to do either and opted for the numbness that ale provided. She gladly let the townsfolk peg her as a lowly bounty hunter who spent her nights at the taverns. There was no telling which of them would sell her for a hefty reward should they learn of her magic.

Tal stumbled into a particularly dark section of town. Cobblestone ended and gave way to dirt and gravel. She knew the area well enough to traverse it in the dark. She'd even memorized the way across the rooftops. Tonight however, she chose to walk on the street. She passed by several dilapidated buildings when a figure stepped out of an alley and blocked her path. The male stood a head taller than her without a scrap of muscle on him. Tal tried to side-step the man, but he followed, blocking her further. Another stepped out of the same alley and moved behind her, while a third guarded her from the side.

"Where you headed, miss?" asked the one in front. His voice grated on her nerves. He flicked a gold coin into the air, caught it, and sent it flipping again.

Tal sighed but said nothing. She made another attempt to step around him, and he blocked her again.

"Woah! Where you off to in such a hurry? This is not a safe place for a woman to be wandering alone at night, especially one with hair as pretty as yours. Would you say there's a bit of red in it?"

She froze. Her eyes flicked from the flipping gold coin to the hand reaching for her hair.

"There're some dangerous criminals in this part of town," said a gravelly voice behind her ear.

Tal spun around to the man who tried to sneak up on her, wrapped her arm around his neck, and held a dagger to his back. He was shorter than the first, but stockier. He stiffened against the blade.

"I know," Tal whispered in his ear. Her breath wreaked of stale alcohol, and the man gagged when it reached his nose. Tal tsked, offended. She took her arm from around his throat and kicked him in the backside with enough force to send him stumbling into his buddy.

"Bitch," he swore.

"What do you say boys? This one looks good enough. You got that red stuff to fix her hair, Gully?" said the man to Tal's right.

The tall one, Gully, nodded. "I think we can have some fun first. They didn't say what condition they wanted her in. Besides, someone needs to show this one her place."

"My place?" Tal scoffed. "I think you boys mistakenly believe that *anyone* can tell me where I belong." She sheathed her dagger. She wanted the satisfaction of knocking them down with her bare hands.

The short one spat and stomped toward her. He swung his arm to backhand Tal across the cheek. She easily dodged, scraping the side of her boot down his shin. He cried out and lost his footing. She pulled his head down to meet her knee with a sickening crunch, and he grabbed his nose, howling in pain. Tal threw him to the ground. She turned for Gully's attack next.

He stalked toward Tal slowly, calculating. Once within reach, he feigned left, making Tal react and adjust her footing. He feigned to the right. Tal shifted again, but all her years of training failed in her drunken state. She stumbled. The third man caught her by the shoulders, and the two attackers snickered.

The stocky one came to stand beside his taller companion. He spat blood on the ground and sneered at Tal with hatred in his eyes. His friend beside him snickered, and despite the low lighting, she could see how rotten his teeth were. She swallowed a gag when he licked his dry lips.

Tal tried to remove herself from the third man's grasp, and he laughed in her ear. He ran the backs of his fingers down her cheek. The smell alone told her it wasn't dirt beneath his fingernails. She managed to unsheathe a knife in her sleeve and jabbed it into her captor's gut, causing him to release her. She spun around and sunk the knife into his neck, then turned to the other two.

They pounced. She spun into a fist that connected with her cheek. Before she knew it, her other cheek slammed into the ground. Darkness briefly stole her vision. In a panic, she tried to call on her fury, but none came. Pebbles dug into her cheek. She cursed the ale that poisoned her blood, nulling her connection to the fiery element.

Tal groaned and tried to push herself up but was kicked onto her back. Two figures stood over her in the dark. She braced herself when one of them kicked her in the middle. She grunted and coughed while they swore at her. Tal swore right back and reached for a dagger, but they kicked her again. She curled in on herself to protect her abdomen. One of the men grabbed her ankle and yanked until she returned to her back. He tugged at her trousers, but her belt held them in place. Her hands fumbled over her weapons.

One of the men suddenly let out a sharp cry, and the other swore, releasing her.

"Leave now, or I will not be as kind as the lady was to your friend over there," that familiar voice warned the attackers.

Tal blinked into the darkness. She couldn't make out the newcomer in the moonlight, but she recognized the voice of the man that was quickly becoming a regular presence in her life.

"You're outnumbered, mate," Gully said in that grating voice.

Tal pushed herself onto all fours.

"Wrong answer." Metal singing through the air filled the night, followed by mirroring cries of pain from the street thugs. Hurried footsteps scraped on the gravel road accompanied by retreating swears and threats. The men escaped.

"I'm beginning to think you like trouble," said the smooth voice behind her.

"They can't get away. They know about the mages," she said to the ground. Despite the spinning and pounding in her head, the flipping gold coin and talk of red hair were clear in her mind.

"I think your health is more concerning. I can track them once we look at your head."

Tal put her feet underneath her and promptly fell over. With a frustrated exhale, she said, "Were you following me, Faron?" She sat and hung her head between her knees to stop the spinning.

He laughed once. "You must have a death wish if that's your only concern."

"I didn't need your help."

"It certainly looked like it." He squatted in front of her. Tal raised her head and met his eyes. In any other person, the sympathy in Faron's gaze would have infuriated her, and yet she couldn't help how her stomach flipped at the way he watched her. "Are you alright?"

"Peachy. I'll be even better when those maggots stop breathing." She gestured in the direction the men had fled. She didn't add that she would torture them until she learned who was searching for a red-haired woman and where they got the coin.

"Well, you got one of them." He nodded to the thug she had stabbed in the neck. Blood pooled under him where he lay sprawled on the street. His body would cause little commotion in the morning, certainly not enough to elicit a manhunt for his murderer.

Faron handed her a vial of yellow healing elixir, but Tal waved it away. "It won't work." He nodded and pocketed it. Healing elixirs were powerful remedies when brewed by the right person, but they only worked when the individual taking it was of sound mind and body. Ale, among other mild toxins, as Septimus described them, interfered with the elixir for the first twenty-four hours. Tal would have to heal naturally, at least for another day.

"Is it dangerous to take too often?" he mused.

"Only to my pocket," Tal quipped and rose to her feet, swaying a bit.

Faron, who stood with her, rested a hand under her elbow briefly. All elixirs were expensive, and her stash dwindled thanks to recent events. Septimus's elixirs were the priciest in town, but also the most effective. She wouldn't dare buy elsewhere for fear the old man would poison her for not staying a loyal customer. She would receive enough grief for taking Faron's elixirs the other day.

"Is it a normal thing for you to get into trouble daily?" They began walking with Tal leading the way. She stumbled a bit, partly from the ale, and partly from the blow to her head. She noticed Faron tensing every time she staggered or swayed, a hand held up to offer stability.

"It only seems to be normal when you're around," she responded.

"Are you accusing me of putting you in danger?" he teased.

"Well, two days ago *was* your fault, but no. I'm accusing you of being bad luck."

"From my perspective, you're the one getting into these situations. You're lucky that I happen to be nearby." Faron winked. "I'd hate to think of where you would be if I hadn't been near during our recent encounters—beaten in some dark alley, held captive by the evil mages, or drowned at the bottom of the Taralin?" He faked a shiver. "Your odds do not look good," he said with a wink.

"I am perfectly capable of taking care of myself," she grumbled.

"Of that I have no doubt. Forgive me for interfering in your efforts to dispatch the criminals," he said, a hint of playfulness in his voice.

Tal nodded. "Apology accepted. I'll get them later," she added with a hint of malice in her voice.

"May I join you?"

She studied her companion. "I wouldn't think my plans to be fitting for a noble. I'd hate to corrupt you."

Faron smiled up at the sky. "Oh, it's too late for that."

After buttering her up with small talk, he convinced her to be seen by a natural healer. The pounding headache that impaired her ability to have a coherent conversation or even walk straight convinced her. She stumbled a few times, and he caught her until she regained her footing again. She didn't even know which way they were walking at that point. She didn't quite trust the man to offer the location of her tunnel hideaway yet, but she would likely get lost on her way back to the tunnels on her own. So, she found herself led by his direction to a house she hadn't visited in months.

The structure looked much like every other building in the docks—run-down, ill-kept, and possibly abandoned. Faron helped her sit against the side of the building while he went around the back. She cocked her head when he didn't knock on the front door, but she didn't bother pressing. Three agonizing minutes later, he came out the front door and picked her up off the ground before she could protest. Waiting at the entrance stood a petite, elderly woman with white hair that usually sat atop her head in a bun. Tonight, it reached well down her back in waves, catching on the long sleeves of her nightgown.

She tsked after recognizing Tal and waved toward the table with an exasperated sigh. "Still starting fights, I see," the old woman chastised.

"Hi Madge." Tal had the mind to show at least a little remorse.

"So, rather than swallowing your pride and apologizing, you'd rather poison yourself with those potions and, gods forbid, doctor your wounds yourself with your shoddy healing methods." She crossed her arms and scowled.

Tal held her head in her hands against the throbbing pain. She sat on the table with her legs hanging over the edge. Thankfully, only a lone candle on a shelf behind the healer disrupted the darkness. "The elixirs aren't poison. They heal faster than your medicines and herbs. Hells, they often use the same ingredients. There's just a bit of magic in them. Besides, you're bleeding expensive."

Madge scoffed and turned her back to Tal, muttering about magic and demons' work.

The whole time, Faron watched the two bickering women, utterly confused. "My apologies, but do you two know each other?"

Madge gestured to Faron. "Best healer in the docks, and he doesn't think we know each other? You don't pick the smart ones, do you?" She placed a basket on the table and rummaged through the items inside.

"Well now, there's no need to throw around insults!" He held his hand over his heart as if taking offense.

"Wake me up well past the witching hour, and I'll be giving all the insults I please." She stuffed a few leaves into Tal's mouth and told her to chew. The leaves tasted awful, but Tal obliged. "And *YOU*!" She wagged her finger at the bounty hunter. "I thought you were giving up the drink."

"I never said that," Tal said around the leaves that were now almost a paste.

Madge held out her hand and instructed Tal to spit. Tal smirked at the face Faron made when she obliged. Then, the old woman humbled her when she slapped the chewed-up leaves onto Tal's bruised cheek. Tal glowered at Faron who quickly covered his surprised laugh with a fake cough. Madge waved her hand at Tal's midsection. "Lift up."

"I can already tell you at least one is broken."

"Girl, next time you try to do my job, I'll make you chew the skunkwood by *accident*."

Tal opened her jacket and lifted the hem of her shirt without another word. Madge didn't have accidents.

The dim candlelight revealed the bruises blooming around her midsection, earning her a few angry tsks from the old woman and a sharp inhale from Faron. Madge set to work poking, prodding, hunting for herbs, and doing what Tal liked to call senile magic for the non-magical. "How do you know Madge?" she asked the noble.

He had stood back since depositing Tal on the table, quietly observing the exchange between the two women. "Pure luck. She happened to find me in distress, and I was happy to pay for her services."

"Luck had nothing to do with it. You were looking like a fool trying to set that dislocated shoulder by yourself," Madge grumbled without taking her eyes off her work.

Tal offered a triumphant smile. "So, I'm not the only one getting into fights around here."

"No. You are," Madge replied quickly.

Faron ducked his head. "I slipped off a roof." Tal's laugh made her wince, but it was worth the look on her companion's face. "I have since purchased a better pair of boots. Good for roof hopping." A pause in the conversation had him making very obvious attempts to avoid seeing Tal's indecently exposed ribcage while she winced, and the old woman worked. "So... how many nights in a row is this for you? Is that a you thing, or a 'docks' thing?"

Tal exchanged a knowing look with Madge before she responded. "Well, both? I guess trouble tends to find me."

Madge narrowed her eyes.

"Okay, so I get myself into those situations," Tal clarified. "But it's also somewhat normal for life here."

"Isn't there a sheriff around here?" Faron shook his head.

"He couldn't stop it even if he wanted to, which he doesn't. The docks are run by the gangs. Or rather, they were. It's all up in the air now that Pochette's gone."

He pursed his lips. "How long has it been like this?"

"As long as I can remember."

Madge chimed in this time, "Life at the docks was rough but fairly safe until the old king died. After that, we were forgotten, and a bunch of shady traders settled here knowing no one would stop them from taking advantage."

Faron narrowed his eyes, but didn't say anything. Instead, he asked, "And the orphans? The beggars? The sick?" He referred to the sad state of nearly everyone unfortunate enough to call the docks home. Illness spread like wildfire, and only those with extra coin could afford help whether from a natural healer, a magical healer, or an alchemist. And with illness running rampant, what children survived were often left orphaned on the streets once the debtors came to collect their due. Good food was scarce, and cleanliness a luxury no one could afford. No one ventured into their part of the kingdom for fear of catching something. And for that reason, Tal had trouble trusting Faron's intentions, even though her friends were less wary.

"Once the money stopped coming in, and Pochette took what was left, the streets were flooded with them. There ain't enough gold in the kingdom or decent people to care for everyone." Madge narrowed her eyes when Tal frowned. "Don't go down that road again, girl. I told you taking on Pochette meant nothing but trouble."

"Tell that to Carrick. He's the one pushing for us to do more. Besides, we have no resources now that his businesses are gone. One issue at a time," she muttered the last part under her breath.

Madge finished treating Tal while Faron stood brooding in the corner. Tal wondered what part of their conversation upset him. This was neither his home nor his responsibility. The docks were an unfixable problem, a lost cause. Anyone who couldn't see that had to be blind.

Despite Tal's protests, Faron paid Madge for her services. The old woman gave Tal some extra herbs, told her to rest until the broken rib healed, then sent her on her way. She had a headache, her midsection ached, and she just wanted to lay down in her own bed.

Faron walked Tal back to a tunnel entrance close enough that she could make it home without incident. "You're sure I can't walk you home?" he asked.

She held a hand across her middle to support her tender ribs. "I'll be fine. The walk is short from here." She gestured off into the distance.

"Then you must promise to rest." He stood with his hands behind his back, kicking his feet like a nervous child.

"I can't." Her mood darkened. "I have to find those men."

Faron held up a finger. "Madge gave strict instructions. I'm sure one of your friends can handle the search until you're well enough."

He wasn't wrong. She already planned to send Egan out in the morning. And Rainier's network must know something about gangs being approached by a mage searching for a redhead. "True, but your concern won't stop me from silencing them myself," she warned.

"Only long enough for you to heal properly, I swear." When Tal didn't object, he asked again, "So, you'll rest then?"

Tal nodded. "Until I can take an elixir—*my* elixir."

"Excellent!" He clapped his hands together, making Tal jump and wince. "Sorry! Sorry!" Faron reached out, but she waved him off. "I'll return tomorrow evening to ensure you've rested."

"Don't trust me?" She chuckled.

"Of course not! You seem to think I'll always come to your aid. If I find you in one more compromising position, I'll have to give up resisting and marry you already."

"Please, not this again." Before he could say anything further, she changed the subject. "Meet me at the longest pier at sunset. And don't for one second think I need you looking after me."

"Wouldn't dream of it, my lady," he said with a bow.

Before he stood, Tal slipped none-too-gracefully into the open sewage drain, cursing her bruised and broken body when she hit the tunnel floor.

14

The hollow *clunk* of Faron's boots on the wooden pier forced a smirk that tugged at Tal's lips. Her cheek throbbed, a constant reminder of the blow to her head the night before. Carrick was none-too-happy that morning while Sybil complimented her blue and purple trophy. Once she'd slept off the attitude and alcohol, Tal admitted her actions were foolish. She owed the noble a great deal of thanks for coming to her aid.

She bit her lip, her own pride keeping her from saying the words she'd rehearsed all day. "I almost hoped I'd finally scared you off last night."

Faron's footsteps vibrated through the planks. "You're happy to see me, just admit it."

Golden sunlight glistened along the water's surface below her dangling feet. Tal inhaled the rank odor of garbage and seawater. She preferred it over the stuffy tunnels she had confined herself to for most of the day. Her ribs screamed with each shallow breath, forcing her to sit with a straight back. Egan's natural healing salve provided minimal relief. He had given her the jar without a word when she instructed him to search for her attackers that morning.

Rainier, on the other hand, had suggested she stay in the tunnels until her injuries healed. "They'll be looking for a woman with a black eye," he had said, gnawing at his top lip.

Tal sighed and turned when Faron's footsteps reached her.

He grimaced when he saw her face. "That's bruising nicely," he said as he sat beside her.

Tal nodded, steeling herself. "Thank you for helping me last night," she blurted.

Faron waved his hand. His flowy white shirt lay opened to reveal his muscled chest underneath. He caught her looking and winked, causing Tal to blush. "Feeling any better?"

Tal nodded, though her throbbing injuries said otherwise.

Faron reached into the satchel on his belt and pulled out a vial of light-yellow liquid.

"I told you I have my own," she shook her head.

"It's the one from last night. Just take it. You're going to need to be in perfect health for what I have planned."

Tal shot him a scathing look, but he just held the vial out, keeping his expression neutral. She pocketed the elixir, a shock running down her hand when her fingertips brushed his. "So, what do you have planned? Don't tell me I've already corrupted you into hunting down those scum."

"I already know where we can find them. Ed is trailing them with Egan for now, but no. I have something less... vengeful planned tonight."

Tal blinked at him. When had he found the men from last night? And why? Her eyes met his and froze. The last rays of the setting sun reflected in the depths of his irises. Green and gold wove among each other like the leaves of her willow tree. *Beautiful*. She hadn't noticed that particular hue in them before. "Care to share?" She cleared her throat. "Or are you going to continue to be cryptic?"

"Are you well rested?" His lips quirked in a half smile.

"Yeeessss."

"Good. Because we can't leave until sunrise." He braced his hands on the dock and tilted his head back, watching the sky turn dark.

"I don't understand."

His tone dripped with mischief when he replied, "That's okay."

Tal waited for more information but received none. After a few breaths, she carefully mirrored his posture and gazed at the first night stars. They sat in silence for several minutes until her broken ribs screamed for reprieve. She collapsed onto the pier, breathing against the pain.

Faron must have noticed the hitch in her breath, but he didn't acknowledge it. After a few minutes, he lay down beside her and rested his hands under his head.

"Why are you here?" Tal couldn't stop the intrusive question.

"I told you. I have made plans. I think you'll enjoy them, though I could be wrong." He shrugged.

"I don't mean tonight specifically. Why do you keep coming back?" she pressed.

"Hmm. Fair question," he mused. "I suppose your perception of nobility is that we only live to gossip and take advantage of those less fortunate."

"I didn't say that."

"No, but you've thought it, and you're not wrong." He turned his head toward her and smirked. "Mostly." When he continued, his expression faltered. "There are members of the king's court who would avoid you, some who would gossip and shun you, and then there are those who would see a lady like you and make a game out of breaking you."

"No one could break me."

"Therein lies the challenge. And they would certainly enjoy the game."

"Would you?" Tal did her best to turn to him without causing pain to her midsection.

"As much as I tease and as little as you might think of me, no. I don't bother with that lot. Their idea of fun is breaking hearts, ruining reputations, and torturing small creatures. I'm disgusted that we are considered the same class."

"Are there any decent nobles in the king's court?"

"Besides me?" The skin by his eyes wrinkled. "There's enough. You just need to be able to read people." He turned his head back to the sky.

"Alright, so if your intentions are *not* less than savory, why are you here?" she repeated.

He paused, watching the stars. "You know, you're unlike any of the women at court."

Tal scoffed. "Gee, I hadn't noticed."

"You're not really like anyone," he said quietly.

"Now you're just trying to insult me."

"You don't follow rules. You make your own."

"Disgraceful." Tal did her best impression of the pompous air of the nobles at the king's masquerade.

Faron huffed. "You don't fear... anything really."

"Corsets." Tal shivered.

A singular laugh escaped Faron's lips. "I fear those too." He met her eyes again and winked.

Tal groaned. "Enough with the double entendre."

Faron chuckled quietly. After a moment, he said, "You throw yourself into situations without hesitation. You live for the moment." He paused again before saying, "Do you have any plan for the future, any hopes or dreams?"

Tal didn't hesitate. "Survive," she responded.

"No husband? No children? No cottage with a garden and servants?"

"No. No husband, no children, just make it through this day, then the next."

"It must be so freeing; to live without expectation. My entire life has been planned out for me, even before I was born. Even now, my day is planned down to what I'll eat."

"Is that why you come here? For freedom..." When he didn't immediately answer, she added, "in your red suit."

"It's maroon actually," he teased, "but yes. At first, I would sneak out as a rebellion against those who tried to control my every step. When I realized the condition of the kingdom outside the—outside high society, I saw the lack of aid. So, I chose to help in a way I could."

Tal bit her tongue on a joke about how *noble* of a choice that was. "With your money?" She didn't try to disguise the disdain from her voice.

His dark chuckle echoed over the water. "I've tried paying people to help, but it somehow finds its way into the wrong hands no matter what I do. And there's not nearly enough to make a difference. I bring what food I can without raising suspicion. I try to keep the criminals away from the innocents. But I have to be careful not to draw too much attention. Those corrupted nobles I told you about? They'd be all too happy to strip me of my title, my influence, and my money if they found out I helped the common folk. And then I'd be no help to anyone."

Tal hadn't considered that. While Faron's life wasn't nearly as difficult as hers, it certainly came with a different set of problems. "So, what are you going to do?"

He rested a hand under his head, scratching his hair. "I haven't figured that out yet. Some things I've done seem to make a difference. I arranged safe passage and a new home for a family trying to escape to the mountains. I've heard the children's health has improved in the clearer air."

"That's just one family. Is it worth the trouble?"

"If I had done nothing, Madge said they wouldn't have survived the next bout of illness."

She searched the darkening sky for what to say. One family. One life. Thinking of the effort it would take to save the whole of the docks exhausted Tal. But she had already started to do just that. Evania and Janin were off the streets and cared for because of one single decision. Would it still feel pointless to save more in need?

Faron continued, "I've made sure Madge has access to the supplies she needs. She hasn't charged a fee in over a year."

"What?" Tal pushed herself up and winced. "She's been charging me near double!"

Faron lifted a finger in thought. "Now that I think of it, her table appeared to be new."

"Yes, because I replaced it."

"Oh?"

"I may have bled all over it and broken a chair." Replaced furniture or not, Tal still hadn't apologized to the old woman for the words she said while in a rage. "I'll steal it back from the old bat if she tries to charge me again."

"You wouldn't. You've got a big heart. You must have saved countless lives at this point."

Tal hesitated. She never went searching for someone to help. She fulfilled bounties and took payment. She survived. But then she thought of the few times she refused payment, or purchased food, and clothing to return to them. The young woman from yesterday came to mind. Tal found herself telling Faron of the husband who beat his wife. His reaction caught her off-guard.

"I hope you gave it back to him ten-fold."

Tal stared at her companion. His voice held no mockery, nor any disapproval. His reaction was so much unlike Daire's that Tal didn't know what to say.

Faron caught her gaze and sat up. "Well, did you?"

She blinked once, twice, and then told him about the man's debts and how she helped Pochette's men collect on them.

He nodded. "And the girl? Her mother?"

"The mother—the mother never recovered. But the girl inherited their home and is raising her family."

Faron didn't question further, which made Talwyn curious.

"He got a good hit on me before I could subdue him. Broke my cheekbone." She tapped the spot on her face, the same spot that swelled in blotchy purple and blue hues.

"And I bet you sported a colorful black eye because you were already two pints in by then." He nudged her shoulder with his own.

"Three actually." She shook her head at the memory. "I was so angry at the world after that, I refused any healing elixir, made a point to let everyone see it so they knew I was the one who stepped in, not them."

"Please tell me how they threw a tantrum at being shown up by a woman." Laughter filled his voice, and Tal couldn't help but join in.

"The sheriff tried to arrest me for breach of the peace, but his men were too afraid to try."

"Truly?"

She nodded, biting her lip. She didn't need to mention that the official had beseeched Daire and his men to step in, but the captain threatened to have him removed from his position. Her friendship with Daire wasn't common knowledge, but he had criticized the sheriff for failing to do his job and wasting the time of the king's guard. "He still has an active bounty out for me, but I'm the only bounty hunter in town."

Faron was in stitches. "Oh, please don't say that. I'll cancel our plans and have us go torment the bleeding sod instead."

"One of my favorite pastimes," she sighed.

They laughed until the sound blended with the water lapping against the pier.

It was refreshing sharing stories with someone who didn't immediately worry over her or remove her independence, and curious even, that she'd found this trait in a noble. She wondered what stars had aligned that caused her to cross paths with someone like Faron, because no one—not protective Carrick, or calculating Rainier, nor even quiet Egan—whole-heartedly believed her capable of handling things on her own. No matter the circumstance, there would always be some shred of doubt or worry that caused them to question her actions.

But with Faron, he had shown at every turn that he trusted her judgement, no matter how reckless it was. It made her want to know him more; to take him on adventures so he could encourage her forward instead of trying to hold her back. Tal wondered what the noble had in store for them. She wasn't ready to part just yet.

She lay on the pier once more, and the gentle timbre of his voice lulled her into an easy slumber where she dreamed of stolen gold, wine, and a pair of horses fleeing into the night.

"The sun's almost up." His voice soothed like waves washing gently on the shore at first sunlight.

Her eyes shot open. When had she fallen asleep? Why hadn't he woken her up? Her hands sought out her daggers as a comfort. When Faron's eyes came into focus, she forgot why she reached for them in the first place.

"Ready to go find some trouble?"

Tal pulled the healing elixir out of her pocket, a mischievous grin reaching her lips. "Tell me what these mysterious plans of yours are."

"Drink the elixir, and I'll show you."

15

Once the elixir healed her cheek and ribs, they left the pier, and Tal immediately recognized the two waiting mares. "These are palace horses."

"You know them?" Faron took the reins from a frowning guard.

Tal's eyes narrowed. "Another friend?"

"Oh, you haven't met Jens? He just *had* to come meet the bounty hunter who fought off three attackers on her own, isn't that right, Jens?"

Jens grunted and his gaze roamed over Tal, appraising. She returned his scrutiny with some of her own. She turned from the guard and greeted each horse by name, letting them nuzzle her with their snout. "How did you get two palace horses?"

"I didn't steal them if that's what you were thinking. I'm a friend of the king's," he reminded her. "I'm free to take his horses for a run if I wish." He mounted the brown mare named Hazel and waited for Tal to mount the gray, speckled mare named Pepper. Jens made a noise beside her, but both Tal and Faron ignored him.

"That's exactly what a thief would say." Tal smirked from Pepper's saddle.

"And yet you still got on the horse," he quipped back.

Tal shrugged. "I've done worse things than ride a stolen horse. But don't you have horses of your own?"

"My horse needs a rest today, and the others are at my estate."

Jens reached his hand out. "M—My lord—" Faron must not have heard, because he kicked the horse into a canter, and Tal jumped to follow him. They reached the edge of town and slowed to a trot through the woods.

"Did Jens have his own horse? I didn't see one," Tal asked.

The glint in Faron's gaze left Tal chuckling. "He'll find one somewhere. He's such a spoilsport. Didn't want us going too far with the palace horses. I promised I'd bring them back before lunch."

"So, you *did* steal them!"

"It's only stealing if we don't bring them back. Let's not waste what little time we have. Hyah!" Hazel jolted into a gallop through the narrow path while Faron yelled back for Tal to keep up.

She snickered to herself and kicked Pepper into motion.

The thumping of the horse's hooves played a rhythm to match Tal's heartbeat as the trees flew past. She relished the wind in her hair. Pockets of sunshine warmed her face, and she turned her head to greet it. There was nothing quite like letting a well-bred horse open up its gait, and she leaned into the saddle without pain in her newly healed ribcage.

Tal thought of the fact that Faron had delayed their plans until sunrise so she could take the elixir. *He knew I wouldn't be able to ride without it*, she thought, heat spreading across her no-longer-bruised cheeks.

The two riders weaved in and out of the trees. They alternated between a trot and a gallop, trying to catch the other. When Faron pretended to hide behind a thin trunk, Tal laughed freely for the first time in ages.

The sun sat fully in the sky when they came upon a well-maintained one-room structure near a clearing. They unsaddled the horses by the attached shed and set them up with food and water. Faron told her to wait while he went into the house. He emerged with bows and quivers filled with arrows.

"Hungry? There's quail usually just past the tree line."

"So, your plan was to ride horses and hunt quail? Forgive me if I was expecting something a little more... precarious." She threw the quiver over her back anyway.

"I'm sure you'll manage to find some mischief."

She chuffed. "Maybe I will."

They stalked between the trees, easily finding their prey. Faron quickly drew back his bowstring and released his arrow, killing two birds at once. Tal missed one shot after another.

She grumbled to herself that a bow and arrow would do her no good in hand-to-hand combat. Faron teased her, "I don't know what kind of quail you encounter in town, but I've never seen one big enough to grapple with."

"No, but I could take down a boar and feed several families."

"That's..." He paused. When Tal didn't deny it, he added, "Impressive."

Another of Tal's arrows missed its mark, and she swung her bow around in frustration. "Damned thing."

"I don't think it's the bow's fault." He laughed.

A flicker in her chest had Tal concentrating on her breaths before she shot a flame at the noble out of spite. "What are we even doing out here anyway?"

He leaned back against the trunk of a nearby tree. "It's peaceful out here. I thought you'd appreciate the fresh air. Besides, I heard the trees can tell us our future."

Tal scoffed. "And what do they say?"

"Nothing yet." He shrugged.

"I guess you're no witch then."

"Ha! No, I guess not." Faron shook his head.

It was no secret that witches lived within the woods. Tal wondered if he knew how close his musings were to their lore.

When they'd caught enough for a meal, Faron set about preparing the birds to be roasted on the fire pit on the far side of the building. Tal picked berries nearby. When they sat to eat, Faron let her have the first bite, and he chuckled when she nearly groaned at the flavor. "I take it you don't eat fresh food often?"

Tal took another bite and spoke with her mouth full, "Only as fresh as they can get at the tavern. The fish are usually pretty fresh, but it gets boring eating the same thing all the time."

"I could tell by the way you enjoyed the buffalo at the masquerade." He popped a purple berry into his mouth.

"So, you *were* watching me then?" she teased.

"You were pretty difficult to miss." He threw the next berry at Tal. She snatched it out of the air and popped it into her mouth.

"Are you going to tell me who asked me to dance then?" She brought up the mystery noble whose identity eluded her. She tried to recall the color of the man's eyes, but that detail remained fuzzy.

"If you don't know by now, I don't think you would want to know."

Tal put down her roasted quail. "What do you mean by that?"

"Why don't you ask your noble knight?"

"I'm hoping to avoid all conversation with him regarding the masquerade."

"Oh, right. I almost forgot." He bit into a strip of quail to hide his smirk.

"Lying is not a good look for you."

He winked at her and opened his mouth to say something but hesitated.

Tal's thoughts raced as she returned to her meal. Who was the mystery man, and why had he taken an interest in her? Why would Faron keep his identity a secret? A thought occurred to her, and she scrutinized her companion. "It was *you*."

Faron barked out a laugh, throwing his head back. By his reaction, Tal couldn't tell if she was right or not. He wiped tears from his eyes. "How much champagne did you have that night that you couldn't tell if it was me?"

Embarrassment warmed her cheeks. She didn't feel the need to remind him that the second time she'd met him had been several weeks before the ball. "Well, who else could it be? And why else won't you tell me?"

"My dear huntress, I am not one for dancing. And I am not telling you who it is because I enjoy seeing you flustered." He ended on a near whisper, leaning close to her.

Tal could imagine the feel of his breath on her cheek and grabbed the food out of his hand. "I'm not flustered," she grumbled before shoving it in her mouth. He was right, though. Her mysterious dance partner had blue eyes, not the mixture of green and tan that she noted in her companion's gaze today.

He held out another piece of meat with mischief in his eyes.

She snatched the quail out of his hand and ate it none-too-gracefully, earning a light chuckle from him.

"His name is James." Faron watched her reaction.

Tal slowed her chewing. "James?"

"As in King James." He drew out the name.

Tal swallowed a large chunk of meat. "The king?"

Faron nodded.

The king? Tal repeated to herself. *Why would the king take an interest in me?* Her mind reeled. She remembered the conversation on the balcony, how she had pulled him into the gardens and lain beside him in the grass. She remembered his hands on her waist while he pulled her across the dance floor, how Daire had insisted she accept his request. Her thoughts darkened. Daire criticized her behavior, called her a barbarian, and yet *the king* had sought her out. Her emotions warred between anger, confusion, and wariness. Daire could be dealt with later, but her earlier suspicion of King James resurfaced.

"Do you wish I hadn't told you?" Faron teased. He took her inner turmoil for embarrassment.

"No. I just—Why?"

"Who wouldn't want to have your attention?"

Tal didn't reciprocate his lighthearted tone. "I'm serious, Faron. After the way I behaved, why would he take an interest in me?"

He held his jaw between his thumb and forefinger, and his eyebrow twitched. "I suppose he likes to cause a stir. You'd already turned a few heads. Dancing with the beautiful woman who ate and drank without restraint sent quite the message to the small-minded elite."

"You mean the woman who retched said food and drink all over the dance floor." She grimaced.

"His opinion of you only improved, I assure you." When Tal widened her eyes at him, Faron said, "Don't worry. I've told him you're off limits."

Tal choked on the berry in her mouth, sending Faron into fits of laughter.

When they'd finished eating, Tal cleaned up the leftovers and smothered the fire while Faron went back inside the house. He emerged with a hard leather case, the same color as his red suit, slung across his back. Faron gestured to the case and instructed Tal to open it.

"What is it?" She studied it with suspicion.

"Open it and find out," he goaded.

Tal set the leather case on her lap and fumbled with the ties. When she lifted the lid, she gasped at its contents. Inside lay two beautifully crafted battle axes. The craftsmanship was unlike any she had seen. Each blade had been expertly carved with ancient runes. The deep brown wooden handle was smooth as the surface of the Taralin at daybreak and secured to the blade with a fine leather strap braided down its length. She'd never seen a weapon so well made, and if she had to guess, the materials used were the finest in the four nations. "Where did you get these?" Tal asked without taking her eyes off the weapons.

"They're a gift from the king for the person who rescued valued members of his staff."

"You mean the king who may be responsible for their kidnapping. And who suddenly has an interest in me. You told him I helped," she accused.

"I had to tell him so he could dispatch soldiers to Silaron, but I promise you, it wasn't him. I mentioned that a skilled bounty hunter and her associates tracked down and retrieved the missing staff with minimal repercussions. He hasn't made the connection to the masquerade." Faron met her gaze. He was an excellent liar.

"And I'm supposed to believe it's a coincidence they were tortured under his palace and in his private summer home." The skepticism dripped from her words.

"He has enough to occupy his every waking minute. Two palace servants are no use to him outside of their duties. It appears someone is hatching their own schemes while his attention is elsewhere."

Tal still wasn't convinced, but her companion showed no sign of doubt in his trust of the king. "What schemes would require the torture of two palace servants?"

Faron tapped his chin with a finger. "Those remain a mystery." He narrowed his eyes at her, lost in thought.

She wondered how long he'd been listening before killing the mage in Silaron. She suspected the mages had mistaken Nola for the woman they were after with red hair and fury, but she didn't voice it. That would require Tal to reveal too much about her own identity.

"I assume he'll be looking into who is behind this then?" Tal wondered what information Faron held back. It seemed they were both keeping secrets.

"Of course."

She turned the conversation to a lighter subject. "Does he know you took his horses overnight?"

He shrugged, unperturbed. "He leaves such things to his staff. And, fortunately for us, Jens will have to come up with an excuse as to why they're gone."

"If I didn't know any better, I'd say you take advantage of the busy king more often than he knows," she teased.

"Only in matters that benefit me of course."

"And how does this benefit you?"

Faron paused, a wicked grin playing with his handsome features. "Because I get to see your face when I tell you the axes are yours."

It took everything for Tal to say, "No. I cannot accept. Carrick and Rainier helped just as much."

"And they've been equally compensated. I assure you."

She shook her head. "We never discussed a contract. This was a favor, not a deal."

"And these," he gestured to the battle axes displayed across her lap, "are merely a thank you gift from a grateful king and his friend. Just accept it, or do I need to conspire with your very large friend to sneak them into your chambers when you're not looking?"

"You stay out of my chambers," Tal retorted, to which Faron laughed. It was a carefree sound, gentle despite its volume. Tal could see herself curling up and falling asleep to such a melody. She had to blink away the distracting haze while Faron replied.

"I wouldn't dare enter your chambers without permission. I am a nobleman and a man of honor. I also prefer not to be stuck with one of your many daggers."

"Which you would be if you came in uninvited." Tal needed a different kind of distraction to clear her mind from thoughts of Faron in her *chambers*. "Alright, nobleman. Then let's go see just how fine the craftsmanship is on these extravagant gifts."

They spent the better part of the early afternoon allowing Tal to get comfortable with the weapons. Faron lounged along a fallen tree while Tal used the surrounding plant life for target practice.

"If I didn't know any better, I'd say you've used a battle axe before," the nobleman mused after the axe *thunked* into its mark yet again.

"You don't think I'm naturally good with a new weapon?" Tal aimed for a patch of dry moss the size of a mouse halfway up the trunk of a tree.

"I've seen you with a bow, so no—Hey!" Tal's throw landed a few inches from Faron's foot.

She smirked at him as she approached. Pulling the weapon out of the dead wood, she inspected it, and a thought occurred to her. "You wouldn't have brought me here to distract me from killing those men, would you?" She turned her attention to Faron.

"I wouldn't dream of stopping you from exacting revenge. As I said, I've located them and have arranged Ed and Egan to track until you are ready to pursue. And I'd thoroughly enjoy accompanying you. However," he paused, sitting up straight, "if they do know about the mages, perhaps it's best we wait and gather more information."

"In case you forgot," Tal flipped the axe in her right hand, spun on her heel, and embedded the blade in the bit of moss she had previously set her sights on, "there were two men. I only need one to give away the mage's location."

"While true, wouldn't the mage become wary, if not suspicious, if another of the thugs went missing?"

Tal sighed. "What would you have me do?" As much as she wanted the satisfaction of watching the horror in those criminals' eyes while the life faded from them, the mages were the more pressing concern. Sybil and Rainier had yet to get any further in their investigation. This was their first direct link to the threat, and she couldn't throw it away for revenge.

"We continue to watch them. Someone is bound to give up more information. Whether they meet with the mage himself, or someone in their gang does, there is something to learn here."

Tal knew this was the right decision regardless of how eager she was to see those men rotting in the gutter. Rainier had said as much the previous morning. She nodded, her anger keeping her from agreeing out loud.

"If it helps, I can gather some sticks and make life-sized figures for target practice." His attempt to lighten the conversation worked only minimally. "We'll call them Dead Gully and D—"

Tal shoved a hand over his mouth. "If I think any more about them, I'll change my mind."

Faron held his hands up in surrender, and his lips twitched on her hand.

Tal became all too aware of their proximity and the feel of his skin under her palm. She stepped away, clenching her fist. She ignored him and focused on a new target.

Faron changed the topic of conversation to Tal's training. "Rainier and his sister taught you? Are they not much older than you?"

"They're from the southern kingdom. Their father was a master warrior of sorts."

"He must have been an excellent tutor for them to then train *you* so well."

Tal rolled forward and threw her axe in one motion, hitting her mark and affirming his statement further. "We learned out of necessity; something your expensive tutors could never teach."

Faron nodded in concession, but didn't give any details of his own training. Tal knew most noble families hired experts of all skill sets for their young lords and ladies. He likely learned to fight in the privacy of his estate. The near perfect way that he moved in a duel, almost like a dance, hinted that he rehearsed each move until it became second nature.

The more they talked, the more distracted Tal found herself. Her companion still lounged on the fallen tree, and Tal's mind wandered to thoughts of his training. She thought of the way he would run his hands through his hair in frustration, how the muscles on his back would flex in the midday sun, having taken off his shirt because of the summer heat. Sweat would drip down his muscled chest. She took a steadying breath when her throw went wide. A sideways glance indicated Faron still watched her. He smirked and raised his brow suggestively as if he knew where her thoughts were. The answering flush in her cheeks made it more difficult to hide her thoughts, and she bit her lip in a futile attempt to regain focus.

When her next throw slipped out of her hands and disappeared in the surrounding trees, Tal swore. Faron laughed and teased her about taking back his earlier compliment. She responded with a rude gesture, earning her more boisterous laughter from the nobleman, and went searching for the lost axe.

She cursed herself while she stomped through the foliage. *Why did I think about him like that?* Despite Faron's suggestive smirks and flirtatious manner, it was foolish to entertain any ideas involving a noble and a commoner. Some would say she shouldn't be alone with the man to begin with, but a ruined reputation meant nothing to Tal, who had given up any expectation of finding a husband many years ago. Someone of his status wouldn't normally seek out her company, but she brushed off her curiosity when rustling leaves to her right demanded her attention.

Not a moment later, a piercing squeal broke the silence in the woods, and Tal realized too late that a large boar barreled toward her.

"Look out!"

Tal was knocked to the ground just as the beast lunged at her. She only had enough time to see Faron kneeling over her, his bow in hand, and an arrow already released. It embedded itself in the boar's rump, earning a guttural screech. The animal turned for a second attack, but before its next breath, another arrow hit home, and the boar slid to the ground a few paces from them. Tal turned her shock from the dead boar to the man above her. She'd been so distracted, she hadn't noticed either of them following her.

Faron released a deep sigh and dropped his bow. His hands fell to his sides. "Some hunter you are." His nervous smile failed to conceal the worry Tal heard in his voice.

Rather than admit he'd saved her from the boar, Tal grabbed his right wrist, locked his leg with her foot, bucked her hips and pivoted to her left. Faron was so caught off guard, he let out a small yelp when he landed on his back. With her right hand on his chest and her left still locked on his wrist, Tal smirked triumphantly at the shock on Faron's face.

Silence hung between them. Tal felt his quickening heartbeat against her palm. His eyes dipped to her lips. The distracting thoughts from before invaded her mind, and suddenly the position of her hips over his revealed his thoughts as well. Their eyes locked again. Heat filled her cheeks. She twisted off him with a jerk and stood, using the freshly killed boar as a distraction.

Faron remained silent while she inspected his kill, attempting to distract her racing thoughts. The animal must have stalked her through the trees. *She blinked at an image of Faron picking through foliage, a predatory smirk on his lips.* She knelt beside the animal's head, eyeing the angle at which the arrow impaled its chest. *She'd spent the better part of the day forcing her gaze away from Faron's own muscled chest barely concealed beneath his open shirt.* Her eyes traveled along the beast's massive body to the arrow protruding from its rump. *The night she met him, her eyes once roamed down Faron's own body, appreciating the way his leather suit clung to his muscles, until she reached*—She exhaled in frustration and stood, facing the subject of her thoughts.

His lack of comment only allowed Tal's mind and her eyes to wander further. She caught herself surveying his attire, imagining how she would remove it, and cleared her throat to stop the thoughts. She composed herself only to find that infuriating smirk returned. He knew exactly what she was thinking.

"I'll get my axe." Tal turned and walked farther into the woods, doing her best to ignore the laughter following her all the way. She found her axe another thirty paces later despite her intrusive thoughts. She returned to the little cottage to see Faron hooking

Hazel up to a cart behind the shed. He lifted the boar into the cart, his muscles straining under the weight.

"It's probably best we return." He faced away from her while fixing the reins. "Jens will be missing the horses, and I suspect the butcher would prefer we deliver our kill before the meat spoils." He turned toward her, and his eyes traveled the length of her body.

Tal knew that wasn't the reason they ended their little adventure, but she didn't push the issue. They should return before she lost all sense. Her lack of self-control seemed to be growing, probably due to the little sleep she received on the pier.

"Will you be okay to ride back?" Faron spoke in a gruff voice as if he too was tormented with inappropriate thoughts.

She nodded. "If you ride, I'll ride."

16

Faron appeared several times in the following week, often joined by Eddard or Waylon. Tonight, the three of them joined her crew for an ale at the tavern. Eddard and Egan were deep in conversation about fresh water in the mountains while Waylon failed miserably at making Sybil blush. Faron sat across from Tal, matching sip for sip until their cups were both empty. Without a word, he followed her to the bar, smirking as she turned to catch his gaze.

"Don't you have crime to fight somewhere? Or maybe some court banquet to attend?" she teased.

"I'm not dressed for any adventures tonight." Faron gestured to his handmade trousers and white shirt. Indeed, he didn't even have his rapier or smallsword with him, though she doubted he'd arrived completely unarmed. He dropped a few coins on the bar top and ordered a round of drinks for their table.

"Keep paying for our drinks, and the night might get adventurous either way." Tal immediately regretted her words. Her cheeks heated and she avoided the suggestive grin on Faron's face, allowing herself to become distracted by conversations around her.

"That's what I'm saying! Two men came in buying drinks and left this here gold coin." The bartender stopped filling their drinks in order to slap the coin on the wooden counter.

A rough-looking man squinted at it. "The king's seal?" He met the bartender's prideful expression. "Where they get a coin like that?"

All mirth escaped Tal. The king's gold made its way into taverns now. When did these two men come here? Were they the same men she encountered a few nights ago? How did they obtain the coins with the blazing willow tree?

The bartender pocketed the coin. "Who knows. Maybe the king himself was here!" He finished filling the drinks and *thunked* them down in front of Faron.

"Come on, princess," Faron called, hugging enough pints to his chest to refill the whole table's drinks. "Let's go see what mischief awaits us tonight."

If he noticed Tal's frown or the sudden change in her focus, he didn't say. While Faron laughed at something Carrick said, Tal sipped her drink and stared at a knot on the wooden table. Days had gone by since she'd found someone with a connection to the mages, and nothing had yet come of it. Her nail scratched the surface of the table. She detested inaction, but they were exhausting all their resources with zero results. Rainier's sources remained tight-lipped, and Egan found nothing unusual of Gully and his associate's recent behavior. She reached into her pocket and rubbed her thumb over the crested coin she'd gotten the night of Pochette's deal.

"She's brooding, Carrick," Faron said loud enough for Tal to hear, nudging her friend in the arm.

"You know, I think she is." Carrick flicked a bit of his ale at her.

Tal flinched. "Do not waste good ale."

"I wouldn't say it's *that* good." Faron sniffed his drink and grimaced. "But it may be your foul mood that's turned it sour."

She dropped her cup on the table loudly, spilling some of her drink.

"Who's wasting ale now, Tal?" Carrick took a mighty gulp.

Faron leaned closer to Carrick as if sharing a secret. "I think she likes to be angry." The nobleman's eyes twinkled, making Tal bite her lip to avoid smiling. "See?" he said.

"Continue talking about me, and we'll see how long that pretty hair of yours lasts, highness."

Faron gasped. "You think my hair is pretty?" He played with the strands that fell into his eyes. "Carrick, if I didn't know any better, I'd say she likes me."

Carrick's amusement rumbled over the noise of the boisterous tavern. "You poor soul."

She grabbed her drink again. "I hate both of you."

Before Tal finished her drink, Faron managed to get a laugh out of her. She soon forgot about the king's coin and the lack of action with the mages. Several hours and rounds of drinks later, Tal and Faron walked together toward one of the tunnel entrances. Several paces ahead, Carrick helped Eddard stumble over the cobblestones. Beside them, Waylon and Sybil walked arm in arm, giving a rowdy rendition of a ballad about an alchemist who never dies. Rainier and Egan followed close behind, deep in conversation.

Faron's pace was considerably slower than the rest of their party. If she didn't know any better, she would have guessed he wanted to prolong the inevitable end of the night.

"Thank you for allowing me to join you tonight," he said.

"Am I to believe that you lowered yourself to come to the docks simply to have a few pints with us?" Tal hated that she liked the idea of the noble seeking her company. It had been over a year since she told Daire not to come by anymore, an order that he often ignored. Tal quite liked the freedom of being on her own, but something about Faron excited her. Her mind swam with thoughts of him, especially after the day in the woods.

"My hope in coming tonight was to gaze upon a beautiful woman and engage her in pleasant conversation." He winked.

"Then why did you waste your time at a table with us?"

Since meeting him, Faron often said ridiculous things. She frequently rolled her eyes at his poetic musings. However, if she was being honest, she'd smiled more since meeting him than she had in the last few years. He was smooth where Tal was all rough edges. He teased while Tal insulted. He laughed and Tal grumbled. Despite her resistance to his charm, Faron kept coming back. Since she'd met him, Tal noticed her hard exterior softening, and she didn't quite mind it after all.

An easy smile pulled at Faron's lips. "Because you are a beautiful woman, and conversation with you is pleasant."

Tal did laugh this time. "You're drunk."

"I'm relaxed and happy to be alive tonight." He opened his arms, palms up. "It is a good day."

She didn't respond, only watched him stumble a few steps with his eyes closed, enjoying the silence of the night and the peace of the moment.

He stopped and opened his eyes, meeting her gaze. "Don't you agree?"

While Faron managed to ease Tal's frustrations over the course of the night, she also came to the realization that she needed action. She sighed heavily. "I'm going to ruin your good day."

Faron raised his brows in response.

"I'm going to get information out of those men. And you're going to help me."

His widened smile came as a surprise. "My day just got even better."

<hr>

Talwyn, Carrick, and Egan met up with Faron and Eddard the following night outside Gale's tavern. Instead of his typical maroon suit, Faron wore fitted brown pants and an oversized, hooded black cowl that made him appear even larger, almost sinister. Tal eyed his new attire appreciatively and received a knowing smirk in return.

"I thought you might like tonight's look. My leather suit got a tear," he explained.

Tal nodded. She willed herself not to be distracted.

Sybil had warned them she could see something unexpected but couldn't identify the finer details. She and Rainier were off searching for more clues into the mages. Carrick had insisted on coming, and Egan, while less insistent, wanted to help.

Eddard must have heard Tal asking how Faron found the men. "I grew up a few streets over. When Faron described them, I knew."

Tal's steps faltered. She noticed Carrick and Egan hesitate as well. "You grew up here?"

Eddard nodded and pointed east toward the water. "Just over there. I joined the guard when I lost my mother and sister. There was no one left for me here. I thought the guard would give me the chance to see the other kingdoms."

"I'm sorry about your family," Tal said after a pause.

He shrugged. "It was a long time ago. I've made my peace."

Eddard often hung around when Tal spent time with Daire. His blissful disposition always grated on Tal's nerves. Now, she wondered if his eternal optimism actually masked the horrors he'd faced as a child.

"Anyway, these guys always caused trouble as I grew up—always picking on women and children. I found them in the same house they've always lived in."

Tal eyed the building in front of her, a short walk from where she'd been attacked. It looked much like any other house at the docks, wedged between similar buildings on either side. They were in the belly of the residential area, where Pochette's men and the rest of the disreputable poor lived. All the buildings along both sides of the street sat in varying degrees of disarray. And, though Tal had grown accustomed to the stinking smell of garbage and stagnant water, it was especially rancid in this part of town.

They crouched on the roof across the street, debating a way in when Faron relayed the information he'd gathered. The two men were in one of the lesser gangs, though they had such low rank it wasn't worth noting. Around the docks, they went by the names Badger and Gully, with Badger being the stockier man and Gully the taller one. It was during Faron's explanation that company arrived. The sight of the cloaked figure sent a wave of unease through the group. She twisted and hissed at Faron, "Did you know anything about this?"

Faron returned her gaze, stunned.

"There's been no communication between them and the mages, I swear." Egan's tone turned apologetic.

"Dammit, we're not prepared for this." Tal's inner thoughts warred over giving up on her revenge scheme tonight or risking a battle with a mage.

"Well, we were waiting for this." Egan seemed too eager to engage their enemy.

Eddard's middle finger tapped nervously on his knee. "Are we changing the plan then? No torture?"

Carrick shifted. "I say we follow, see where the mage hides during the day, attack him, then come back tomorrow for your marks." Carrick's plan did not surprise her, but Tal had set her mind on action with minimal risk. She wasn't willing to let the two men walk away again.

"We can't engage the mages here, and I don't like the idea of going after them without Sybil's input. We could be walking into a trap." She watched the door open, and sure enough, one of her attackers, Badger, stood in the opening. Fire burned in her chest. She gritted her teeth and took a deep breath to calm the fury making its way to the surface. By the time the cloaked figure entered the building and the door shut behind them, her magic had calmed within its cage.

Faron chimed in, "Or we listen, Ed follows the newcomer when he leaves but doesn't engage, and we stay. You still get revenge. Ed can get back to us when he finds the mages."

"Two birds, one stone. I like it." Eddard's childlike smile returned.

"Works for me. I'll take the first floor." Tal couldn't wait any longer. She hopped down from the roof onto a windowsill and into the side alley.

Faron followed behind her, close enough that the skin on her neck prickled.

Together, they ran across the street, crouching below an open window to the left of the front door. She pressed her back to the side of the house and craned her neck to peer inside. Two shadows crossed in her periphery. She jerked her attention in time to see Carrick and Egan find new vantage points on adjacent rooftops. Eddard remained across the street.

Every now and then a door slammed. Someone yelled at a nearby tavern. However, Tal's focus remained on the conversation inside the house and Faron's quiet breathing beside her.

"Yeah, yeah. I've seen her. I wanna see the money." The man's voice set Tal on edge. Memories of that night flashed in her mind, and she recognized the voice of Gully, the taller one. She stared at the ground in front of her and focused her hearing. Beside her, Faron had gone still. "We heard you were payin' Amos, and now he's in the wind. I wanna know what's in it for me."

A jostled coin purse responded to Gully's demands. The scene of Pochette and the apparition in the alley came to mind. If an apparition instead of a mage stood inside, its maker would be nearby. Was he watching them right now? She realized too late that she ran into this situation without enough thought.

"What's so special about her anyway?"

"We have business to settle. Where can we find her?" The visitor's smooth voice held no inflection. It oozed over Tal's ears, and she wondered if the sound carried a spell with it.

"Hells if I know. She got away. She had a buddy with her, a red swordsman."

Tal's gaze shot to the right, and her eyes locked with Faron's. He rolled his eyes and mouthed, "It's maroon."

Tal swallowed her laughter and widened her eyes at him. Silently, she responded, "This is serious!" which earned her another eye roll.

The emotionless voice interrupted their silent conversation. "Can you describe either of them?"

"Yeah. He wore red. She wore black. Both pains in my ass." Heatedly, he added, "Cut off two of my fingers!"

With a tilt of his head, Faron shrugged his shoulders, as if to say "He deserved it."

She shook her head at him, but a grim satisfaction settled in her chest.

"Anything else?" the voice asked. The disconcerting lack of emotion confirmed an apparition stood inside. Tal scanned the street but saw no sign of a mage.

"She was piss drunk. I reckon she was coming from Gale's."

Tal swore silently. If the mage could draw any conclusions, they only had to wait at the tavern to find her. She'd have to start stocking up on ales to bring back to the tunnels.

"And you? Do you have anything to add?"

Even without seeing who the apparition addressed, she instantly recognized the short, stocky man's voice. It grated on her ears and made her want to clear her own throat. "She could fight," he ground out.

"Thank you for the information. It has been most... interesting." The metallic thud of coins falling onto the wooden table interrupted the conversation. "As promised."

Footsteps sounded, and Tal realized they were exposed. They only had a moment before the guest reached the door. She dove into Faron who, at the same time, grabbed her and launched the two of them around the corner of the house, turning as they went. He landed on top of her, and they stared at each other. Tal prayed to the gods they wouldn't be noticed even with their feet sticking out past the side of the house. The door opened and closed. She held her breath and focused on Faron's determined expression, as if he willed them to become invisible.

Finally, the crackling of footsteps on the gravel street faded. The entangled pair breathed a sigh of relief. Tal's thoughts returned to the woods when Faron didn't move. Instead, he quirked his lips.

"We really must stop meeting like this. It's not good for my reputation," he whispered.

Tal rolled her eyes. Faron's breath caressed her face, sending chills throughout her body. She felt herself blush. It should have been too dark to see the pink color of her cheeks, but his smile grew larger.

"If I didn't know any better, I'd say the fearsome bounty hunter has grown shy," he added.

"If I didn't know any better, I'd say your dagger is digging into me," she whispered back.

"Are you sure that's my dagger?"

Tal scoffed and pushed him off her. A large shadow fell by her head, and Carrick crouched beside them.

"Not to interrupt, but are we still going after the two lowlifes who live here, or are we going to let them disappear?"

Tal jumped to her feet and swore at the sight of her two targets sauntering down the street. "How did they get by us?!" she hissed.

"You looked a little distracted." Carrick's response was short, clipped. While he'd gotten used to Tal's drunken carelessness long ago, alcohol had no part in her more recent mistakes.

She glared at Faron and wanted to wipe the smirk off his face. "Don't look at me like that." She smacked his arm. "Come on. We're going after them." She stalked in the direction the criminals disappeared without waiting for her companions.

They caught up to her, each at her shoulder. She eyed the rooftops to her left and saw Egan's form leaping from building to building as he overtook the trio.

She gazed down the street and knew the men's destination. They were beef-witted louts with unexpected coin. They were likely headed to the nearest shady tavern. While they wasted their reward on a few pints, Talwyn would convince Carrick and Faron to drag the bastards to the kiln. *Forget the chair this time. I'll let them try to fight back.*

"Eddard's following the apparition." Carrick tried to get her attention. "We should wait until he's confirmed the mage's location before we take action."

She stopped in the middle of the street and rounded on Carrick. "You want me to just let them go? Do you know what they tried to do to me?" The logical part of her brain abandoned her. She told herself torturing them was a means to gain information, but her fury demanded revenge.

"I want them to suffer just as much as you, but these mages are dangerous. And they want *you*. These guys could be our way of tracking *all* of them down before they get to you."

Faron cut in, "He has a point, princess—"

"Don't start with me," Tal shot back. She pointed at the noble who held both hands in the air. "You were the one who said we would let the visit take place, and then I could take them out." She gestured down the street. "If we let them go, they could just as easily attack someone who can't defend themselves, and that would be on *me*, because *I* didn't stop them."

Eddard came jogging back, briefly interrupting the conversation. "The apparition disappeared a hundred paces down. I see no evidence of the mage."

Silence hung between them as the new information sank in.

Carrick's gentle voice cut through Tal's thoughts. "They won't be able to attack anyone because we'll be watching." He had always been her voice of reason and talked her down from the edge countless times. It infuriated her as much as it helped her.

"Jens will help with shifts," Eddard offered.

Faron leaned closer. "We won't let them get away."

Tal said nothing for three breaths while her eyes wandered the street, and she deliberated. Finally, she sighed and gritted her teeth. "Fine. But once we find out what we need, they're dead."

"Agreed," said the two men in unison. Eddard simply grinned.

"And a tail on them at all times."

"Of course," Carrick said.

At the same time, Faron replied, "Obviously."

Tal shot a pointed glare at Faron for the slight attitude. "We'll monitor. If there is *any* sign of the mage or its apparition, we consult with Sybil. If she says to attack, we don't hesitate."

17

J anin begged Tal not to leave. "Please play with us! We'll give you honey tarts!"

"Why don't you go play with the other children?" Tal suggested. The brother and sister had settled right in according to the baker's wife. She smiled at Evania, who hid behind the older woman's skirts.

Tal spoke to the baker briefly about the ongoing search for his niece. It had been nearly a year since the man's brother had beseeched Tal for help. The family had stopped asking for updates, but Tal still informed them every few weeks of her continued search efforts. The baker thanked her, his resigned tone sobering her mood. She tried to offer money to cover the children's needs for the next few weeks. The baker refused, saying they were more than compensated. Tal assumed Rainier had taken care of it and bid farewell.

It had been two days since their decision to continue watching Badger and Gully. Her mind wandered while visiting the children. Her daggers hung heavily in their sheaths, almost commanding her to bring the men to their knees. It wouldn't be easy to sit back during her watch today.

The door to the baker's shop smacked against its frame.

"I'm not answering that, Faron." Carrick's unmistakably deep growl carried over the noise of the busy street.

"I can't help you if I'm left in the dark. Is this because of Nola's rescue? Are they looking for revenge?" Faron's back faced Tal. She didn't expect his concern.

She could see the tension in his shoulders through his thin white shirt. Her stomach squeezed at the sight of him—the first time since Badger and Gully's house. She pursed her lips and fought the urge to get his attention.

Carrick's eyes flicked to her, but he didn't acknowledge her presence. His hulking form leaned against the front window. "You can help by keeping your mouth shut and finding the mages."

Faron ran a hand through his hair. "You're almost as impossible as Tal, do you know that?"

Tal scoffed. "Is that what you think of me?"

Faron spun, shock quickly morphing to delight when their eyes met. "There you are! I was just telling Carrick—"

"I heard. Are you ready?" Faron had offered to tail the two thugs alongside her. The anticipation of spending nearly a whole day with him caused her to toss and turn all night.

"Once I learn what it is you're not telling me." The corner of his mouth quirked.

Tal crossed her arms and met his unwavering stare. "We only found out they were after me the night of the fires. I don't know why yet." She could feel the heat creeping up her neck. *Dammit*, she thought. She was usually an excellent liar.

"But you know *something*," he drawled.

"And we don't have time to discuss this. We're going to be late." She brushed past the noble, a shock of electricity jolting down her arm at the contact. "I'll see you at the tunnels," she called to Carrick.

Tal sipped her ale in a shadowy corner of the run-down tavern. Badger and Gully blathered to nearby patrons while she and Faron sat in near silence all afternoon, a small relief. Faron had plagued her with questions the entire walk to the dodgy side of the docks. More than once, she stopped herself from blurting about her power. The man was nothing if not persistent.

He gained focus once they'd taken the watch from Egan and Sybil. Her mind warred over the decision to tell Faron. He'd proven to be trustworthy time and time again, but revealing her magic would be putting her life in his hands. *Does he deserve to know?* she asked herself. *Do I* want *him to know?* Her finger tapped the metal cup, and she was reminded of Eddard. She'd known the guardsman for longer, and he seemed to trust Faron. Tal bit her lip and turned her attention to the noble beside her, catching his stare.

"You're supposed to be watching them." She lifted her cup in the direction of the men sitting by the barkeep.

"You're unusually broody today."

"You pestered me the whole way here," she shot back.

"Pestered is a strong word. I like to think I... questioned? Interrogated? Asked when you were being less than forthcoming?" He drank his ale, hiding his smirk.

Tal ignored Faron and focused her attention on Badger. He was in a particularly jubilant mood. The two men had done little more than spend their coin on food and drink for the last two days. They'd become predictable and gave no indication they'd see the mage or its apparition again.

Unbridled laughter drowned out the rest of the tavern.

"Hey Gully, tell us again how you lost your finger!" someone called over the chatter.

"I heard it was a woman!" another called.

"Fuck off!" Gully threw his drink at the responding chorus of jeers. "I told you; it was some bastard with a sword! Besides, the bitch is about to regret it. They both are!"

Faron stiffened beside Tal. The tendons in his hand strained as he gripped his cup.

"Oh yeah? How do you figure that?" The barkeep's tone belied his lack of patience for the man.

"We got big friends—powerful friends. Ain't that right, Badge?" He nudged the man next to him.

"Yeah, where do you think we got the money to pay for these drinks?" Badger held up his ale.

"Next time we see her, we get to keep her for a night before handing her off." His dark chuckle set Tal's teeth on edge.

Her fury crashed against its walls. The single mug of ale she'd drank that day did little to tamp down its influence.

Beside her, Faron leaned forward on his elbows, his gaze fixed on Gully. A muscle in his jaw flexed.

Someone threw food at the goon. "Like you would know what to do with a woman!"

Tal couldn't listen to Gully's reply. She gripped the dagger sheathed to her thigh. They needed him alive to find the mage. She inhaled the stale air, which did little to quiet her turbulent fury.

A hand on her arm pulled her from the inner turmoil. "They will not touch you." Faron's voice hovered barely above a whisper, his rage simmering behind each word.

She held his gaze. The noise within quieted to a simmer. "I know."

Cheers of greetings reached her ears. Daire entered the tavern in plain clothes, a frown on his face. He ignored the heckling crowd and searched around the tavern.

Tal swore and sunk into her chair. She pulled her hood further over her face. She noticed the way Faron angled his body, concealing both himself and Tal from view.

"If he sees me, the whole tavern will know I'm here," Tal spoke into her cup. Her eyes darted between Daire, Gully, and Faron. The tavern had only one exit and nowhere to hide. Their presence could not be revealed if they hoped to continue monitoring the two men.

When Daire stepped away from the door, Faron grabbed her arm and, in unison, they rose to their feet. His hand slid to hers, and they picked their way around the outer edge of the establishment. Every step closer to the door felt like the beat of a warning drum. Five steps, and she would be out the door. Daire spoke to the barkeep, his back to them.

"Hey, Captain!" a man shouted as Tal passed. "I hear your fancy lady dumped you at the king's ball! Gully has one he can share with you!"

Tal tripped over the leg of a chair and knocked someone's drink over. A cacophony of yelling and wood scraping on stone pulled everyone's attention. Faron tugged her through the door. She lost sight of Daire around the outside wall as he turned toward the noise.

Faron pulled her around the side of the tavern and swore. "What are the chances the captain stumbles into *this* tavern?"

Tal let her head fall back against the building. "He's always around the docks. And no matter where I am, he always seems to find me."

"How unfortunate for us."

The door to the tavern burst open and slammed against the building. Tal and Faron's heads both snapped toward the sound. When the chatter from inside the tavern faded as the door closed, slow footsteps *clomped* on the cobblestones. They approached the alley where Faron and Tal hid.

Faron turned his back toward the entrance, blocking Tal from view. He towered over her. Their eyes met, the alarm on Faron's face mirroring her own. The footsteps reached the alley, and Tal froze. The stifling air surrounded them like an invisible, clove-scented cocoon. Tal hadn't noticed exotic spice on the noble until now. She found herself drawn to it.

Faron reached an arm around her waist and gently pulled her into him.

Her eyes flicked toward the movement and back to his face.

His lips parted in a silent, "Shhh." When the intensity of his stare remained, she understood. Two lovers locked in an embrace would be less conspicuous. His muscled abdomen pressed against her. Chills washed over her as his other hand came up to her neck, sliding into her hair.

She exhaled, leaning into his embrace.

"You there!" Daire called from less than ten steps away.

Faron's hand tensed against her neck. His shoulders curled around her further.

The tavern door slammed into the building again. "Hey, Captain! Come have a round!"

Faron shifted again. His fingers disturbed her hair, sending another wave of chills down her back. His eyes scanned her face as if searching there for an escape.

She bit her cheek, willing herself to remain focused.

Daire's footsteps retreated. "One drink, and I'm not paying this time."

The tavern door slammed closed, and Tal breathed a sigh of relief.

Faron's hold on her relaxed. "That was closer than I would have liked." His voice rumbled in his chest.

"I've never had so many close calls until you arrived. I'm beginning to think you're bad luck."

Faron pulled back, clutching his chest. "Now, now, beautiful. As I remember it, the danger is all brought on by *your* associations."

"Call me beautiful again, and you, too, will lose a finger." Her words sobered her.

Faron's face fell. "They're lucky I respect you. If I had any less restraint, they would not be leaving this establishment with their heads, much less their fingers," he growled, and his arms twitched around her.

"I'll let you take a pinky." She tested his reaction. Would her dark desire for revenge scare him away? How far would be too far for the noble?

His lips quirked. "You're too generous."

Tal matched his smirk and bit her lip. She hadn't expected that response.

His arms remained around her for a breath longer before dropping. He took half a step back. "With Daire around, it will be difficult to watch the two closely. We should go find Ed and Waylon. It's almost time for their shift."

A twinge of disappointment clenched Tal's stomach. Their day was coming to an end. She walked past the noble with her chin up, hoping to disguise the emotion. She could feel his gaze at her back. Once they were past the tavern and out of sight, she turned. "Are you coming, or not?"

Faron's eyes shined with words he didn't say, but he moved to her side, his arm brushing hers with each step.

They apprised Ed and Waylon of the events of the afternoon. An awkward air hung between them on the return to the tunnels. Faron had yet to bid her farewell, and Tal refused to look at him. She could feel his eyes on her. Finally, she'd had enough and turned to tell him off.

"Did you have a run-in with them before? Maybe you angered them somehow?" he blurted.

"What?"

"The mages. They've been after you since before the rescue at the mansion." His eyes widened. "And before the incinerator. They were after you then too." His voice trailed off. "You're sure you haven't done anything to warrant this hunt?" His voice held genuine concern.

Tal stopped in her tracks, causing Faron to step past her and then backtrack. Her resolve wavered. "I—no. They've been hunting me since the night Pochette's burned down, likely even before."

"So, they're not hunting you for attacking them. Then why—?"

Tal started walking again, slowly. Her companion jolted to keep pace with her. After a breath, she reluctantly explained, "They made a deal with Pochette to capture me. He and I had... a business agreement. I'd periodically check in to make sure he upheld his part. He was going to use one of the meetings to ambush me and sell me to the mages."

His utter astonishment almost made her laugh. "Okay... I'm going to assume that you did not take that lightly. I'd love to hear about your reaction, but why hunt you in the first place?"

Tal paused. That same question from before plagued her. Could she trust him? For her own safety, she had refrained from sharing her ability when they first met, but after spending so much time together, she'd grown to accept the noble as a regular in their crew of misfits.

It had been years since she'd shared her secret with anyone new, not even Daire had been awarded that privilege. She showed Carrick after only a few days out of necessity. She'd taken a few months to open up to the twins. Egan had witnessed her fury when he stumbled upon Tal in a skirmish. She immediately accepted him into their group for jumping in to help her. She'd only known Faron for a few weeks, and so much about him still remained a mystery. But something about the noble drew her to him. She steeled herself and said, "Come on."

***

The Kiln was the safest place to practice her fury. She'd occasionally used magic elsewhere in the tunnels or even on the surface, but she always ran the risk of being noticed or starting a fire. Tal ushered Faron into the small room and closed the door with a screeching metallic *thud*. His unease did not come as a surprise. Scorch marks marred the floor and ceiling, and questionable burnt remains sat in a small pile at the center of the room.

"Okay, so they're after you because you own a really great torture chamber?" He laughed nervously.

"I'm about to trust you with something that, if it got out, would put a price on my head higher than anything you've ever seen before."

"A bounty hunter with a bounty?" he attempted a joke once more.

Rather than telling him, she held her palm, face up, in front of her. His brows furrowed.

Tal called to her fury. Pulling at the energy within, she felt a low tingle in her chest. Slowly, it crawled to her shoulder and walked down her arm. She exhaled and the weight of a pebble sat in her palm. It warmed as the pressure built. Soon a light glow emitted from the center. She studied Faron's reaction. When his eyes widened at the appearance of light, she pulled more fury into her hand, and the glow rose into a single flame.

Faron's mouth opened in astonishment. The single flame grew into a ball the size of her fist. He stiffened as her fury reflected in his eyes. She let the fireball double in size until she tamped the energy feeding it. By then, Faron's jaw had hit the floor.

Tal played with the ball of fire, letting it roll to her fingertips, and to the back of her hand, before returning it to her palm. She often performed the trick to combat boredom. If she really concentrated, she could toss the flame in the air and catch it like a ball.

"Bleeding hells, Tal! You have fury!"

"I've noticed," she said darkly.

"You have *FIRE* fury!"

"Yes, I know."

He ran his hands through his hair, turned around, took two steps, then turned back. He fidgeted, running a hand over his face. "They're after you because you have fire fury!" he exclaimed. "Oh hells, they're after you because you have fire fury," he repeated with grim realization.

She nodded coolly. "I'm aware. By the way, you can't tell anyone, not even Ed or Waylon."

"That part's obvious. What are we going to do?"

Tal chuckled. Her prior hesitation to tell him seemed silly now. "We? Are you involved now?"

"Aren't I?"

"Are you?"

"I'd like to bet my coin on 'yes.'"

She snuffed out the flame. "I'll consider it. What do you bring to the table?"

"Good with a sword? A winning smile?" He tilted his head waiting for a response. "Battle axes?" he drawled.

"Hmm." She tapped her chin, feigning deep thought. "Those are decent arguments. There's one problem though."

"Name your price." He narrowed his eyes, pretending to be dreadfully serious.

"You are terribly distracting."

Faron straightened and couldn't help the smug expression on his face. "Am I?" He stroked an invisible beard. "That *is* a dilemma. But I don't think you have much choice. Now that I know," he took two steps toward her, "you'll need to keep me close to make sure I don't do anything..." he took two more steps until the tips of his boots knocked her own, "compromising," he finished.

Tal had to crane her neck to look into his eyes. Her mouth suddenly felt dry. She bit her bottom lip, and his pupils expanded. That infuriating smile suggested he could read her mind.

He slid his thumb along her jaw, sending goosebumps down her arms. He leaned down and paused before their lips touched, eyes locked on each other. "The question is," he breathed, "can you focus enough to stay out of trouble?"

He stepped back unexpectedly, the space between them cold. *What a tease.*

Irritation flared, and she swallowed the flame that threatened its way to the surface. Her cheeks prickled.

Faron's smile faltered. He blinked three times and opened his mouth to say something when someone pounded on the steel door.

"Tal, you in there?" The metal door muffled Carrick's voice.

Tal blinked a few times to clear her head. She watched Faron as she walked to the entrance. His brow pulled down in confusion, and he seemed distracted by something. She wrenched the door open.

Carrick filled most of the doorway and briefly flicked his eyes from Tal to Faron and back again. "Rain has new information."

She crossed her arms. "About?"

His gaze caught Faron again before answering. "About what Sybil saw," he answered vaguely.

Tal remembered Sybil's vision involving the Pyrie. They hadn't gained any information about the legend in weeks. "Is everyone back?"

Carrick nodded but didn't say anything.

"Then let's go." She started pushing the enormous man out of the way. After two steps, she turned her attention over her shoulder and jerked her head in the direction of their tunnels. "Come on, you too. You might as well hear this." Carrick protested, but she silenced him by saying, "He knows, Carrick."

His eyes grew wide. He again flicked his gaze between his friend and the noble. "Tal—" he began, a hint of warning in his voice.

"Oh, get over it, Duckie. It's amazing he hasn't figured it out already."

The use of his nickname made Carrick snap his mouth shut. Tal walked past, followed by Faron who watched Carrick, barely restraining a laugh.

"Duckie, huh?"

"Don't make me dislike you, swordsman."

"Wouldn't dream of it," he singsonged, skipping after Tal with his hands clasped behind his back.

Carrick half-groaned, half-growled and followed after them.

18

Faron sauntered into the common area, welcomed with shocked silence. Sybil's head jerked in his direction, and Rainier jumped to his feet, eyes darting between Faron and his sister. Egan dropped the wooden branch he'd been carving. It clattered on the tunnel floor with a hollow *clack, clack, clack*.

Tal stalked past him and introduced everyone to Faron as if they hadn't met before. "Everyone, this is Faron. Faron, this is everyone." Then she held her palm out in front of her and instantly called a ball of flame much like she had in the Kiln. There was no point delaying the ensuing drama.

Egan's jaw dropped as his eyes darted between Tal's flame and Faron's unsurprised face. Rainier backed into the tunnel wall and yelled her name. Sybil slapped her palm to her forehead. Carrick narrowed his eyes at her from the archway.

"Everyone, Faron knows I have fire fury. Now, can we get to Rain's new information?"

No one spoke. Eyes darted around the room. Finally, Sybil sighed and muttered something that sounded like "might as well," and said rather loudly, "If you must know, I'm a seer." This earned her a wide-eyed stare from Faron.

"Syb!" Rainier's shock matched Faron's. His fingers scratched his nail beds nervously.

"Well, if the fire fury doesn't send him running for the highest bidder, I don't think a seer is going to entice him to betray us," Sybil reasoned. She had a point.

His hands stilled. "Unbelievable," he sighed under his breath. "Fine." He turned his attention to Faron and admitted, "I can coerce."

Faron's jaw could not fall any lower than it already had. He turned to Egan and asked, "And you?"

"Uh, I don't even know. I'm a bit... *wild*... in a fight." He shrugged.

"Uh huh." Faron turned to Carrick who still stood in the entrance. "And you? Are you going to tell me you're half bear?"

Sybil snorted, but Carrick shook his head. "I'm just plain old me." He cracked his knuckles.

Faron's eyes circled the room before settling on Tal. "You've certainly gathered quite the talented crew here."

Tal shrugged, never being one for fanfare. "Can we get to the important part now?" she asked Rainier.

Rain gave Faron the briefest of explanations. "The night after the rescue at the incinerator, Sybil had a vision of Tal standing opposite the Pyrie amid a group of nobles. She couldn't see any identifying features nor understand their purpose."

"It was bleeding vague, is what it was," Sybil complained. He and Sybil had been checking sources for anything on mages, the Pyrie legend, and any connection to the noble families. With the information gained from the books she stole on the night of the masquerade, Sybil had been unsuccessfully attempting to force a vision about the Pyrie. Her struggle wasn't uncommon, especially given that the details were obscure.

"The Pyrie? You mean the children's story?" So, Faron had heard of her.

"Legend. She was real, but a really long time ago," Rain clarified.

"How can the vision be possible? She's dead, right?"

Sybil chimed in, "Visions don't always have to be literal. Sure, I could see events happen before they unfold, but they can also be symbolic. I'm guessing this one is something symbolic involving the three of them."

"Well, what do they have in common?" Faron asked questions they'd already investigated at length.

"Blazing pigs, can we get to the new information please?" Tal grumbled.

"Hold on, Tal." Rain held up a hand to stall and received a nasty glare. "Now that Faron knows, I think we can look at this from his angle," he spoke animatedly. "So, obviously, both Tal and the Pyrie have fire fury, which is extremely rare. With the nobles surrounding them in Syb's vision, I'm inclined to think that has something to do with their powers being exploited, especially now that we know the mages are after her." He turned to Faron. "Do you know about anything that would connect nobles with fury—especially fire fury?"

Faron paused, his expression darkening. "Ever heard of the Fury Rings?"

No one answered.

He clenched his jaw and inhaled. "One of the reasons fury is rare is that those in power have always exploited it. It's a wonder you haven't been warned about them." The attention he turned on Tal sent a flurry of butterflies through her middle.

"My earliest memories are of the man who housed me here. He made it very clear that to reveal my fury would ultimately bring my death. He never said why, and I never asked."

"Frankly, I'm surprised we haven't heard of Fury Rings before." Rain would have been the first to know about them. The fact that he didn't learn until now must have been frustrating.

"Only those with an invitation can participate, and only those with something to offer the most powerful people in all the kingdoms get one."

Tal wondered if Faron would be counted as one of those powerful people.

"Rain, the invitation the other noblemen mentioned at the king's masquerade..." Egan remembered their conversation the day after Tal's performance at the palace. Rain nodded.

"What invitation?" Faron's attention whipped between the youngest of the group and Rainier.

"I attended the masquerade under the guise of a foreign dignitary and spent what I could of the evening among some of the noblemen. There was a brief mention of an awaited invitation, but nothing specific. One of the men shut down the conversation quickly."

Faron frowned. "Do you know who spoke of this? Could you point them out if you saw them?"

"Briggins brought up the invitation to Lighton, and Mordency told them to save the topic for another setting."

Faron's expression darkened further at the mention of the three names.

Tal didn't recognize any of them. She wouldn't get involved in matters of the king's court, but she wondered what Faron would do about it. "Do you think they were talking about this special Fury Ring invitation?" she asked Faron.

He shook his head. "I can't say. I wouldn't expect any of them to know about them. It would be a serious offense if they were involved somehow. Fury Rings are forbidden in elite circles, but many still strive to get the chance to join." After a pause, he explained why. "Receiving an invite means you're given the opportunity, and expected, to attend an auction... of elementals. With the dwindling numbers of magical folk, I expect a Fury would fetch a pretty high price, not to mention two with your talents." He tilted his head toward Sybil and Rainier. A heavy silence hung among them. "These people are kidnapped, beaten, starved, sometimes raped," he gulped, "and then thrown on a stage and auctioned like livestock."

Tal's nostrils flared. All this time, people like her suffered, and she had no idea. Perhaps she could have done something about it if she'd known. Her fury flared in agreement. "And what happens after? What does it mean to be the highest bidder?" Her voice was gruff with the suppressed anger and effort it took to hold her power in.

"They become the person's master. The elementals are confined to a life of servitude, at the mercy of the buyer." He didn't mask the disgust in his voice.

All around the little common area, Tal's friends wore looks of horror, disgust, and anger. "The mages. Do they work with the Fury Rings? Are they rounding up Furies and magic folk for this slavery auction?"

The nobleman shook his head. "I don't know. Everything I know is from a book I found as a child in our family archives. It was incredibly cryptic, but didn't mention any mages."

Rain perked up at the mention of more information. "Any chance we could read it?"

"Sorry." Faron frowned. "My father caught me reading it and burned it. I searched everywhere and never found any other mention of it."

Once again, silence fell among the group as they considered the new information. Tal's mind swam with questions. Why did Faron's family have a book about the Fury Rings? If his father knew enough about the book to burn it, where did he stand on the matter of its contents?

"So, one of these noble friends of yours wants an elemental of their own." The threat in Carrick's voice would be enough to make almost anyone reconsider crossing him.

"These are no friends of mine. I don't even think anyone in the kingdom has enough in their coffers to be offered an invite."

"Maybe they've tipped the mages off about Tal, or at least a rumor of her in hopes of earning an invitation?"

Faron's lip curled. "It's plausible. But who would be dense enough to get involved? Being so powerless would mean death once they're no longer needed. These elite circles are bad news. Once you're in their sights, the only reason they keep you alive is because you're useful."

Rain laughed. "We thought the same thing."

"Which of those nobles is that stupid?" Tal half teased.

"Most of them, honestly." Faron sighed. "But I don't know any of them that have ventured far enough outside their part of society to learn about you," he said to Tal.

Rainier crossed his arms. "With Pochette's betrayal and what we know about Badger and Gully, it's likely there are others at the docks with powerful connections."

Sybil changed the direction of the conversation then. "So, my vision—maybe Tal ends up in these Fury Rings, or maybe she destroys them. That's fine." Her nonchalant tone received a series of concerned looks, grumbled warnings from her friends, and one very appalled expression from Faron. "But that doesn't explain the Pyrie. What does a long-dead Fury have to do with it?"

"Well, we've considered it's a warning for Tal to master her power before it consumes her," her brother cut in.

Tal shrugged when Faron turned his horrified gaze to her.

Rain continued, "But maybe it has something to do with what I learned tonight. Sybil got a book from the palace that mentions the legend," he said to Faron, who gave Sybil an impressed look, and the seer bowed dramatically. "But it doesn't really go into any sort of useful detail. There are a few families here whose ancestors were around during the Pyrie's power. I've been talking to them and going through old manuscripts for information on her. As far as I can tell, the disappearances of elementals didn't really happen in her time. Magical and nonmagical folk lived harmoniously. In fact, elementals were practically worshipped."

"That's interesting," Carrick said from his spot in the doorway.

"What's even more interesting, is it seems that around the time the Pyrie was killed, tensions between the two groups spread like wildfire. Magical folk started disappearing in droves. Which leads me to believe these Fury Rings didn't exist *until* then."

"Do you think she was protecting our kind then?" Tal asked.

Sybil, ever the one with a dark disposition, added, "Or maybe she's the reason they created these Rings in the first place, to protect themselves against someone like her."

"Either way, I think the vision has something to do with the Rings," Rain concluded.

"Is that all?" Tal expected something more prophetic.

"Mages also didn't exist before the Pyrie," Rain added with a hint of annoyance.

"Let me guess, they *also* appeared shortly after her death." While this information provided some enlightenment, it didn't indicate their next steps, or what dangers lay ahead.

Rain held up the other book Sybil managed to pilfer from the palace. "This book details foreign relations and conflicts. Right around the time she became too powerful, reports started coming in of villages being destroyed—entire villages in a matter of a few hours—a handful of attacks once every five years." He paused until understanding dawned on Sybil.

"And accounts of elementals going missing started right before the attacks?" she asked her brother.

He nodded. "Reports of disappearances followed by sightings of powerful beings always precluded the attacks on the villages."

"They *were* collecting for the Rings then." Carrick clenched his fist hard enough to crack his knuckles.

"Seems like it," Rain affirmed. "The good news is that every single attack seems to indicate three mages, no more, no less."

Faron frowned and narrowed his eyes. "That's oddly specific. I wouldn't trust that bit of information. Especially with it being so long ago."

"I would have thought so too, but there's hundreds of accounts in this book, the most recent being fifteen years ago."

"What?!" Sybil's attention snapped to her brother. "Was it—"

Rainier nodded, eliciting a swear from his sister.

Inaction had made Tal restless. "Well, if that's the case, then we only have one left to worry about. Maybe we *should* go after this mage and eliminate him."

"You can't be serious." Faron stared, dumbfounded.

"I am absolutely serious. You and I have each killed one already. What's one more?"

Carrick pushed off the wall. "What happened to keeping our heads down? Didn't you say they're too powerful for the five—six," he added with a glance at Faron, "of us to handle on our own?"

It was no surprise that Rain didn't agree with Tal's sudden change of heart either. "We need to find out more. So, we have the history. That doesn't teach us how to win against them. We don't know the full extent of their power, or did you forget that you were nearly killed by a single spell from just one mage?" They repeated the argument from the night after Pochette's failed betrayal all over again, except this time, Tal was the only one in favor of going after their enemy.

"And yet, we've eliminated two of them with daggers, no less. Even his royal highness over here can handle that." Tal gestured to Faron who looked around at the group like he didn't want to be brought into the conversation.

"We can continue following Badger and Gully. The mage is bound to appear at some point," Egan piped up for the first time.

No one seemed to hear the teen. Carrick threw his arms up in frustration. "Tal, you said it yourself. We can't do this alone. The twins' entire village wasn't enough to hold them back."

Faron's head jerked. "Their *entire* village?" His attention shot to Sybil, who cleaned dirt from her boot with a knife, and Rain. "Where are you from?"

Tal sighed and sat in the corner while the twins recounted the timeline of attacks from the mages. To his credit, Faron was horrified at the extent of the devastation and lack of news in the king's circles. When they compared the events in the docks, he concluded it was happening all over again in Meladair. "Tal, you're right, we have to stop the remaining mage. But we can't go in blind, and we can't do it alone."

Rainier must have been hoping for this ever since Faron walked into the common room. "Do you think you can get support from the king? You said he's a friend, right?"

Faron nodded. "I'll try to get an audience with him." His eyebrow twitched. "Though, you're aware he doesn't have much to offer even if he agrees? If the villages in the southern kingdom were no match, I'm not sure how much resistance we can provide. Then again, we do have a Fury." He smiled at Tal. Unfortunately for him, Tal only scowled back.

"Are you forgetting Sybil's revelation in the palace? The torture chamber underneath? The summer home infested with mages? How can we trust the king after everything we know?"

"What revelation?" Faron eyed the seer.

"Well, we probably should have mentioned it first." She peered sideways at her brother. "But my vision definitely has something to do with one of the rooms in the palace—off the Great Hall, big rectangular table, window on the north side that takes up most of the wall."

Tal noticed Faron tense when Sybil described the room. "Do you know it?"

"No," he shook his head slowly, scrunching his brow. "You think this vision has to do with the palace then?"

"I think it has to do with that room. We need to find out what it's used for."

Faron hesitated. "I can speak to James, but most of the rooms off the Great Hall are used for whatever they need to be." He rubbed his brow in frustration. "I can't say we'll learn anything significant."

"No." Tal stood. She grew tired of conversations that went in circles. "We haven't confirmed we can trust the king. Whatever you do, don't let him know about any of this." She gestured around the tunnel.

"I know I've said it before, but you can trust him. I'd bet my life on it."

Silence hung heavily in the room while everyone waited for Tal to respond.

"The evidence is pretty incriminating."

"Maybe it's meant to be," Rainier muttered under his breath.

Tal scoffed. "If you don't need my input, I'd like to sleep before the gulls start shrieking."

Faron jumped at the opportunity to follow Tal. "I'll see what I can find out. I should get going before my servants notice I'm gone."

Egan scoffed and mumbled something that sounded like "privileged."

Tal didn't say goodnight to the others or see if Faron followed her. She left the common area and trudged to her room. When Faron caught up to her, he tried to strike up a conversation, but she was too tired to engage.

"So, this is where you live?"

"Yup." She yawned.

"It's pretty impressive." Somehow, he sounded sincere.

"Not as impressive as your mansion I bet."

"If that's what you would call it. I didn't realize you lived like this. I have hundreds of extra rooms and several houses. You could all stay there. It would be safer."

Tal laughed. "And you don't think there's anyone rich enough in the kingdom to be a contender for power?"

"Most definitely not."

"It's a generous offer, but I can't accept. The others might, but we have responsibilities here. We can't travel long distances every day to meet them."

He nodded. "Understood. Have you ever thought about living elsewhere?"

"No. Have you seen the rest of the houses in this part of the kingdom? We're better off down here. No one bothers us."

"You really have made a home for yourselves." He observed the hanging blankets and curtains separating their bedrooms from the main tunnel.

Tal stopped in front of her own and turned her back to the entrance. "Thank you for your help with this. I have nothing to offer you, so if you decide you don't want to get involved, I understand."

"Even if you offered something, I wouldn't accept. You need help. I'll do what I can."

"Why?"

"Why wouldn't I accept, or why am I helping?"

"Both." It wasn't like anyone, much less a noble, to help someone like her—poor, orphaned, and a nobody.

"Because you need the help," he said as a matter of fact. When Tal didn't respond, Faron attempted to lighten the mood, "And hopefully, if I stay close enough, I'll get the undivided attention of a beautiful woman." He winked and received an eye roll in return.

19

Tal swiped her bedroom curtain aside. "I smell sausage."

Faron leaned his back against the tunnel wall, failing to keep his face neutral. He held a pastry between them. Before he could respond, Tal held up a finger as if to say, "Don't you dare."

Faron nodded to his hand instead. "I saved this one from Sybil."

Tal swiped the offered treat and bit into it, scowling. "If she drank all the rose water this time, I'll singe her bedsheets."

It had been three weeks since Tal welcomed Faron into their home, and every morning since, he'd arrived with a basket of food. Aside from the masquerade, they had never eaten food so fresh and delicious. From the bread with jam, still-steaming meats, quail, ripe fruit, and many things they didn't recognize, they didn't let a single crumb go to waste.

The first time Faron offered the gift, they didn't know how to react. While Tal still slept, Carrick had been struck dumb at the delicious aroma emanating from the basket. Sybil, on the other hand, didn't hesitate to take it out of Faron's hands and dig in. When Tal finally awoke, Faron had already left, and she lost her chance to give him an earful. Her pride gave in once she tasted the chocolate cakes he included. They accepted every delivery after with only a little reluctance. Tal once asked Faron why he brought the food, but he shrugged and said it would go to waste if they didn't eat it. She could read the lie on his face, but didn't reject his help.

"I caught Syb and Egan on their way out. They're taking over our shift—something about a vision last night?" They made their way into the common area where Rain scrutinized something in his notebook. He greeted the two, grabbed a slice of bread and returned to his work. Faron and Tal sat on the floor, the basket between them.

Sybil had a vision the previous night of Tal entering a dark room with fire in her eyes. Despite her assurances, the group decided Tal should no longer track Badger and Gully for fear she would take matters into her own hands.

"Anything interesting happen during Ed and Jens's watch last night?" Rain asked without tearing his eyes away from his reading.

Faron stretched his legs out in front of him. "Still nothing. Jens has been a big help in looking further into the thugs, but they're as predictable as ever. Nothing on the mage, and no apparition sightings either."

Tal searched through the basket. "Did Syb take the custard?"

He held up both hands in surrender. "I tried to stop her, I swear." His eyebrow twitched.

"Liar."

Faron shoved a sizable chunk of salted meat into his mouth and stared pointedly at the ceiling.

"What are Ed and Waylon up to today?" Tal took a large bite of jellied toast.

Faron's mouth turned down as he shook his head. "Ed has been sent on a mission by the council, and Waylon's father has had him locked in his study for the last week."

"Sounds dreadful," Tal mused around a mouthful.

Rain set his quill down. "Still no luck with the king? How about information on that room in the palace?"

Faron sat on the floor in their common area, staring at the wall while nearly chewing a hole into his lip. "No. I'm no help there. But I have other news."

Tal perked up. "News?"

"Where is Carrick today?" Faron's voice didn't hold its usual cheerful tone.

Rain closed his notebook on the quill. "He's on a job. He won't return until tomorrow."

Normally, Tal would have expected that revelation to pique the noble's interest, but it appeared he had been expecting more of an audience. "That complicates things," he sighed.

She placed the toast back on the cloth napkin in her lap. "Why? What does it complicate?"

"I've been looking into that invitation." His head dipped toward Rain.

"The one the nobles mentioned at the masquerade? Is it related to the mages?" Rain leaned forward.

Faron hesitated. "It's for something tonight."

"Tonight?!" Tal jumped to her feet. "Why aren't we getting ready then?" She stuffed a few more treats into her pockets, about to get into her leathers and grab her weapons.

The noble reached for her hand. "Woah! Slow down. I only learned of it today. And we're not going."

She froze. "What do you mean we're not going?"

"I only know when and where. I don't know what the invitation is for, who or what will be there, or even how to get in there ourselves. Weren't you the one that chastised me for running into the incinerator without any kind of plan?"

Tal opened her mouth to brush off his logic. She couldn't pass an opportunity to gain information, but she also couldn't deny his reasoning.

Rain shook his head. "You're right, but we've had no development in weeks. We can't lose this chance. Is there time to wait until the others get back? Or any way the two of you can sneak in—just to observe," he added when Tal's face brightened in a mischievous grin. "We need to take advantage of this."

"The two of us?" Faron asked. "You won't be joining?"

Rain gathered his things and stood. "I'm off to interview another family from this list." He held up the notebook.

Faron sighed and nodded to himself. "Alright. But we are only going to gather information."

"Right. I'll get ready," Tal called over her shoulder, already running to her room.

Faron's chuckle followed her through the tunnels.

"Tal, focus. You need to know the layout before we go traipsing about the grounds." There was something about Faron's serious tone that Tal found adorable.

A miniature model of the mansion sat on the tunnel floor, erected out of whatever they could find. Faron's basket stood in the middle, representing the extravagant house. Inside, rolls and croissants were placed strategically to signify different rooms of import. One of his shoes sat a short distance from the basket. Faron used a charred piece of wood to draw the path they would take through the surrounding forest, and another line connected the basket to his shoe. Tal's dagger jabbed a rolled pastry with a delicious brown spice and sugar drizzle.

"So, the study is here, next to it is where they dine, and over here is a second house." She pointed the pastry-tipped dagger at the shoe.

"It's a dovecote, but I know for a fact that Mordency lost all his doves. The beetle-headed barnacle can't run a house to save his life." The nobleman in question appeared to be the one at the center of this invitation business.

"Remind me what a dovecote is again?" She waved the dagger around and took a bite from the impaled pastry.

"You're sprinkling icing all over the grounds."

"Maybe it's snowing." She took another bite, and more of the drizzle landed in their display.

"In the dead of summer." His hair fell into his eyes when he shook his head at her. "A dovecote is where the doves are housed.

Mordency's is empty, at least of doves. He's been hosting something there that he doesn't want some of the other nobles to know about."

"And that's what we're going to find out," Tal added around a mouthful.

They planned to sneak into the main building through the servant's quarters and try to eavesdrop on the house staff. If they were lucky, they may even be able to catch conversation among the guests. Once the event started, they would make their way to the dovecote.

"Do we engage? Will they recognize you?"

"As much as I'd love to indulge your fantasies, this is one I'm afraid that we will have to exercise restraint."

"I don't know what fantasies you're talking about."

The banter didn't stop the whole way to the mansion. Monitoring Badger and Gully proved frustratingly boring, and Tal's hatred for them did nothing but grow as the days passed. Now, a wave of excitement coursed through her. The hilt of the dagger in her hand kept her mind calm. It flipped in the air and landed back in her palm. She yearned for a fight, but these men were not the bottom of the barrel scum she encountered in the docks. It wouldn't be wise to cross them.

A pine-scented breeze blew hair into her face. The surrounding forest provided the perfect cover for observing the property, and Tal could almost see it in its entirety from the branch she perched on. A twig snapped below as Faron crept through the leaf-littered ground. Branches bowed underneath her, and her palms scraped on the bark during her descent.

"It doesn't seem large enough to hold any kind of auction," she noted. The dovecote appeared exactly as Faron had described. The small stone structure was barely larger than a one-room home. At most, she expected no more than ten people would fit comfortably inside.

"I did find it odd he hosts there. Though, it does offer more privacy than anywhere else on the grounds."

Faron relayed his observations regarding entrances and exits as well as the number of visible staff and visitors. They had arrived well before any guests and spent the afternoon getting a better layout. At the appearance of the carriages, Faron moved around the house to recognize any faces while Tal kept an eye on activity within the smaller building.

He returned with a newfound tension in his shoulders, his nostrils flaring.

"What is it?" Tal asked.

"Waylon is here."

"What? Here?" Tal searched the grounds as if she would see him standing there.

Faron seethed. "I've known him since we were children. I would have trusted him with my life."

Tal swallowed. Her usual snide comments died on her tongue as confusion blasted through her. Had Waylon betrayed them? "Who else is here?"

"Briggins and Lighton—the two nobles Rain mentioned—along with one other noble and a foreign dignitary." His jaw ticked listing off each man that arrived.

"Are any of these men capable of buying human slaves?"

"If they are, I'll personally take them to the palace to be humiliated in front of the whole court, and make sure their titles and lands are stripped from them." His voice grew deep with anger. His hands gripped the handles of his knives, his knuckles white.

Tal wasn't used to seeing him anything less than jovial. If Faron had fury, he most certainly would have lost control of it by now. "You can do that?"

He replied with a grim nod.

"And Waylon?"

Faron searched the space around them, and the muscle in his jaw flexed.

"I'm happy to cook him if the situation calls for it." Tal tried a tentative smile, but the noble merely pursed his lips. Faron didn't

need to talk, he needed action. "Well, no sense in storming over it."
Tal ran across the grounds without a backward glance.

Outside the door to the servant's quarters, they hid behind a
wooden cart and a barrel of water. They pulled their hoods low
and used a cloth to cover their faces. The guests ate dinner while
the clanging of dishes and servants chatter accompanied the smell
of roasted pheasant and buttery vegetables drifting out the open
window.

Tal sat next to Faron with their backs against the outside wall.
Running across the grounds had done nothing for the noble. His
knee bounced erratically against her own leg.

Tal placed a hand on the offending limb.

Faron's attention shot to her hand, and his leg immediately stilled.

Her eyes softened, as if to implore him to calm his nerves. Faron
took a slow, deep breath in response. She eyed him, concern blooming over what Waylon's arrival would mean for Faron. When he
caught her staring, he exhaled and looked away.

Chatter about dessert reached their ears, and soon, silence filled
the kitchen. They waited five more minutes before sneaking inside.
The table in the center of the room held piles of newly washed dishes
on one end and two platters of leftover desserts and glasses of wine at
the other. Tal reached for one of the miniature blue tarts and stopped
halfway to see Faron's reaction. That seemed to ease some of the
tension in his shoulders. She winked and pulled her hand away. She
passed a carafe of magenta colored wine, a shade she'd never seen
before. Faron regarded the liquid for a moment before continuing.

He flinched at the sudden noise when she quietly whispered,
"What is it?"

"Not sure."

Outside the kitchens, they paused to let one of the valets pass
down the hall before heading toward the great room. When they
reached a corner, approaching voices sent the pair back into the
shadows.

"—must get back an' clean up 'afore they begin."

"I'm nervous. What if someone finds out?"

"That's not fer ye to worry 'bout. Did ye take yer mixture?"

Tal couldn't hear a response, but the first woman gave a throaty giggle.

"Ye'll be forgettin' yer nerves in no time."

Two female servants walked quickly arm in arm past the spot where Tal and Faron hid. The more they learned, the more confused she became. A glance at her companion indicated he too couldn't interpret the overheard conversation. They stepped through the doors of the great hall only to find it completely empty.

"What now?" Tal turned. They were in the open and without a plan. "Have they left already? We didn't see them pass."

"Try the study." Faron placed a hand on her back to urge her in the right direction, and Tal tensed at the warmth from his touch. Faron either didn't notice or chose not to comment. His hand remained.

Eerie silence filled the house, which didn't bode well for Tal's nerves. Something about the whole night felt off. Finally, noise reached them from the study. The spicy, sweet scent of tobacco reminded Tal of the brothels at the docks. Fading echoes of laughter filtered through the closed door. "Why is it getting quieter? Is there an exit on this side of the house?" she whispered outside the door.

Faron's confusion offered little comfort. "Something's not right."

Tal eased the door open and thanked the gods the hinges didn't groan. Inside, a single candle cast a dim glow from a desk on the far wall. Moonlight filtered in through the floor-to-ceiling windows as Tal's eyes adjusted to the dark. Small tables and upholstered chairs littered the room, arranged for entertaining. Movement behind the desk caught Tal's attention. A well-dressed man only a few years older than Egan fiddled with the buttons on his jacket and puffed erratically on a pipe. A moment later, he faced the bookshelf along the back wall and pulled out one of the books. A metallic *click* reached her ears. The bookshelf swung forward with an audible groan, and the nobleman slipped behind it before the shelf swung back into place.

Tal's hand shot back and grabbed Faron's. The men had left the house through the study, and they just found the secret passage they used to do it. She dropped Faron's hand and swept into the room. She weaved around the labyrinth of furniture, finding herself in front of the grand windows.

A hand suddenly covered her mouth, and an arm around her waist spun her behind the heavy, floor-length curtain. She reached for one of her daggers until a near-silent "shhh" sounded in her ear. Faron's expensive leather sleeve felt familiar in her grip.

A feminine melody hummed just a few paces from where they stood. Glass *thunked* onto one of the wooden tables. Chair legs scraped on the wool rug. One of the servants tidied up the study. Tal completely missed her cleaning in the far corner when she went after the noble.

Faron released her, and Tal spun to face him. His muscled torso pressed against her in the confined space. She ripped her hood back and pulled on the cloth covering her face. Faron did the same. The moonlight filtering through the window reflected in his eyes. Faron responded to Tal's wide-eyed look by mouthing, "What were you thinking?"

"I was going after him!" she mouthed back, gesturing in what little space they had between them.

He pointed to the corner of the room and silently replied, "The woman is *right there*!"

Tal stood on her toes to get closer to his eye level. "Well, I didn't see her!" She swayed into Faron, and he caught her around the tops of her arms.

"Obviously." The corners of his lips pulled into wry smile.

Tal narrowed her eyes, but something in her chest clenched to see that expression returned. Nerves had them both breathing heavily in the tight space, and Tal swore she could feel his heartbeat against her chest.

The maid brushed by the curtain, stirring the air around them. Tal expected the exotic spiciness of clove, but noted fresh lavender and rosemary instead. "New soap?" she mouthed and sniffed dramatically.

Faron grimaced. "It's all I had."

Tal scrunched her face to hide her smile, but Faron mirrored her expression.

While the maid worked around the room, the two hid in the near-dark, exchanging looks of feigned annoyance. Faron still held Tal's arms, so she turned her contemptuous gaze to his hands. This only encouraged him to begin massaging circles into the leather at her shoulders. The sensation sent goosebumps running up and down her body, and she hoped the dim lighting concealed the flush that filled her cheeks.

Faron slid one foot to the side of Tal's leg, pressing her up against the window. He leaned his head down until his breath brushed across her lips.

Tal pressed into the window and let her head fall back. It hit the window with a distinct *thud*. They froze. They waited for the servant to discover their hiding spot. The silence of the room beyond stretched until Tal couldn't take it anymore, and she poked her head out from behind the curtain. Cool air blasted against her face, and she realized how stifling it was in their hiding spot. A quick glance confirmed the woman had left. Tal stumbled out of Faron's grasp and into the cool study air. She wrenched one of her daggers into her hand and brandished it against the noble.

"You! Knock it off," she whispered hoarsely. She wanted so badly to smack the smirk off his face... or kiss it. *What?* She inhaled. Did that thought just cross her mind? Instead, she walked over to the bookshelf by the large wooden desk and eyed the shelves.

The hair on the back of her neck stood on end when Faron stepped close behind her. He reached over her shoulder and pulled at the binding of one of the books. The same metallic *click* echoed through the room, followed by the agonizingly loud groan of the bookshelf. Tal glanced behind her.

Faron's hand gestured for her to go first. "After you." Cold surrounded her when she stepped out of his space.

Behind the bookshelf lay a large stone tunnel. It sloped downward toward the northern side of the property in the direction of the dovecote. She took out a second dagger. A quick glance confirmed Faron's swords were also in hand. They stalked down the tunnel, past the occasional torch illuminating the way.

A deep, quiet voice echoed, stopping them in their tracks. Tal could barely make out the form of the young noble up ahead. He paced back and forth, mumbling to himself. She afforded Faron a single look then took off toward the gentleman, silent as an owl in the night. She pulled up her hood and face covering mid-step and sheathed one of her daggers, staying to the shadows along the wall.

When the nobleman turned away, she ran the remaining distance and pounced, covering his mouth with her free hand and holding the dagger to his neck with the other.

He yelped against her hand and jerked in her grasp.

"Remain still or your neck will be slit open," she hissed.

He froze. Sweat on his upper lip coated Tal's fingers. He panted against her hand.

"Scream and you die. Understood?"

He nodded vigorously.

She removed her hand from his mouth and pressed the dagger tighter against his neck to prove her point. "Who are you?"

"L-Lord Lighton."

"Where are the others?" Tal eased the pressure behind her dagger. Lighton shook so much he nearly cut himself on the blade.

His unsteady hand pointed further down the tunnel. She could see they had reached a valley, and the stone began to slope upward beyond where they stood.

"P-P-Please. They told me we weren't doing anything wrong. They said they wanted it." Sweat made his near-blonde hair stick to his forehead.

"Did you ask them that or are these your friends' words?" she snarled.

"Ple-ease. This is my first time. I s-swear I haven't even touched one of them yet."

"Tch—People like you disgust me. You think you can take advantage of someone because you have more money than them?"

The man blubbered, and Tal's anger grew. She gripped the hilt of her dagger harder and gritted her teeth.

"What are they doing in the dovecote?" said a deep growl behind them. Tal spun with the man to find Faron in shadow. He had disguised his voice to the point where even she didn't recognize it.

Smart, she thought. A small part of her felt guilty for jumping into the situation against their previous agreement. She risked exposing Faron to his fellow nobility. She would have to make it up to him somehow.

"What?" Lighton's voice reached a new octave on the one word.

"What. Are. The men. Doing. In. The dovecote?" he enunciated each word in his disguised voice.

"You—They—Don't you know?" His eyes darted between Tal and Faron.

Tal didn't know what to say, and Faron's dark-shrouded figure only offered silence.

"It's the Communal," he said, confusion lining his features. When Tal and Faron shared a puzzled look, Lighton continued, "The—the servants. They join us and they—They say they want to, I swear! We drank the Unfruitful Wine and everything." The man made no sense. Tal didn't know what to do.

Faron decided for her. He stalked forward and slammed the pommel of his sword into Lighton's head, knocking him out. Tal slid him to the ground. "What was he going on about?"

"I think I have an idea." He turned and made his way up the tunnel. Tal ran to keep up.

Halfway up the slope, whimpering and guttural moaning rebounded along the stone passage. Tal could only imagine the amount of torture someone had to go through to emit such sounds. Before Faron could stop her, she sprinted up the slope, bursting through the door without a second thought. She blinked against the sudden blazing light of the dovecote, searching the room for the source of the pained cries—and froze.

Clothes scattered around the floor and draped on the furniture as if they'd been torn off in haste. But what had Talwyn's jaw dropping of its own volition was the sight of both men and women stark naked and tearing into each other as if they'd been starved of bodily pleasures. Her eyes flickered from one group to the next in utter confusion, wondering what the hells she had barged in on. The moaning and wailing only increased the longer she watched. And there, in the center of four other men and women, Waylon stood propped against a cushioned seat, jostled by the assault. Pure ecstasy lit his face.

"Well, this makes much more sense."

Tal jumped. Faron stood at her shoulder, his own mask covering his face, and his eyes reflecting a humorous gleam. He pulled her back into the shadows and closed the door, the animalistic cries still penetrating the thick wood.

"WHAT THE F—"

Faron burst out laughing before Tal could finish her sentence, causing her to jump.

"DID YOU KNOW—"

Faron doubled over, hysterical.

"This is some sick joke. On display. In *groups!* You nobles are positively disgusting." She smacked him.

"Don't look at me! I didn't get an invitation."

"You knew what was behind that door!"

He backed up against the stone wall and placed his hands on his knees for support. "I swear to you I had no idea. I recognized the wine and have heard of an appleberry tart for enhancing pleasure, but I didn't make the connection until Lighton started blubbering."

"So, you let me barge in there knowing full well that I was about to intrude on such feral behavior?!"

"I did not," he wheezed. "You threw yourself into that."

"I cannot stand you." She stomped down the passageway back toward the main building, his laughs chasing her the whole way.

Tal shoved the bookshelf open to an empty study. "I feel like such a prude witnessing that. And I'm not!" she added, glaring back at Faron and making her way through the room.

"I certainly feel violated." Faron brushed the front of his shirt.

"Did they not see us? How did they not notice?" She peeked through the study door, watching for wandering servants.

"The appleberry tart focuses their minds on the needs of the flesh. They're essentially in a pleasure-driven trance until the effects wear off."

Tal's lips pulled up in disgust. "And the wine?"

"The Unfruitful Wine prevents... ah... surprises?" Faron ran a hand through his hair, avoiding Tal's gaze.

"A child, you mean?"

"Yes, a child. The wine prevents the... conception... of a child." He coughed and rubbed the back of his neck.

"Are you okay over there, your lordship?" Tal pushed open the heavy wooden door and eased into the dark hall.

"Barely. Let's get out of here before anyone catches us."

***

Pepper's saddle became a constant remind of the scenes replaying in Tal's head the whole ride back. She had to threaten to cut the smirk off Faron's face. They had escaped the grounds without issue as most of the servants and all the guests were otherwise indisposed.

"Would you like to share my saddle? I can assure you it's quite comfortable." The amusement in his voice infuriated her.

"One more suggestive remark and I swear, I'll slip one of those damned tarts into your pastries when you aren't looking."

"Do that, and you'll surely regret it, I promise you." Something in his voice had Tal thinking of the scene at the dovecote, and she had to shift in the saddle again. "Unless you'd like to eat one as well."

"I don't need to eat a pastry to enjoy a man, or a woman for that matter."

Faron lost his laughter to a coughing fit. In a raspy voice, he said, "Hells, woman. Don't speak like that."

"Don't tell me you've become prudish," she scoffed.

"Just the opposite. You test my wavering self-control."

Tal shifted in the saddle again. This time Faron didn't remark on the movement. The moonlight silhouetted him, and Tal knew if she could see the gleam in his eyes, she would throw caution to the wind and kiss him in the middle of the forest. Hells, ever since they left the mansion behind, her body had urged her to even more.

Out of sheer frustration, she sent Pepper into a full gallop to get out of that forest as fast as she could. *I need to focus*, she told herself. She couldn't let Faron distract her. What should have been a night of answers turned into a dead-end. They were still no closer to finding the mage, and she felt like a sitting duck.

Annoyance flared within her. Families were fleeing to the mountains. Children were starving. Hells, they were living in *sewers*. All while the nobility ate, drank, and fucked without a care in the world. *What can I do?* Tal asked herself, hoping to find the answers among the trees. When none came, she was left with an itch in her chest and a fire burning through her. She grabbed at the itch, firming her resolve. Her fury purred at the attention. It lapped against its cage, urging Tal to set it free.

She pursed her lips, ready for tomorrow to come. She didn't find the mage. But she could prepare for the day when she would.

20

"Oh sure, I've been to the Communal a *few* times." Waylon leaned back and rested his feet on the tavern table three days later. "Why didn't you ask?"

Faron shook his head at his friend. "You've been locked away all week. And how would I have known to ask you?"

Waylon groaned. "My dear father will not give up on my hopeless education. But Mordency has been hosting for ages. You've heard about them." He gestured back to his friend.

Faron's brows reached his hairline, bewilderment filling his features. "I have not."

"Of course you have! I've been trying to get you to join me since last summer. Don't you remember?"

"You mean the 'fun time' you've been suggesting? *That* was your idea?"

"Of course!" Waylon slapped the table.

"Forgive me if I prefer other forms of entertainment."

Tal watched the two men argue and couldn't help feeling deep satisfaction that Faron had not wished to join Waylon to such an event. Was that jealousy flaring inside her?

"It's great! The wives don't know about it, and his servants love to participate."

Tal didn't hide the skepticism from her face.

"What? Don't look at me like that. They get to choose their partner. We simply sit and wait."

"And the... utter lack of control is enjoyable?" Tal had no issue with the man's choice of partner or *partners*. It was the feral nature with which they had attacked each other she couldn't stop seeing. They'd all been consumed by it. She barely released her hold on her power. She'd never allowed herself to be so... free.

Waylon licked his lips just as Faron's leg brushed against her own. "And you're friends with him?" she asked Faron over Waylon's laughter.

"Waylon has always been, shall we say, carefree." He took a sip of ale and choked at the gesture Waylon made.

"Did Lighton say anything?" Tal's guilt over risking Faron's exposure had plagued her since that night.

The noble shook his head. "Not a word. In fact, he hasn't been as cheerful as of late. What on earth did you do to the poor sod, Faron?"

"Tal attacked him. I only knocked him out." He threw an arm around her shoulders, and Tal fought the heat that filled her cheeks.

"Hells. I need to find a woman like that." Waylon dropped his feet and leaned onto the table. "Are you sure you don't want to share?"

Tal certainly failed to hide the redness in her cheeks after that. "What makes you think I'd want a man who supports adultery?" She turned her nose up at the noble.

Mischief filled Waylon's features. "But you don't deny you want him?" He gestured to Faron, eyeing the arm around Tal's shoulders.

Faron peered at her sideways and drew circles on her arm. Chills ran up and down at the point of contact.

"Is it the blue eyes?" Waylon asked.

Blue eyes? Tal furrowed her brow. Faron's pale green gaze held hers. She found the gold specks there. As the contact lingered, the color shifted. It darkened. And, as a shadow crossed over his features, there it was. Not green. *Hazel.*

"What?" he said, his voice like a caress.

"Your eyes are hazel."

Faron nodded a fraction, his face lit with amusement.

"They always look green. I never noticed the blue." Even then, Tal could barely catch the deep hues.

His attention flicked to her lip as she bit it in concentration. "Well, the blue is mixed with light brown. So, looking at you, they'd probably blend together."

Before she could ask what he meant, a commotion near the entrance distracted her. Entering the tavern were Daire and a few other guardsmen, including a worried Eddard. Tal felt Faron's finger twitch on her arm. She sighed. "I do *not* want to deal with him today."

Faron leaned closer to whisper in her ear, "Then let's get out of here." His warm breath on her skin only added to the thoughts still plaguing her mind.

Waylon stood with a loud scrape of his chair. "Well, looks like I'll be needing to find my own entertainment tonight. You two have a good evening." He bowed, winking as he stood, before joining the crowd by the door. The guards greeted him noisily. A familiar mop of thick chestnut hair joined him, and Tal caught the captain's attention. Recognition flooded his features. His gaze flicked behind her, and his eyes widened in surprise.

Faron took his arm from around her shoulder and stood. He held his hand out to her. "Ready? I know another way out."

His skin was smooth against her palm. Faron squeezed her fingers, and Tal smiled despite herself. She stood, and they snuck out through a door along the back wall. They dropped hands once they'd exited but walked side by side back to the tunnels.

They didn't talk about the Communal or Waylon's question, though the glances they exchanged told her it gripped both their minds.

"I apologize for Waylon's forwardness." Faron turned to face her.

Tal waved a hand at his apology. "There's no need. I like him."

Faron cried out and placed his hand over his heart. "Damn him. I'll strike him down for stealing your affections."

"Still your sword, oh jealous one. I must focus on preparations. I don't have time to mend your wounds, nor your fragile ego." Tal pushed him playfully.

"Oh, how little faith you have in me." His shoulders heaved with a dramatic sigh. "Alas, your training awaits, milady." He dropped the highborn tone. "I look forward to the day when you've mastered that fire."

Tal searched his face for a hint of humor but found none.

"Remember that time you were so mad at Duncan for interfering with a bounty that you stomped straight home to Carrick's room, and before you could get one sentence out, your hands shot flames that burned his bedding to nothing but ash!" Sybil barely managed to finish her story before she lost herself to a fit of laughter.

The group sat scattered around the common area and shared stories, as had been their new routine for the last week when the search for the mage proved fruitless.

"I slept on the floor for a week after that." Carrick chuckled.

Tal groaned behind her hand. "I offered for you to sleep in my room!"

Rain tipped his drink in Carrick's direction. "He probably should have. The bed sat empty since Tal went missing for the next five days."

Sybil cackled. "Not missing, just drowning her fury with Pochette's Mud Water at Gale's."

"Is that why you're always drinking?" Faron asked.

Talwyn sipped her ale to hide her shame. "It doesn't block my fury completely—"

"Unless you're four pints in!" Sybil interrupted.

"Which she usually is." Carrick shook his head.

Tal held her hands up in surrender. "My fury calls to me. The stronger the call, the harder it is to resist. The more ale I drink, the easier it is to ignore it, and the harder it is to pull my fury out."

"And then when you get good and pissed off, nothing but a batch of the revolting poison that is Mud Water can keep the flames at bay," Rain chimed in. He shivered at the mention of the bitter drink that could knock out a horse.

Tal shrunk further into her spot against the wall. "It's not *that* bad. You gain a taste for it eventually."

"Sure." Sybil threw a bite of bread at Tal. "Just don't plan on kissing anyone for a while."

Tal's gaze shot to Faron, and she noticed the way his lips twitched. She forced her focus to the cool drink in her hands before she turned as red as a rose.

Faron shook his head. "And none of you are concerned that a Fury spends a majority of her time surrounded by highly flammable substances?"

He received blank stares.

"Honestly, I hadn't thought about it." Tal shrugged. He had a point.

"And no one tells Tal what to do," added Egan.

That was the last night Tal drank anything to dull her fury. She'd had control of her magic for weeks now and had built her stores significantly as she practiced each night.

***

A week later, she and Faron sat in the common area working on Tal's hold on her magic. "Alright, wise tutor, what new task will you have me do today?" She set down her faerie water, a mix of mashed up fruits, fresh water, and honey.

Faron stopped bringing ale when he learned it dulled Tal's fury. "You need a clear head to train properly," he'd said.

Tonight, the faerie water offered not only a substitute to her usual pint of ale but also a reprieve from the stifling summer's heat. Tal wore a torn-up shirt with ties up to her shoulders to give her arms some air.

Faron stretched out across from her, his back against the wall. "What did we master last? One flame on each finger?"

"Almost." Tal called up the flames and stared pointedly at the noticeably flame-free pinky on her left hand.

"Poor little guy. He's trying."

Tal grunted and snuffed out the flames.

"You and your flaming toes will get there soon." He winked when Tal stuck her tongue out at him. "You know what would be really impressive?"

She crossed her arms. "Do I want to know?"

"I can see it now. Talwyn the Fearsome, engulfed in flames, stalking the streets as her enemies run in fear."

She snorted and shook her head. "More like Talwyn the Turbulent. It's easier than concentrated spots, but I've only managed full body flame when I can't control my fury."

"You've already done it? Fascinating! You really are incredible, do you know that?"

Tal didn't answer.

"What happens to your hair?"

"Nothing burns except my clothes." Tal anticipated the mischief in his gaze and responded with what had become her signature eye roll. She found his lips, noting the way he licked the faerie water from them.

She recalled that moment in the alley where his hands pulled her into him, his body pressed against hers, and his mouth flirted with the distance between them. The memory had been tormenting her since that night. She dreamed of him. Sometimes her dreams brought her back to the afternoon with him in the forest; other times, she relived the near kiss behind the curtain at Mordency's.

And then there were the dreams of things that hadn't happened yet, dreams in a stone tunnel with a blue tart on her lips. She would wake with the memory of his touch as if he had been there moments before. Those images plagued her mind day in and day out, sitting across from him in the common area. "I know what you're thinking, and no." She grabbed bread from Faron's basket and shook her head at him.

"What?" He feigned innocence. By the way his eyes roved up and down her body, she could guess Faron wanted her to attempt it.

"I told you it won't work. It's too dangerous." She held a flaming finger under her bread to create a lovely golden-brown toast.

"But you've had so much practice now," he pleaded.

She bit into the toast with a satisfying crunch. "It takes too much energy, and I can't hold it long enough."

"Long enough for what? Even a moment is plenty long enough to prove you can do it." He tossed her another piece of bread, his only indication that he wanted it toasted as well.

She obliged and tossed the piece back to him before saying, "Long enough to get somewhere so I'm not *indecent.*"

"Oh, you won't bother me, I can assure you." He winked, taking a large bite of his freshly toasted bread. He closed his eyes and groaned. "Even better than out of the kitchens," he mumbled to himself.

"I'm sure you'll do the gentlemanly thing and turn away." She threw the remaining piece of untoasted bread at him.

He tossed the bread right back at her. "I thought you knew all nobles are rakes." When he caught the smile that Tal tried to hide, he continued, "When are you going to admit you've wanted to kiss me since that night? You've been torturing me with those eyes ever since."

She spared him another eye roll and shook her head with a laugh. "Are you confessing your own desires?"

"Obviously."

From where she sat against the tunnel wall, she watched him, the last piece of bread a few inches from her mouth. He mirrored her from his spot just a few paces away. She watched as he licked his bottom lip, pulled it into his mouth, and bit the skin there. His chest heaved from the deep breath he took. He rested his arm on his propped knee, letting his hand hang. Despite his relaxed posture, his hand fidgeted.

He rubbed his index finger along his thumb, and Tal felt the hairs raise on the back of her neck. The images from her dreams taunted her from within as much as he did. *Fuck it*, she thought.

Dropping the piece of bread, she shifted her weight forward and pushed herself onto her hands and knees. She watched the knot in his throat bob when he gulped at her approach. The cool floor against her palms contrasted the heat pulsing through her. She closed the distance between them slowly, watching his every reaction.

Tal enjoyed silencing the flirtatious noble as she took the reins. It had been weeks, and he had yet to make a move, despite the suggestive commentary and smoldering looks. She would beat him at his own game, and she would enjoy it.

Lavender and rosemary filled her nose. She smirked, inhaling, and crawling into his space. Her hand brushed his inner thigh. Their eyes met and his warm breath brushed across her lips. For a moment, she stared into his eyes and saw the hunger there. His pupils dilated. She heard, rather than saw, his jaw clench. She licked her lips, and his eyes flicked to them before returning to hers. "So, what are you waiting for?" she half-whispered.

He offered a wolfish grin before responding. "You."

She needed no further invitation. Tal closed the one-inch distance between them and pressed her mouth to his. Instantly, Faron reached up to her neck and pulled her into him. His arm hugged her, and Tal melted into him. She crawled into his lap, straddling him. Their mouths parted and she tasted the deliciously sweet faerie water on his tongue.

Faron gripped the hair at the base of her neck.

Goosebumps traveled down her spine. She wrapped her feet around his back and pulled her hips into him. Her fingers threaded through his infuriatingly silky hair. She needed to be closer. Despite the summer heat, Tal reveled in the warmth from his body, an odd comfort she never thought she would crave.

His arms were sure and strong. He kissed her hungrily, as if the last few weeks had been as much torture for him as they were for her. He ran a hand up her back, and an animalistic groan escaped Tal. She gripped him harder and pushed into him. In a flash, Faron had Tal on her back. The shock of the movement had Tal opening her eyes. He cradled her head to protect against the stone floor and pressed into her.

Faron stopped kissing her then. Their eyes met. She drank in the sight of him, studying the swirling colors she'd missed for so long. *So beautiful.* And there, among the blues and greens, were her gold flecks. She recognized now that they shifted in different lighting, but now that she'd seen them, Tal knew she'd always find them.

For a moment, Tal wondered if she should stop him. After all, what right did she have to link herself to the noble, even if for a night? But the pull to him had started that night at the incinerator, and it had only gotten worse ever since. She reached up to kiss him again, and he pulled back out of reach.

"Tal, I—" he began, but she didn't want to hear anything.

"Just kiss me." She closed her eyes, pulling him down to her, and he obliged. She kissed him as if her fury could be embodied within his embrace. In fact, something strange grew within her chest. Her fury uncoiled in a way she'd never experienced before. The magic usually stormed like a caged animal clawing to be set free, but kissing Faron felt like a warm blanket being wrapped around the two of them. If she didn't know any better, she'd say her fury had managed to get out on its own and filled the space around them.

She suddenly realized the warmth and brightness behind her eyes wasn't imagined. Tal's eyes shot open, and she turned her face away from Faron. She stared at the golden glow that surrounded them, terrified for a moment that she had set the two of them on fire.

"You're glowing," Faron said with a hint of wonder in his voice.

"What? No, I'm not. It's in the air."

"No, it's definitely you. Look." He gently grabbed her arm from around his neck, and indeed, it glowed a glorious shade of deep orange.

She pulled her arm out of his grasp and stared at it in shock. "What in all hells—?" She scooted out from under him and sat up. The light shone through her shirt and trousers as well.

Faron pushed himself off her. "That's never happened before?"

She shook her head, trying to remember a time she'd ever been able to release light without flame or heat before. When the light faded from her skin, she warily met his gaze.

She should have known the playful noble would handle it without issue. When his knowing smile turned his concern to satisfaction, it was all she could do to stop from groaning.

"So, is that how I make you feel?" He leaned back on an elbow, all but inviting Tal back into his embrace.

"It doesn't bother you?" Tal didn't know if she cared either way. It certainly concerned her.

He nodded emphatically. "Oh yes. In fact, it bothers me so much, I think we should do it again to see how bothered I am."

"Oh no!" She feigned concern. "I would hate to cause you any distress. We should avoid the bothersome behavior at all costs."

"No, no. Please. I beg you. Bother away." He reached for her, which only made her laugh and pull against him when he caught her arm. He kissed the top of her wrist. "My lady." When she didn't pull away, he kissed halfway up her forearm, letting his lips brush her skin as he worked his way up, regarding her with hooded eyes. When he reached her bare shoulder, Tal bit her lip against the goosebumps that traveled along her skin. With his free hand, he reached up and pushed the hair away from her neck. He placed a kiss below the corner of her jaw, and Tal exhaled a nervous laugh. She closed her eyes.

Faron kissed along her jaw until he reached the edge of her lips. He paused, waiting for her to take the final step. She could feel him grinning against her skin, and she mirrored the expression. With a deep breath and an exhale, she turned ever so slightly, and their lips met. Instantly, it hit like a shock to her system. Her breath hitched in her throat. Kissing him felt like the world dropped away, and only heat stood between them. Her fury quieted within her, almost as if it had finally found peace, something she had never experienced.

Tal had never been one to enjoy kissing, but the way she felt then, she could have spent forever in this man's embrace. She needed to. The space between them ached with a desperate hunger. She gripped his shirt in both hands and pulled him on top of her. After weeks of intense glances and carefully planned caresses, Tal had grown tired of waiting, tired of waking up from dreams she would much rather dive back into. Heat filled her at the memory of all the things her unconscious mind had already done to him. Tonight, Tal would make at least one of those fantasies a reality.

She kissed Faron with urgency, and he responded in kind. But as much as Tal demanded more from him, she could tell he held himself back. Just as he had all these past few weeks, Faron let Tal take the lead. Perhaps their power imbalance forced his restraint. According to societal standards, it certainly wasn't proper for them to be alone in a room together, much less kissing.

However, those few weeks they'd spent ignoring their attraction let Faron observe more about Tal than she would have freely revealed. He knew she liked to be in control, and he was all too happy to surrender it to her. When Tal realized, it sent her head spinning. Never had she met a man who allowed her to be herself so completely, and she certainly didn't expect to meet such a man with his social status. She'd found someone who perfectly complemented her.

She pressed against Faron, and he responded with a maddeningly satisfying groan. He stopped kissing her and fisted his hand against the ground, holding himself over her. His head dropped slightly. "Hells. You're treading on dangerous ground."

Tal smirked at him. "I'm not treading on anything. I'm on my back."

Faron chuckled darkly and shook his head. "If kissing you always escalates like this, I'm afraid I won't have enough restraint for much longer."

"I'd like to see you with a little less restraint."

His eyes burned into her, and his nostrils flared. Tal tested his resolve. "Do not ask for things you aren't truly ready for," he growled.

"I'm not asking." She lifted her chin up, so her lips were a hair's width from touching his. "I'm demanding." Tal narrowed her eyes in a challenge and waited for Faron's answer. But she was caught off guard when, instead of meeting her lips, he pulled away.

Faron sighed heavily and rolled off her. He lay on his back on the floor, seemingly struggling over something. Tal sat up on her elbows and watched him. Frustration built within her over his sudden change in behavior. She wanted to accuse him of taunting her these past few weeks and then backing down when she took action. She watched Faron's chest heave, unable to gather her thoughts.

"We have an audience."

Tal's attention snapped to the opening where Egan, to his credit, looked away, blushing. "How long have you been standing there?" she asked with a harsher tone than she intended.

Egan opened his mouth to answer, but didn't say anything.

Tal crossed her arms over her chest, fists clenched. "You knew?" she snapped at Faron.

"I tried to warn you." Faron shrugged at the ceiling.

"What part of all that was a warning?!"

He smirked to himself. "The part where I didn't undress you."

Egan coughed from his position, and Tal scoffed. "Tal, the gals had some information for me."

Tal groaned and stood with effort. "Let's talk by the river. I need air." She ignored Faron's chuckle and stormed out of the tunnel.

———

"Oona's been feeding me information from the brothel. Two of the girls went missing the night of the... uh... Communal," Egan began. He rubbed a hand behind his neck nervously.

Tal swore. "It's been over two weeks! Why are we learning this now?"

"I'm sorry. I was on duty that night with Syb. Badger and Gully kept to their usual routine. Nothing strange at all, I swear. Oona thought the girls escaped. It's why she never mentioned it. They had already been planning it. But she overheard the headmistress last night threaten someone about stealing her girls without compensation."

"Who?" Faron snapped.

"She couldn't tell. A client called for her before they stepped into the hall."

The three of them sat at the tunnel opening. Nearly two months ago and almost every day since, Tal practiced her newly discovered talent of breathing fire. She thought back to that night and the hope they had felt. So much and nothing at all had changed since then, but she could feel a crossroads on the horizon, and she didn't feel ready for it.

"There's more," Egan continued. "One of our little problems has developed a bit of an addiction." Egan's main source of information came from the brothel. The women there favored him. He claimed they preferred his kindness to their usual patrons. Tal wondered if he simply enjoyed a change from the tunnels.

"Was he there when the women went missing?" Tal's eyes shot daggers at Egan.

"No, that meeting was in the morning. He only goes at night. He's been using his newly earned coin to visit Nemina almost every night this week, and he talks. He has been summoned to the palace for a meeting with his associates, as he calls them."

Both Tal and Faron stiffened. "The palace?" they asked in unison.

"With the king?" Tal asked.

"With who?" Faron said at the same time.

Egan shook his head. "Someone important, that's all he implied. He was very proud of himself."

Faron frowned while Tal swore. "And what of his coin? Did you get a chance to look at it?"

Egan nodded. "Gold coin with the king's seal. Just like Pochette's."

"The king's seal? You're sure?" Faron's voice twisted with worry.

Tal pulled out the coin she kept in her pocket and handed it to him. "The apparition gave this to Pochette. We've tracked several other coins, just like this one, around the docks."

Faron inspected it and shook his head. "This is not the king's seal. It's a good attempt, but it's fake." He handed it back to Tal.

"Can you prove it?" Egan asked.

"I'll see what I can do."

Tal crossed her arms. "I'm still not convinced the king isn't involved. Everything has been pointing at him this whole time."

Faron's eyes widened at her. "Tal, think about what you're saying. Why would the king ally with the mages? Do you know what that would mean for the kingdom? For him?"

"Yeah, power." Tal already ran through the reasons in her head. Meladair suffered from violence, unbalanced classes, and a significant amount of poverty among other things. They were constantly in danger of being overtaken by any of the foreign powers, even from those within. A partnership with the mages could provide the protection the king didn't have access to locally.

Egan tilted his head, thinking. "If power is what they're after, why wouldn't they just overthrow the king? What would he have to offer that they couldn't easily take on their own? I mean, Rain and Syb lived in a village full of warriors, and they didn't stand a chance. We need their take on this one."

Tal stood. "I don't know. Maybe he's offering the throne without a fight. Or the secrets of our enemies. Think. Syb's vision has to do with that room in *his* palace. The two servants were tortured underneath it in a secret dungeon. And then we found the girl in *his* own private residence, guarded by mages. And now, this urchin is going to the same godsdamned palace. There is no way the king doesn't know about it." She headed off to her room. She had a bounty she needed to fulfill before the others returned.

Faron caught up to her. "Tal, don't jump to any conclusions here. We don't have all the information."

She stopped and faced him. "Look, Faron, I know he's your friend. But can you really look at all the facts, and tell me you don't suspect he's behind this? Can you honestly say he would never do whatever it takes to keep power?"

Faron shook his head. "You don't know him."

She turned and started walking again. "Well, maybe you don't either."

"Tal, wait." Faron reached for her arm and slid his hand down to hers. The satisfying chill that spread across her skin distracted her momentarily.

She turned to him and could see the concern in his features. "Don't worry. I'm not going to storm the palace," she teased. The lines on Faron's face softened.

"What if I could prove to you that it's not him?"

"Aside from finding who is responsible, I don't see how you could." She wanted to believe him, wanted to believe that the king didn't invite mages into their land, but the evidence suggested otherwise. Either the king was corrupt, or he was completely oblivious to what happened right under his nose and wasn't suited for the role. "I trust you," she said. "But until you can prove it's not him, he's the first person I'll blame for anything mage related."

Faron nodded. "Understood."

She sighed, wishing they had a little bit longer to explore what had happened between them before Egan interrupted. "Sounds like our evenings are about to get exciting."

Faron stepped into her and forced her back into the wall. "I thought things had already started to get exciting." He leaned down and brushed her lips with his.

She let him tease her a moment more. When he didn't deepen the kiss, she put her hands on his chest and pushed him away playfully. "You've been coming here for weeks, and *now* you're ready to make a move?"

He walked backwards toward his exit to the street above. With both hands up in surrender, he said, "What can I say? I've had a taste. Now I want more." With a bow and a wink, he headed off and left Tal to her responsibilities.

21

Talwyn blinked in surprise when Faron stood in her doorway early the next morning. He had a mischievous gleam in his eyes while he waited for her to finish sheathing her knives in the holsters strapped across her back and on her thighs. "I think you may be a little overly prepared."

"Did you forget that we're in the slums? I piss off every criminal at least once a day, and the mages are still hunting me down." She sheathed the last dagger inside her boot and pulled the leg of her trousers down over it.

"You're safe as long as I'm with you."

His playful tone caught her attention, and she chuckled. "Wasn't I the one that saved you at the incinerator?" She stepped into his space. He propped one arm along the doorway and leaned over her. His proximity made her face flush, and she couldn't stop the easy smile that pulled at her lips.

He leaned dangerously close to her. "I seem to remember a certain someone needing to be pulled out of the river," he whispered.

Talwyn's heartbeat pounded in her chest. She didn't dare breathe.

"I have a surprise." He pulled back.

Tal couldn't help her disappointment, but she could see the mischief in his gaze. He motioned for her to leave first and followed close behind. She peeked at him over her shoulder. She bit her lip, trying to compose herself, but his tongue glided over his own lips, and her fury roared southward. She clamped her teeth shut and worked to rein it back in.

The small exchanges continued as he led her to the bakery, saying they needed food before he brought her to their destination. "You've been delivering baskets every day. Did you forget to pack?"

"That food was for everyone else. I want to have a taste from this amazing baker Egan keeps talking about."

Tal secretly wondered if he made the excuse to support the business owner. When they arrived, Evania squealed at the sight of the swordsman who had first come to her rescue. Despite being without his maroon suit, she recognized him instantly. Faron hugged the siblings and pulled a trinket for each of them out of his pocket. When they ran off, he greeted the baker and his wife. By the exchange between them, Tal guessed the noble had visited the children before. She suspected Faron's penchant for gift giving extended to the family.

Shortly after, the two of them stood on either side of a display while Tal sampled a roll. She locked eyes with Faron when she bit into it. She noticed the tick in his jaw, how the corner of his lips lifted. He took a deep breath. "Now, now," he breathed, his voice hoarse, "behavior like that is going to get you in trouble."

Tal chuckled and stepped around the display until she stood in front of him. She opened her mouth to say something that surely would have gotten her into the kind of trouble he referred to when footsteps behind her signaled a newcomer. Faron tensed and stared over her shoulder.

"Your Majesty," Daire commanded from behind Tal. She turned to catch him straightening from a bow. "The council requests your presence and has sent me to escort you back to the palace."

Talwyn stared at Daire in confusion. She laughed. Daire must have been mocking Faron. But his face remained the mask of a captain, and he refused to meet her gaze. She turned back to Faron who clenched his jaw and pursed his lips. His whole body went rigid. Tal gaped between the two men.

"What?" she breathed.

When Faron didn't respond, the knight persisted, "I really must insist, Your Majesty."

"Majesty?" she asked Faron, her voice rising an octave. He closed his eyes and sighed without relieving the tension in his body. "Majesty?" she said, louder now.

"Tal—" Defeat coated Faron's voice.

She laughed incredulously, turned to Daire who still refused to acknowledge her, then to Faron who reached for her. "No." She pulled back and tossed the bread on the ground. She darted out of the bakery past a wide-eyed Eddard. Faron yelled at Daire to give him a minute then called after her.

Tal hurried down the street, unsure of her destination. Her mind raced with thoughts of betrayal and confusion. Her breath hitched. She pulled a dagger from the sheath at her hip; the familiarity of the handle helped her focus to keep her fury at bay. She paced toward the water, where the sound of her boots on the wooden planks of the pier provided a rhythm to focus her thoughts.

"Tal, wait!" Faron called behind her. He grabbed her arm, turning her around.

She ripped it out of his grasp. "Majesty?" she spat the word at him. He flinched. "Please, Tal."

"The king!" She ran her empty hand through her hair and turned her face to the sky. "Was this all a joke? Have you had your fun pretending to slum it with the poor orphan from the docks? Am I a joke to you?" Her voice shook with anger.

"Let me explain," he pleaded, holding his hands up in surrender.

"Explain what, Faron? Hells, I can't believe I trusted you. I was a fool. The *king*! The rake king who spends his mornings sneaking out of women's beds. Gods, I should have known someone like you would never—" She wouldn't finish the thought aloud.

"Tal, please." He reached for her again, but she pulled back.

"Don't touch me," she snapped. Tears burned in her eyes, but she willed them to stay put. A thought occurred to her. "Is that why you were at the incinerator that night? Did you plan for that to happen?

Try to get close to me, so you can get me alone? Take me back to your dungeons? Hells, did you order the mages to come after me? You did a fine job acting surprised when I showed you my fury, didn't you? When did you really learn about my magic? What were you planning to do with me?"

"Gods no! Tal. I had no idea. How could you think that?" He stepped closer to her again when she tried to back away.

"You lied, Faron. You lied to all of us. You lied to me. You—" Her voice broke. "You kissed me, Faron. Was that a lie too? Dammit I can't believe I actually thought—" A tear fell onto her cheek, and she cursed herself. She dropped her dagger and wiped at it angrily with both hands.

"Please, just let me explain."

"What is there to explain? You had your fun slumming it with the commoners, watched us starve and suffer in filth and violence, then went back to your pretty palace with your overflowing plates, and stupid balls. Did you go back to your noble friends and laugh about the commoner who reeks of rubbish and thinks the king lo—" She caught herself on the last word.

"It wasn't like that, and you know it." His tormented gaze burned into her.

"Do I? Because I don't even know who you are. Isn't that right, *James*?" She used the king's name like a weapon. Another tear fell, and she let it. She clenched her fists at her sides.

"My name is Faron." He stressed each word. "Let me explain," he pleaded.

"No."

"Tal—"

"I said no! I don't want to hear it." She bent and picked up her dagger, flipping it in her grasp for comfort. She couldn't look him in the eyes. "Don't follow me," she said at last and continued down the docks until she could find a tunnel entrance. She didn't glance back, but she knew Faron stayed where she left him. He called after her twice but didn't follow.

That night, Tal sat in Gale's Tavern. There were places closer to the tunnels where she could get a pint, but none that she could get away with swinging a fist at a few patrons. She needed the rush of adrenaline to distract her from her anger. She curled her hands around the metal cup and hunched in her seat. Her eyes scanned the patrons, searching for one who would fight back, and her gaze caught on a familiar face with sandy hair near the bar. When their eyes met, he turned his head in an obvious attempt to appear occupied. Tal narrowed her eyes at him, noting the nervous tapping of his fingertip on the bar top.

"So, what if he's the king?" Sybil broke Tal's concentration and gnawed on a greasy piece of mystery meat. She had returned from her bounty earlier that afternoon, and it took both her and Carrick to stop Tal from burning down half the docks. "I say that actually works to our advantage. He's got even better connections than we thought. Hells, he's the most powerful person in the kingdom. What's wrong with that?"

Tal stared at her drink but remained silent.

"Oh, I see. It's because you kissed him, isn't it?" Sybil leaned forward, excitement in her deep brown eyes.

"Drop it Syb," Carrick warned while Tal seethed.

"No, no. That's it!" She slapped the table. "Our little ball of fire is *embarrassed*. Did the pretty royal hurt your ego?" She smirked.

Tal, who had taken a swig of her ale, slammed her pint on the wooden table. She leaned across and hissed, "If you want to keep the pretty hair on your head, I suggest you shut your beak."

Sybil's grin grew further as she sat back. "Ooh ho ho! Wait a minute, I think she *likes* him! She thought she had a chance! Don't worry, you can still be his mistress."

Tal shoved her chair back as she planted her feet and stared at Sybil with fire in her eyes. She clenched her fists, and almost hoped Sybil would challenge her to a fight.

Carrick pushed away from the table. "Grab your drink. Let's go."

Tal stomped to the bar. She shoved Eddard's shoulder. "Following me? Has he sent his pups after me?"

To his credit, the guardsman did his best to appear dumbfounded. "Goodness, Tal, what's with all the hostility? I lived here, remember?"

Carrick grabbed her arm. "You're not mad at *him*."

She ripped her arm out of Carrick's grasp and pushed out of Gale's, grumbling that she didn't even get to throw *one* punch. The tavern door hit the wall with a satisfying *crack*.

Carrick let her walk down the street, following closely behind, and then stepped beside her. "Let's go to the pier." He didn't wait for her to respond, but she followed him anyway. They made their way to the water and Tal marched down the wooden planks. She glared at the large ship docked there and kicked at its moorings. Mice scurried out of her way.

At the end of the pier, Carrick turned and took out his knives. He eyed Tal expectantly until she took out two of her own. Reluctantly, she stepped beside him and turned her back to the open water.

"You first." He elbowed her.

Tal let out a frustrated sigh and threw her knife with as much force as she could. It hit with a loud *thunk* in the second wooden post on the right. Her aim was sloppy, landing two inches from the bottom, on the right side of the surface facing them.

"Should we go to the Willow for an easier target?"

Tal scowled. If she focused, she could almost see the enormous tree in the distance, another reminder that the life they lived veered so far from the one they planned all those years ago.

Carrick threw one of his own knives, and hit the third post on the left, an inch to the side, two inches from the top. They continued like that, each taking a turn to out-throw the other. When they had each thrown four knives, they walked down the pier and silently picked the weapons from the wood. They continued to the beginning, turned, and started again.

They'd played this game since stealing their first dagger. It had been a way to pass the time. Then, as their skill improved, it became an exercise to protect themselves or hone their hunting skills. The twins taught them even more when they showed up one day, two malnourished teens stowed away on a ship alone but with extensive fighting knowledge. Their skillset eventually outgrew the game at the pier, but Talwyn and Carrick often still went there when something troubled them.

"She has her motives for goading you on like that." Sybil had a knack for pushing someone toward an event that would make one of her visions come true. However, the seer never revealed her reasoning.

Tal threw another knife, landing four posts down but slightly off-center this time. She nodded. "It would be easier if she would just tell me her visions, and I can decipher them myself."

"You know she doesn't work like that." Carrick's knife crossed over the invisible line down the center of the wooden planks and landed dead-center on Tal's post. He smirked, and she answered with a scowl.

"Right, she's told us a million times," Tal mocked. "I don't see how it's much different than telling us where to throw a knife in a fight," she grumbled. The hollow *thunk* of Carrick's knife punctuated the momentary silence. "But what is she getting at? Is she trying to get me to hate him? To confront him? To marry him?" She scoffed at the last part.

They walked back to the end to pull their knives out. When they readied to start over, Carrick asked, "Well, do you like him?"

Tal glowered at him.

"Come on, Tal. We could all see it. And I know you kissed him last night." He held onto his knife, ignoring his turn.

She grumbled something about Egan being terrible at keeping secrets.

"Why can't you just admit it? There's nothing wrong with caring for him."

Tal's next knife went wide and landed in the water. She swore then turned to Carrick. "Because it's pointless, Carrick." She threw up her arms in defeat and turned to him. "He's the king! Not some insignificant noble with few responsibilities. Even if I did like him, it wouldn't change anything. Or did you forget that commoners aren't supposed to even be in the same room as royalty, let alone fall in lo—" She stopped herself. *What a stupid thought.* She didn't love Faron. They barely knew each other, even less so than she thought. But she couldn't lie to herself that, at one point, she had wondered where her developing feelings could lead, and if Faron would feel the same.

Carrick worked at a nail in the wood with the toe of his brown leather boot. "He likes you too, you know."

"Not enough to tell me the truth apparently." She started picking at the handle of her knife. "No matter how either of us feels, it doesn't change the fact that he lied to us. He could have been misleading us this whole time so that we don't find wherever these mages are hiding or maybe he's been giving us false information to protect himself."

"I think you know that he has no involvement with that. Everything he's done up to this point has given us more information than we could have gathered on our own. He may have been protecting himself at first, but I think he just didn't know how to tell us the truth yet. Not to mention, would we have believed him? And what would we have done to him, what with our accusing the king of being at the center of everything?"

Tal sheathed her knives and sighed. "It doesn't matter, Carrick. He lied. We can't trust him." She walked to the post where her knife had entered the water and glared at the dark surface. With a groan, she stripped off her clothes and dove into the frigid waters to retrieve her weapon.

For the second time in as many days, Faron came to the tunnels to talk to Talwyn. The first time, Sybil gladly would have let him in, but she relented when Talwyn threatened to burn off her eyebrows in her sleep.

"I only want to explain. That's all. Then I'll leave." His voice carried to the bend in the tunnels where Tal hid. She peered around the corner and saw nothing but Carrick's enormous form filling the space.

"She doesn't want to talk to you." Carrick crossed his arms.

Silence rang through the tunnel, and Tal could imagine the resigned slump in his shoulders. "I know. I'm sorry. Can you at least give this to her for me?"

Tal took a step out of the shadow to get a better view only to see the top of Faron's head as he retreated toward the exit. Carrick remained, ensuring Faron didn't turn around, and Tal used his body as a shield.

"What is it?" she asked when her friend turned and joined her. Wordlessly, Carrick handed Tal a small object wrapped in a thin cloth. Embroidered on a corner in maroon thread were the words, "I'm sorry." She pulled the cloth open and frowned at the sugared pastry.

Carrick clapped a hand on her shoulder. Since the night on the pier, he began inviting Tal to his bounties like they were kids again. They didn't talk about Faron, and Tal was grateful her friend always knew what she needed. She shoved the pastry into her mouth in two bites and let the cloth napkin fall to the tunnel floor.

They had discussed at length the new information Egan provided. Rainier reminded them of Sybil's vision taking place in the palace, and Tal's mistrust grew further. Tal wouldn't openly connect the faceless royal with the man she'd spent half the summer with. And, while she insisted they couldn't trust the king, Rainier disagreed. "We can be cautious, but one rumor of a meeting at the palace isn't enough to prove Faron is involved, especially given who the rumor is coming from."

Tal flinched at the use of his name.

Rain's dagger picked at something under his nail. "Honestly, it's more possible that someone else at the palace is sneaking behind Faron's back and trying to usurp power. Remember the falsified ledgers? Syb even said her visions of Faron have all proven he's on our side. Trust him, Tal."

Tal glared at the seer. "What visions?" Her friend hadn't mentioned seeing anything regarding the noble—*royal*, she mentally corrected herself.

Sybil threw her shoulders back and narrowed her eyes. She threw her hair behind her shoulder as if this new information wasn't important. "Since the night at the incinerator, I've been trying to force visions like you asked. Sometimes he's in them. Anything involving the mages shows him fighting on our side, *against* them," she added.

"Are these visions of the future or symbolic fights?" Carrick joined the conversation.

"It's hard to tell. My guess is both, given what we've seen in the past and the fuzzy details."

"What fuzzy details, Syb?" She hated how cryptic the woman could be. Tal suspected she knew more than she let on but could never get clear answers.

Sybil waved her hand dismissively. "Just my understanding of it all, maybe something about a building, or who is there. I can't say for sure."

Tal crossed her arms, but Rain interjected before she could say anything. "We need to be diligent, get information, and look at the facts objectively. Nobody goes barreling into a situation without all of us discussing it first, got it?" Everyone except Tal nodded. "Right, Tal?"

She grumbled out an affirmative and stormed off to her room.

22

For the next two weeks, Tal tried to keep busy by taking on as many bounties as possible, but she still brooded over her conflicting thoughts. Madge hired her to gather a few different herbs that could only be found a few hours' ride outside the kingdom. It would have been a good day away from life at the docks. It should have been, but Tal was a glutton for punishment. While packing her weapons, her eyes brushed past the two battle axes laid out before her. She considered chucking them into the river, but it would have been an insult to the talented blacksmith who crafted them.

"Where did you get those?" Sybil stood in the opening, curiosity filling her features.

"They were a gift." Tal eyed the design stamped into the metal. "From F—"

"I could take them off your hands if you don't want them."

"You can take them off my dead body." Tal grabbed the axes and strapped them onto her back. She hefted her satchel, filled with enough food for the day, and faced Sybil. "What's with the face?"

Sybil's eyes shifted from a glazed stare at the wall to focus on Tal. She blinked, like she hadn't been paying attention. "If you want to chat, you know where to find me." She lingered, blocking Tal's exit.

"Thanks, but I'm fine."

Sybil waited a moment longer then stepped aside. She watched silently as her friend passed.

Tal ignored Sybil's odd stare and left the tunnels. The weight of the axes pressed against her back, and she vowed to find some beast to sink the blades into. Perhaps the fight would calm her fury a bit.

Madge had already paid for her to rent a horse from a nearby stable, but Tal had other plans. Adrenaline rushed through her system when she snuck into the palace grounds. She'd done it plenty of times to meet Daire. The palace stable was relatively quiet aside from the horses left in their stalls. She snagged a bridle, saddle and reins and found the gray speckled mare. Pepper recognized her and snuffed out a greeting. Quietly, Tal prepared the horse who nuzzled her playfully. When she mounted the saddle, a pang of disappointment clawed at her stomach at the ease of her escape.

She urged Pepper forward, and Eddard stepped out from the side of the stables, blocking her path. Tal pulled on the reins and slouched in the saddle. "Move aside, Ed. I'm going for a ride."

His finger tapped on the handle of his sword, his palm resting on the pommel. "You know I can't let you go alone, Tal."

"He can't stop me from fulfilling my bounties." She narrowed her eyes.

"I won't interfere. I could use a little fresh air." If his reason for stopping her had been anything other than Faron's orders, Tal may have considered allowing him to join. But she needed to get away from the constant reminders. She needed to free her mind.

"I just need a moment, Ed, a quick ride north. I'll be back in a few hours."

His finger drummed along in the waiting silence. *Tap. Tap. Tap.*

"I'll bring back fresh water from the stream," she offered in a sing-song voice.

He sighed. "Fine. Take my waterskin. It's bigger." He stepped into the stable and rested a hand on Pepper's shoulder. "If you're not back in four hours, I'm coming after you."

"Good luck finding me."

Eddard stepped back, shaking his head. "Faron is going to kill me," he said under his breath.

Jens waited outside the stables. When Ed told him to let Tal go, he narrowed his eyes at her before wordlessly marching to the gate.

Tal gritted her teeth and kicked Pepper into a slow trot past the guards that watched her with apprehension in their eyes.

Once she allowed the mare to open up, a sense of release came over her, and she relaxed into the ride. Pepper, it seemed, was all too eager to be set loose. Tal's recklessness gave her an adrenaline rush that eased some of the tension she'd been feeling. She'd purposefully chosen Madge's bounty when Rainier listed off those remaining. He hadn't questioned her judgement, and Tal appreciated the return to normalcy. The mountains were full of predators, animal or otherwise, and she welcomed the danger.

She leaned into the horse, smiling at the wind. It was a small jab at the man who had lied to her the whole summer, but Tal felt some satisfaction. She would return Pepper as soon as she finished the job. Though, a part of her hoped Faron would fret over the missing horse for a little while.

The long ride to the mountainside required several stops to allow Pepper to rest and hydrate. Difficult terrain sometimes demanded a slower pace, and once or twice, the mare's ears pricked up at something that caused her unease. Tal also felt the familiar chill on the back of her neck from being watched. But other than a mere feeling, they encountered no trouble on their journey.

They reached their destination, and Tal dismounted. She grabbed the horse's lead and walked ahead as she scanned for the signs Madge mentioned. The first herb proved easy enough to spot. The tiny blue flowers grew on the western side of a cliff face. She dug up the plant, roots and all, and placed it carefully in the pouch Madge had insisted she use to transport the item.

The second herb grew on the edge of a stream. "Don't go grabbing the first mossy rug you see. This one has gray hairs growing in it, like the hair of a woman a few years past her prime," the healer had said.

Tal walked Pepper to the water and let her drink. She regarded the mare while she sat on a rock and indulged on bread and a bottle of ale. Tal found nothing but peace this far from home. The shouting of fishermen and sailors didn't cover up the calls of the birds. The air here was crisp and clean, not muddled by garbage and filth. And the painted landscape displayed colors unlike anything Tal would find by the docks.

Life flourished in the misty mountain air—life ruled by a set of laws that man disobeyed. At the docks, the hierarchy constantly changed, creating danger everywhere she turned. While Tal's fury could save her from almost any situation, she'd complicated things when she'd opened her heart. Without fury like hers, her friends were vulnerable. And Tal would be much happier with them far away from a kingdom like Meladair.

She finished her refreshment and searched for the hairy green moss, telling Pepper not to wander off. As she cut the moss away from a river rock, she noticed how eerily silent it had become. Pepper no longer grazed along the bank of the stream. Tal jumped to her feet and quickly searched the area to no avail. She cursed herself for getting so distracted. Quickly packing up the moss and tossing her satchel across her back, she pulled out a second dagger and went in search of the wandering mare.

The tracks were easy enough to follow. As the mud turned into grass, signs indicated something very heavy passed through. She found Pepper grazing on the other side of a rocky outcropping. Tal shook her head at the mare. "While I don't think he'll be too upset that I borrowed you." Pepper lifted her head at Tal's approach, "I'm not sure the man will forgive me if I lose y—"

Before Tal could finish her sentence, the horse let out a frightened whinny and took off toward her. She barely had time to jump out of Pepper's path. She hit the ground and rolled, landing back on her feet. Not a moment later, a dark blur shot past, followed by several more. Tal swore and took off after them.

She sheathed her two daggers and reached inwardly for her fury, praying she had built up enough magic stores to avoid crashing out here by herself. She launched one fireball after another, missing all but one of the predators. It erupted in a column of flame as the others ran past.

A massive brown wolf circled back and turned its attention on her, snarling viciously. It leapt at Tal as she dropped to the ground. She thrust her dagger upwards as the wolf passed overhead. Its pained yowl died when it landed in a bloodied heap.

Tal jumped to her feet and followed the snarling wolves, holding onto hope with each of Pepper's distressed whinnies. The mare found herself cornered against the high walls of a cliff face. Five wolves surrounded Pepper. The sixth, a smaller black wolf, lunged and received a hoof to the snout. It yelped and jumped back, shaking its head.

Without a moment to catch her breath, Tal threw a flame high above and sent a prowling predator crashing into the stone behind it. It fell to the ground with a sickening thud. Ten eyes snapped to Tal and a chorus of answering growls filled the area. She grabbed her axes off her back as the pack stalked around her. Her chest heaved with each breath, her fury pulsing with each thunderous heartbeat.

A rusty orange wolf lunged and forced Tal into the path of another. She pivoted and sunk an axe into the black furry neck. A third wolf's brown muzzle clamped down on her arm, pulling a shriek from Tal. She shot off a blast of fury into the wolf's face. It released her, and Tal wasted no time pulling her axe out of the black wolf. She swung her weapon into the beast again for good measure and turned in time to ram it up into the brown wolf's jaw. Its head and snout displayed a gruesome series of burned fur and flesh. With a fierce cry, Tal spun and hefted her attacker over her shoulder. The sight of the dead animal did little to soothe the searing pain in her arm or the tightness of her lungs.

Growling behind Tal precluded a sharp pain at her shoulder. She cried out and her knees buckled. The animal thrashed Tal around. The orange wolf joined the fray and latched onto her ankle, pulling her in the other direction. In a desperate attempt, she concentrated her fury on her shoulder where stinking fur brushed her cheek and teeth ground into bone. She recalled the training sessions in the tunnel with Faron not so long ago and willed her magic to burst from her shoulder. It pulled painfully at the fury within her chest. A short stream of flame exploded into the wolf's face, blasting it backward. Melted fur and flesh overpowered the mountain air as flames engulfed the unmoving body.

The orange wolf dragged Tal backward, spears of pain blinding her every time it tugged. She swung her axe, but the beast dodged her attack. A snarl from the cliff wall above had Tal throwing her axe in front of her face. Black fur appeared by Tal's head when a fierce roar drowned the wolf's snarls, and Pepper stampeded into the fight. The snarling wolf could only turn before being trampled by the mare's hooves. Pepper continued her battle cry as she stomped and kicked her would-be attacker until it was good and dead.

Jaws corrected their grip on her leg, and Tal cried out. The orange wolf took Tal's distraction to jump on top of her. It lunged for her neck and latched onto her axe's handle. Her shoulder wanted to give out. Her fury pulsed weakly in her chest. She searched for her magic stores and screamed at the wolf as it snapped and snarled around her weapon. A painful itch in her throat reminded Tal of the night so many weeks ago by the water with her friends cheering her on. With her hands barely holding the wolf at bay against her axe, she took a deep breath and released her remaining hold on her fury as she exhaled. The magic warmed Tal as it exited her body, and a stream of flame shot into the wolf's mouth and down its throat. Several moments passed before the animal realized, only too late, it had made a grave error. It stumbled backwards, snapping at nothing, and then dropped dead onto the ground.

Tal lay bleeding, gasping for breath, and exhausted from the fight. Her chest hollow, her fury quieted. Pepper nuzzled her head. "Thanks for the help." When the mare nudged her harder, Tal reached up a hand and rubbed her snout. "I'm okay."

She groaned as she sat up, the sight of the shredded flesh along her leg enough to send a wave of nausea washing over her. She would need an elixir if she wanted it to heal at all. The wound would turn green before it ever healed properly on its own. The injury to her shoulder appeared less gruesome, but by the amount of blood seeping through the bite marks, the wound must have been deeper.

Thanks to her earlier drink, Tal's pain dulled slightly, but that also meant she would bleed more and couldn't take any elixir to heal quickly. She cursed herself and the damn ale.

She wrapped her wounds slowly, using her axes to cut her favorite jacket. It was a waste of a perfectly good jacket, and Madge would call it a shoddy job, but it helped to stem the blood flow.

Getting on the horse proved a task in and of itself even when Pepper bent down to help her into the saddle. Reluctantly, Tal went back through the woods to retrieve the satchel she had dropped at some point in her pursuit as well as the remaining herb for Madge. She would have abandoned the bounty if she thought the old woman would still help her, but the healer was spiteful. She would let Tal bleed out on her doorstep if she returned without those herbs.

By the time she turned Pepper homeward, she'd bled through her makeshift bandages and swayed in the saddle, too dizzy to stay upright. Tal found the clear summer sky and asked the gods to give her a little help just this once. She needed a miracle if she hoped to survive the amount of blood she would lose over the next few hours.

On the ride back, the aftermath of using her fury and her injuries proved to be too much. She struggled to stay conscious fearing she would fall off the mare, and by their pace, the ride back would take a full day. She used the strap from the satchel to secure herself to Pepper's saddle, and soon lost track of reality as she gave into the darkness.

"Blazing hells! Tal! What happened?!"

Someone yelled at her, but the pounding in her head, the pain in her shoulder, arm, and leg, and the sheer exhaustion pulling at her body won her attention.

"Tal! Wake up! Can you hear me?!"

"Madge," she groaned. Her tongue stuck to the roof of her mouth. She needed water.

"You need an elixir. Where aren't you hurt? Can I carry you?"

Tal let out a pained grunt, and the voice took it as an invitation because suddenly arms pulled her out of the saddle that she had somehow managed to stay seated in. She yelped at the fierce ache in her shoulder.

"Sorry, sorry! Hells, woman, what happened to you? If I had known when you left this morning that you would come back like this, I would have stopped you."

"This morning?" Her head fell back, and she grimaced. She'd hoped that she would have slept off the time it took for the ale to leave her system. She still had half a day to wait before she could take an elixir to heal her wounds. She groaned again.

"I'm taking you into the palace. We'll get you an elixir."

His words and voice finally registered. Faron. Of course it was him. Here he stood, as if he had been waiting for her to come back. "No." She shook her head. "I need Madge." Even talking hurt. She wanted to go back to the dark oblivion, but the pain awakened her senses with each breath.

"Don't be stubborn. You've been bleeding for what looks like hours." When Tal shook her head again, the voice stopped then sighed. "Dammit, Tal. You and that godsdamned ale. I'll flay Ed and Jens, so help me."

Had she any energy, Tal would have felt remorse for her part in their coming punishment. Her head pounded within the fog that tried to pull her back into nothingness.

Getting her in a saddle was even more painful the second time. When he climbed up behind her and pulled her into him, Tal inwardly cursed her body for curling into his embrace.

Faron took off at a gallop, apologizing the whole way every time she grunted through the pain. She wanted to let her anger surface. She wanted to call him a liar, and a bastard, and so many other things, but she was too damn tired to do any of that. Instead, she remembered what she felt those weeks that he came to the tunnels, and his hold around her middle offered a small comfort.

Once again, they arrived at Madge's in the middle of the night. This time, Faron didn't bother waiting outside. He brought the horse to the back, pulled Tal down, and kicked the door in with her in his arms. If she wasn't trying to stay mad at him, she might have made some suggestive comment.

"Madge!" Faron yelled as he gently deposited Tal on the front table. "Madge, down here! Quick!"

"There's no need to tell me where you are, you dewberry. There's only two rooms in this whole house." The elderly woman walked down the stairs and scowled at her intruders.

"She's hurt, and she's had ale. An elixir won't work." He stumbled over his own words, his tone frantic.

Tal eyed the noble—*king*—and thought he might be overreacting. His hands ran through his hair, gripped his neck, then returned to his dark waves. His eyes roamed over her body, his movements growing more agitated by the second. He shifted his weight from foot to foot.

"You and your cursed elixirs. You barge into *my* house at all hours of the night, worked up like the woman's dying, and you insult me by suggesting you would prefer elixirs?" the healer chastised. "Go and secure your horse before I tell you both to go rot in the river." She shooed Faron out the door and turned to Tal. "Now you know why I don't get my herbs myself." She tsked.

"You could have warned me there was a wolf's den on that mountain," Tal griped from the table.

Madge lit a candle by the cupboard, then turned back to where Tal lay. "Would you have listened? You're as stubborn as that boy out there. Ain't no way anything I say would give you pause. Did you get the herbs at least?"

"In the satchel," Tal said through clenched teeth. Talking through the pain felt nearly impossible but so did doing much of anything.

The old woman rummaged through the satchel at Tal's side. She pulled out a bloodied axe and fixed a stern eye on Tal, then deposited it on the chair by Tal's leg. "I'll bet you went alone, didn't you?" When Tal didn't answer, she shook her head. "You've got a fearsome man out there who cares about you, and you are too stubborn to let him help you."

Tal sighed. She didn't come here to be lectured, but she also didn't have the energy to argue. "He's the king, you know."

"Aye, and what of it?"

She turned her head to the woman. "You knew?"

Madge put her hands on her hips and cocked her head. "You didn't?" She tsked again. "Girl, how do you not know who your own king is?"

"Seriously, Madge? The guy never shows his face at the docks; nobody from the palace does. How would I know who he is?"

"That man has been coming to the docks every night for the last two years. Don't tell me he doesn't show his face."

"Really? To do what? Laugh at the poor?"

"To feed them, girl. Have you not seen the baskets he brings every night? Has since the first night."

"And what is this I hear about you not charging anyone?" She tried to sit up, but Madge pushed her back down. "I can barely afford your prices!"

"I charge what can be afforded. If you didn't waste your money on the drink, you'd be rolling in gold."

"Is she going to be alright?" Faron asked from the doorway.

Madge waved a fern at him menacingly. "You bring her here in this state, give me all of ten breaths to wake up, and start making all these demands. King or no, I'll kick you both out on the street."

Faron's face softened. He walked to Tal's side and saw the axe on the chair. His lips twitched. When he searched Tal's face, she turned away from him. "What happened?" he asked gently.

Tal swallowed. "Wolves."

"Wolves? Plural?" He sounded impressed and concerned at the same time.

"They attacked Pepper while she grazed."

"And let me guess," Madge said from her cupboard. She was hard at work with rags, herbs, salves, and a mortar and pestle. "You thought you could save the animal against a bunch of born predators." Tal could see the woman shaking her head. "When will you learn that you're not invincible?"

"You hired me for a job. How was I supposed to get back without a horse?"

Madge came over to the table and started cleaning Tal's wounds with a rag dipped in some yellow and green paste in her pestle. "Sure, use that as your excuse. Damned fool is what you are." Madge chastised Tal more while she worked. She complained about the state of Tal's wounds, how much blood she'd lost, everything she could think of.

Tal began to think that the woman did it to distract her from the pain. She tensed each time Madge dabbed at her ravaged skin, and the woman set off on another rant. She tried her best not to make a sound, but occasionally a grunt or whimper slipped past her lips. When Faron grabbed her hand and squeezed, she squeezed back. She turned to see his face, finding the expression unreadable.

"Don't blame them."

Faron's lips pressed into a thin line.

"They tried to stop me, and I nearly ran them down."

"You don't need to lie for them. Ed has a soft spot for you. It compromises him." Tal tried to interject, but Faron continued, "It'll gut him when he hears what happened to you. He and Jens have been gone for hours looking for you."

She turned her head to the ceiling, swallowing down the emotion that clawed at her throat. "I'm sorry," she whispered.

Faron squeezed her hand with both of his.

Tal stared at the shadows flickering along the wooden slat ceiling while Madge tended to her wounds, and Faron drew circles on the back of her hand.

She didn't say anything, and neither did he. It wasn't time for apologies, and Tal was in no condition to accept them.

23

Whatever Madge did, it helped with the pain, and Tal soon relaxed enough to fall asleep. She awoke in her bed the next day with Carrick by her side, like so many times before. He scolded her for barreling into danger without hesitation. Described the terror at seeing her carried in by Faron, unconscious, battered, and bloody.

"I'm tired of seeing you hurt," he said.

"It was wolves, Carrick. I had a bounty to fill. Mages had nothing to do with it, just bad luck, something that could have happened any day."

He pursed his lips before saying, "And what am I supposed to do the next time you bleed out because you're too drunk to take an elixir?"

Tal raked a hand over her face. "Did you forget that we live in the docks? Life here isn't fair, nor is it lengthy. I could turn a corner tomorrow and run into an angry client with a knife and nothing to lose. You can't protect me from reality, nor from the mages. Stop acting like everything will somehow be okay."

Carrick sighed, but didn't say more. Instead, he told her about Faron, how the man was torn up over her, and Tal rolled her eyes. Faron had described her state when Pepper burst into the stables. There was so much blood, he initially thought the mare had also been injured. She collapsed in her stall upon their return, after what must have been a nonstop journey home. Tal made a mental note to visit Pepper and express her thanks.

"He brought three vials of healing elixir and a basket full of food for you. Said he'd be back tonight."

"I don't want him here," Tal snapped.

"Hells, Tal, the man probably saved your life. The least you can do is hear him out."

Rather than have this argument, Tal turned her head and closed her eyes. After a few minutes, Carrick sighed and left the room. Tal let sleep find her again. She woke up sometime in the afternoon and instantly regretted it. Her wounds throbbed. Any movement sent spears throughout her body. She was dehydrated, ravenous, and had a pounding headache.

Tal scowled at the sight of the basket of food and healing elixirs. She tried to convince herself she didn't need any of it, but Madge's words from the night before came back to her. "Your leg will never be the same. And good luck throwing those knives without pain," the healer chastised as she worked.

Tal bit her cheek but ignored Faron's gifts.

"Just accept it and get back in this fight, or infection will kill you before the mages do," Sybil criticized from the doorway.

"Oh, you've seen that, have you?" Tal retorted.

Syb exhaled sharply and shook her head before grabbing one of the healing elixirs and walking it over to Tal. She pulled the cork out and held out the vial. "Just drink it already."

Tal pursed her lips but did as she was told. When the yellow liquid hit her tongue, a wave of electricity washed through her body. After a few moments, her headache began to subside, and soon the pain from her wounds started to dull.

Sybil handed her a second bottle and nodded for her to drink that one as well. Satisfied, she left the room, but not before turning back to order Tal around some more. "Make sure you drink that third one and eat everything in that basket."

It took an hour for Tal to feel well enough to walk around, but she complied, albeit a little reluctantly. Hydrated, fed, and healing, she found her friends in the common area, not at all surprised to see them waiting for her recovery. Already anticipating their concern, she told them she needed to go see the horse. The men all tried to insist on someone joining her while Sybil ignored everyone. Ultimately, Carrick chose to accompany her.

Tal limped through the streets, Carrick at her side. He knew better than to offer help, but that didn't stop him from walking close enough to catch her. Movement in her periphery caught Tal's attention. A head full of dark brown messy locks disappeared around a building. She waited for the man to appear around the other side. Sure enough, a familiar face came into view, and Tal scowled at Waylon's mischievous grin. The noble bowed and flourished his hand, inviting her to continue.

"They're following me," she grumbled.

"Have been for a while now," Carrick murmured in a deep voice.

Tal made a rude gesture at her stalker, receiving riotous laughter in return.

"We noticed them the day after you were attacked." When Tal mumbled something about boundaries, he continued, "I confronted him. He said they were not to interfere unless you were in trouble. He's only worried about you."

"Oh, is that all?" she quipped.

Waylon followed them to the palace walls, and waved farewell with a cheery smile. Tal only narrowed her eyes in return.

Carrick walked her to the palace stables, where he waited outside.

"What? You're not going to follow me too?" she teased.

A smile cracked across his face. "Unlike our red leather wearing friend, I know better."

Pepper poked her head out and whinnied before Tal reached the stall. "Hey there, beautiful." Tal scratched the bridge of the mare's nose.

"I've got something for you." She pulled a carrot out of her satchel, and Pepper ate it without hesitation. "I hear you didn't stop until you got home." She scratched behind the horse's ears, and Pepper leaned into her hand. "Thank you. You saved my life." Tal hated getting emotional, but she would never forget how Pepper somehow knew that Tal needed help and then stopped at nothing to find it.

"She was meant to be the princess's horse," Faron said from behind.

She jumped back to face him and winced when she landed on her bad leg. Faron's eyes cut to the injury, then traveled the rest of her body, taking stock of her other wounds. She could feel the weight of his gaze and the memory of his kiss heated her face. She didn't want to acknowledge his lies, but she didn't want to forgive him either. Instead, she kept the conversation on neutral ground. "The princess?"

Faron nodded and stepped to the other side of Pepper's stall, almost brushing Tal as he passed her, causing her to tense. He focused on a spot on the horse's head, scratching her snout. "Pepper would have been Elora's birthday present, but she died in the fire before the celebration. When my father was appointed king, he gifted the horse to me, but I couldn't claim her. It didn't feel right. So, I rode other palace horses until I acquired Hazel." He nodded in the direction of the brown mare's stall. He watched Tal scratch Pepper for a few breaths. "She likes you," he noted. Tal didn't know what to say. Instead, she remained silent. "You're welcome to ride her whenever you like. I think she would enjoy having the same person in her saddle."

"You didn't give her away?"

He shrugged. "As I said, it didn't feel right."

Tal could tell he debated what to say. Her thoughts warred between her attraction to him and the betrayal she felt. The past two weeks felt strange not to have him around the tunnels. He was still Faron, the joyful swordsman who made his own clothes, but his secret life that he rarely shared with her turned out to be much grander than she expected. A small voice reminded her of the rumors of his philandering and the possibility that he was responsible for the mage attacks.

"I am not the one who hired the mages to come after you," he said as if he heard her thoughts.

Tal inhaled deeply, her worries interrupted by the pain of the knife in her heart that day at the bakery. Sighing, she turned harsh eyes on the king. "I didn't come here to have this conversation."

"I need you to understand that you are not in danger with me." His voice wasn't exactly pleading, but Tal could see the desperation in his eyes.

If he had been the one to tell her, she might have wanted to forgive him more easily. But Tal could not easily forget that Daire, of all people, revealed Faron's secret. And even if he hadn't hired the mages, he had deceived her. Trust was not easily given. Tal had yet to ever forgive someone who had lost her trust so completely. "Then tell me this, why is that scum meeting at your palace?"

Faron gritted his teeth. "I don't know."

"Then I suggest you find out, *your majesty*. Seems to me like you have a rat." She gave Pepper one last scratch behind the ear and refused to look at the king when she turned. She limped out of the stable. Faron didn't follow, nor did he say anything further. When she found Carrick beyond the wall, he stayed quiet.

Faron didn't come to the tunnels that night as he said he would. Tal guessed her coldness that afternoon changed his mind. She had no plans for the next day except to visit the cobbler and a tailor. She noted the state of her bloodied clothes. The boots and leather jacket would be expensive to replace.

Tal sat on her bed and tested the condition of her shoulder, rolling her arm around. She tested her ankle next. Not a single ache or pain. Her calf showed no signs of injury and bore her weight easily. She felt refreshed and fully healed thanks to the three vials of healing elixir and tried not to feel gratitude toward the man who gifted them to her. She tied up an old pair of boots and followed the echoing voices to the common area.

She stopped in the opening at the sight of the familiar handmade shirt and brown trousers with a missing pocket and uneven hem. Conversation halted and everyone avoided Tal's accusing glare except Sybil, who stuck her beaklike nose up in the air, a challenge. Tal stepped into the room and ignored the man sitting in his usual seat, directly across from her own spot. The basket of fresh food she had seen so often sat in the middle of the floor, and she spotted the jam cakes that she loved so much. Her eyes flicked from the breakfast treat to the man whose lips twitched like he wanted to smile at her. With effort, Tal looked away.

Her friends were all in various stages of eating their meal. They'd been spoiled during the weeks Faron had supplied food for them, and Tal realized they couldn't expect it to last forever. The king couldn't continue to gift them food when she refused to accept any apology of his.

Her stomach protested loudly, and Tal decided she would stop at the baker's before completing her errands.

"Oh, take the damn cake, you stubborn cow. No sense in letting delicious food go to waste because you don't want to seem grateful." Sybil rolled her eyes at Tal while everyone else stared.

Tal glared as Sybil shoved a powdered roll into her mouth. Her stomach growled again, and her resolve evaporated. She grabbed two of the jelly cakes, a piece of bread covered in different seeds, a block of white cheese, a boiled potato rolled in herbs, and a thick slice of salted hog meat. Tal savored the cake first, taking great pains to keep the satisfaction off her face as the sugary treat blasted her taste buds. She licked each finger thoroughly and washed it down with several gulps of goat's milk. Then she ravaged the remaining food, barely taking time to taste or chew anything and leaving a mess of crumbs and grease over her pants.

"It's no wonder everyone stared at you at Faron's masquerade. You eat like the baker's sow—Hey! Don't waste that!" Sybil ducked to avoid the bread Tal threw. She stuck her tongue out.

Tal focused on her food, ignoring the man across from her. She tried unsuccessfully to keep her thoughts from the masquerade that should have found Faron a bride. *A bride!* Yet, he entered their tunnels every night for over a month toying with her.

Her fury boiled in her chest, and she swallowed a particularly large bite of potato. The thought of Faron wedding another woman and so many other images she never wanted to see had her grinding her teeth on a very well-mashed bite of cheese. Her eyes sought him out only to find his own lit with silent laughter. Her nostrils flared, and she pretended to find a spot on the potato particularly interesting.

Rain broke the silence. "The coins are spreading like hailfire. Someone paid the baker with one this morning, and the locksmith has received three in the last week."

Tal frowned and bit her lip. "There's no way Badger and Gully had that many."

"We're thinking it's not just them this time," Carrick said. He leaned against the tunnel wall near Tal, thick arms crossed over his chest. Despite his words yesterday, he still watched the king with barely concealed animosity.

"Wonderful." Tal chuckled darkly. "So, the mages have recruited the whole of the docks to come after me, and now they're taunting me by leaving breadcrumbs everywhere."

Faron spoke for the first time that morning, "Actually, that may be my fault." His sheepish grin did nothing to dispel Tal's resentment. "I've been paying for Ed and Waylon's food and drink while they're in the docks. And I may have given them a few bags of my coin to spend at their leisure."

Rain's mouth hung open. Sybil stopped chewing the pastry she just bit into. Carrick pushed off the wall and stared in bewilderment.

"A few?!" Tal scoffed.

"How many coins in all?" Rain asked warily.

Faron shrugged. "Fifty? Maybe a hundred?"

Sybil choked. "*Hundred*?!"

"They're hungry scoundrels who like to take advantage of me." His attempt at humor had no effect on Tal, and his snicker died quickly.

Tal exhaled sharply. "So, this whole time Rain has been looking into the sudden appearance of this coin, and it's been you behind our backs?"

Rain came to the king's defense. "No, we've confirmed the mages are paying with their own counterfeits. Though it does hinder the investigation." He approached Tal and handed her two coins. "This is the one found in the rubble after the fires, and this is the one Faron brought himself." Tal inspected the gold in the candlelight. The fake version swallowed the light while Faron's coin reflected bright honey-yellow across her clothing. She took her own coin out of her pocket and noted the differences with the real one—the smaller willow, the lack of detail. While the two daggers crossed on both, the detail on Faron's showed the leather grip on the handle, and the blades protruded more from the surface.

"If we can figure out how to track only the counterfeit, we may be able to trace it to the mage or even who hired him." Rain took the coins back from Tal. "I'm still concerned at how many have been hired to look for you. Even with Faron's gold thrown into the mix, there is no denying the mage has paid others to find you."

Tal pocketed her coin. "It still doesn't prove the palace's innocence either." She shot an accusing glare at the man she refused to mention by name. "The mages could have been given fake coins so as not to take from the kingdom's coffers."

Faron exhaled a frustrated sigh.

"Is Egan searching for more of the mage's coin?" Tal noted his absence. "It's not his watch tonight."

Carrick's voice held a note of unease when he said, "Faron sent him off to confirm the location of apparitions."

"Daire and I intercepted a correspondence that alerted their presence in the kingdom," said the royal.

Fury roared through Tal at the mention of the captain. Flame enveloped her empty hand.

Faron held up his own hands in surrender. "We were discussing the orphans."

Skepticism coated Tal's face.

"I'm looking for a few reputable individuals who would be willing to take the children under their care. They would be compensated, and I would provide everything the children should need. I was hoping Daire could gather that information for me."

Tal rolled her flame around her palm. "You think we haven't tried that already? Anyone willing to take in a child is either in no condition to do so or has the worst intentions."

"It's a problem that more than just money and resources can solve," Rain added dejectedly.

"There has to be a way," Faron said.

"Yes, burn everything and start over," Tal added under her breath.

"There are more corrupt than honest people. If we still had Pochette's businesses under our control, we may have been able to turn things around, but it all went to shit," Carrick added.

In a tone that Tal considered gentle even for Sybil, the seer said, "It's a problem for another day, highness. Tell us about that letter."

Faron sighed. "A courier approached us looking for someone by the name of Sceleratus."

"That sounds familiar," Sybil mused.

"It's the name you found on the palace ledger," Rain offered.

"Right. The one noting the large sum of gold." Sybil nodded to herself.

Faron ran a hand over his tired features. "It appears even my ledgers need to be monitored. I'll speak to someone on the council, but there isn't anyone by that name under my command. It's likely an alias. Regardless, I took the letter, and it confirmed that apparitions would begin appearing within the docks."

The new development increased her focus and chipped away at Tal's anger. When she spoke next, her voice lost its edge. "So, we find the courier and have him tell us where the letter came from."

"It's handled. I've located the mage's hiding spot."

"What?!" Tal jumped to her feet. "Why are we sitting around? Let's get the bastard." Tal snuffed her flame with a flick of her wrist.

Rain narrowed his gaze at the king. "How long have you known?"

"I came as soon as I had confirmation. He's holed up at the incinerator, apparitions at every entrance—*including* the tunnels," he added when Tal opened her mouth to speak.

Tal reached for her dagger. "Fine. So, we go in like last time. Use Sybil to guide us."

"No." "Absolutely not." "Sounds like fun!" "Are you serious?"

The chorus of replies to Tal's suggestion echoed around the room. Faron's gravelly "No," caught her attention. He had never before refused support for her decisions, and his change of heart did not go unnoticed.

"So many things could go wrong with that plan," Rainier explained. "We don't do things rashly, not now."

"Have you forgotten that you were just beaten and bloodied by a pack of wolves not two days ago?" Carrick loved to remind Tal of how often danger found her.

She threw her hands up in frustration. "Then I don't know what you want to do. Why are we discussing this if I'm not allowed to do anything about it?"

Hurried footsteps echoed through the tunnel, and Egan burst into the common area out of breath. "They know," he panted. "They know you have fury!"

"What?!" Terror gripped Tal's heart. Her fury pounded against its walls, frantic and warning.

Faron's eyes grew wide with panic. Carrick pushed off the wall, fists clenched at his sides. Rainier's back straightened, and Sybil rested her food on the ground.

"Badger received a letter." Egan gasped, hands gripping a stitch in his side. "He knows why the mages are after you. Gully didn't return home last night, and he's spooked. He's going to demand more payment or find someone who will pay him more."

"Demon's snare, what else will the gods throw at me?!" Tal gritted her teeth against the fire threatening to overpower her.

Faron stepped toward her. "We'll figure this out. We'll find out who told—"

"Dammit, I don't want to figure this shit out!" She stepped back. "I don't give a damn who told him. I don't care who sent the fucking mages. I don't care about the godsdamned Fury Rings. I'm done sitting around. His time is up," Tal ground out the last part, her voice hoarse with the effort of containing her fury.

Egan stopped her with a hand. "Apparitions are everywhere. One watches the house day and night. One hides in the alley behind the tavern they frequent. And one trails him around the docks. Others hide in the shadows along the streets."

Tal crossed her arms. "I'll take out the one by the house."

Faron paced the small space. "And risk the others noticing?"

"We need to take the mage out first. It cannot wait." Carrick cracked his knuckles.

Tal should have been worried. When Carrick suggested action, the situation was dire, but she only felt relieved anticipation.

The king stopped pacing. "None of you should go after him. This is a problem for the whole kingdom. I'll lead the Guard to the incinerator, and we'll handle him while you go after Badger. I'll have Eddard search for Gully and secure him for you."

Tal nodded. He would save the kill for her. She gritted her teeth. The king sure made it difficult for her to keep her resolve.

Everyone else stared at Faron in shock, except Sybil, who remained unaffected. Carrick shook his head. The Guard rarely deployed within the docks. "You'll be putting all of them in danger. They're no match for a mage."

Tal may have killed one with a dagger, but the soldiers were trained in a different form of combat. They'd never met an enemy like this.

"It's what they're trained to do. Protect the kingdom. I cannot ask any of you to put yourselves in harm's way when I have the resources to handle it myself."

"Why now?" Impressively, reticent Egan questioned the king, a man he always seemed to admire.

"The council controls our armed forces. They won't deploy the men within the kingdom without clear proof of a threat. It's too dangerous for our people. Until now, I haven't been able to provide that proof."

Tal's mind blanked at this new bit of information. She assumed the king to be all powerful, and the council simply offered advice.

"What proof do you have?" Egan continued.

"I have a witness." For what felt like the hundredth time that night, Faron shocked Tal. He locked eyes with her when he continued, "The sheriff has met with a mage on several occasions, and he's more than happy to relay that fact to the council."

Tal had shared with Faron her dislike for the sheriff. She once revealed how the man essentially told her to learn her place when she asked him to intervene with a client's abusive father. It came as no surprise that the sheriff had met with the mages, and an unlikely coincidence that Faron had singled him out to find the evidence he needed. Tal wondered whether Faron went after the sheriff for neglecting his duties or for what he had said to her.

"What happens if the council still chooses not to send the Guard? Is a witness enough to convince them of the threat?"

"I'm a fan of asking for forgiveness."

Tal snorted and Faron's signature smirk returned for the briefest of moments. "Doesn't mean you'll get it," she countered. An awkward silence fell on the room, and Faron's smile fell.

"I've already spoken with Daire. He's ready to go at my command."

Tal ground her teeth at the mention of the captain. "Fine." She took in the eager expressions around the room. "How soon can we move against Badger? Do we risk attacking at his house?"

"Actually," Egan chimed in, "he still visits the brothel nightly. Oona says the apparitions aren't allowed inside. The headmistress only allows her girls, her guards, and her clients. It's fairly secure, but we'll need to be wary of the guards. They monitor every hall."

Sybil picked at something in her teeth with one of her daggers. "So, we send one of us into his room."

"What, you mean for one of us to bed him?" Carrick laughed.

"He'll think that, yes. Which will make it the perfect opportunity to tie him up and strip him, skin and all." Sybil stared at Tal when she said the last part. Her eyes did not blink, did not waver. She'd had a vision.

"And who are we going to send in there? You?" Rain asked his sister.

"Me," Tal answered.

"No," Faron snapped at the same time Carrick said, "Absolutely not."

"He's my kill. The easiest way to get to him is inside that room."

"After what he tried to do to you, you're going to simply walk in there, knowing what he's expecting?" Faron shook his head. "You will not be posing as some whore and locking yourself in a room with that filth," he growled, the first sign of possessiveness he'd ever shown. Something heated in the pit of Tal's stomach, but the more stubborn part of her spoke louder.

"You have no power here, your highness." She sneered at him. "I am perfectly capable of defending myself. You think I can't handle one street thug?"

"Rain would be the ideal person to go in. He could coerce the man to give up information and then to keep silent," Egan pondered.

"Except we know for a fact that he prefers women," Rainier added grudgingly. Apparently, he too thought himself the better option over Tal.

"We could always ambush him before he goes inside once the apparition disappears," Carrick threw out, always more suited to action over espionage.

"No. The commotion would draw attention. I get in there, kill him, and get out before anyone realizes the new girl escaped."

"New girl, huh?" Sybil smiled. At least *she* supported Tal's plan.

Tal smirked. To Egan, she asked, "Can you and Oona get me in?"

"There's got to be another way. Can't Rain coerce everyone to forget they saw him?" Faron gripped his waterskin a little too tightly.

Tal gritted her teeth. He had always been supportive of her choices before, but now he wanted to shut her down. She would have none of it.

Rain shook his head. "Memory coercion takes a lot of energy with only one person. I couldn't coerce a whole brothel. Believe me, I've tried large groups in other situations. Besides, there's ways around a silencing coercion that would allow one of them to say they saw me. I'm better with actions. I could tell someone to look away, but there's the chance someone else comes down the hall and sees me before I can stop them. I'm better one-on-one."

Sybil's head whipped in Faron's direction. "Oh no, loverboy. Don't bring me into this. Tal's made up her mind."

"She's not going," Tal ground out, knowing that Faron wanted to suggest Sybil go instead. "Syb, what do you see?"

"Not much. It's too dark to really tell. But you get in there alone with him."

"I can get you in tomorrow," Egan added.

Tal nodded and walked to the outer tunnel.

Faron followed after her. He reached for her arm, but she pulled away. "Tal, this is too dangerous. Don't do this." After a pause, he released a pained whisper. "Please."

His tortured expression threatened to break Tal's resolve, but she gritted her teeth. "Did you forget? I'm a bounty hunter. I hunt criminals for a living. I've killed them if I've been hired to. I'm not one of your princesses who needs someone to save them."

He ignored the jab. "You're deliberately offering yourself to someone who attacked you. Someone with a mage actively watching them. Don't you see how mad that is? I'll dig deeper. Hells, I'll kidnap him if I have to." He threw his arms wide in frustration.

"You can't just flaunt your authority or throw your precious gold around and expect it to solve our problems. If you want to be the hero, go back to your palace and find homes for the poor. Hire a sheriff who will actually stop the violence. Tell your damned council which pawn will be your bride so you can save this kingdom from itself. Who knows, maybe one of them comes from a country that can bring in the resources to stop the mages if more of them come."

At the mention of a bride, Faron flinched like she had hit him. If she had been a better person, she would have apologized for being so harsh. Instead, she stormed off toward her room. Faron didn't follow her, and she didn't turn back to see the hurt on his face.

24

"I'm Oona." A slight blonde woman grabbed Tal's hand and shooed the guard out of the room. She stood a few inches taller, perhaps five years older than Tal. Egan trusted this woman most within the brothels, the one who arranged for Tal to be captured by the Netters early that morning.

She pulled Tal through the room past women of all ages in various stages of undress. They wore silk robes with sheer chemises underneath and sat on chaise lounges with plush cushions while they applied makeup, ate fruit, and sipped wine. Her gaze caught on a frightened figure huddled in the corner and her blood boiled. The girl couldn't have been more than fifteen. It took every effort not to burn the place down right then and there.

Oona pulled Tal around a curtain at the back to reveal a washroom with a filled bath. When the curtain fell behind them, the woman sprang into action. "Your robes are over there." She gestured to an upholstered lounge chair in the left corner. "Make yourself presentable, or you'll never be allowed out of this room."

Tal removed her clothes. "When does he usually come?" She had spent the better part of the morning preparing for this. She forced herself to forget her anger at Faron and focus on why this man needed to die. He had attacked her. He joined forces with the mages. He knew about her fury and planned to sell the information. He could not make it through the night.

"Before dinner. He likes to work up an appetite. Egan and I will be in the room beside you." She squeezed Tal's hand briefly before gently running a brush through her hair.

The thought of the many evenings the man had spent in the brothel paying for one of the women in the room beyond, building up an appetite, as Oona had said, made Tal's fury rage inside her. Her thoughts landed in places she didn't want to visit and brought questions she didn't want the answers to. She washed away the thoughts as she sunk into the bath and cleansed her skin. She wouldn't gain answers to those questions tonight or any night. Tonight, she'd get revenge.

They wasted time in the big room as the other women were summoned one-by-one, all except the young girl who hadn't moved from the corner. Tal's attention flicked to the girl frequently, silently urging the gods to keep her hidden.

When the women returned, they would disappear into one of the curtained washrooms before returning to the main room and reapplying their makeup. The atmosphere felt relaxed, carefree even, despite most of the women having been forced into this life. Here, they had food, water, and a roof over their heads. They were safe to a degree. The headmistress didn't entertain violence against her girls. Tal wondered if the loss of freedom was worth it to them, knowing she would never interfere unless asked. The teenager tentatively nibbled on a plate of cheese, still in her corner, and Tal clenched her jaw. That one, however, *would* be freed. *Tonight.*

The guard summoned Oona once around lunchtime. She returned twenty minutes later with a smirk. After cleaning up, the blonde sat beside her on the lounge chair, sharing fruit and making small talk.

Tal's knee bounced as the sun set. Women left the room more frequently, only to return and wash up to resume the process. She watched the door expectantly and sat up straighter each time it opened. She jumped out of the chair when the guard gestured to her. Oona adjusted Tal's chemise, then slipped one side of her white silk robe off her shoulder. She pulled the hair off her bare shoulder, exposing her pale skin. With a wink, Oona sat back down.

Tal afforded one last glance to the corner of the room, then walked past the burly man at the door and waited in the dark corridor for direction. He led her further into the building, away from the back entrance she entered through. She counted the doors as they passed, three, four, five. On the sixth, the guard opened it and waited for Tal to step inside.

Darkness enveloped the room. Curtains covered the windows. A single lamp with a low flame sat on a wooden table beside two chairs, a bottle of wine and a plate of food on top. An upholstered seat, similar to the ones in the ladies' room, sat along the wall. And in the center of the wall opposite her stood a medium sized bed with white blankets. A shadowed figured sat at the foot of the bed. Even in the dim lighting, she could identify his tall, muscular frame. Tal froze. This was not the man she came to kill. Badger was short and stocky. A hand pushed her shoulder from behind.

"Get on with it," the guard said.

"Aren't you going to close the door?" Tal tried to form a plan.

"The mistress wants to ensure you do your job." He crossed his arms over his chest and leaned against the door frame, unmoving.

Tal's mind reeled. She hadn't planned for this. The man should have been secured before he could even lift a finger. Bile rose in her throat at the thought of having to perform for this guard, of letting this unknown man on the bed touch her.

She searched the room for a way out and couldn't find one. Forcing the guard to leave would raise alarms. She needed to get her revenge and get out as quietly as possible. She clenched her fists, wishing she had thought to bring a weapon.

The guard cleared his throat, and Tal gritted her teeth. Pursing her lips, she crossed the room. She would form a new plan. If the guard wanted a show, she would give him a show.

Shadows hid the man's face. He didn't move when she threw a leg over his lap. Her chemise hiked up over her thighs, and she thanked the dark lighting that the man wouldn't be able to glimpse her naked body underneath. She ran her hands under the lapels of his jacket over his muscular chest and slid it off his shoulders. Carefully, she searched for inside pockets or hiding weapons—anything she could use if it came down to a fight—but came up empty-handed.

Turning in his lap, she swallowed down the bile that rose in her throat when she brushed up against evidence of his arousal. She sat with her back against his chest and leaned into him, resting her head on his shoulder. Lavender and rosemary saturated the air around him.

Tal stopped. Fury clawed at her chest. Faron. Why was he here? She wouldn't listen to him, so now he'd inserted himself into their plan? Where was Badger? It took all her will not to elbow him in the ribs.

The guard at the door cleared his throat meaningfully.

Her robe slipped off her shoulder and clung to her forearms, exposing the skin of her back, shoulders and chest. Faron inhaled deeply, but didn't reach for her.

Damn the gods that mocked her. Her chance at revenge skirted out of reach once again. They threw the royal at her at every turn as if his lies meant nothing to them.

The dark figure shifted by the door. "Get on with it," he urged.

She pursed her lips against the words she wanted to say to both the guard and the bastard beneath her. Tal exhaled forcefully. She ran her hands down the outside of his thighs. Her fingertips brushed against the handle of the dagger along his calf, and she considered taking it.

She could turn it on him, demand answers. It would serve him right. He knew the seriousness of tonight's plan. Hells, he knew she didn't want to see him. And still, he interfered, refusing to give her the space she needed.

Fine. If he insists on joining me, I'll show him how unhinged I can be.

She brought her hands back up over his inner thighs, and the king stiffened on the bed. He turned his face into her neck, and Tal could feel his labored breath in her hair. She decided head-butting him would be an adequate response if he tried anything with his hands. She could have the dagger in the guard before anyone could blink—collateral damage that no decent person would miss. One hand reached down Faron's thigh toward the concealed dagger. But before she could strike, his hands came up to her forearms and pinned them in place.

She wanted to hit him, to scream at him. She wished she had never learned his identity. She wished he *was* only a noble. Maybe then they could have enjoyed a moment in the dark, *her* bed beneath them. Anger rose in her, betrayal at her own mind for wishing she'd never learned about his lies, for wishing she had been left in the dark a little longer.

The click of the door latch invaded her thoughts, and the guard disappeared. She pulled against Faron's grip on her arms, struggling to get out of his grasp. In an instant, he had her on her back, his body pinning her to the bed.

"Tal."

She ripped her hand free, pulling it back to punch him in the temple, but he caught it easily.

"Quit fighting me, dammit."

"Fuck you!"

She tried to bring her leg up around his neck in a maneuver that would flip her over and hopefully break his hold on her wrists, but he locked her legs with his own.

"Will you stop? Listen, it's a trap!"

"Get off me!" She thrashed against him, her fury practically begging to be set free, but she held onto her control.

He released her and stood back. "It's a trap, Tal. They knew you'd be here."

"Of course they did." She stood, fixing her chemise and brushing past him. She would find Badger on her own. She threw open the door and stormed out of the room, not really thinking about the guard who had left only moments ago.

A dark figure appeared at the end of the hall and stalked toward her. Before she could react, she was thrown up against the wall, a hand splayed by her face and a body pressed into her back, pinning her.

"There are apparitions everywhere." Faron breathed into her neck. "Don't move."

He pressed up against her as if he would take her right then and there. She could feel evidence of his desire to do so at her back. She tried to push against him, but he held her firm, one arm around her stomach and the other blocking her face from view.

A door down the hall burst open and a half-naked male stumbled out. "Fire! She's on fire!" Waylon's deep, silky voice called down the corridor.

The dark figure hesitated, then spun on its heel and rushed past the man into the room.

Waylon slammed the door shut and waved his hand at them frantically. "Go!" he called after them.

The door next to them opened, and Oona poked her head out. "Come!" She waved them over. "You must go!"

Tal twisted and pushed against Faron as he lifted and carried her into the room. He set her down once the door closed, and she pushed against his chest, swearing at him.

Egan paced the floor while Oona opened a window and waved them over.

"Flaming hells, what happened?" her friend asked.

"I'm going back out there." Tal tried to step around Faron, but he blocked her advance. She stared at him, wishing he could see the hatred in her eyes. He had betrayed her, and here he was, interfering with her chance at revenge because of what? Jealousy? She wouldn't let him stop her.

"The man you're looking for is dead. They both are. You won't find any closure tonight. We must leave now."

"What do you mean they're dead? Did you do this?" This could not be happening. She'd behaved. She'd spent weeks holding herself back from proving to her attacker, to herself, that she wasn't some weakling he could take advantage of.

"You know I would never take that from you."

She could feel his breath on her face and her anger grew when she realized she enjoyed it.

"My men found them an hour ago. The mage knows you're here. He wasn't at the incinerator. I got here just before the apparitions arrived, then paid the headmistress for her newest girl."

Tal's eyes burned into him, but Egan doused her anger with his sharp tone.

"Get over it, Tal. We had to get you out of that room, which, by the way, was guarded by someone playing with a gold coin. We never would have gotten to you or Oona before the mage did."

Sweet Egan had never spoken to Tal like that, and it cut through her inner rage. She swallowed her pride, if only for the moment. She stepped up to the third-story window, stopping with her foot on the sill.

"Tal, there's no time!" Faron warned. "Waylon can't hold them off forever."

"I'm not leaving. There's a girl, younger than Egan. She's a worker here. I'm getting her out."

Faron swore, but Oona's hand on her arm pulled her attention. "Go. I'll protect the girl. We'll get her out, but tonight is not the time."

"No." Tal refused to move.

"Bleeding hells, Tal." He placed three coins into Oona's hand. "Tell your mistress to put her in a room for the night, and she is not to be disturbed." He turned to Tal. "Is that sufficient? I'll buy her freedom tomorrow, but we have to go *now!*" Faron ran his hands through his hair, watching the door warily.

Leaving the girl for even one night angered her enough to make her want to burn the whole place down, but with the mage here, she would be hard pressed to get the girl out safely. Biting her lip, she turned to Faron. "Tomorrow," she said and waited for his confirmation. Then, without a word, she climbed out the window.

The three of them reached the ground quickly, using ledges and gutter pipes to leap down. They paused only briefly to ensure no apparitions waited outside the building and ran as fast as they could. They turned a corner when shouts rang out from the brothel. Waylon's distraction had run its course. Tal prayed that Oona's part in the night remained undiscovered, that her and the young girl would be safe.

They ducked down alleys and sprinted down streets until they found a tunnel entrance that would lead back to their home. Convinced of Tal's safety, Egan went after the twins who had been nearby before everything fell apart. Tal breathed easier, still filled with anger over the turn of events.

Faron had taken off his shirt and not relented until Tal covered herself. It reached the skin above her knees and covered her chest, a great deal more than her chemise offered.

At first, they said nothing. Faron stayed several paces behind while Tal stalked home. Each step added fuel to the fire raging within her. Someone else killed Badger and Gully. Someone else took away her retribution. And who had been the one to tell her? Not only tell her but force her to *satisfy* him before he revealed himself.

"I promise, I'll get the girl out tomorrow."

Tal stopped and turned around to face him. "Did you enjoy it?" she asked.

"What?" He jerked to a stop.

"Did you enjoy having me pressed up against you?"

"Tal—The guard was paid off. We couldn't risk him knowing," he pleaded.

"How about when I touched you?" She ignored him and stepped closer. "Did you enjoy it when my hand ran down your thigh?"

"What are you doing?" he asked warily.

"Or when my chemise came up over my hips? Did that ignite anything in you?" She bunched the fabric of Faron's shirt in her hands until the hem reached above her mid-thigh.

"Hells, Tal, what's gotten into you?" He backed into the tunnel wall, and she followed.

"Did you ache for my hand to venture closer?" She now stood chest to chest with him. She reached between them, smiling wickedly when his body answered her question. "Does it feel good now?" she whispered.

Faron gripped her shoulders and whipped her around to press her against the wall. With both forearms resting by her head, fists clenched, he growled out, "You're playing a very dangerous game."

She reached behind her and continued stroking. "Is it? Is it just a game to you? Because I can play too, and I don't lose." She spun to face him again and raked a hand up his bare chest, his neck, and into his hair. She fisted his hair in her hands and pulled until he grunted against her. Part of her enjoyed teasing him, and another part of her wanted to torture him. She reached her other hand up from where it worked against his trousers and slipped it into his waistband.

His mouth came crashing down onto hers, and his body pinned her hand between them, keeping her from teasing him further. He kissed her greedily and wrapped his arms around her, fisting her hair the way she had done to him. She moaned against his lips.

His hands dropped to her thighs, and as he lifted her, she wrapped her legs around him. He crushed her against the tunnel wall and groaned when she bucked her hips into him. They tore into each other as if the recent distance between them finally became too much to bear. Tal didn't know if her anger or her desire fueled her, but it didn't matter. Right now, she only wanted to touch him and be touched by him, to torture him with desire and let him do the same.

Fire raged within her. She scratched a hand down his back, eliciting a shiver across his body, and rolled her hips against him with vigor. He answered in kind. Her magic pounded within its cage. She threw her head back, exposing her neck. Faron took the opening, and the sensation of his lips on her skin sent pleasured chills to her core.

She pressed her hips into him, wanting more. She had fantasized about his kiss over the last few weeks, the feel of his body against hers. She had only just begun to enjoy the thought of his touch when everything had come crashing down. Her body wanted to forget her anger. Her fury wanted to consume him. Tal ran her teeth over his bottom lip and ground against him again and again.

Faron exhaled a frustrated breath. Suddenly, his arms were under hers, lifting her above his head. He guided her legs to his shoulders and held her aloft with his hands under hips. Tal gasped when his mouth connected. The warmth of his tongue matched the inferno burning within her. Her hands went to the ceiling of the tunnel, and the shock of his mouth between her legs made her want to twist away. Instead, she pressed onto his tongue, needing more. Her dreams of the man were suddenly lacking. She had never known passion like this, and she hated him even more for it.

She groaned at the intensity building between her legs. Faron only fueled the fire. His hands held her against his mouth with a desire that had been burning for too long. Tal closed her eyes and saw red. She grabbed a fistful of his hair and guided him. Her legs started to go numb from the building pressure. She held her breath and tensed.

An animal-like cry escaped her lips when she climaxed with his tongue inside her. Her fury bellowed within, thrashing through her blood with each pounding wave. She pushed against him, but Faron didn't stop. He demanded her pleasure until she shook against him. Her echoed moans escaped down the long tunnel. She prayed for relief and for it to never end.

When her pulsing slowed enough for her to catch her breath, her power quieted, and her body relaxed. Faron lowered her carefully. He kissed the skin below her jaw and inhaled her scent.

Tal stood breathlessly, her legs shaking. She pushed him off her, breaking the seal of his lips on her neck. He blinked, his chest heaving. Tal caught her breath, and her thoughts of him sobered. She tore off his shirt and threw it at him. "You'll want to clean yourself up before you return to the palace," she said, noting the wetness around his mouth and on his chin. Without another word, she turned to head home.

"Blazing hells, Tal. Really?" He stood with his arms out, shirt in hand, a rising anger in his eyes.

"Let's see how you like it when someone plays games with you." She continued walking.

Faron swore and muttered that he must be crazy. His hurried footsteps echoed down the tunnel. He grabbed her arm and turned her around, and she didn't fight him. "It was never a game. How can you not see that?"

"How? How can you expect me to believe anything you say when you lied about being the blazing *king*! How am I supposed to trust anything after that?"

"I was going to tell you, okay?! That day! When did you expect me to bring it up? When we fought the mages? Or maybe while we hid under that window listening to the apparition talk to those thugs? I'm sure they would have loved to overhear us then. When Tal? When do you think I should have told you that the king snuck around at night to try to take back control of the kingdom that he lost power over? The kingdom I should never have ruled in the first place?" He ran his hands through his hair and his head fell back.

"I don't know, maybe before you kissed me? Before you tricked me into believing a noble liked me?" she yelled in his face, but he didn't flinch.

"It wasn't supposed to happen like that! I didn't mean for it to go that far before—"

"Before what?" she pushed him in the chest. "Before you left? Before you disappeared back into your palace once you'd had enough of playing pretend?"

"Before I fell for you!" He swore before gripping her shoulders. "It wasn't supposed to go that far before I fell for you! Okay? I tried to find a way to tell you. I tried to take you somewhere that day to tell you and ask for your forgiveness, but Daire showed up and ruined the whole damned thing."

"Don't blame him for your carelessness," she spat.

"Carelessness? You think I don't care? Do you not see how much I've risked being here to protect you?"

"Then don't. Go back to your palace. I don't need your protection, and I didn't ask for it." She lit a flame in her hand to remind him of the power she had at her disposal. "Leave before I set fire to your beloved trousers." She stared at him with such hatred, willing him to see the seriousness of her threat.

His face turned from frustration to confusion, and finally... hurt. He released her and took a step back, but didn't say a word. When she continued to hold the flame, her stare unwavering, he huffed and continued backwards, giving her the space she demanded. Before he'd walked five paces from her, she turned and walked off, pretending not to listen for his retreating footsteps, even though the sound never reached her ears.

25

Footsteps thudded on the cobblestones. Tal ignored her permanent shadows. They had followed her since she'd left the tunnels, now dressed, and in search of a drink. She was glad to see Waylon unharmed, though she didn't say as much.

"For someone who wants nothing to do with high society, you sure have moved up quickly." Daire's voice slithered out from an alley and her fury flared in answer.

One godsdamned thing after another. Alright you cursed gods. What else have you got? Tal sighed in exasperation.

Daire pushed off from the house he leaned against and approached her. "I thought you weren't interested in marriage."

"You have impeccable timing." She tried to walk past him, but the captain stepped into her path.

He splayed his arms wide. "And yet here you are, bedding the *fucking* king of all people. You *are* aware that he's looking for a wife, yes? Or perhaps you prefer to be his mistress."

Tal swung at the captain, but her arm stopped. Waylon stood beside her, her forearm in his fist. He pushed Tal behind him without a word.

"Respectfully, my lord, thi—" *CRACK*! Waylon's fist collided with his nose. Daire stumbled backwards, clutching his face.

Immediately, Eddard stepped in to distract his captain. "Oh dear, you're bleeding all over! Here! I have something to clean that up!" He waved Waylon and Tal away.

Tal ignored Ed and tried to take her own swing, but the noble gripped her around the middle and threw her over his shoulder. "Hells, Waylon! Put me down!"

"Sorry, Tal. I'm saving you from yourself." He jogged down the street until Daire's angry insults were drowned out by the sounds of nearby taverns.

When he put her down, Tal rounded on him. "Why did you stop me?!"

"For Faron. He would have killed me if I let you handle that bastard."

Tal scowled. "That's what you think." She stomped toward the taverns, but not before yelling over her shoulder, "Don't follow me."

Gale's proved to be exceptionally boisterous that night, and exactly what Tal needed. Nothing but ale, testosterone, and blood to distract her. After two pints, she started to feel guilty for leaving on her own. Her friends should be in the tunnels by now and would be worried.

Gale returned behind the bar after knocking out a rowdy customer's front tooth for smacking her ass. "Another?" the burly woman asked. She placed a hand on her hip. The knuckles shown red in the dim light.

"How about a swig of something stronger? Then I'm off." A quick glance at the door confirmed Eddard stood guard, his middle finger once again tapping the handle of his sword. At her attention, he suddenly found a very interesting spiderweb above his head. Tal rolled her eyes and turned back to the bar. Waylon was nowhere in sight, likely still searching the surrounding buildings.

Gale nodded and pulled a bottle of dark amber liquid from under the bar. She uncorked the infamous Mud Water and poured barely two gulps into a small glass. Before it reached Tal's lips, the smell accosted her senses and sent her into a coughing fit.

"Best if you do it quick, love," the barkeep said before stepping away to yell at two drunks having it out near the window.

Tal heeded her advice and tossed it back. The spicy, sweet liquid burned down her throat. It destroyed her tastebuds. Breathing fire wouldn't be a problem for anyone drinking that liquid flame. Her body shivered of its own accord, and she realized how long it had been since she had tasted the drink. She slammed a few coins onto the bar. Before she could hop off the stool, a hand on her arm had Tal reaching for the blade at her thigh.

"You're not safe yet, friend."

Tal squinted at the girl whose delicate hand rested on her forearm and slowly lowered her weapon. She shot a quick glace to Ed who made his way through the crowd, hand on his sword. She shook her head minutely and turned back to the newcomer.

She'd seen the girl before, but never at Gale's. The curly chestnut hair and dark brown eyes aged the girl. "Gwendolyn will not be pleased to find you on this side of the docks, child. Go back home before the grass tells her you've left." Finally, Tal had found a member of the local coven, but the timing couldn't be worse.

"It's the trees that speak to us, and you know it. And I'm no child. I've nearly come of age. I'll have my powers before the next full moon." She looked no more than fourteen, but by her admission, she must have been about Egan's age.

"And yet you're still too young to be *here*." Tal nodded to the rowdy patrons around them.

"I've come to warn you. Danger is near. Too near for you to be alone."

Tal narrowed her eyes. "Did the trees tell you about the mages? What more did they tell you?"

The young witch's attention darted around nervously. She squeezed Tal's arm. "Mage. Just one. At least only one now. But you must be careful. The trees—they speak of something to come. They speak of *you*."

Tal leaned in then. "What do they say?" Tal kept her voice low even though the surrounding ruckus drowned out all conversation.

The tavern door opened, and a cool breeze blew the girl's hair from her face. She stiffened, and her eyes grew wide. "I must go. Be safe. Please." The little witch spun and bolted toward the door around a group of sparring men. Tal tried to go after her but was thrown off balance by a drunk stumbling into her. Eddard immediately helped right her with a hand on her arm.

"I'm fine." She pulled her arm out of his grasp and stomped out the door. Neither the girl, nor Waylon were anywhere in sight. She swore and went to check around the side of the building.

Not three steps out the door, a dark figure blocked her path and reached for her head. The force of a stone wall barreled into her, sending her crashing to the ground.

Eddard's sword knocked the mage's hand aside, but didn't break the skin. Before he could strike, a cloaked arm flew up, and the guard went rigid. Warm liquid slapped across Tal's face. The smell of copper hit her in a rush, and Eddard's body collapsed in two pieces.

Tal sat frozen, staring at the growing puddle of blood that soaked the ground. It filled the cracks of the cobblestone, reaching the tip of the guard's sword. Too much blood, too soon after the blow.

Tal was distantly aware of the footsteps approaching her. The hem of a dark cloak dragged through the puddle, staining the ground in streaks of crimson. Eddard did not get up. His chest did not rise with his breaths. His hand lay unmoving.

Cold fingers gripped Tal's chin and turned her gaze. The mage's face lay in shadow but for a wide smile that pulled at sunken cheeks. Tal's eyes sought out her friend's body lying prone in the street as the mage's hand reached for her forehead. The moment it touched her, a blinding pain made her elbows buckle, and everything went black.

She woke to a pounding headache. She attempted to reach for her head, but her arms wouldn't move. A candle emitted a soft glow somewhere near her feet. She tried and failed to turn her head. She couldn't feel her limbs, couldn't feel the clothes touching her skin or the hair at her neck. Her breath sounded muffled, like listening underwater. Light suddenly illuminated the ceiling. A door had opened.

"My elusive little friend. It's about time we met."

She couldn't see who entered the room, but she recognized the voice. She'd heard it plenty of times before, except then it sounded off, emotionless. It was the same voice used by the apparitions that had been plaguing the docks the last few months.

"My apologies, the spell immobilizes you." Movement in the corner of her eyes precluded a brief tingling sensation on her jaw and neck, and the deafening silence of the room blasted her ears. She turned toward the voice and finally saw the mage. He was ageless. The bone white hair and eyebrows were in stark contrast to the flawless skin. "A pleasure to meet you." The mage smiled, and it all came back to her. The tavern. The witch. Eddard.

Eddard was dead. His body lay in pieces outside Gale's. Had anyone found him yet? Where was Waylon? Was he dead too? Anger flared within her, a dull feeling. Did the spell mute her fury?

Tal tried to move her arms again to no avail. She swallowed. "What have you done? Where am I?" Her voice was hoarse as if she hadn't used it for several days.

"That doesn't matter anymore. Tell me, are the rumors true?"

Rather than answer, she turned her head, taking in the limited details of the room. There were no windows, no other furniture, no sounds outside, nor smells to indicate where she might be.

"You won't find any chance of escape. Nobody knows you're here."

Eddard sliced in two. His busy hand stilled forever.

"Fuck you."

He chuckled darkly. "Thanks to you, my associates are no more. She'll be pleased to see that I captured you all by myself."

"Who will?"

"You'll see," the mage crooned. He grinned audibly, his lips scraping along his teeth. The dry skin cracked, and a drop of blood seeped through.

Blood crawling between cobblestones. Too much blood.

Tal swallowed with difficulty. "What do you want with me?"

"Show me." His eyes widened greedily.

"Show you what?"

"Your gift."

Waylon. Waylon missing. Waylon searching for her. No red. No gold. No fire.

"You mean my singing voice? Sorry to disappoint. This bard doesn't work well under pressure." The same searing pain she felt outside the tavern split her head again. She screamed, straining against her invisible bonds, and just as suddenly, it was gone.

"You'll find that I don't have patience for nonsense. Now, if you please." He waved his hand to signal for her to proceed.

Sybil's vision. The Pyrie standing opposite her.

Tal took a deep breath, paused, and began to sing, "The cold wind blo—" She screamed again. She closed her eyes and only saw blood behind the lids. Her head burned. But this wasn't the fire she knew; this was like poison. It ate at her mind and slithered into every inch of her body like the blood that coursed through her veins. When it stopped, her captor brought his face to hers.

"I can continue like this for weeks. I assure you that you will not outlast me. Now, show me your gift." His breath accosted her, and Tal gagged.

"Have you ever considered chewing mint leaves? You would make more friends if your breath wouldn't frighten them away."

Aside from pursing his lips, the mage showed no sign that he heard her. He sighed heavily. "One more time?"

Carrick at her bedside, chastising her for getting hurt again.

Tal screamed until her throat burned. Her brain must have swelled until it grew too big for her skull. She tried to thrash, punch, and kick, but her body refused to respond. When it stopped, she gasped a ragged breath. The mage asked again for her to reveal her craft, and she spat in his face.

He stayed silent as he wiped away her saliva but then gripped her head in both his hands and maintained eye contact through the agonizing barrage of a powerful spell that felt like a thousand needles impaling her eyes.

Calm and calculating Rainier, worrying a spot on his nails, anxious he missed something—a detail, a clue.

It continued like that for what felt like ages. She slipped in and out of consciousness, and lost track of time. When she woke, she taunted her captor, and he slowly lost his composure. First, he pursed his lips. Then, he gritted his teeth. Before long, he began pacing the floor. At some point, he adjusted his paralyzing spell so that she could feel pain without being able to move. He switched to alternating between one spell that bludgeoned her body and one much like the slicing spell she had experienced at Silaron.

Sweet, tortured Egan looking to her for answers she didn't have.

She imagined the bruises and gashes that must cover her body and wondered what bones were broken and how much blood she'd lost. The sight of her must've been horrendous. Her energy sapped, her throat raw from screaming. There wasn't an inch of space that didn't hurt. When she'd finally had enough, she waited for the mage to get close to her. He'd slapped her across the face this time. She turned back and he got in her face and screamed, "Show me!!"

Faron.

Tal took a deep breath and concentrated what remaining energy she had left. She met the mage's eyes and blew into his face. She called her fury and willed it to burn the mage where he stood. But none came. There was no heat, no rumble in her chest. She felt nothing. Her fury had gone. No, not gone. Impaired. The alcohol still flowed in her system. Where her fury should have been, laughter bubbled up in her chest. She burst out an exhausted, hysterical sound. Her eyes sprang with tears that she couldn't wipe away. "How long ago did you take me?" she croaked.

Faron fighting alongside her. Faron exasperated, running a hand through his hair. Faron and his telltale smirk, filling her space, tangling his hand in her hair, kissing her.

The mage stormed out of the room and slammed the door. Not a moment later, he rushed back in and grabbed her head, eliciting the most excruciating pain she had ever felt, like her head being ripped apart by his bare hands. Tal didn't even have a chance to scream before she passed out.

She was dreaming. She knew that much. The small room and the mage were gone. She stood in a forest. In front of her, with her back turned, stood a woman with flaming red hair. She stared at a mirror image of herself. *Am I dead?* she wondered. She reached for the other Tal, but the woman did not turn. Instead, she walked away, setting the forest around her ablaze.

Water splashed onto her face. It filled her mouth and nose. She coughed and choked on the liquid. She turned her head to get out of the stream of liquid and continued to splutter.

"Why do you make this so difficult?" asked her captor.

"You do realize you picked me up at a tavern?" Her throat felt like fire, and she continued to cough. "Do you not know anything about magic?"

"I know a great deal more than you will ever know," he spat.

"But apparently no one ever taught you the first rule."

He slammed his hands down on the table beside her head. "You cannot taunt me. You are weak. You are insignificant."

"And you are an asshead."

The mage lost his control at her insult. He slashed his arms down over her body, and she felt heat before the pain. She couldn't see it, but she felt the gash across her middle. Tal hoped he hadn't cut too deep, or her insides would pour out onto the table beside her. He didn't even bother torturing her mind this time. With a wave of his hand, she once again fell into unconsciousness.

Darkness surrounded Tal. She tried to blink it away and couldn't tell if her eyelids responded. She spun on her heel and found a soft white glow in the distance. A step in its direction forced the light to concentrate into a pinprick. Another step, and it grew to the size of her palm, pulsing as if it called to her. As she neared, its color changed to a soft yellow, then deepened until it matched the color of her sunset hair. She stood opposite a flame. The light, now her own height, should have blinded her. Sparks of red shot throughout, some breaking free before dying on their own. As her heart pounded in her chest, so too, did the red sparks. She reached for it, and the fire mirrored the movement.

Tal cocked her head. The top of the flame tilted in the same direction. She placed a hand on her chest, only now noting how empty it felt. She watched as the flame, her fury, moved in tandem.

"It's you," she said.

The flame tilted forward, nodding.

"How do we get out of here?" Tal sobbed.

Her fury did not respond.

"Please, you have to help me." She stepped forward, hoping to pull the flames within her, but hit an invisible wall. She pushed against the barrier to no avail. "What is this?" she cried.

The flames grew slowly, as if carried on a wisp of smoke. Her fury filled the surrounding space, reaching its borders. Each effort to push through caused it to flash and flare. It tried and failed to break free of a box barely large enough to contain Carrick. The fury grew agitated, lashing against its walls, growing brighter with its fruitless effort.

"What do I do?" Tal's fist banged soundlessly against the cage. "How do I get you out?"

She could barely keep track of the flames now. They moved too fast. She squinted against the light that now burned too bright.

"Please!" She closed her eyes, blinded. "Tell me!"

The wooden door banged against the wall. Pain accosted Tal's senses. She gasped air in short bursts, not sure which was worse: dying or the pain that greeted her with each agonizing breath.

"The others. We took them. Yes, it is with them. The red. They had red. It must be with the others. It follows the red."

Warmth poured over her middle. The gash at her abdomen throbbed.

"Red hair. Red eyes. Red patches. Red marks. Yes, we've caught it already. It's back there. It's not here anymore. It can't be."

Her knee was shattered. She could only imagine the bone broken into a thousand pieces that now floated within the cavity of her leg.

"The children. The girl. *Yes! The girl.* No. She had yellow. Wait! Strawberry. Yes, strawberries are red. It must be her. They took her back. I *knew* it was her. I *knew* she had it. I must take her again. I must bring her to the—"

Something warm bubbled up Tal's throat, and she choked on the liquid. She turned her head and coughed blood onto the table.

The mage stopped his mad rambling and tsked.

The *pop* of a cork filled the small room, and her captor shoved a warm glass bottle to her lips just as he had so many times already. She swallowed the healing elixir greedily, but it was gone too soon. The mage pulled back before she could drink enough, always too soon. The pain lessened. She welcomed the familiar itch of her wounds stitching themselves closed, but despair returned when the itch stopped and the burning, aching pain remained. She wasn't healed. Only kept from dying.

"You know the rules. You live. You suffer." His gaunt face came into view, crazed eyes wide. "Unless you reveal!" His throaty whisper hinted at something sinister, eyes searching Tal's face. His lips cracked as they pulled wide into a terrifying grin. "I shall pull the memories from you, yes. I shall remember them *for* you." His hands gripped the sides of Tal's face, digging into her temples.

Something scratched within Tal's mind. It doubled and tripled. It clawed within her thoughts, and she began seeing the moment in reverse. The mage took his hands away from her face. *When did he get so close?* The memories played like a mirror image of themselves. He whispered in a demonic language she couldn't understand. Each barb-coated memory was wrenched from her, tearing and slashing through everything in its path. And when the hooks tore free, the memory was lost. His cracked smile fell as his eyes searched her face in a frenzy. The pain remained, but she didn't know why. *Was that a healing elixir?* Her knee, broken into a thousand pieces. *What was he rambling about?*

The claws dug too deep. Tal screamed. She remembered the blood in her throat. She registered the copper on her tongue and spluttered.

Red spattered across his face, and he stopped the assault on her mind. He blinked, eyes focused on nothing. Then they widened, and disgust pulled his mouth into an ugly, warped line. He used the sleeve of his cloak to wipe her blood, only succeeding in smearing it across his pale skin. He roared at the ceiling while Tal watched in silence. He turned to her, panting and snarling, before gripping her head again. He lifted her off the table with a force that made her neck crack and then shoved back down. Tal didn't hear nor feel her skull smack against the wood. Everything went black.

She remembered everything. Every moment she had ever suppressed her fury and the utter exhaustion she felt as a result, every time she wielded her magic as if holding it by a rope, every time it called to her from within flashed before her. *Is this what death feels like?* The rumbling in her chest felt distant and near at the same time. Her fury was there with her, suffering alongside her with each memory. It whispered to her, but she couldn't hear the message.

Torture was strange. There came a point where the pain washed over her, coating her soul in poisoned fire. It became a part of her. It never dulled, never became easier, but Tal reached a point where she couldn't muster the energy to *feel* it. Her screams dulled to a cry, a whimper. Her fury had returned long ago, but she couldn't call it. It hid within her, beaten into a shadow of itself. It could not comfort her. Tal was alone. With nothing to give but blood, she was ruined. And each time the mage returned, she anticipated the burning pain of the slashes, no longer braced herself for it. She welcomed it. She *was* pain.

26

Everywhere Tal looked, she found nothing but ash. Beside her stood a familiar figure with hypnotizing eyes and a playful smile. He reached out a hand and she took it. A sensation like electricity traveled up her arm and filled her body. *Let go*, his voice whispered. It filled her mind like a warm embrace. She felt the tension in her chest release and his face lit up with a glow that emanated from her. He held up her hand to show the glow on her skin and kissed it. Tal took a deep breath and closed her eyes.

She opened them to the same wooden ceiling. The pain crept its way back into her senses and she groaned. She needed water. She needed healing elixir. She needed a lot of things. Tal wondered how long she'd been tortured for. How long had she been missing? Did her friends realize she'd been taken? They had to have noticed her absence by now. Did Faron know? Did she care if he knew? She silently scoffed at herself for that last thought. Of course she cared. She wouldn't be so angry at him if she didn't care.

She tried not to imagine them coming for her. She didn't want them risking their lives for her sake. She didn't want that even if it meant she died there on that table. No, Tal would get herself out of this mess. She needed energy.

And then, there was the paralyzing spell. It had held for days, without needing to be recast. Would killing the mage remove it? Did the mage have defenses she couldn't sense? Would she be able to gather enough energy to kill him on the first try? Because gods knew if she missed, she'd never get another chance.

There had to be another way to release the spell. She took a deep breath and would have doubled over in pain if she'd been able to. She forgot about the raking claw marks across her chest, the dislocated shoulder, the slash to her middle, almost like he had whipped her with his magic.

Tal remembered the last time a mage had used a spell like that on her. She had almost died from the blood loss the night she had helped rescue the servant girl. Nola had also been restrained by magic, though they had used a magicked rope that couldn't be cut. Tal actually had been attacked by the slashing spell because she tested out her fury on the rope—

Her mind reeled. She forgot about the rope. Her fury could burn through the magic on them like a flame to a string. It might be able to burn through the spell paralyzing her too. She closed her eyes and reached into herself, searching for her fury, and there it was, brushing against its walls like a gentle caress. It never abandoned her. It bided its time until Tal knew what to do. Tal focused on it and called to it, but it slipped back into her with each pull. She was too weak. The magic was too heavy. She exhaled a defeated breath. She needed her energy back.

A noise outside her small prison alerted her to something new. She stiffened, anticipating the mage's return, but the door didn't open. Instead, someone cried out and then chaos ensued.

A bright flash of green light showed through the gaps around the door and illuminated the room around her. When it dimmed, the noise outside the room erupted. All at once, it sounded as if a small army fought beyond her door.

"Check the rooms!" yelled the familiar voice of her intelligent, calculating friend.

Weakly, Tal sobbed out her relief. They'd come for her. She tried to call out to them, but she had no energy. All the fight had been tortured out of her. What hope did she have of burning through the spell if she couldn't even call out to her friends?

A door slammed in the distance amid the fighting. They sounded so far away. Tal could only wait while they fought their way through the mage's defenses.

"Syb! Some guidance!" Carrick yelled.

"Somewhere dark, west side!" came the seer's response.

Tal closed her eyes and forced herself to concentrate. If they made it to her, she would still need to break through the spell. She pulled at her fury, but it was like trying to grab onto water.

Another two doors slammed, but not hers. "Come on," she urged them, tears in her eyes. The fighting continued, and her worry over them increased with each clash of metal and every battle cry.

Her door burst open in a spray of wood and dust. The fighting accosted her ears, but it was the frantic, "In here!" that she focused on. An enormous form blocked out the light, and Tal fought back tears.

"Tal." Carrick's hands reached for her face.

"Carrick," she croaked. "I'm sorry. I shouldn't have gone out." Her breath came in short gasps.

He shushed her and brushed the hair away from her face. He assessed her injuries, horror destroying his boyish features. He shook his head. "Shit, Tal. What did they do to you?" He placed a gentle hand on her shin, and she cried out. His hand flinched away. "Where are you hurt?"

"Everywhere."

Without a word, he stomped to the door and called out, "Faron! Elixirs!"

At the mention of his name, Tal sobbed. She had hoped, but didn't expect him to have come. Carrick ran out into the fray when another figure filled the doorway. In a moment that took less than a breath and entirely too long at the same time, he was there, touching her face, kissing her forehead, hands hovering over her broken body. She could think of no words to say to him about her recent behavior.

She could only cry and pray they survived long enough for her to apologize.

The *pop!* of a cork being removed from a small glass bottle filled the space. "Drink." He held the elixir up to her lips, and she swallowed the honey-sweet liquid greedily. In mere moments, she could feel sweet relief from the pain. And with it, her fury began to build within her chest. The renewed energy calmed her agony and gave her a renewed purpose. The mage would burn.

"Gods, Tal. What happened?"

"Aren't you going to say how tired you are of rescuing me?"

He smiled gently. "Exhausted."

"Faron, I'm sorry. I—"

A shadow filled the doorway. "I'd love for you to enjoy your sweet little reunion, but we have to go, NOW!" Sybil demanded and then jumped back into the fighting.

"Faron," she began. "Faron, it's Ed. He—"

He brushed hair out of her face. "It's alright." He met her gaze with tears in his eyes. "I know." He offered a second vial of elixir, and her knee started to reform.

Tal's face crumpled in a broken and bloodied mess. Tears burned on the cuts along her temples. Every gasping breath felt like her ribs had been ripped open and her heart was laid bare on the table. But tension grew in her sternum accompanied by a warmth she knew so well.

Faron caressed her hair. "Can you walk?"

She shook her head. "It's a spell. I'm paralyzed." A tear escaped and dropped down the side of her face into her hairline. Her fury battered its cage. She was ready.

Faron swore and began rummaging in his knapsack. Tal could hear the tinkling of several glass bottles being jostled around. "I don't have anything for that. Can I carry you out?" He tried to get his arms underneath her, but some invisible barrier connected her to the thick wooden table. "What in the hells?"

"I might be able to burn through it. I need you to step back. I don't know if I can control the fury right now." Her voice shook. Her strength had not yet returned. Once she released her magic, she would likely lose consciousness again. She needed to stay awake long enough to get her friends out.

Her magic clawed at her throat like a wild beast. She barely held onto it by the time Faron had stepped into the corner of the room, eyes glued to her. Rather than open the gate containing the magic, Tal instead inhaled and eliminated the gate altogether. She embraced her fury with a sigh as if it had been gone for eons.

Suddenly, a new sensation filled her—one she'd never felt before. Usually, when she used her fury, a tightness remained within her that helped keep some of her power at bay. This time, she didn't have the energy to hold back. Instead of feeling like a foreign thing warred within her, vying for control, Tal felt at peace, as if she and the fury were one and the same.

It started in her chest and built like flood waters being released. A soothing warmth spread to the ends of each of her limbs and grew in intensity. It was a heat unlike any other she'd experienced, like sunbathing on a summer's day. It clawed its way to the surface and warmed the skin there while healing the body underneath. It grew hotter and hotter until it turned cold.

"Tal?" said a voice in the corner.

She sat up. The spell melted away, leaving a rotten odor in its wake. Her fury still burned, but she didn't try to control it. For once, she felt comfortable in her own skin, like she finally knew herself. She swung her legs over the side of the table, and that's when she noticed the flames.

Her entire body was covered in them. No, her entire body *was* flame. The broken bones and bleeding, bruised skin was gone, and in its place burned a brilliant, golden fire that flicked this way and that. There was no distinct line between where Tal ended and her fury began.

She set her feet on the ground and stood, expecting to find the table turned to ash. The wood was nearly unrecognizable under all the blood staining it, but not a single burn marred the surface. She held a hand up in front of her face. Five distinct digits wiggled. She turned her hand over and could just barely see the bones and tendons working.

She turned back to the table and placed her hand on it, then pulled it away. Nothing happened, not even a scorch mark. She did it again. This time, she pushed the flame into the wood. A perfect charred handprint appeared. She repeated the action, blasting her power into the surface with all her might and a stream of flame burst through the wood, burning a hole in the spot she touched.

"Tal?" Faron repeated.

"The mage. Where is he?" Her voice sounded distant, almost ethereal.

He took in the sight of her. "He's in a back corner. Trapped behind a layer of apparitions." He gestured in the direction.

Tal nodded, though she didn't know if he could tell. Slowly, she walked out of the room. It felt graceful, like gliding. The sight out in the hallway would have terrified her if she had a mind to be. As it were, she felt at peace, as if all would be well.

Apparitions filled the open space, pushing to reach the six fighters scattered throughout the room.

A guard roared as his sword sliced through two apparitions at once. Tal blinked and thought she saw a ghost, only to realize the stoic Jens had joined the fight. Waylon, too, dispatched one foe after another. His usual jolly nature was replaced by a ferocity akin to Tal's own fury.

Her friends yelled to each other, calling out strategies and warnings. Something flew across the room and apparitions fell in its wake. Egan landed on top of one and tore its head clean off with claw-like hands. She blinked and noticed how free he seemed, releasing the beast within. It was beautiful to watch, but another problem demanded her attention. Tal turned away and walked in the direction

Faron had indicated. Carrick caught sight of her and did a double take. "Blazing pigs, what in the hells is that?!"

"It's Tal!" Faron appeared in the doorway behind her. "It's Tal!" he repeated.

"Tal?!" Carrick replied incredulously.

She continued her approach. As Talwyn walked past apparitions, she brushed them with a hand, and they burst into flame. She found the mage holed up in the last room, surrounded by more apparitions. She easily walked through his defenses, burning them to nothing with the slightest touch. A cape of flame and smoke followed in her wake until it disappeared upon the apparition's death. As she drew closer, she could see the mage frantically spelling more apparitions into existence, but he wasn't fast enough to block her approach. Soon, he gave up on the apparitions and began throwing curses at her directly. She felt the slashing spell hit her in the chest, but her flame burned it away. His arms waved this way and that with the spellcasting, but Tal continued her approach without disruption. When she reached the mage, he screamed in sheer terror.

What a shame. She much more preferred to kill him when he was the unfeeling man who tortured her. She lifted a hand and caressed the back of her fingers down his petrified face. He choked out a scream and his eyes glowed yellow, then flames burst from them.

Flames escaped his body from his eyes, his mouth, his ears, and soon they shot from his fingers. They ate away at his skin. Tal watched as her fury slowly consumed him. The screaming stopped and his burning form collapsed on the ground. The building grew quiet. She turned in time to see her friends running into the room, all apparitions gone now that the mage was dead, no bodies nor cloaks left behind. Her friends were in quite a state, all showing signs of an intense battle, but all thankfully still accounted for.

Their eyes went wide when they caught sight of her, jaws dropped in wonder and amazement. When Faron pushed his way to the front, concern lined his face. His eyes searched her. Whether he searched for any sign of injury or evidence that the living flame in front of him was still the stubborn woman from the docks, she didn't know.

He had come for her. She had pushed him away, played with his emotions, and threatened him. But still he fought for her. There he stood, face full of concern for her. She walked toward him. With each step, she thought of his smile, his kindness, the feel of his hands in her hair, his kiss on her lips. And with each memory, she felt her fury retreat into her. First her hands and feet returned to skin and bone. Then, slowly, the flames returned to her chest, concentrating their form over her heart until a single blinding, beating ember remained.

Tal stood naked before the king, her clothes having been burned away when she released her fury, and with the last beat of her magic, a single tear escaped her eye and traveled down her cheek. All at once, she felt too tired to continue.

Faron reached for her, and she collapsed in his arms, sobbing with what little energy remained. Egan came forward and covered her with his shirt. Faron wrapped the fabric around her and held her tight. "It's over. You're safe. We've got you," he comforted.

Tal fought the exhaustion for a few more breaths and then finally relaxed in Faron's arms, letting a peaceful darkness pull her under.

27

Tal stood next to another version of herself. The two observed the forest surrounding them, the same one from two nights ago. Soon, people started coming out of the shadows between the trees. Men, women, and children stalked toward them. They didn't say anything. Their expressions remained flat.

They approached slowly, forming a circle around the two Talwyns. Her mirror met her gaze and smiled, letting go of her hand, and stepping into the group. She gently brushed her hand along the shoulder of the first person she reached, and the woman burst into flame, her face to the sky in a silent scream of agony. To her horror, the other Tal continued to set fire to the entire forest—trees, people, and all. She watched, rooted to the spot, as every last living thing around her died a gruesome death.

Hours later, the ground lay black with smoke rising to a cloud covered sky. It blurred her vision. She coughed but made no sound. She stood next to a middle-aged man with a button nose. His warm brown eyes peered down at her with pure devastation in his gaze. The handsome face was ruined by his grimace. He didn't try to talk to her. Instead, a single tear created a track through the soot on his cheek. He nodded and Tal's own eyes welled up with tears of their own. She blinked, and he disappeared.

She stood alone in the open field ruled by destruction. When a light breeze blew the smoke away, she saw the bodies among the ash. Death surrounded her. She walked for hours. Ash left the ground in clouds with each careful step. A hand grabbed her own, and she met

Faron's eyes. His mouth moved, but she heard nothing. The silence was deafening. She tried to tell him she couldn't hear him, but he kept repeating. Ringing started in her ears. It grew in volume. Faron kept trying to tell her. The ringing became painful. It would burst her eardrums.

"What?!" she screamed at Faron.

"You have to stop it! You have to save them!"

Her eyes searched the scorched field around them. The bodies had disappeared. She turned back and Eddard stood in Faron's place. Grief pulled at his features.

"I'm sorry! I'm so sorry!" Tal cried.

Warmth slapped across her face. A red line split Eddard's head and his body fell away. Behind him stood the other Tal, a bloody, malicious grin on her face.

Sobs shook her awake. She clung to the blanket that enveloped her, muffling her cries into the tear-stained pillow. Strong arms held her tight, grounding her to the space that she once called home.

"I've got you." Faron spoke in a low cadence.

The sound reverberated through her system. Her fury clung to it. Her body relaxed in its waves.

"You're safe now."

She tangled her legs in his, wishing it was enough to keep her from drifting into the dreams that tortured her every time she closed her eyes.

"You're home."

Home. That word. She knew he meant the tunnels. She knew he meant among her friends. But what was that word? Shelter? Among family? Home was supposed to mean safe. Yet her own mind brutalized her. Nowhere was safe. *Nowhere* was home.

28

Chills tickled Talwyn's scalp and crawled along her spine. "When did you learn how to braid?" she asked the king.

Faron's soft chuckle had become so familiar the last two days. "Did you know that braided rope is stronger, more flexible, and less prone to kinking?"

Tal leaned into him and rested her head on his shoulder. "Still answering a question with another question." She breathed in the lavender and rosemary that filled the air around him. She didn't know if he continued to use the feminine soap for her sake, or if he truly ran out of the clove and citrus like he claimed.

His arms came around her, and he nestled into her neck, a gesture that had quickly become familiar since Tal's rescue.

"He's still here?" Egan asked from outside Tal's room. It was now common to have an audience in the tunnel. The group had taken it upon themselves to ensure Tal knew she was not alone. The only time she'd been afforded privacy was when she promised to gift each of them a rotten fish under their pillows if they didn't go to their own rooms.

"I don't see him leaving until the end of summer," Sybil yelled, her tone sardonic. "At this rate, we won't find the witchling until she's died of old age."

Tal sighed audibly, attempting her usual tempered tone, but it fell flat. "Fine. I'm getting up."

Faron's hold on her tightened for a fraction of a second before he kissed her neck and released her.

"Good!" Sybil called. "You need to thank her for sending that note."

Tal slipped into her new clothes, delivered by Faron after the mage and her own fury destroyed her old ones. She missed the elasticity of her old clothes. These new ones were tight and scratched her fury-healed skin—skin that felt like an even more restricting suit. "You said the note had been signed 'The Grass.'" Tal tied the laces on a pair of leather boots that likely cost more than everything she owned and then some.

The seer finally poked her head into the room. "You and I both know that was some sort of joke between you and the witchling. Now, go put your face out there so maybe she'll come out of the woodwork, and we can thank her for saving your life."

"The witch saved my life; you saved my life. Even the king has saved my life. When does Tal save her own life, huh?" She meant to be funny, but her voice broke on the last word. She hadn't been the same the last few days. She'd struggled to smile, food didn't hold its usual flavor, and sleep was riddled with nightmares of a soldier in pieces and a crazed grin with cracked lips.

Rainier walked by her room. "Maybe when she remembers how she transformed into Living Fury." His voice trailed after him.

Tal stood, her new boots laced and feeling like they would give her blisters. "I told you, I don't know! I called my fury, and it answered! Like *always*." Without seeing him, she knew her friend's narrowed eyes and raised brow reflected how little he believed her. "It's nice to know that almost dying doesn't change how you treat me!" she called after him.

He hadn't said it yet, but she knew the vision of the Pyrie, and the legend of her magic-induced madness, weighed heavily on his mind. The worry of it ate away at her idle thoughts. She had felt it—that blissful detachment in the moment she let her power free. She could have burned it all if she hadn't been so focused on the mage. And that thought terrified her more than anything.

"It's because we love you and couldn't let you die. It didn't feel right when your grumblings didn't echo throughout the tunnel," Egan said.

"I don't grumble."

Arms wrapped around Tal from behind and she fell into the warmth. "Don't worry. I'll help you learn how to be cheery. Your first lesson is to remain neutral when speaking to that alchemist of yours."

She turned in his arms. "I'm not ready to talk to him yet. But there's something else I need to do."

Faron squeezed her hand. He guided Tal through the streets to a dilapidated shack on the northern side of the docks. In its prime, it would have had a perfect view of the Taralin. Tal imagined Eddard growing up watching the ships sailing by, pretending he joined the sailors on their adventures across the world. Now his childhood home stood abandoned and broken.

A soldier stood in front of the doorless entry, his back to her, and Tal's heart stopped for a moment, thinking her shadow hadn't died after all. Then, she noticed this man's height, the way he stood as if a rod had been jammed down the back of his shirt. His hand lay still on the pommel of his sword.

Misery seized her heart once more. A seagull flew overhead, gliding on a breeze she couldn't feel. She took a shaky breath. Mildew and seawater hung on the air, an unfamiliar smell after the days hiding in her tunnels. Faron squeezed her hand, and Tal steeled herself.

She clung to the waterskin in her arms. The soldier showed no signs of detecting her approach, nor did he react when she stood at his shoulder.

Inside, sun rays shone through holes in the roof and walls. Signs of furry inhabitants littered the wooden floor. Those items deemed useful or worth anything had long since been looted, but a few scraps of cloth and broken furniture remained. She left the waterskin by the entrance; a parting gift she never had the chance to give.

"I didn't stop it." Tal's voice clung to her throat as if the words didn't want to be released. She tried to swallow, but the muscles in her throat wouldn't cooperate.

Jens took in a shaky breath.

"He pushed me out of the way, and before I could even turn, it was over." Her vision blurred through tears she'd been shedding since her rescue. Eddard didn't deserve this. The whole damned kingdom fought tooth and nail to bring him down, and he still smiled like the air in his lungs was its own victory. He should have seen the mountains. He should have seen the world. Instead, the last thing he saw had been a dreary tavern on these damned dirty streets. Tal's fists clenched at her sides. She bit her cheek and let her head fall back. The sun burned her eyes, and she welcomed it. "I'm sorry I didn't stop it."

Jens's callused hand closed around her shoulder. He didn't turn to her but kept his gaze on the rays of sun lighting the forgotten home. Waves of muscle tensed, marring his stony features. "It was his duty to protect you. When the captain called off the investigations, Ed enlisted my help. He knew the threat still remained." He cleared his throat. "You killed the bastard. He'd be proud."

Tal could only nod. She reached across her chest to grip Jens's hand. This singular point of contact comforted her more than his words. She let the tears fall, let the waves of grief wash over her body. She sent a silent plea to whoever would listen that Ed had found his adventure even if it wasn't in this life. She apologized to the empty house, vowing her pride wouldn't put anyone in danger again. Guilt saturated every broken piece of her. She turned her face to the sky, imagining Ed's warm smile, forgiving as always.

Jens held steadfast, an anchor against the tide. Together, they said good-bye to their friend while the seagulls cried above, and the sun shone on his childhood home.

———

Tal studied the faces she passed. She'd left a letter inside a bird's nest, given a token to a crow, and fed fish to a black cat. The witch coven preferred to be left alone, but she'd learned a few tricks over the years. If they accepted her requests, she would know.

Faron put his arm around her shoulders. "Are you sure you don't want to go anywhere else?"

She leaned into him and shook her head. "I'm tired. I want to go home." She eyed the road that would take them to the palace. "Don't you have to return?"

"I have a meeting with the council in two days. As far as they know, I'm on a hunt until then."

She watched a young woman with curly brown hair cross the street. It wasn't Dierdre. "How important is this meeting?" She dreaded the thought of him going back to the palace. He'd only left her side once since she'd been attacked, and that had only been long enough to find someone to send a letter. Once he left, she knew things would be different. The little haven they'd created the last few days was only temporary.

His voice held no tension, but she felt it in his arm. "They're angry with me for deploying the guard."

Tal had almost forgotten. If Daire and Faron had dispatched the mage while Tal took care of Badger, perhaps no one would have been hurt. Ed would still be alive. Something nagged at her thoughts. It wasn't the horror of her torture, or the despair of Ed's death. It had something to do with Faron's meeting with the council. She pulled on that thread until it was taut, and her head snapped back with the invisible force. "Where is Daire?"

"Bastard!" Tal's fist connected with Daire's jaw. His head whipped to the side, and he turned back to her, gaping. Her second fist found its mark.

"What the blazes?!" Daire reached to cup his jaw.

Tal reared back for another blow when Faron caught up to her. He grabbed her around the middle and hefted her behind him.

The captain flexed his jaw, rubbing the reddening spot with an incredulous look. "Lovely. How much have you been drinking this time, Tal?"

"You told the council about the attack on the mage!" She kicked and fought against Faron's hold on her.

Daire narrowed his eyes then flicked his gaze to the king. He stood at attention, but the hatred in his eyes was unmistakable. "Apologies, majesty. I was only doing my duty. They requested an update on my investigation of an active threat to the kingdom."

"You're a godsdamned liar, and you know it. You called off the investigation weeks ago." Tal felt the realization reach Faron, and he set her on her feet.

"Did I?" A glint in his eye set Tal off.

"Did you know they were after me? Is this because I rejected your proposal? Are you trying to get back at me for ruining your precious reputation?"

He scoffed. "What would mages want with a nobody bounty hunter at the docks? I thought they wanted to hire you."

Faron bristled beside Tal. "So, you set her up anyway. Because of you, Eddard was killed, and Tal was tortured for nearly a week!"

Daire blinked. Unease crept into the captain's expression. His eyes showed the slightest hint of worry as they searched Tal up and down for signs of injury. When he found none, he crossed his arms, sticking his chin in the air. "I haven't the slightest idea what you're talking about."

"Coward!" Tal had to be held back once again. This time, Daire flinched. "Are you helping mages kidnap elementals now?"

Daire snorted. "Elementals? Really? You're really on something today. If the mages wanted elementals, that would mean that you—" His eyes flicked between Tal and the king until they widened in shock. His jaw dropped, forming a silent "oh" as he tried to back away from the pair.

Faron closed the distance and gripped the captain by the collar. "Not a word," he growled. "I should have you hanged for treason."

"Oh, so *he* knows?" he addressed Tal. "And you didn't tell me? Real nice, Tal. I courted you for years. Wasted my time, treated you like nobility, and this is the thanks I get? Dumped in the river like trash the moment anyone with a title swoops in and promises you riches? How does it feel to know you replaced loyalty for someone who can't keep his cock out of every wom—"

Daire's head snapped back from the force behind Faron's fist. He hit the ground with a satisfying thud.

Faron stood over him, flexing his right hand. "You're a disgrace of a captain and a pathetic excuse for a man."

"And you're a fool of a king. If you knew anything, you'd know my duty is to the council, the true saviors of the kingdom. It's an insult to have to follow you around and report back to them."

Faron stilled. "The council has you following me?"

Daire's silence spoke for him.

Faron swore. "How much do they know?"

"They know you sneak out at night. And that you steal food from the kitchens."

Faron pinched the bridge of his nose. "It's my godsdamned palace. How is it stealing?" he griped under his breath. "Do they know where I go?"

"I can't be bothered to babysit a boy tyrant."

"Watch your tongue." Tal stepped beside Faron.

"The council isn't saving the kingdom. They're destroying it. If you opened your eyes, you would see that." Faron's voice warred between anger and exasperation.

Daire's defiance faltered. His eyes searched the surrounding area, and Tal could see the hatred in his eyes replaced by stubbornness.

"I steal from the kitchens to feed the poor. I sneak out to find out what's going on in *my fucking* kingdom because the council refuses to tell me." He paused, gritting his teeth. "I'm taking back control of this kingdom one night at a time. And you're going to help me do it."

29

"**I** don't like this, Faron." Tal argued with him the entire walk back to the tunnels. "The bastard helped the mages find and torture me. They *killed* Eddard!"

He reached for her hand, but she pulled away. "I know. I'm sorry, I know! But my allies in the palace are in the dark. I need someone the other members trust."

"But *we* can't trust *him!*"

"He values his duty and his reputation more than anything. The council convinced him I did nothing but waste the kingdom's resources. If he realizes we're trying to fix things, he'll do as I say. And if he tries anything, I'll have his title publicly stripped and leave him in the stocks for a week before hanging him." He pleaded with Tal. He knew she would rather gut the prick. "We need to know what the council is planning, and he's going to tell us."

"He knows about my magic, Faron. What if he tells them?" Tal cursed herself for revealing her secret.

"Jens and a number of soldiers are fiercely loyal to me. They will keep the captain in line."

They argued the whole way back to the tunnels, and the peace that surrounded them for the last two days shattered. They joined everyone for dinner in the tunnel common area, sitting side-by-side, but not speaking. She knew her friends noticed the change between her and the king, but no one asked. She wanted to get the attention off the new distance between them. "I don't think he knew what magic I have."

All heads snapped to where she sat in the corner eating a roasted potato with bone broth. Faron tensed beside her.

"He kept telling me to reveal my gift, but he never said fire, or even fury, for that matter."

Unease hung in the air, but it was no surprise that Rain responded first. "So, it's possible they're only after you based on mere suspicion of your ability. That could be good or bad news."

"Why is that?" Sybil asked her brother.

"It's good that fewer people know about her fury. Otherwise more than just mages would be after her. It's no secret that anyone with power would go to any lengths to have a fire fury in their arsenal."

"I'd never let that happen," Faron said darkly. This whole possessive side of him was new to Tal. She was so used to the carefree noble who followed excitement wherever it went. She didn't know how to respond to the sudden change. Part of her wanted to slap it out of him and tell him she belonged to no one. But a small part of her liked his protectiveness. Carrick felt a similar responsibility for Tal, a familial bond, but with Faron, it bordered on territorial. The idea of the king—disheveled and out of breath—standing above her with lust in his gaze—lust for *her*—sent a heat through Tal that made her shift in her seat. Faron noticed.

"There are more powerful kingdoms and more morally corrupt kings out there, your majesty," Sybil warned.

Faron narrowed his eyes, but didn't argue. Meladair's weakness was no secret. His council continued pushing the issue of marriage for that reason. An alliance with a powerful kingdom could ensure their safety for a whole generation.

"The bad news," Rain continued, "is that they pursued you so vigorously without even knowing you have control over the fire element. If they ever find out, we'll be in a world of trouble. Let's not forget we still haven't figured out Sybil's vision." He turned his attention on Faron. "I'm assuming you know which room her vision is referring to?"

Faron swallowed and turned his gaze to the floor. "The council chambers, by your description."

Tal didn't want to address the matter of him withholding this information, but Carrick did so anyway. "Rain has been asking for the significance of this room for over a month, and you knew all along?"

"It would have raised the wrong suspicions and wouldn't have changed anything."

Faron's apologetic tone did little to appease Carrick's irritation. He pressed his lips into a thin line before opening his mouth to respond, but Sybil interrupted.

"I had another vision while Tal was missing," Sybil revealed.

Tal tensed. Out of the corner of her eye, Faron clenched his jaw. Rain stared at the floor, but Carrick and Egan both braced for more information.

"A letter, with your signature." She nodded to the king. "It was addressed to a Lord Niktovaz. Something about regret."

Faron hung his head. "Lord Niktovaz is the father of the woman my own father arranged for me to marry when he took the throne. I wrote that letter last winter to end my betrothal."

"Why would you have a vision of the letter now?" Tal ignored the unease in her stomach at the mention of Faron's betrothal.

Sybil bit her lip and locked eyes with her brother before returning Tal's gaze. "When the vision of the letter faded, I saw Pochette's deal with the mage, then my vision with the Pyrie again."

"What is that supposed to mean?" Egan asked.

"I think," Rain concluded, "that the ending of the marriage contract caught the attention of someone powerful."

"So? What does that have to do with Tal?" Carrick stood with his arms crossed, fists clenched. The muscle in his jaw flexed, and Tal wondered if he'd ground his teeth to nothing with all the anger he'd harbored since her capture.

Rain opened his mouth to speak, but Faron interrupted. "I foolishly thought there would be no consequences. I was wrong. Of course her father would be furious. Of course he would demand retribution." He clenched his fist and tapped his foot restlessly.

"Don't be so hard on yourself," Rain said. "I've heard whispers from traders that foreign powers have turned their eyes to our kingdom, wondering why you have no need of an alliance. But more importantly, there's talk of other alliances your council is making that the others view as a threat."

"The mage claimed to be working with a woman," Tal offered. Perhaps this woman was in talks with the council. Or perhaps she was one of the curious rivals hoping to discover Meladair's secrets. Rain asked for more information, but Tal had none to give. Silence hung within the small tunnel room.

"Maybe we should go somewhere safer. People are already moving to the mountains in droves. We could move out there." Egan surprised everyone with his suggestion, but no one spoke against him.

Tal scowled. They had to know that she would never leave the docks. "Absolutely not. I will not let them drive us from our home."

"Even if it costs us everything?"

There were no words to say to Egan that could explain why Tal wouldn't leave. Even she didn't understand it herself. With Faron by her side, Tal watched each of her friends, knowing they wouldn't leave her, wondering which of them she would eventually get killed.

Egan had started to come into his own this summer. The once quiet teenager now spoke his mind. Rainier had become more of a leader than Tal in the months since the mages showed up. Sybil's adolescent sense of humor had gotten her into trouble plenty of times, but she was learning how to balance it with the maturity of someone her own age. And Carrick, her enforcer, her rock, remained unchanging. Just as he did from the first day when she had been a sickly child; he saved her day in and day out.

He helped her when she made stupid decisions and put herself in harm's way, when she was too stubborn to make the right decision, and when she became too hard on herself, he saved her. She remembered that he found her first. She recalled how he came barreling into the room like not even a wall could stop him from getting to her. She wouldn't have expected any less, and she couldn't have thanked the gods enough for bringing them together.

At some point, Faron had reached his arm around her, and she relaxed into him. He rubbed his thumb on her shoulder, lost in thought, staring at a slit on the ground a few paces ahead of them. She knew he must be thinking of what Rain and Egan had said. Danger lurked within his kingdom, and he had a responsibility to fight it. He couldn't run away. He would stay here until his death. And if that threat happened to be mages or kingdoms searching for more power, that time may come sooner than they all knew.

Tal stood and pretended to yawn. She excused herself and walked a few paces toward her room. She stopped and turned around when Faron didn't follow. He hesitated, and it hurt something within her that he didn't automatically think to join her. She tilted her head and looked meaningfully in the direction of her room, waiting for him to catch on. Almost comically, when he did catch on, he jumped to his feet and bid everyone goodnight.

Back in her room, Faron stood by the hanging curtain, a wariness creasing his brow. Tal removed her boots, socks, and her weapons belt, then hesitated at her trousers for a moment before letting them fall to the ground, the hem of her shirt falling to her upper thighs. Faron quickly apologized and tried to step outside to give her privacy.

"Faron," she said, her tone full of admonishment.

He stopped and turned around hesitantly.

Tal rolled her eyes. "You've slept beside me for two days now. And you've held me stark naked."

He rubbed a spot on the back of his neck and appeared embarrassed. "Well, yes, but you were clothed the last two days and before that we weren't in your bedroom."

She chuckled. "That didn't stop you before. Stop being such a gentleman." She left her shirt on and climbed into her bed. She closed her eyes as she hid under the covers. When he didn't join her, she opened them and huffed. Pulling the blanket down, she said, "Are you coming or not?"

His face lit with the knowing smirk she enjoyed so much. He began removing his boots. Satisfied, Tal returned to the comfort under her covers. When they lifted, she added, "May as well remove the trousers too. You've been sitting on the ground." She smiled under the blanket at his pause before his belt *clinked* as it hit stone.

A moment later, the covers lifted, and the bed shifted with his weight. She faced away from him, but she could imagine how un-characteristically nervous he must've looked. She could see right through his devil-may-care attitude. The man could act all cool and confident, but when it came to Tal, he was like a lost puppy. Slowly, he eased up behind her and wrapped an arm around her middle. She curled into him and tangled her feet between his legs. After a breath, Faron relaxed and nuzzled into her neck.

They lay like that, listening to the other's breathing, feeling each other's heartbeat. Tal didn't worry about the outside world. Her mind was at ease, her body without pain, and her heart where it was meant to be.

Faron shifted. He inhaled deeply, preparing to talk about some-thing she did not want to face. "Tal, I want you to know, I—"

"Can we not talk about it for one more night?" She turned to face him. "Please?" she asked quietly. The last two days, they hadn't said a word about Faron's lies, or done much of anything besides enjoy each other's presence. He was content to let her heal, and she was happy to just *be*. "For one more night, I don't want to think about the fact that I have the godsdamned king in my bed."

He searched her face. Tal reached up and smoothed the crease on his brow and placed her hand on his cheek. "Let it be us tonight," she whispered and kissed him.

Faron melted. The arm he had draped around her middle held her tightly and pulled her further into him while the other came up to her neck and caressed along her jaw. The sensation sent a wave of fire through Tal's core. She tangled both hands in his hair, crushing her lips to his. Tal wrapped a leg around Faron's hip and pressed into him. The feral growl that escaped his throat had her smiling against his lips and only encouraged her to continue.

She ground her hip into him, almost content to simply feel him through the thin fabric of their shirts. His hand explored her body, pulling her into him again. Tal smiled for a brief pause and climbed on top of him. With a hand to his chest, she forced him onto his back. Their shirts still tangled between them, but that did little hide the evidence of their desire from each other. Faron gripped her hips and held her steady, a warning on his face.

She leaned down and kissed him again, this time snaking her tongue into his mouth. She needed more. The days spent angry with him, spent without him, now left her with an emptiness that she needed filled.

She needed to feel his arms around her, holding her, comforting her, *choosing* her. She kissed him until tears welled in her eyes. She couldn't let him see. She reached down between them and rubbed her hand over his length. His hand shot to her wrist, but she gave him a wicked smile. "Don't worry. I'll behave." She kissed him again before finishing with "mostly," and left a trail of more kisses down his torso.

His breath hitched when she reached the trail of hair below his middle. She reached up a hand and scratched his chest. Goosebumps covered his skin. Tal couldn't help the mischievous smile she gave when he let out an involuntary sound.

Their moment in the tunnels after the botched plan at the brothel fueled her desire to pleasure him. She'd been too harsh with him, and yet he said nothing of it. He deserved more than what Tal could give him. But while Tal held his attention tonight, she would let her mouth, her lips, and her tongue reciprocate what her mind and her heart couldn't.

Faron's body tensed under her, but she didn't relent, not when he let out a deep, almost pained groan, and not until his body relaxed into the bedding, and an exhausted exhale reached her ears. She let the sound wash over her before she crawled up his torso. She kissed his neck then lay on top of him with a smile on her face.

Faron's arms came around her and held her tightly. He tried to kiss her, but she turned away from him. Instead, he kissed the top of her head and collapsed back onto the pillow. "Blazing hells, Tal," he sighed. "You—"

"Are unlike any woman you'll ever meet?"

He nodded. "That too."

Tal laughed against him. "What were you going to say?"

"You unravel me." He tightened his arms around her and kissed her head again.

Tal didn't say anything because she feared what it would mean. *This man.* This man had barreled into her life when she'd grown content to block the world out. He made her forget her anger when she wanted to burn it all to the ground. He showed her how to laugh. He made her want to forgive him when she had never allowed forgiveness in her heart for anyone else. She found herself counting down the minutes to when she would see him again. It was an entirely new sensation, letting someone else dictate her happiness. Tal would never admit it, but she didn't know how she would ever say good-bye.

She moved to the bed, laying with her back pressed into him. Faron's hands caressed the exposed skin on her legs, sending chills racing through her body. She closed any remaining distance between them and opened up for him. Faron didn't hesitate. His warm hand explored what pleasured her. He kissed her neck and sent another wave of chills that clashed with the building momentum between her legs.

She wanted to tell him what to do, where to touch. She ached to be filled by him, to feel him thrust into her, but she lay frozen in a state of expectation. She didn't dare say anything for fear of losing her hold on the growing tide. Her fury beat in rhythm with his strokes. She held her breath for one heartbeat, two. In the third, the wave of electric ecstasy crashed over her again and again until she had nothing left to give and her body melted into the bed. Tal breathed until the pounding in her ears and in her heart quieted.

She rolled over in his arms and met his gaze. The low candlelight reflected in his eyes, and she found the flecks of gold there. Her eyes traced the lines of his face, the dark hair that was much too unkempt for a king, the expressive brows, the length of his nose, the sharpness of his jaw, and the fullness of his lips. She reminded herself that for a moment, this moment, this beautiful, stubborn, brilliant man was hers, and she would not waste it.

A soft glow filled the space around them. "You're devastatingly beautiful, Tal." He traced a finger from her brow to her jaw, down her neck, across her collarbone and placed his palm on her chest where her fury glowed the brightest. It pulsed with her heartbeat, and she knew it beat for him.

She kissed him with a gentleness that even she didn't know she was capable of. The passion of a few moments ago burned away. Faron didn't grip her with barely concealed restraint. Tal didn't press her body into him. Instead, Faron wrapped his arms around her while she rested her own palm over his heart. It beat a steady rhythm against her hand and the song called to her. This kiss, this moment, felt like coming home to a warm fire on a cold winter's night. And right there in Faron's arms was the closest Tal had ever come to finding a place of her own.

Faron's heartbeat pounded against her ear while she lay with her head on his chest. She could hear the moment he fell asleep, when it slowed to match her breathing. His arms around her relaxed and his body sunk further into her bed. Something about the act touched a chord within her. A voice in her head told her to remember this moment. This man, this king, *her* king, could be anywhere, and he chose to be here with her. In two days, he would likely have to go back to his duties, back to running the kingdom. And she would pick up the pieces of her life and figure out what to do next. Would the mages return for her tomorrow? The next day? How long did she have before they came crashing down on this life she'd built? Would some other threat ruin it all?

She sighed. For now, the threats were too far away to do anything about. She was safe. Her friends were safe. And she fell asleep listening to the heartbeat of a man who knew all her misgivings and still wanted to be by her side. She inhaled deeply and exhaled slowly. The world melted away and for a moment, Tal was content.

In the early hours of the morning, Tal felt the covers lift. A cool air disturbed the warmth underneath. Faron's clothes rustled as he put them back on. He kissed her gently on the temple and left the room in darkness. The bed felt colder without him, and she tried not to think too much about what it meant.

She tried not to think about what the future held for them. She tried not to think about last night. She tried not to think about him fighting a mage for her or staying with her during the aftermath. She tried not to think about their fight or him lying to her. She tried not to think about all those times they'd had together before she discovered his title. She tried and she failed at all of it. With him near, it had been easy to live in the moment and not think about the future, but with him gone, she feared she couldn't ignore the inner turmoil.

She tossed in bed and noticed a paper on the pillow next to her. On it sat a note. "Stay in bed. I'll be back." *When did he write that?* She smiled to herself, glad to know he would return soon. Her mind quieted, and she burrowed further into her bed. Soon, she dozed off again.

30

Poison filled Tal's mind. It reached into her, gripping her fury with dagger-like claws, and squeezed. She suffocated on it, trapped inside her paralyzed body as her fury writhed within her. It wrung her dry until she was nothing but a husk.

She opened her mouth in a silent scream and freed her power. It exploded outward in a white light, clinging to everything. All around, agonized wails pierced her eardrums. An entire forest crackled under the flames. Tal gasped, and it wrenched the magic back toward her. Everything within its grasp was sucked into her as the flames disappeared. Everyone around her was gone. She'd killed them.

She should be frightened. She should feel sorrow. But she only felt hollow. Her fury exploded outward again—this time without her bidding. It burned the sky until Tal was left in darkness. When the magic died, Tal collapsed. She lay prone and empty without her magic. The poison ate through her body, melding with every part of her until she didn't know where she ended and death began.

"Tal? Tal, wake up. You're safe. Wake up."

Faron brushed the hair from her face. She blinked, and he came into focus. Her heart raced. A weight sat on her chest that made it difficult to breathe.

"You're okay. You're safe," he repeated.

Her eyes swept the room, and she sucked in a deep breath.

"It's alright. You're safe," he repeated.

She nodded because she didn't trust her voice to hide the truth. The dream, the sense of impending doom, felt so real. What did it mean?

She sighed at the familiar thrashing energy within her chest. Her fury calmed when she acknowledged it, as if the magic had been trying to wake her from the nightmare. Tal clung to Faron, counting the beats as her heart pounded. She stared at a spot on the blanket, worried about what she would see if she closed her eyes.

"I brought you breakfast," Faron said softly when her racing heart had calmed. On the table in the corner of the room sat a plate full of breads, jellies, meats, fruits, and all manner of foods Tal had only tasted a handful of times in her life. He moved slowly, eyeing her reaction, and brought the plate to the bed.

Tal ate slowly, not quite tasting anything, but feeling her belly fill and energy return to her sleep-filled limbs. Faron combed his hands through her long hair, humming one of his usual tunes. When she hadn't taken a bite in ten minutes, he moved the plate to the end of the bed. "We can save the rest for later."

Tal nodded. "I'd like to see Septimus today."

The old man seemed to be waiting for them when the two arrived, though he didn't say anything to indicate it. He greeted them delightedly, his usual air of elderly impatience absent.

Tal relayed her capture and, as expected, Septimus appeared to have already known. "He cast a spell that rendered me immobile and stuck to the spot. Can you create something that would burn through the spell without injuring the victim?"

The alchemist nodded for a moment while lost in thought. "Give me three days," he spoke in his smooth voice.

"Are you not going to ask how she escaped the spell?" Faron eyed the alchemist with poorly concealed suspicion.

Septimus had a glint in his eye. "Your majesty," he began, at which Faron had a coughing fit, "you'll find there isn't much in this kingdom that I do not know, including a fairly dangerous secret that our fire-haired friend here holds closely. I do not feel the need to have her air it out unnecessarily for all to hear." He leaned across his counter to the couple and whispered, "There are unwanted eyes and ears everywhere." He straightened and continued in his normal tone, "You would do well to remember that."

Faron's eyes widened at Tal who shrugged.

"Am I the last person to find out who he is?" Tal's attention switched back and forth between the two men. Faron had the mind not to make eye contact.

"There's much about this kingdom you don't know, child. If you ventured further out of your tunnels more often, you'd see." Septimus gave her a curious grin.

She exchanged glances with Faron briefly before turning back to Septimus as a thought occurred to her. "Do you know anyone I can speak to about my... craft? Someone who can provide guidance?"

Septimus shook his head. "There is no one who would help you that knows how."

She considered his choice of words. Did that mean there were others with fire fury? Why wouldn't they help her? Perhaps she might be able to convince them.

Faron was a bit less inclined to drop the conversation. He later told Tal that he would ask the palace alchemist for a similar elixir to destroy a paralyzing spell. Tal teased that he didn't trust Septimus, and he didn't deny it. "He has kept my fury a secret for gods knows how long. I have no reason not to trust him."

"Has he though? Do we know that he isn't also providing information to the mages behind our backs?" They walked through the town away from the tunnels. They still hadn't discussed the matter between them, but Tal could feel the urge to say something bubbling at the surface, a feeling much like when her fury demanded to be let loose.

"Sybil said we can trust him, and Rain has tracked him closely to ensure he's not a threat. The man is as innocent as the baker. *I* trust him."

"There's something about him that seems off."

She nudged him with her hip. "You're just upset that he saw right through your lame disguise."

"I'm surprised that you didn't." His gentle smile fell the moment he said it.

"Well, maybe I didn't want to."

"Hello! Hello! Please! Stop!"

Tal turned in time to see a head full of blonde hair run around a cart and straight for them. The girl seemed out of place in her fine clothes and clean hair. She beamed at Faron, hands behind her back.

"Clara! You should have left for the mountains days ago." Faron leaned down to speak at her level.

Something clicked, and Tal recognized the happy teen as the same frightened girl at the brothel that she insisted on going back for. Faron had said he paid for the girl's freedom that same night, not knowing Tal had been taken. She should have been on a wagon to the mountains with a sweet older couple and a chest full of necessities.

"I asked them to wait so I could thank you!" Clara bounced on her feet.

Faron chuckled. "Well, don't thank me. It was Talwyn over here," he pulled Tal over by the hand, "who insisted we get you out of there."

The girl's eyes widened in recognition. "You were there! I saw you!"

Tal smiled awkwardly. "I was."

"You helped free me?"

"Uh, well, I told him to." Tal gestured to Faron.

"'Demanded' is more like it." Faron nudged her.

The air rushed out of Tal when Clara slammed into her with a crushing hug.

"Thank you," she whispered into Tal.

She hesitated but found her arms reaching around the girl as if by their own accord, and Faron's cheeks dimpled. Slowly, Tal smiled back.

<hr>

Faron refused to reveal their destination. They walked through the docks, then the slums, then fields of wheat grass and wildflowers, and finally, rolling hills. At the top of the biggest hill stood the enormous white willow tree.

Tal placed her hand on the rough bark. Her fingers easily found the grooves of her and Carrick's initials carved into the trunk long ago. *Hello, old friend. I pray you've been well.* It had been many years since she last sat beneath the tree. While so much in Tal's life had changed, the willow kept its many branches and grew the same leaves every spring.

A light breeze blew its draping branches in an elegant dance that she couldn't peel her gaze from. They sat underneath and listened to the leaves as they swayed in the wind.

Sweat dripped down Tal's brow and off her lip. Faron took off his shirt and enjoyed the cooler air. The summer sun glistened along the sweat dripping down the muscles of his back. He caught Tal admiring his bare skin and winked at her. She shoved him and laughed.

The faint sounds of life at the bottom of the large hill carried on the wind to their spot beneath the tree. Seagulls screeched at sailors. She always hated the sound. It pierced her eardrums. But at this distance, it was almost beautiful. People went about their lives below, entering shops, scrambling about, unaware of the danger that walked among them a few nights ago. *How peaceful it must be*, she thought, *to live a life free from such violence*. Tal didn't have that luxury. She had chosen violence as her profession, or rather, it had chosen her. But sitting up here under this willow, she could almost imagine what that kind of life must be like.

"I come up here to think," he said to the wind. "No one can interrupt my thoughts or demand a decision I don't want to make."

"It must be lonely."

"You have no idea."

His gaze remained on the town. Things had quieted between them. Tal could feel it in her heart. The tumultuous waves of excitement and near-anxiety of those first weeks had dissipated. The poisonous betrayal of his secret and what his identity might mean for them remained absent. Right then, she only felt peace.

"What's it like?" she mused. "Having all that power?"

"Nothing like you would think." He paused. "I'm not allowed to make many decisions on my own. I can't even eat breakfast without someone approving. Can't have their precious king do anything that could put him in danger. And you think the king has power? I likely have barely more power than you do." Bitterness crept into his voice. "The council has to approve of anything I do, and they most often do not."

"Then what's the point of you being king?"

"To have someone to blame when their policies backfire," he said harshly.

Tal blinked, having expected a different answer. "So, you weren't merely coming to the docks to escape life at the palace?" She thought of his maroon suit and the first night she had seen him, a naive swordsman eager to save the first person he saw in danger.

He nodded. "I didn't realize how bad it was. No one told me anything. And when I questioned, they assured me everything was being taken care of. But even my first time outside the grounds proved they lied."

"So, what now?" Tal had always thought the king didn't care, that he called all the shots, and his council only advised. All the times she silently blamed him for the kingdom's condition, not knowing it had actually been Faron, only to learn he'd been deceived by his own council made her wonder if things could have been different. "Now that you know how bad it is," she added.

"Things are going to change," he said, staring out at the run-down homes. "I've already started pushing them to show me evidence of their improvements. Some of them will have to go. But I'm going to be more involved. I have allies on the council. I'm seeking allies abroad. They'll help me take the kingdom back."

Hearing him talk about Meladair like that gave Tal a strange feeling in her chest. She had spent so long thinking of him as this spoiled but charming noble. And as king, he had responsibilities to uphold. He would need to attend meetings, entertain foreign dignitaries, visit other kingdoms, as well as continue the royal bloodline. A rock formed in the pit of her stomach at the last thought. What did this mean for them? For her? What was she even doing?

She couldn't be running around with the king. It would spell disaster for him. The council had already made their intentions of marrying him off well known. He would wed some royal princess from a wealthy foreign country. There was no fighting it.

They would never approve of him marrying an orphan from the docks. Even if it were a possibility, would she want that? The fancy balls, the meetings, the reputation to uphold—Tal wouldn't survive that kind of life, nor did she want to.

She had already made a name for herself earlier that summer. Even if she wanted to join Faron, the council would never approve, nor would the public accept a queen who behaved the way she did. She sighed. She shouldn't even think of such things. It's not as if they had discussed what they were to each other when she thought he was simply some random nobleman. She frowned at her thoughts' downward spiral.

"I planned on bringing you here that morning." He didn't need to say which morning. She knew. "I had a plan. I would tell you that I come up here when I need somewhere to think without being bothered. Sometimes I come up here when I'm stressed, or worried. But I come here to be happy too. This place brings me peace. And then I would say that my life requires a good number of important decisions that could affect many people. You would ask something like 'What important decisions do you have to make? If you want your fresh croissant buttered or with jam?' And I'd say 'No, that's usually decided for me,' which you wouldn't believe."

She chuckled at his impersonation of her.

"I'd get all serious and say there was something I needed you to know. I've been wanting to tell you for some time, but didn't know how. I came up here for weeks wondering if and when I should tell you. I honestly didn't know how you would take me being serious, and if I would have been able to say it if you couldn't. But you deserved to know, and I'm sorry you found out like you did after so long. I honestly thought that first night without my mask you would have known. And when you didn't, it was nice to be just... me. I got a glimpse of what life would be like if I wasn't the king, what it could have been like if that fire hadn't burned the east wing of Silaron and everyone in it. And when I decided to give it up and tell you, I couldn't bring myself to do it. I started to so many times. But I kept finding a reason why the time wasn't right. Honestly, can you think of a point when I could have told you and not have it go badly?"

Tal inhaled deeply, not sure how to respond. "I don't know, Faron. What do you expect me to say? Just because it wasn't easy, doesn't mean you shouldn't have tried to explain. And it doesn't mean I can't be upset about it."

His lips thinned, and he nodded.

She pinched the bridge of her nose and took a deep breath. "Maybe it's for the best. If telling me hadn't upset me somehow, we probably would have continued down some road we had no right to be on."

Faron's head snapped to meet her gaze. "Wait, what?"

"I mean, you can't expect me to think we'd continue this charade after finding out who you really are?"

"Charade? That's a bit harsh, don't you think?"

"Is it? I mean, I should have understood what was going on even before then."

"What do you think was going on?"

"We were just having fun. It could never last, even if you weren't the king." The title felt foreign on her tongue.

"Is that what it was to you? You were just having fun?" He narrowed his eyes.

She could see he wasn't happy with the turn in conversation. She too wondered why she talked to him in this way, perhaps to protect herself. She anticipated the inevitable rejection. She wanted to be ready for it. Maybe she wanted to be the one to do it first. He wouldn't have to feel guilty, and she could walk away with her dignity and call it a fun but temporary distraction.

She stood and brushed off the grass stuck to her pants. "I—thank you for coming for me, for fighting for me. You really—" She inhaled a shaky breath. "For someone who grew up in such a different world, I never would have thought I'd enjoy your company." She turned to leave.

He stood and grabbed her elbow. "Are you really that upset with me that you would walk away?" The hurt on his face made her bite her cheek to stop the tears from coming.

"What's there to walk away from, Faron? You're the king. You have a life to live."

"You're walking away from us, Tal!" He grabbed her other arm now. "Don't act like we didn't have something. Was it all nothing to you?"

She didn't voice her thoughts—that it didn't matter what she felt. Instead, she took a deep breath and said, "You shouldn't come by anymore."

"Are you sending me away?" His voice shook with barely restrained emotion.

"You have a kingdom to run. I can't distract you."

"I'll choose how I spend my time. I will not be ordered away," he growled.

She called her fury to light a fireball in her palm. "Is that a challenge?" She remembered the night in the tunnel not even a week ago. This time, she would send him away for good and save herself the heartache.

"Demon's snare, woman. I swear, you'll be the death of me." He released her and stalked a few paces away before turning back to her. "You are the most infuriating, pig-headed, brilliant fool that I've ever met. Swallow your stubborn pride for once and listen.

"Every moment of my life has been spent bending to their will, paraded from meetings to dinners and dances from one meaningless day to the next, an ornament to their machinations. I was *suffocating* in that idleness until you barreled into that room. You brought a light into my world when I'd spent my whole life drowning in dullness.

"From the moment I saw you fighting to save that little girl, a fire has awoken within me. That flame has pulled me to your side every day, and I ache to be near you when I'm away. You are the light that guides me. I can close my eyes, but I still see *you*. Talwyn, I love you. I love your anger, your passion, your fury, your stubbornness, your selflessness. I love your mind, your spirit, and your gods-damned infuriating body and the way you use it against me. I love you. And no amount of your anger is going to drive me away.

"Take me at my word. I love you. I have since the first night you rescued Evania without hesitation, to the night you wrestled with your dress and nearly fell off that balcony, to the night you destroyed that mage who attacked you, and even though you are hells-bent on destroying me, I love you for it. You've ignited my soul, and I will fight like the hells to keep it from being snuffed out."

Tal stood wordlessly and stared at Faron. The orange glow from her flame reflected in his hazel eyes. Her gaze followed the crease in his brow, down his nose, and to the full lips that closed as he swallowed. She let his words sink in one by one. Her eyes danced between the willow, the docks in the distance, and back to him. She studied the outline of his muscled shoulders, how the light of her flame reflected off his bare chest.

Her mind reeled, trying to make sense of his words and tamping her anger over his lies. She had never been any good at reasoning when her emotions ran high, and it took great effort to do so now. A thought occurred to her. "That *was* you at the ball."

Still breathing heavily, he let out a soft laugh and shook his head. "I just poured my heart out to you, and you want to know who danced with you?"

"You told me it wasn't you."

He shook his head. "I told you it was the king. I didn't say he *wasn't* me." He took a tentative step back to her. "You intrigued me before but seeing you so carefree that night unlocked something inside me. I needed to see you again, to get to know you."

"Wait, does this mean the king makes his own clothes?" Tal remembered the handmade trousers he coveted.

"Well—" Another step.

She didn't let him answer, and instead said, "And all those favors you were owed. They weren't really favors, were they?"

"No. They weren't," he answered reluctantly. "They were well paid commissions." He stood a few paces away now, and Tal's heart beat in her throat.

Tal's eyes went wide. "The axes?!"

"Those were a gift to me, but I knew they were more suited to you. Anything else you'd like to know?" He chuckled.

"Did you really name your horse after your eyes?" The question had been bothering Tal since she'd made the connection.

Faron laughed freely now. "You can blame Waylon for that one. I didn't know the color, and he convinced me it was a beautiful name for a beautiful horse."

Tal bit back the humor in her voice. "He's a menace."

"He's an asshole."

Tal took a steadying breath to gather her thoughts again. "Your name? Should I start calling you James now?"

"I was anointed King James when I took the throne. My birth name, the name my mother gave me, is Faron. I'm only called James when I'm performing royal duties."

Tal tilted her head at that revelation. "What about the rumors? The nights you supposedly spend in women's beds?"

"It's a ruse. Waylon runs around pretending to be me. How else would I get away with sneaking out every night as the masked maroon swordsman?" He stopped his advance.

"Why did you kiss me, if you knew you were lying to me?" Hurt broke through her voice, and she hated herself for the show of weakness.

"You kissed me, remember?"

She felt a grim satisfaction at the pain in his eyes. "But you kissed me back." She couldn't understand why she struggled to breathe.

He was close enough to reach out and touch. His hand twitched as if he too resisted the urge. "Do you really think I could resist you?" That easy smirk returned to his face, and Tal felt a bit of relief. He'd grinned in the weeks since she'd learned of his true identity, but never this one, never the sweet, carefree, almost boyish grin that he used to give her so often.

"I don't know how to do this. I don't forgive easily," she said, either as a warning or an opening, she couldn't be sure which.

"I wouldn't expect anything less." He took a tentative step toward her. One more and he would be close enough to wrap his arms around her.

"And what about your responsibility? The council would never approve of a relationship between the two of us."

"I'm the king, remember? I'll dismiss them and make my own laws."

When her shoulders slumped, he closed the distance between them and pulled her into a gentle embrace, like he had after she killed the mage. Before him, she had never known such tenderness accompanied by warmth and trust. He held her head against his chest for a moment, then pulled back and placed his hands on either side of her face, cupping her jaw. "I'll spend every moment fighting for your forgiveness if you let me." He kissed her, gently, and she let him.

31

Tal's dagger landed in the wooden pole with a solid *thunk*. She turned her smug grin to Carrick. "Oh? What were you saying?"

Carrick answered with a perfectly placed dagger in the next pole. "I was saying that you're going to pay for tonight's round."

Sunset glared off the Taralin, painting the pier in red and orange hues. A warm breeze gusted on the water. It stunk of trash and seaweed, and Tal breathed it in gratefully. Each exhausted exhale pressed heavily on her sternum, but she welcomed it.

A week had passed since her afternoon under the willow tree. She found the town's guardian in the distance. The leaves hung motionless despite the breeze at her back. It seemed that the willow always lived in contrast to life below the hill.

Unease turned Tal's stomach. Every night since that afternoon, she'd had nightmares filled with images she hadn't known to fear until now—a ship with sails as black as death approaching her shores, Faron eyeing her with nothing more than indifference, the palace in ruins, Carrick's beautiful face marred with a bloody grimace.

Every night, Tal's dreams ended in the same devastated forest. She opened her eyes to gray skies and charred remains. Her heart hammered in her ribs—or was that her magic? Echoes of screams rang in her ears, and bodies lay at her feet. Panic gripped her by the throat. She couldn't breathe. Ash coated her lungs. She collapsed in still-warm embers, coughing and retching. Her hands turned black as they searched the ground—for what, she didn't know. At last, they connected with a power so great, it pulled her in and sent a shockwave through her, jarring her from the dream. The last thing she saw before the panic dissipated was the willow tree looming over her.

"Are we finishing this game, or what?" Carrick's voice cut through her exhausted haze.

Tal blinked. *It's just a dream.* She retrieved her daggers and joined her friend at the other end of the pier. "Maybe I can trick Faron into paying tonight," she attempted her usual flippant tone.

"You won't even have to try. He pays every night." Carrick's dagger landed high. "So, are you going to tell me, or do I need to drag it out of you?"

Tal's throw landed square in the center of her post. "Tell you what?"

"If you two had a chance to talk or if you're both pretending you didn't want to break his nose." The next dagger landed low, and Carrick swore.

"We talked." Tal flipped her blade in the air, feeling like herself once again.

"And?" Her friend turned his broad chest to her.

"And he's an ass for keeping it a secret." She paused to take her turn. "But I guess he's made up for it."

His thick arms crossed over his chest. "You guess?"

Tal sighed. "Okay. Yes, I forgave him."

He bit his cheeks to stop a smile from splitting his lips. "Good. So, I expect to see him around—*with* his eyebrows intact." He added the last part as Tal threw another dagger and sent it wide.

She pushed his arm, but the brute didn't budge.

"I told you tonight's round is yours!" he chuckled.

"You did that on purpose!"

"I most certainly did—Hey!" He dodged Tal's next throw.

Laughter came easily in that moment. She grasped onto the feeling and let it embrace her. There was no telling how long it would last. Tal balanced on a knife's edge, and the blade demanded that she fall.

"So, what about all that marriage business?" Carrick's throw bested Tal's again.

She answered with an impeccable throw of her own. "He's got the council off his back for now."

"And later? Will they let him choose?"

Tal flipped her weapon in the air. "If you're suggesting I marry him, don't. Marriage is not for me, least of all to a king."

"Even if that king is Faron?"

"Forget it, Carrick. I am not fit to be a queen." She threw her next dagger with more force than she meant to. It soared past the intended post and embedded in the next. Tal sighed heavily. "I am not fit for marriage at all."

"He might be able to convince you otherwise. Besides, you really know how to turn heads in a dress."

Tal elbowed him in the ribs, and Carrick retaliated by shoving her off the pier. She shrieked before hitting the water. It chilled her bones. The river engulfed her, and she stilled in its weightlessness. Despite the sun overhead, darkness filled her senses, the kind that swallowed all thought and left her with only silence. It was peaceful.

She paused a moment longer, relishing the coolness caressing her skin. When she resurfaced, Tal let the water brush across her face and smiled at the sun's contrasting warmth.

"Hells, woman! Don't scare me like that!"

Tal grabbed his outstretched arm and let him pull her to the pier. "What? Did you think I forgot how to swim?"

"Or something." He stepped back and leaned against the nearest post.

"Or *something*? Are you alright, Duckie?" Water pooled beneath her while she checked her weapons and wrung out her hair. His frown gave her pause. He wedged a dagger in the wooden post and twisted it audibly. "You're going to split the wood if you keep at it."

"I'm strong, but not that strong." His smile didn't reach his eyes.

"Alright." She sat cross-legged and slapped the wood in front of her. "Sit."

Carrick sighed heavily. "You know—"

"*Sit.*"

He plopped in front of her and folded his legs, resting his elbows on his knees.

"Now, spit it out."

He hesitated. The corners of his eyes wrinkled against the emotion he refused to release. "When you—" He frowned.

Tal held his gaze for three long breaths. She rested a hand on his knee, waiting.

His head fell into his hands. "When you were taken, it was—it felt *wrong*. You're supposed to be *here*. I didn't—" He lifted his head. "How are you so okay?"

Tal knew Carrick heard her screams every night. He knew she wasn't okay—that she was pretending nothing had changed. He needed to hear the truth. She steeled herself with her next breath. "In truth? I'm not." She willed herself not to think of the visions she'd revisited just moments ago.

Carrick's hands fell on top of hers.

"I cry every night. And when I don't cry, I have nightmares. I see cloaked shadows in the dark. I smell Ed's blood on the wind. I spend every moment waiting for the next blow to bludgeon my body. And when my power surges in my chest, I wonder if this will be the last time. Will it finally drive me mad with the need to *consume*. I'm not okay, and I don't know when I will be." Her words grew thick. She struggled through her next breath and felt the sting of tears waiting to fall.

Carrick squeezed her hand. His eyes glistened with tears of his own, and Tal couldn't muster the energy to tease him.

"I don't know when I'll be okay again," she repeated. Her next breath washed through her like the water that crashed over her head. It crested over her aloof facade and left her vulnerable. She swallowed the sobs that left her broken and raw each night while Faron hummed a deep melody. She hadn't opened up about this. Not to Faron. Not to anyone. Not until now.

It terrified her to admit she had no control over her thoughts, her fears, her own magic. She would do anything to go back to the Talwyn that drank herself into a stupor and stumbled over the cobblestones until trouble found her. The world around her had become foreign. She awoke from the terror only to fall asleep to a sense of foreboding. She couldn't navigate this alone, and Faron wouldn't be there for every moment of it.

"I'm sorry," she whispered.

Carrick frowned. He opened his mouth to speak, but Tal stopped him with a shake of her head.

"I'm sorry for my stubbornness, and that I couldn't see how my actions had consequences... for *all* of us. I'm sorry for making you worry and having to save me because I couldn't follow my own damn rules. I'm sorry you got this *shit* life. I wish—" She inhaled against the tightness in her chest. "I wish I could give you something more, that I could wave my hand, and we'd have everything we could ever want, or at least that I could stop being such a dewberry."

"Hey, if anyone is a dewberry around here, it's Daire."

Tal laughed through her tears. "Don't get me started."

"Once Faron has no need of him, I'll enjoy breaking every single one of his bones." Carrick's eyes lost their light at the mention of the traitorous captain.

"And then he's mine."

Their fickle alliance with Daire, if they could call it that, still made Tal uneasy. It felt more like they had to threaten the man into feeding false information to the council while reporting back to Faron. She hoped, at least, they would learn who hired the mages and ensure the danger had passed.

"I'm sorry too." Carrick broke Tal from her thoughts. "You shouldn't have been left alone. With everything you've been through this summer, I should have been there with you."

Tal wiped her nose with her wet sleeve. "You have nothing to apologize for. And I wasn't alone. I had Ed and Waylon."

"And they were still no match for the mage. It was too much to ask them to protect you. Waylon is devastated enough as it is. He still hasn't come by."

"And you think putting yourself in danger would have been much better?" She nudged his arm.

Carrick released a frustrated sigh. "I don't know. I just—" He curled his hands around hers. "I just wish I could change it all. When I thought something had happened, I was lost. Don't look at me like that. I need to say this," he chastised her when she grimaced. "We built this life *together*. I don't want it if you're not there to see it through." His eyes pleaded.

"Are you confessing your love to me, Duckie?" Tal tried to hide her grin.

"I confess that if you die on me, I'll beat you to a pulp." He released her hand and poked her shoulder.

"There he is." Tal rubbed the spot that would definitely bruise. "Don't make it awkward. Apparently, I'm taken, and I'm not made for sharing."

"Faron can have you." He pretended to turn away.

"Hey!"

"As long as he brings you back by dinner," he said with an ear-splitting grin.

"I can't promise dinner. Definitely sunrise... give or take an hour." She tapped her chin in pretend thought.

Carrick sighed. "Don't leave us, Tal. Okay?"

"Are you kidding? You aren't that lucky. I'm not going any-where." Tal stood and offered her hand.

Carrick took it and stood beside her. He wrapped his muscled arms around her and squeezed.

Tal closed her eyes and returned the embrace. When he didn't let go, she said a silent prayer to the gods to protect them, all of them. Whatever dangers lay ahead, she prayed they would face it together. As she fought the tears that threatened to spill yet again, her fury lapped at its walls in a gentle caress. *We'll be okay,* she told herself, and her fury swelled for a heartbeat before quieting.

They gathered their weapons in silence and left the pier. Tal busied herself with securing one of her sheaths when she was tugged toward the water with a force that had her stumbling into a newcomer. Something cold and sharp bit into her neck. Tal released an exasperated breath.

"Alisaire wants to speak with you."

Carrick tilted his head—an offer to step in—but Tal had already resigned to handle the situation herself.

She lifted her shoulders in a slight shrug before saying, "Fritz, I told you, if you put your hands on me again, you're dead."

The blade bit into her neck as the thug shook. Warm blood trickled down to her collarbone. A dark room with a wooden ceiling filled Tal's mind. She held Carrick's gaze to steady her thoughts.

"You're coming with me."

"Good-bye, Fritz." Tal fisted her hands. She didn't bother removing his knife. Pain didn't register in the recesses of her power where she traveled. It didn't take any effort at all. Between one breath and the next, pure fury exploded out of the man. He collapsed in a ball of flame before he could cry out.

Carrick gaped while Tal brushed remains from her sleeve. "Blazing pigs, Tal. You didn't touch him. You barely moved."

She picked Fritz's blade from the ashes, inspecting it and deeming it worth keeping.

"Are you at all fazed?"

She met his stare. No. She was not fazed. In fact, she was so unaffected by the use of her fury that she was terrified. The magic coursed through her, enticing her to use more. And she would.

Something changed in her on that table, and Tal didn't know whether to cling to her friends or tell them to run. So, rather than admitting the war within her, she said, "I'm fine."

"Uh huh." Carrick grabbed a nearby bucket and washed away the evidence of Tal's fury. "Looks like the gangs are getting restless again?"

"I'll deal with Alisaire when I'm ready. We have other plans tonight."

"Well then, come on." He dropped the bucket and threw an arm around her shoulders. "I hear the king is at Gale's. Something tells me he has a thing for redheads."

Tal smirked. "Is that so? Do you think he likes stubborn bounty hunters with a healthy appetite? Maybe I can swindle a round of drinks out of him."

"Something tells me he'll offer more than that."

Tal shoved Carrick again, and still the man was unmoved. They turned north toward her favorite tavern.

"Do you think he brought dessert? I'm starving." Carrick's voice echoed over the Taralin.

"He better have. And if Sybil eats my custard again, I'll be furious."

Epilogue

Faron

"With all due respect, *Your Majesty*," Councilman Gregor spat the word like poison on his lips, "your blatant disregard for policy and tradition has been downright insubordinate and has left many of us wondering if you're even fit for the throne." The bloated and balding man stood proudly, as if he had already won the argument. His swollen finger jabbed a page on the ledger in front of him. The sneer he directed at Faron should have been treasonous.

"With all due respect, *Councilman*," Faron threw the title back at him, "our kingdom would benefit more from an alliance providing lumber and wool to house and clothe our people, *not* from steel. The alliance that *you* insist on will provide enough metal to outfit every citizen with a weapon and suit of armor. Do you plan to declare war on the three kingdoms at once? Or did the eastern kingdom promise you something else with my marriage?" Faron splayed his hands on the table in front of him. The wood beneath his fingers helped ground him. Gregor's contributions to the council were always self-serving. Despite being part of the group that appointed Faron's father to the throne, Gregor would better serve the kingdom in his grave.

Radomir leaned forward in his seat, waving for Faron's attention. "What Councilman Gregor means, Your Majesty, is that our kingdom has thrived on adhering to certain... expectations." He nervously searched for Gregor's approval.

Faron threw his hand toward the east. "You call this thriving? The people are *starving*, their homes are collapsing on top of them, or worse—they're living on the streets. Gangs have taken root in our port and corruption and violence are rampant. No one here is thriving except the so-called *nobility*." Faron sneered. The pair disgusted him; Gregor, the boorish fuck and Radomir, his sniveling pet rat.

Gregor scoffed. "We're handling the situation in our port. You've been told not to concern yourself with the matter, and you would do well to listen."

"You're handling *nothing!*" Faron shouted. "As the king, I demand you turn your sights from foreign affairs and fix the mess you've made."

"You're in no position to make demands, boy." Councilman Mackenzie didn't bother to stand from his seat to deliver the veiled threat. While he claimed his hunched form hindered his mobility, Faron knew it was a farce so he wouldn't have to pay the proper respect to his king.

"Calm down, Mackenzie, before you make a fool of yourself." Connell waved a shaking hand at his fellow councilman.

Faron gritted his teeth against the insult he wished to sling at Mackenzie, allowing Connell the room to speak. The elderly councilman had been the chief advisor for four separate monarchies, and he respected the man more than anyone. Over the last decade, his old age had forced him to relinquish much of his power on the council, but he was still the most venerated member.

Connell pushed himself forward in his chair with difficulty, his frail arms shaking with the effort. "Your king is concerned, *as he should be.* And, while breaking his betrothal without our knowledge was ill-advised, and deploying the guard broke our laws, *he had good reason.*"

Radomir cleared his throat. "Our laws are in place to protect the monarchy, Connell. If we allow these actions to go unpunished, we risk him making a decision that destroys the people's trust. We'll lose the loyalty of the guard, and all our livelihoods could be forfeit."

"Oh, come off it, Radomir. Did you rehearse that pile of horseshit or is Gregor's hand so far up your ass, you've become his puppet?" Raedan admonished.

Faron didn't bother hiding his smirk. Out of all the council members, the short-tempered noble was Faron's favorite.

Raedan leaned back in his chair, arms crossed. "If you dickheads would shut the fuck up for once, perhaps we can all agree on a solution and get out of here before your miserable wives finish fucking the steward." The auburn-haired councilman delivered the insult with a straight face and a glint in his eye.

Faron thanked the gods that Raedan's position on the council could not be revoked thanks to a link to the old bloodline. His fiery disposition and penchant for speaking his mind endeared him to Faron, especially in recent months.

Radomir puffed his chest like an angry fowl readying an attack, but Connell stood from his seat, silencing the room. "The issue at hand is that we now have a regiment questioning the decisions made within this chamber, a dead soldier, and a would-be ally that is now threatening war."

Faron deflated. He expected a fallout, but war? They would never survive.

"We will meet with the soldiers, display a united front, and pay respects to our fallen man."

Gregor huffed and received a glare from Raedan.

"There is nothing to be done about the betrothal. Lord Niktovaz will never agree to another contract." Connell met Faron's gaze when he added, "That particular agreement no longer served our kingdom anyway."

Faron sighed. Even with Connell's admission, his own actions brought trouble to Meladair, the full scope of which had yet to be revealed.

"We will open negotiations with the eastern kingdom to repair relations. We do not have the resources to offer as a concession, therefore a marriage alliance, under *different* conditions, will be our goal."

"Councilman, if I may," Faron interrupted, "if we were to acquire resources by other means, we may be able to appease the eastern monarchy and repair our alliance."

"As much faith as I have in your intentions, Your Majesty, a *mountain* of resources and gold could not undo the damage to Lord Niktovaz's ego. And, being a distant relative to the eastern monarchy, they *must* take the slight as a direct insult. Marriage is the *only* solution. It is decided."

Two hours later, Faron left the chamber ready to ask Tal if she would incinerate Gregor. The prick didn't even attempt to hide the fact that he had his sights set on the throne. If he thought he could get away with it, Faron would have thrown him out the window. Hells, he'd been ready to throw Connell too. The elder may command respect, but he stubbornly refused to listen to Faron. That is, until an hour after arguing, when Faron presented the treaties he'd been working on. And still, Gregor pushed his own agenda. The squabbling continued. Nothing was gained, but it was a start.

Some days, he didn't care if he lost his title. He never should have had it in the first place. If he had remained Lord Faron of Dohaern, someone else could worry about ledgers, alliances, and the threat of being overthrown. And he would be free to marry a woman of his choosing.

Faron rounded a corner to find a sullen Waylon leaning against the opposite wall.

"If I had known you dragged me out of my house to listen to those self-important assholes drone on about themselves for hours,

I would have told you to eat my mother's cooking." He pushed off the wall and joined Faron as they made their way to the palace's exit.

Faron shivered at a childhood memory of something resembling bread that stunk of feet and tasted like dirt. Waylon's raised finger stopped him from commenting. The king gave his friend a once-over. Stubble had begun to grow on what was usually a clean-shaven face. His clothes looked like they'd been under his bed for ages—and smelled like it too. The shadows under Waylon's eyes gave away the sleep he'd lost, as did the sharper angles of his cheekbones and near-sickly pallor of his skin. "I dragged you out of the house because you've ignored me for almost two weeks."

Waylon shrugged. "I've been studying."

Faron would have laughed if the lie wasn't hiding something darker. "You needed to get out of that house." He sniffed. "But maybe you should have bathed first." Faron laughed when Waylon shoved his shoulder. "You're coming to the tavern with me."

"With Tal, you mean." Anguish twisted his friend's features.

"With everyone. They're meeting us later." Waylon hung his head, shaking it, but Faron spoke before he could offer an excuse, "I'm not letting you back out this time."

"Fine." Waylon fixed the buttons at his wrists. "But I need to stretch first."

The pair emerged from the training yard two hours later. Faron's lip was bleeding and swollen, his bare chest gleaming with sweat. Waylon sported a new black eye.

"Wait until I tell Tal how you screamed like a child." Faron jabbed his friend, happy to see the light return to his eyes.

"You threw me over your shoulder! And you ruined my good shirt." Waylon fit two fingers through a tear over his heart.

"That thing has seen one too many deplorable acts and should have been burned long ago." Faron avoided his friend's half-hearted punch to the stomach. He grabbed his own shirt from a wooden fence post and pulled it over his head.

Waylon fidgeted with the damaged shirt. "The least you could do is replace it."

Faron shook his head, a smile on his lips. "I'll buy your drinks tonight."

"You buy my drinks every night." Waylon gripped the fabric by his abdomen, tugging on the hem. "I could always just go without."

"Do that and the commotion you cause will definitely start a brawl."

Waylon shrugged. "It's not easy being this desirable. Besides, unlike you, *I* don't have someone to warm my bed every night. I've got to improvise."

Faron plucked a handful of flowers from a bush as they walked toward the palace kitchens. "Is that jealousy I hear?" He smiled at the bouquet, thinking of the cutting remark Tal would offer as thanks for the gift. The woman hated to be treated like a lady, and he loved her even more for it.

"You're damn right it is. Look at you, smiling like a bleeding fool. You've had that goofy expression on your face since the beginning of summer." Waylon threw his arm around Faron and lowered his voice, "The servants have started to wonder if you fell off your horse and hit that giant head of yours."

Oh, Faron had fallen all right. From the moment he'd caught Talwyn whirling on an apparition, a dagger in each hand, he'd been desperate to catch her attention. He nearly killed himself trying to impress her when he jumped off that roof the night he first heard her laugh. He'd spoken truthfully under the willow. One glimpse was all it took. His heart was lost to her.

Faron didn't bother telling any of this to his friend. Waylon had teased him countless times the past two months over how quickly he fell for the bounty hunter. Each time, Faron just smiled and agreed that he never stood a chance. "I'm not convinced you aren't just trying to further anger your father," he said instead.

They reached the kitchens and slipped in through the servant's entrance. Faron nodded to each person as they bowed, letting him pass. Waylon walked past them without a glance. He grabbed an apple from a bowl and leaned against a long stone counter while Faron gathered a basket of food. "Can't I find love *and* become a disgrace at the same time?" he said around a mouthful.

Faron placed as many desserts as he could into the basket, taking extra care to grab two more custards for Tal. He hid them under the rest of the food and placed the bouquet of flowers on the top. He imagined the way she would purse her lips, calling him a hopeless romantic for bringing her flowers but not the custard she loved so much. He couldn't hide the smile that pulled at his lips thinking of how he would tease her once she found the dessert.

When Faron didn't respond, Waylon asked quietly, "What would your parents have thought of her?"

The question hung between them. He didn't ask with spite in his tone. Waylon's father had tried to leash his son from the moment he could walk, to mold him into some vision only he could see. And Waylon had spent his whole life rebelling.

"Mother would have lost her mind over a lady in trousers." Faron's face softened thinking of how she would waste no time teaching Tal an appreciation for finer fashion. His father would love her, naturally. "Father would have been fascinated by her skill with a dagger," he added, knowing the former king would ask Tal to teach him to throw. He wished they could have met her, just once. Faron knew, even if he *was* king, they would approve of her.

Waylon lowered his apple, as if reading Faron's thoughts. "We'll figure out a way to get the council off your back. You're the fucking king! They can't force you into anything."

Faron leaned back against the counter beside Waylon. "You'd think that would count for something." His exhale betrayed the exhaustion he'd been masking since his first night visiting the docks.

"I'll send Jens to the mountains in the morning. Father's journals mentioned rumors of fire and steel. If steel is what Gregor wants, I'll bleed the damn hills dry." He refused to consider a future where he would bend to the council's demands.

Connell may have the most respected opinion of all the council members, but there had to be a different way. Any alliance with the eastern kingdom would come at a cost to Meladair, and Faron wouldn't be their willing sacrifice. And speaking of alliances, he couldn't forget to send the stable hand to intercept a correspondence from the western kingdom. He expected their letter to arrive any day.

A heavy silence hung between them, and Faron knew it was more than just worry for him that plagued his friend's thoughts. They hadn't spoken since Tal's rescue, hadn't discussed what happened to Ed. Waylon had claimed his father was keeping him busy, but he had never obliged the old man for more than a few days.

"What happened to Ed was not your fault." Faron stared ahead as he spoke.

Waylon stiffened.

"Whether it was myself beside him or Jens, or anyone. There was nothing you or any of us could have done. And Tal doesn't blame you."

"Saying it and believing it are two very different things, brother." Waylon's voice held every bit of self-loathing Faron knew he had directed at himself since the attack.

He turned and gripped Waylon's shoulder. "Then we'll spend every moment reminding you."

Before they left the kitchens, Faron passed a note to one of the servants, instructing Daire to meet him on the west wall at mid-morning. For the last week, the captain kept his word and fed false information to the council while relaying their instructions back to his king. It did nothing to change Faron's opinion of the man. Faron didn't consider himself violent, but every time he met with the captain, he remembered Daire's sneer when he spoke to Tal after her capture.

If he hadn't been useful, Faron would have welcomed the pain of breaking every bone in the man's face with his bare hands. He would even gladly sit back while Tal let her fury consume him. The only thing keeping him alive was the possibility that the information he gathered might lead them to whomever sent the mages after Tal. Once his purpose was fulfilled, Faron would find a new captain.

The pair made one last stop at the tanner's for the gift he'd been planning. The wolves destroyed Tal's old holster for her axes. So, he had a new weapons belt made from the hide of the boar they'd killed. It was sentimental, but he knew Tal would see its practicality. The belt would be her favorite gift, of course, followed directly by the custard. She was a woman of action, and he was the poor sod who couldn't keep his eyes off her.

As they passed through the gates, Faron peered northeast to the willow tree, as he did every time he exited the grounds. It was a habit—one he convinced himself was for good luck. He had done so the first night he saw Tal and had every day since. He blinked when his eyes found the massive trunk. Under its swaying leaves stood a figure—a woman, if the height and long hair were any indication, but the willow was too far for him to discern anything further about her. In all the days and nights Faron had looked to the tree, he had never seen anyone beside its trunk. As its leaves swayed in a wind Faron had no doubt carried the salty brine from the Taralin, he could have sworn one of the branches bent down to the woman's face. He blinked, convincing himself the distance was playing tricks. A moment later, he lost sight of the woman as she descended the large hill.

"I could have retrieved these things for you." Waylon pulled Faron's attention away from the willow.

Faron gave his friend an easy grin. "And let you take all the credit? Not a chance." They made their way to Gale's with a basket of food, a bouquet of flowers, and a boarskin belt in hand. Despite the outcome of the meeting, Faron's duties for the day were fulfilled, and he would spend the night with his friends and the most incredible woman he'd ever met. Tomorrow, he would try to solve the kingdom's problems. Tonight, his only hope was to see the stubborn bounty hunter smile.

Acknowledgements

This book would not have come about without the support and love from so many incredible people. This is for you.

Firstly, thank you Taylor Swift for the rain show at Gillette that planted an idea in my head about a woman who kicks ass for fun and gives zero fucks. You won't see this, but a thank you is warranted nonetheless.

Jordon, my real-life Faron, thank you for the coffees after late nights, for sending me to the bookstore on your only day off, for saying absolutely nothing when "I told you so," was warranted, for acting out scenes with me, and always asking "When do you need the money?" instead of "How are we going to afford it?"

For my children: Kaison, you don't know how much it warmed my heart that you started your own book beside me on the couch. Keaton, Tal's spunk comes from you. Never lose it. For Ellie Lou, thank you for being with me every step of the way. You three don't know it yet, but all those times I was tired or at my computer, I was following my dreams to show you that you can follow yours.

Thank you to my loved ones who have always supported me: Ruthie, Norman & Nana for taking the kids so I could write. Dad, thank you for teaching me everything, for never questioning me, and for making sure this book happened. You've believed in me since the beginning, and I'm forever grateful. Mom, thank you for being my biggest cheerleader. You've always wanted me to be happy. Look at me now!

Thank you to my unhinged stick figure supporters. Without your ceaseless love for my lack of artistic talent, I would not have enjoyed this journey nearly as much as I have.

Thank you to my Alpha, Beta, and ARC readers. Your feedback and unhinged comments are what kept me going. Thank you, especially, to Shay for being my number one hype gal, Kirstin for loving the story more than I thought anyone would, and Anyssia for your incredible knowledge and feedback—thank you for taking a chance on this fantasy.

To my spleens, especially: Ellie for finding me before I'd created my own brand of cool, and putting up with my crazy, Dahlia for not laughing at my grandma dance moves, for giving everything unconditionally, and for the AMAZING promo goodies; I'll never be as badass as you, Pedigo for matching my sarcasm and making it easy for me to be myself (I forgive you for the pickles, but when's the D&D campaign??), Erin & Amaris for always lifting the rest of us up and reminding me I'll always have a home—even if it's online.

Thank you to my editor, Mallory, for your invaluable feedback and bringing the excitement. I may have loved this story from its infancy, but you showed me others will too.

Thank you to LazyHunnyBee for the flawless cover and interior artwork. *Chef's kiss*

And finally, to Brea, my furious coconut, my kindred spirit; you loved this story when it was a wee sapling. You watered it, brought out the sun, and now we have a whole world we can get lost in. For the enthusiasm, the unhinged chats, the idea swapping, the cannon lore that is everything to me, the beautiful and flawless artwork, and so much more, thank you for taking a chance on me and my stick figures. Now, it's your turn.

About the Author

Milli C. Vieira is a lifelong dreamer of magical worlds and life-changing stories. She channeled her creativity into designing engaging curriculum as a high school mathematics teacher until she retired to raise her children. Nowadays, you can find her surrounded by her family, her books, and countless journals with story ideas waiting to be completed. She lives with her husband and three kids in Florida. Visit millicvieira.com for information on upcoming works.